the shadow of your smile

the Shadow of Your Smile

Susan May WARREN

a deep haven novel

TYNDALE HOUSE PUBLISHERS, INC., CAROL STREAM, ILLINOIS

Visit Susan May Warren's website at www.susanmaywarren.com.

TYNDALE and Tyndale's quill logo are registered trademarks of Tyndale House Publishers, Inc.

The Shadow of Your Smile

Designed by Erik M. Peterson

Edited by Sarah Mason

ISBN 978-1-61793-724-8

Printed in the United States of America

For Your glory, Lord

Acknowledgments

God showed His unfailing love to me once again as I wrote this story. I am deeply grateful to the following people for abiding with me on this journey:

Sarah May Warren, my beautiful daughter, who let me use her amazing poetry and song lyrics as the foundation for Kelsey's. Your talent makes me cry with joy. I can't wait to see what God does with your obedient heart.

Andrew Warren, my beloved husband, who is Eli and more. Thank you for all your guidance on the "man's POV" in this story.

Peter and Noah Warren, my basketball stars who helped me forge an appreciation for the game. (Peter, you are not allowed to tackle in basketball!)

David Warren, who lets me blather on about my plots and knows just the right questions to ask. You'll make a fabulous editor someday.

Rachel Hauck, my writing partner. Stop arguing with me! (Or rather, thanks for pushing me and making me a better writer!)

Dick Dorr, who listened to my crazy plot with his "I'm not sure I buy what you're saying" cop look and then helped me straighten it all out. It is a gift to know you. Thank you for your patience, stories, and expert assistance.

Kathy Johnson (and family), who let me into her life and taught me about deer hunting, ice fishing, snowplowing, and north shore living. You are a true north shore woman, and I'm delighted to call you friend.

Marybeth Farley, basketball buddy. Oh, were we supposed to watch the game? Thanks for helping me with my "research"!

Jim Miller, Lynn Shulte, and Margarquet Fortunato, friends at SA. Thanks for your encouragement and being the friendly faces I detour to every day. (Jim—your joke made it into the book!)

Steve Laube—"Breathe, just breathe, Susie" (how he answers my phone calls). Thanks for being calm.

Karen Watson, for your steadfast encouragement. I am too much like a puppy, hoping for your pat on my head. Thanks for loving this story.

Sarah Mason, for again smoothing out my words and story into something readable. I am blessed by your talents!

My reader friends, for your kind letters, your testimonials of how God has spoken to you through my stories, and for the encouragement to press on in truth. Thank you for reading.

1

NOELLE LONGED FOR the redemption that came with a fresh snow. The way it blanketed the northern woods of Minnesota with lacy grace, frosted the shaggy limbs of the white pine, turned the grimy dirt roads and highways to ribbons of pristine, unblemished white. The crisp bite of a shiny morning after a blizzard had the power to woo a new spirit to life inside Mrs. Eli Hueston, mother and wife of the former Deep Haven sheriff, when she stood on the deck of her woodsy home, steam from a cup of coffee swirling into the chilled air.

In moments like those, she almost believed that everything could be made new.

But this snow offered no such redemption. This snow, a mixture of sleet and flake, bulleted Noelle's windshield, crusts of ice piling in the corners, turning her wiper blades to razors. This snow transformed the highway into a lethal slick of black ice as she crawled along the shore of Lake Superior to her tiny north shore hamlet.

Eli would surely discover her transgressions now.

Noelle turned her wipers on high to sweep the sleet faster, cranked the defrost to full. She should have scraped her windshield better before leaving Eric's office, but she'd checked her watch, calculated her route home, and bargained on her car heating faster than the storm.

Again, she'd opted for survival mode.

But that's what this trip was about, wasn't it? Surviving?

Or maybe it was about living again.

The road from this stretch of northern Minnesota into the northeast corner of the state appeared eerily vacant, the storm turning the late afternoon to pewter gray. She had switched her lights to dim, the brights only making the snow appear three-dimensional as it buffeted her. Deer lurked under the cover of black pine, poplar, and birch trees that walled either side of the road, ready to throw themselves into traffic.

In this weather, a touch of her brakes might spin her right into the ditch.

Maybe she should have spent the night in Duluth, but then she'd certainly have explaining to do.

In the cup holder of her ancient Yukon, her phone buzzed. Noelle fumbled with the earpiece, glancing at the road, then back to the phone. Lee. She finally wedged the earpiece in, clicked the button.

"Lee? Are you still there?"

The voice, splotchy with the poor reception, cut through the rhythm of the wiper blades, the pummeling of the sleet. "Noelle, where are you? You missed yoga this morning. And Sharron said she's covering your visitation at the care center."

Not yet. She couldn't tell Lee just yet.

It would be a big enough scandal when the news did surface. She hoped to hold it in for at least five more months. Just until Kirby's graduation. Then she could exhale.

They'd all exhale, probably. Especially Eli. She wasn't deceiving herself—he would be as relieved as she with her decision.

"I had to run to Duluth." True enough.

"Today? There's a winter storm advisory. Didn't you listen to the weather report this morning?"

She could picture Lee, always beautiful with her long auburn hair, a trim body that needed no yoga, probably sitting in her immaculate home, staring through the window at the lake as it pounded the rocks outside her house.

Her lonely house. Noelle admired Lee for her strength, but Lee had filled her life with so many activities since that horrible day that being snowbound could curl her into the fetal position if it weren't for the telephone and her son, Derek, classmate of Kirby.

If they had a snow day tomorrow, Kirby would dig out the snow machine and spend the day carving trails in the woods. How they used to relish the rare snow days of the north. One year— Kirby had been about ten—he and Kyle and Kelsey had spent the day building a snow cave . . .

The memories could rise like knives to skewer her, carve her breath from her lungs. *Focus on the future.*

"I heard we might have snow, but I had an appointment." Also true. Noelle lifted her foot from the gas as she rounded a curve.

"Oh no, it's not . . . ," Lee said, worry in her tone.

Bless her for remembering. The last few years had turned their friendship stiff, but Lee had tried all the same. Noelle should remember that.

"I got an all clear from the biopsy—the report came in the mail a couple weeks ago." Noelle should have mentioned it to Lee, but she'd been so busy preparing for today. In a way, the clean report had only confirmed for her that it was time. "But I had some follow-up to do." Like figuring out how she got here, a forty-six-year-old woman who longed to start her life over.

"Are you going to be okay?"

Yes. She had to believe it. *Yes.* "I'm fine. Did you say they called a winter storm advisory?"

"Yes, although I'm sure the basketball team will stay for practice in hopes their game won't be snowed out tomorrow."

Noelle made a face. Perfect. Sometimes her family's devotion to small-town sports could make her bang her head against the dashboard.

Still, if it weren't for Kirby and his athletics, she might have lost herself completely.

"I hate Kirby driving home in this storm in that decrepit Neon. I told Eli to change his tires out for winter treads, but . . ." If she'd been home, she would have put on the four-wheel drive in her SUV and trekked to the school.

She hated to ask, but that's what fellow sports moms did for each other. "If Kirby lands in the ditch, can you pick him up?"

"Where's Eli?"

The obvious question, of course. And in earlier years, the answer might have been easier. In town. At the station. Or in his cruiser.

But since he'd retired a few months back, who really knew? "He said he was going up to the lake, fishing. I expected to be back before he returned but—"

"Absolutely, Noelle. Don't worry about a thing. I'll make sure Kirby isn't left alone."

"Thanks, Lee. How's Emma?" Noelle managed to ask without a hiccup in her voice, although a burr filled her throat. Someday, perhaps, she could ask without the pain.

"She's fine. Still playing her music in the Twin Cities. I think she has a gig this weekend."

She *thought*? Sometimes Noelle hated Lee for how easy it all came for her.

Noelle heard the sound of the dishwasher being unloaded, plates scraping together. Lee probably only had to load it once a week nowadays.

Maybe Noelle should have invited Lee to go with her. But she had to do this alone.

Would do it alone. After all, who else did Noelle have who might understand what it felt like to look in the mirror and not recognize the woman she'd become? Lee had survived, even become stronger after that terrible day. She couldn't possibly understand what it felt like to want to leave it all behind.

To want to forget.

Not that Noelle wanted to erase the last twenty years of her life. Just parts of it.

Heart-wrenching, horrible, breath-stealing parts.

But not even God could heal the wounds and put their family, her marriage, back together again.

"I'll be home soon." Ahead, Noelle spied the lights of the next town shining out of the grayness. "I'm going to stop and get some coffee. If Eli shows up looking for me . . . just tell him I'm on my way home."

Silence, then, "He doesn't know you went to Duluth?"

Noelle tapped her brakes as the speed limit decreased. "I meant to tell him, but . . ."

No, actually, she hadn't, and she could nearly hear her pastor in her head. *A lie of omission is still a lie.*

But was it a lie if they never talked about *anything*? If she and Eli had been reduced to two barely compatible roommates? He'd been sleeping in the den for more than a year now. It had somehow ceased to matter if she informed him what she was doing.

Ever again.

"Be safe," Lee said, her voice sounding distant, even odd.

But it could be the storm, the pitch of her tires as Noelle slowed to pull into the Mocha Moose coffee shop along the highway. She could use something to keep her awake for the rest of the two-hour drive.

"Thanks, Lee," she said, but her friend had already clicked off. Probably she'd simply lost the signal—it happened too often up here in moose country. She parked, grabbed her purse, and trekked across the lot. She shouldn't have worn her three-inch dress boots. But she hadn't been thinking of the storm when she'd dressed this morning.

She'd been trying to find a pair of suit pants that didn't pinch at the waist, didn't appear to be from the eighties—the last time she'd interviewed for anything that mattered. She'd been trying to remember how to fix her blonde shoulder-length hair into anything but a swept-up ponytail, and rehearsing her answers.

Why do I deserve enrollment in the Duluth Art Institute?

She had some feeble replies, none that seemed overly compelling. Eric Hansen had seemed nice enough about her responses, however. Said he'd contact her.

She stamped her way into the coffee shop, the warmth fogging her sunglasses. She pushed them on top of her head and walked to the counter. A cheery gas fire crackled in the hearth, leather chairs for reading propped before it. A chalkboard along the back listed the specials.

"Just in time. We're about to close," the girl behind the register said.

Noelle scanned the board. Oh, why not? "A white chocolate mocha with extra whip." She dug into her purse. "And can I have those little chocolate chip sprinkles?"

The perky cashier, a blonde probably fresh out of high school, grinned at her. "Celebrating?"

Perhaps she was. The restart to her life, the road to something she could live with. Noelle nodded as she paid, then walked to the next counter to wait for her drink.

When the mocha arrived, she added a cozy to the cup, then took a sip, emboldening herself for the storm outside. The chocolate warmth seeped into the empty crannies inside, fortified her, if only for a second.

She could do this. With or—and this was more likely—without Eli.

She'd come to accept that, at least mostly. If only she could go back in time, figure out when it had started to unravel, maybe they'd still have a marriage worth saving.

One last stop in the facilities and then she'd head for home. She ducked into the ladies' room, and that's when she heard the noises. Shouts, raised voices. She cracked open the door and froze.

Standing in front of the counter were two men wearing ski masks—or one she'd call a boy because his stature didn't resemble the broad-shouldered girth of the other man. The larger held a gun on the cashier. Noelle recognized a 9mm Glock.

The skinny one handed over a paper bag. "Fill it up, then get on the floor."

Really? A coffee shop holdup?

Still, petty thieves lurked in the north woods too. Look at what had happened in Deep Haven.

Well, no one was going to die today.

Noelle's heart slammed against her ribs as she fumbled in her purse for her cell phone. Shoot, she'd left it in the car, in the cup holder.

But there was the door, two steps away . . .

She took a breath, then flung open the restroom door and raced for the exit.

"Hey!"

One of them turned, and she might have heard a shot as she leaped onto the sidewalk, diving for her car.

A hand caught her arm, yanked her back. "Where do you think you're going?" She clawed at his ski mask even as he dragged her back into the coffee shop.

Inside, he slapped her hard, her jaw ringing. Brown eyes, a tattoo on his hand in the webbing of his thumb.

The cashier was on the floor behind the counter, crying. She had a welt across her cheek, open and bleeding. The boy stood over her, scraggly blond hair peeking out from his ski mask. He looked at Noelle, and she chilled at the pale blue-gray of his eyes.

The larger man now grabbed her by the neck, pushed her face into the floor. "Open the safe or we'll kill her," he growled to the employee.

The girl whimpered as she crawled to an office in the back.

Please, God, I don't want to die on the floor of a coffee shop.

Or a convenience store. The thought nearly choked her. Her family couldn't go through that again.

"We got it," the boy said.

"Good. Now shoot her." He held out his Glock to the boy.

The boy stared at it. Shook his head. "I can't."

The bigger man stifled a curse word. Then he disappeared into the back.

Oh, oh, please, no—

Noelle jerked as a shot rang out.

The boy met her eyes, his own wide.

She felt it inside then. Instinct, maybe. A voice.

Run.

Run!

She sprang up, leaping for the door. Shouting chased her, but she fled down the sidewalk for the road.

There—headlights! A semi plowing through the blizzard.

"Help! Help!" She scrambled into the road, waving her hands above her head. "Stop!"

That's when her boots betrayed her. They slipped on the black ice, her foot flinging out in front of her. The jolt jerked her other foot free. Her body launched into the air.

Her scream joined the screech of the semi.

Noelle slammed into the pavement, pain exploding through her.

Then, darkness.

2

Eli Hueston would like to live alone forever in his ice house. He could, couldn't he? At least for four months out of the year. The house, dragged out into the middle of McFarland Lake right before Thanksgiving, now accessible only by snowmobile, had all the trappings of home sweet home.

Without the icy, impenetrable chill.

About as big as his bedroom in their Cape Cod, the ice house contained oak cupboards, a stove, a microwave oven, a refrigerator, and a new HD flat screen, not to mention his submersible camera capable of monitoring the bottom of the lake, the bait, and fish.

If he wanted to, he could spend the night on one of the four bunk beds, the house turning so toasty warm from the propane heat that he'd on occasion had to open one of the vents near the ceiling for air.

Of course it had facilities. Oh, and six holes for catching fish. Which, sometimes, he did. Like today. Four perch—one a keeper—and a northern who couldn't escape the lure of a flathead chub jigging in front of its wide, hungry mouth.

The pike Eli had cleaned and fried up in a batter of shore lunch. He downed it with a Coke. He wasn't the type to haul a six-pack to the woods anymore. He'd been the alcohol route, found it empty when he woke to a worse fate every morning. Besides, he'd seen too many anglers toes up from hypothermia to tempt fate by bringing alcohol out to this lonely planet.

Indeed, the smooth white of the lake, marred only by the tracks of his Polaris, seemed its own constellation, the surface crystalline and shiny under the blue sky now mottled by the twilight settling over the horizon. It spilled magenta over the ice like syrup.

He could stay here all winter. And in the summer, pull the custom-made trailer off the lake, park it on the Huestons' little undeveloped plot of land, and fish from the shore, camping out, surviving on fresh walleye, northern pike, and bass over a crackling campfire.

If only life were as easy as fishing.

Out here, a man loaded his hook with the appropriate bait— waxies, moth larvae, chubs—then plopped his line in the water and waited for the fish to bite. He didn't have to ask the fish how it might be feeling, guess at what he'd done wrong to elicit its cold shoulder, didn't have to worry if the fish might be crying itself to sleep in the middle of the night.

He hated standing outside their door, listening to Noelle's sobs. He'd moved to the den so he could escape the hollowing out of his soul, night by night. He had no idea how to comfort a wife who'd lost so much of herself, her future.

If he could, he'd take back that dark midnight or replace it with a different loss. Yes, Eli would like to live forever on this forgotten lake, tucked inside the lush, snowy forest, thirty miles from civilization, and allow, in time, the voices inside his head to quiet to a murmur. To let him think.

Feel.

Forgive himself.

Perhaps he might even figure out how to repair their lives. Or decide if he even wanted to. It had occurred to him, more than once, that they should just admit defeat.

Lee had even voiced it—that they could all start over after the boys graduated. Eli had been chopping wood for her heater—a job Derek could have managed, but with his basketball schedule, he had little time for household chores.

Besides, a man had responsibilities to the widow of one of his deputies.

She'd been dressed in Clay's red-and-black padded flannel shirt, her auburn hair peeking out of a gray wool cap, stacking the cordwood as it fell from his ax. "How do you want to spend your retirement, Eli? Alone? Or with someone who cares about you?" She'd pushed her hair back from her face with her wrist, then smiled at him, and there seemed to be an invitation in her expression.

He didn't answer her, but the question lingered. Followed him to McFarland Lake. Dogged him as he'd watched his bobber, the fish scurrying about on the screen.

Alone?

He wasn't alone, was he?

Eli finished washing his cast-iron pan, dried it, and set it in the cupboard. The ice house still smelled of the bacon grease he'd fried the fish in, so he opened the door to air it out as he locked up his tackle, his equipment. The house, so heavy it had hydraulic wheels to haul it onto the ice, could turn into an impenetrable fortress once he locked it.

He loaded the cooler with the rest of the fish onto the seat of the snowmobile, drained the sink and the facilities in the back, then turned off the heater and locked the house. To the west, the sky appeared darker now, as if a storm might be rolling in. A gust of wind skimmed snow from the surface of the lake, splattered it on his parka. He shivered at the change of temperature as he started the snowmobile.

Hopefully Kirby had made it home okay in his clunker old Neon. Near the lake, the storm could roll in faster, turn fluffy snow to sleet. He picked up his cell phone, but he was still out of range.

Thankfully, Noelle would pick the boy up if he needed help. She practically hovered over their youngest son. But really, who could blame her?

Eli opened the throttle over the ice, drinking in the power of the speed. His truck came into view, a black hulk on the shoreline. He pulled up to it, dragged out the ramp, drove the snowmobile onto the bed, then strapped it down.

He let the truck warm for a moment, setting the cooler on the seat beside him, holding his hands in front of the heater.

Alone? Or with someone who cares about you?

Lee's voice rumbled around in his head. That, and her laughter, the way she looked at him that made him feel twenty years younger, without tragedy in her gaze. She had her own tragedy, of course, but in her eyes he saw himself reflected as a savior.

Instead of a tormentor.

But she had been Clay's wife.

No. Eli's heart thumped.

No.

And oh, boy, he was married. He hated himself for thinking of that second. But what was a marriage, anyway? Certainly not what he and Noelle had. Coexistence? Tolerance?

Sometimes, not even that.

He could probably drop right through the ice and she wouldn't miss him. Let the ice freeze over, erase him from her life without a blink.

He eased the truck onto the dirt road. As he drove south, the weather turned sour quickly, thick flakes landing on his windshield, melting as they slid off. He turned on his wipers. No doubt near Lake Superior, he'd find the highway icy and traffic in the ditch.

He was being too hard on her, and he knew it. The responsibility for keeping a marriage strong rested on the man's shoulders— he'd heard that sermon enough to believe it. But what if she didn't respond to him? What if his attempts actually caused her pain?

God, I don't know how to love my wife anymore. How to fix this. How to be the husband she needs. I think we're beyond hope—

His cell phone vibrated in his parka.

He scooped the phone from his pocket, his cold hands fumbling with it, and held it up. He didn't recognize the number.

Touching the brakes, he angled for the side of the road, deserted as it was, and opened the phone.

"Eli Hueston." Oh, he still had his sheriff's tone. But twenty-five years spent taking bad news didn't dissipate from his system overnight. Or even in three months. He could feel his stomach tensing out of habit even as he pressed the phone to his ear.

"Sheriff, it's Anne Standing Bear."

He hadn't heard the EMT's voice in nearly five years, since she and her husband, Noah, had moved back to Duluth for her to add an MD to her nursing degree. He always liked her, the way she knew how to take care of a trauma. But she'd needed more than what Deep Haven could give her, and after the birth of their son, Clancy, she and Noah had moved away to pursue her dreams.

Much like Noelle had done for him once upon a time.

"Hey, Anne," he said. "I'm not sure if you heard, but I'm not the sheriff anymore."

She didn't comment, and something in the way her voice emerged, tight and cool, the way they must have taught her at St. Luke's, made him catch his breath. "I'm sorry, but there's been an accident."

Oh, please, not Kyle. Hadn't he told the kid that law enforcement wasn't for him? That he didn't wish that life on any of his children, even his oldest? But after Kelsey, Kyle wouldn't hear his objections. It seemed almost as if he had to prove something to himself.

Or work off his own grief.

Eli steeled himself. "How is he? What happened?"

She paused. "It's . . . it's your wife, sir. She fell outside the Mocha Moose."

The Mocha Moose . . . "In Harbor City?" What was Noelle doing there? "I thought she was at home. Did she hurt herself?" He realized as soon as the words left how stupid that sounded. Of course she hurt herself—otherwise, why would she have Anne call for her?

And how did Anne find her, anyway?

"No, I'm afraid she did." Anne's voice softened. "She hit her head, hard. You need to come to St. Luke's in Duluth. . . . Eli, she's got eight staples in her skull."

"Oh, my." He pulled onto the road, trying to picture Noelle sprawled on the snowy, dirty parking lot outside the coffee shop, bleeding. She always had to stop there, regardless of the time of day. He shook the image away. "Are you calling from the hospital? Can I talk to her?"

"I'm calling from ICU, Sheriff. But I . . . I don't want to talk to you about this over the phone—"

"Anne, just tell me."

"She's . . . had a major head trauma. In fact, Sheriff, I'm so sorry—your wife is in a coma."

&

This was not the life Emma Nelson had planned on living.

No, the dream she'd conjured with Kelsey Hueston as they jammed together, creating their band, the Blue Monkeys, in the upstairs attic of her north shore garage, certainly never included neon beer lights, hairy bikers dressed in black leather, and a woman doing shots out of her deeply vee-d red T-shirt three tables from the stage.

Emma averted her eyes as she stood behind the lead guitarist of Retrospect, her bass guitar over her shoulder, playing a twelve-bar blues riff as they covered hits from Led Zeppelin, Fleetwood Mac, the Stones, and even Stevie Ray Vaughn. The rank odor of cigarette smoke embedded the black Hard Rock Cafe T-shirt she'd inherited from her best friend, and a line of sweat dribbled down her spine despite the icy air outside.

If she had to play "Stairway to Heaven" one more time, she just might pack up her Fender fretted four-string and flee. Maybe all the way back home, back to Deep Haven.

No, no, she was simply tired. And smelly.

And broke, or she wouldn't be stuck filling in for the various rock and blues bands around the city in need of a bass guitarist. A *female* bass guitarist, which, according to Ritchie Huff Management, could land her enough gigs to keep her in rent money this month.

What she wanted was her own gig. Alone under the spotlight, playing her own music on her first love—her electric guitar. Sadly there wasn't quite enough demand for a bluesy folk singer from northern Minnesota with a hot talent for improv to keep her in solo gigs. Or any demand, really.

She watched the lead for a rhythm change, ended the song at the nod of his head.

"Ten-minute break," he said to her over his shoulder. Bobby? Billy? She couldn't remember his name but she nodded, glad to set her bass on its mount, climb off the stage of the packed 400 Bar, and head out through the back to the alley, where the crisp winter air might clear her head.

Why, exactly, hadn't she taken her guidance counselor's advice and gone into teaching? Or stayed in school, pursuing a music degree at the university?

She *might* have been propelled by the memory of her father, standing just outside the door to her studio, ready to hop in on the drums, treat her to a drum jam that kept the attic studio rockin' all night. Or sometimes he'd just plop himself on the ratty green sofa and lean his chin on his hands, listening.

She hoped he was still listening, even to the iffy music of Retrospect. For her dad, she'd played her heart out, even if it was only for old covers.

The drummer stepped out behind her, propping open the door

with a can. "You're pretty young to be so good," he said. Tommy? Ted?

"Tim," he said, to her obvious frown. "We have another gig next Thursday. I'm sure Brian would love to have you join us."

That was it—*Brian*. She leaned against the metal railing outside the door, lifting her face. Overhead, smoky clouds mottled the sky; only a few stars broke through. Even then, with the city lights, she could barely make them out.

Once upon a time in Deep Haven, it seemed she could see all the way across the universe.

She shivered. "Ritchie mentioned you needed a bassist. I'll have to check my schedule." She knew already what her schedule read for next Thursday night—a big, fat nothing. But what if something came up—a chance to play at one of the local hotel lounges, or even at the Fine Line Music Cafe, with real listeners, not the kind that just wanted a beat as they guzzled down whiskey Cokes?

"I'll bet you're pretty booked with those wicked riffs."

"Thanks. My dad taught me those."

"A blues player. I'll bet he's proud." Tim looked old enough to be her uncle, if not her father, and the smile he gave her wasn't in the least creepy. She liked him with his balding comb-back, his bulky waistline. He lit a cigarette but blew it away from her.

"He would have been." She smiled at him. "He passed away three years ago."

He wore the look most did when she told them the news. At least she spared him the gruesome truth. *Murdered.* She hated that word.

"I'm sorry," Tim said.

"Thanks. He wanted me to pursue music, even left some cash for me to live on while I figured it out."

Except that was almost gone. Or at least her portion. Her mother still had her share, and Derek had banked his for college, although he just might land himself a basketball scholarship if he kept racking up points for the Huskies.

"Where are you from?"

She rubbed her hands on her arms, the sweat now freezing down her spine. "Deep Haven."

He studied her with kind brown eyes. "Seriously? I love it up there. They have a blues festival every summer."

"I know. I played a couple years ago."

"I probably saw you. I go up every year, park in the municipal campground, me and the missus, our two kids."

"I always play in the tents—and on the main stage for local talent night. I used to play with a friend. We called ourselves the Blue Monkeys. Dumb, I know."

He drew on his cigarette. "I think I remember you. You had a crooner—"

"Kelsey. Yes. She could really rock the house." She could say it now without as much pain. Moving five hours south helped.

"Are you still together?" He threw the cigarette on the ground and flattened it with his shoe.

"Nope." She left it at that. But the answer could elicit a moan inside if she let it.

"Too bad." He opened the door for her, ushered her inside. The heat of the bar, the swill of alcohol, the brine of sweat could sweep her breath from her chest.

Someday she'd hit it big and her days playing blues joints would end. She hoisted the guitar over her shoulder. Smiled into the audience.

No one smiled back.

"'Pinball Wizard,'" Brian said and Tim picked up the beat.

The Blue Monkeys had cranked out a few Who covers, but she'd never been a rocker at heart. She'd preferred the older stuff—Gladys Knight, Mavis Staples, Aretha Franklin. But she hadn't ignored Janis Joplin, Joan Baez, and Joni Mitchell either.

And she could get lost forever in her arrangements of the kings of the seventies: Joe Cocker, B. J. Thomas, even Simon and Garfunkel. They probably couldn't be improved on, but she liked to try.

She liked the sound she'd developed, and so had her manager, Ritchie, it seemed, when she met him while playing at an open mic night at the Mad Fox. Then why, a year later, was she still gigging for AWOL bassists around the city?

Probably because she still couldn't conjure up her own words. Sure she could nail the riff, jam up and down the frets, keep up with any Chicago blues piano, but finding the words to croon along?

That had been Kelsey's job.

On the dance floor in front of the stage, a couple of fans had begun to move to the beat, one of them pretending to play the air guitar, the other now zeroing in on Emma. He danced toward her, wearing a Guns N' Roses T-shirt and a drunken come-hither smile. He winked and she hid the roll of her eyes.

Awesome, a groupie. She shot him a look, no smile in it. *Keep moving, pal. Nothing here to see.*

A figure rose from a table near the back door and she nearly dropped a beat. Tall, with football shoulders, tousled bronze hair and hazel eyes that, like a heat-seeking missile, landed right on her and tharrumphed her heart out of rhythm. He wore his signature Levi's, an insulated jean jacket, and looked like a redneck from the hills in his hiking boots.

No, it couldn't be Kyle Hueston.

But the man had Kyle's lean hips, a saunter that could part a crowd, an aura of power around him that could make her forget her own name. No longer the boy she'd worshiped from across the lunchroom or from the bleachers where she played the flute while he made his name on the basketball court, this Kyle had grown, had a man's hands and a man's swagger.

What was Kelsey's amazing older brother doing in a biker watering hole in the Twin Cities?

Good thing she wasn't at the mic. Emma swallowed, but her heart blocked the way. She glanced toward Kyle. Smiled at him.

Did he meet her eyes?

Suddenly the groupie whirled around, on target to take out the competition. He stumbled forward, tossing his drink onto Kyle's jacket, saying something she couldn't hear.

Kyle didn't even blink, just kept that cool smile, grabbed the man before he fell, and set him on a stool.

But Emma's admirer wasn't having it. He threw the rest of his drink down Kyle's back. It splashed over a man dressed head to toe in black leather sitting at a nearby table.

She wasn't sure exactly how the fight broke out then—a chair flying across a table, men launching themselves, women screaming, as Brian churned out the last of the lyrics.

She stopped playing when a glass flew over her head and shattered on the paneled wall behind her.

Kyle vanished in the crowd. Or maybe she hadn't seen him at all. Maybe the mention of Kelsey in the alley had stirred to life all her crazy high school fantasies. Kyle storming through a crowd to catch her in his arms. Or seated front row center at one of her performances, his beautiful eyes pinned to her.

After all, a girl didn't so easily forget her first crush.

"Grab your gear!" Tim yelled above the chaos as he rose from behind the drum set, reaching for a leather pouch, his sticks.

Emma shrugged out of the guitar, unplugged it, fumbling with the case as she shoved her guitar inside. Another glass shattered behind her, but she didn't look.

Two men fell across the stage, slamming Brian into the drums, the keyboardist hollering.

Protect the Fender, protect the Fender—Emma clutched her guitar to her chest and scooted toward the edge of the stage.

She hit the floor, grimy with spilled whiskey, foamy beer dregs, but a couple brawlers banged into her, pitching her to her knees. She caught herself with one hand and hugged the guitar to her body, her brain pulsing one word.

Run.

Her heart tattooed the command inside her head as she scrambled to her feet, only to be knocked down again. Wetness saturated the knees of her pants. She managed to find one foot.

Someone slammed into her. She flew forward, her hand missing the edge of the stage. She caught it headfirst.

The world bowed in, shadows flickering as pain speared through her. Her hand went to her forehead, came away slick.

She dropped her guitar.

Oh.

The pain dumped her back on the floor, the ruckus around her deadened in the pulsing of her head.

Help—

Arms closed around Emma, pressing her guitar back into her arms a second before they swooped her up.

She scrabbled to hold on to the guitar, her other hand against the searing heat in her forehead as her rescuer pushed through the crowd toward the back door.

The cold air shook her free from the chaos, the pain vanishing for a brilliant moment as she looked up, the alleyway lights illuminating his face.

Oh, she hadn't dreamed him at all.

And in that crazy moment, with the smell of him around her, that breathtaking look of concern in his gorgeous eyes . . .

She kissed him. Simply leaned in and pressed her lips to his, a moment she'd dreamed about for years that just seemed right and perfect as he held her in his arms.

Kyle. He'd noticed her. Maybe he always had. She ended her kiss with a smile, looked into his eyes. "Hey, Kyle."

His eyes narrowed and he frowned. Setting her down, he reached into his pocket, pulled out a handkerchief, and held it to her forehead. Then, quietly, "Do I know you?"

3

SHE HURT EVERYWHERE—her arms, her legs—her entire body ached, right to her bones. And her head. As if a vise gripped it, pain screwed through her, eliciting a moan from places deep inside.

"I'm right here, Noelle."

The voice brought her forward, from the webbed blackness, from the place where pain held her prisoner. Her eyes blinked open, just for a moment.

Where . . . ? Noelle sank back into the cushion of darkness as she rooted for comprehension. She searched the smells—the biting tang of antiseptic, the cottony clean of freshly washed sheets. A hospital? She bit back the taste of panic, sour in her throat, and cracked her eyes again. A sky-blue curtain hung beside her bed, and next to her, a machine beeped her vitals. A glass wall with a half-drawn curtain obscured a dimly lit hallway. Muffled sounds betrayed activity beyond.

"Noelle, shh, you fell."

The voice made her fight through the final threads of unconsciousness, and she made a noise of effort as she fixed on the source.

A man. Tall, with wide shoulders, wearing a gray wool stocking cap glistening with moisture. She had the sense that she knew him, a shadow she couldn't quite make out. A doctor? No, he couldn't be because he wore a pair of brown padded coveralls, held what looked like worn work gloves in his hand. He looked familiar, though, and something told her not to be afraid.

Until he squeezed her hand. She stared at his meaty, hot grip and swallowed. Pulled her hand away. The other hand pinched with the sting of an intravenous pipe in her veins.

Her mouth was so dry that even when she opened it, nothing emerged. He must have noticed because he picked up the cup from her bedside tray, brought the straw to her mouth. She sipped, the water seeping into her parched throat.

"What—?" Her voice emerged raspy, nearly inaudible.

"You fell. Outside the coffee shop in Harbor City. And you hit your head pretty hard." He leaned back, swiped off his hat. Ran his hand through grizzled, unkempt brown hair. He wore a weekend beard and looked to be around fifty or so, although she had never been a good judge of age. "You had me pretty scared. I just got here, and they said—" He blew out a breath. Met her eyes with a sort of shake of his head. "What were you doing out in this storm, anyway? You didn't even tell me you were leaving."

He had nice eyes—deep brown—and they ran over her now, concern in them. Yes, she felt as if she knew him, but whether due to the searing pain in her head or the bright lights making the room swirl, his name wouldn't form in her mind.

She stared at him, waiting for recognition to set in, but—"I don't know what you're talking about. And *who* are you?"

Again the frown; then he leaned close, peered at her eyes.

She lifted her hand to keep him away. "Listen, Mr.—"

"Hueston," he filled in, leaning back now to press his fingers to his forehead. "It's me . . . Eli. Don't you know me?"

"I don't know . . ." Oh, it hurt to speak. Every word pinged around inside her head. She grimaced, closed her eyes.

When she opened them, he was gone. Maybe he'd gotten the wrong room. She reached up to the throbbing in her head and found a bandage there. What had he said about her falling?

And coffee? She didn't even like coffee. It was vile, black and acrid. Clearly he didn't know her because anyone who did knew she was a straight Diet Coke girl.

Noelle went back to her last clear memory, trying to sort it through. She'd been walking across campus; she remembered that much. No, no, wait; she'd been on the Washington Avenue bridge. Huddled against the wind. The snow bit into her face. Why had she agreed to live off campus? She'd stopped at the light, shivering.

Had someone hit her with their car?

She did feel bruised, all the way through, and her jaw ached, too. She tried to move her arms, her legs, and found them intact.

Maybe he was a security guard at the university. That's why she knew him. She rolled the thought around in her mind, found a warm fit.

She should ask them to call her parents. However, she didn't have the strength to root around for the nursing call button.

"Noelle?"

A pretty doctor—short auburn hair, hazel eyes—stood over her. She was wearing a lab coat, her stethoscope around her neck, and flicking a penlight into Noelle's eyes. Noelle winced and couldn't deny another groan.

The doctor leaned back. "How are you feeling? You took a pretty bad fall." She lifted Noelle's arm, took her pulse.

"My head hurts," Noelle managed. Her gaze slid past the doctor and her heart gave a tiny jolt.

The man stood across the room, arms folded, his expression nearly brutal. Maybe this Eli just wanted to know she would be all right.

"Thank you," she said quietly to him. "I'm not sure how I got here, but I guess you had something to do with that."

His mouth opened, and what looked like panic swept across his face. "Uh, no—I think someone found you. They called me. I was up at the lake." He came close, took hold of her ankle through the blanket. "Don't you remember? I told you this morning I wouldn't be home until late."

The doctor slipped a blood pressure cuff on Noelle and began to pump it up. She moved her ankle away from his too-familiar grip. He frowned.

The lake. Maybe he worked for her father? Wasn't he building onto his cabin up in Brainerd? But why—

"Your blood pressure is a little high, but that's not unexpected." The doctor replaced the cuff.

"Where are my parents? Maybe . . . Should you call them?"

The man stared at her without moving, just the tiniest flicker of a muscle in his jaw.

The doctor was pulling out a thermometer, sliding it into

a plastic sheath. She held it above Noelle's mouth as she asked, "Noelle, do you know where you are?"

"Yes, of course. I'm in the hospital." She opened her mouth to receive the thermometer, held it under her tongue.

Her gaze tracked back to the man. Yes, he must work for her father. He had strong carpenter's hands, a burly look about him, as if he knew how to handle himself outside.

The thermometer beeped, and the doctor removed it. "It's within normal range." She threw the plastic case away. "Do you know how you got here, Noelle?"

"I . . . I was coming home from class. It was snowing. Did I get hit by a car?"

"Oh, my—" At the end of the bed, the man began to back away, pointing at her as if accusing her of something. "No, no—"

The doctor turned to him. "Sheriff, just stay calm. This happens sometimes. Give us a minute here."

Sheriff? Did he believe she'd committed some crime? The thought sent a scurry of fear through Noelle. "I want him to leave," she said to the doctor. "Please. Make him leave."

"Listen to me, Noelle. You fell outside a coffee shop on your way home. You're in Duluth. And you really don't recognize the man behind me?"

Noelle frowned at him. He seemed to be pinned to her words. "He . . . looks vaguely familiar. But no, I'm sorry. Should I?"

The doctor slid her hand onto Noelle's arm. "This man is your husband."

Everything inside her stilled. Her gaze went to him, the way he watched her, the longing suddenly on his face as if he waited for her to confirm it.

What kind of man was this? What kind of stunt was he trying

to pull? "I'm sorry, but he is lying, Doctor. I'm not sure why, but this is ridiculous. I'm not married, and I have no idea who that man is."

"Mrs. Hueston—"

"Don't call me that!" The pain flared in her head. She made a face, groaned.

The doctor shot a look behind her, then back to Noelle. "Okay, calm down. It'll be okay."

Noelle covered her eyes with her hand. "Listen, maybe he's the one who's injured. He's got me confused with someone else. Just . . . please, call my parents. They'll come and pick me up."

No one moved. The ticking of the clock opposite her bed made her draw her hand away. The doctor stared at her, the expression on her face frightening Noelle a little.

The man spoke. "Noelle, your parents, they're—"

"Eli, let's talk." The doctor patted Noelle's arm. "We'll be back. Try to get some rest."

Noelle watched them leave, then closed her eyes. Oh, she needed an aspirin. The sooner they called her parents and she got home to her bed, the better.

She had classes in the morning.

❦

"Kyle, it's me—Emma. Emma Nelson."

Emma Nelson.

Kyle stared at her, the kiss she'd just landed on him ringing in his head, and that niggle of familiarity he'd experienced as he'd watched her onstage clicked. No wonder she had a small-town look about her—no piercings, her dark hair pulled back in a messy ponytail. Of course it was Emma behind the bass guitar that nearly ate her whole. He should have recognized the easy way she managed the twelve-bar beat.

He didn't need her clarification as she looked up at him with wide blue eyes.

"Emma Nelson, Kelsey's friend? She and I sang together in the Blue Monkeys?"

He remembered her now, a skinny girl with brown pigtails and a tie-dyed shirt, sitting in his sister's room, working chord progressions. The Nelsons' daughter. To his surprise, the realization didn't hurt as much as he'd expected.

Miss Emma Nelson had developed a few curves—and from the kiss she'd given him, more than a little big-city in her spirit.

Oh, boy. "Right. Hey, Emma."

When she grinned at him, it whisked him back to high school, walking through the lunchroom to the jocks' table, a weird hush emanating from Kelsey's table of freshman girls.

He hadn't deserved their awe. Now it churned inside him a strange, unidentified emotion. So sue him, he liked it.

"What are you doing here?" She trembled, the residue of their escape.

"My buddy likes the band." He didn't add that the scene at the 400 Bar didn't exactly qualify as a place he might like to hang out on a Thursday night—he would have preferred a game of pool down at Lucky O'Tooles, but his buddies had picked the location for his good-bye party, and he wasn't driving. Or perhaps now he was, considering his Diet Cokes versus their Heinekens.

Kyle pressed his handkerchief to her bloody forehead again.

She made a face. "Sorry about the fight. That guy must have been drunk."

"He definitely looked like trouble, but I was just trying to use the restroom in back. I hate bar fights." And the fact that even in a crowded bar his law enforcement instincts wouldn't ignore the scent of trouble. Most of all he hated the memory of Emma crouched on the floor, clutching her guitar to her chest. He figured her bloody forehead accounted for why he'd scooped her up and charged to safety. He lifted the handkerchief from her cut. "I think that needs a few stitches."

"I hate hospitals."

He gave her a sad smile. "Who doesn't? I'll drive you."

An hour later, she lay on the table in the ER of the Hennepin County Medical Center, betraying not a hint of pain as the trauma doc put the fourth stitch in her forehead, just under the hairline.

"You know, you can squeeze my hand if it hurts," Kyle said, not sure why he'd offered that. But she hadn't complained once—tougher, clearly, than she looked.

"Really, I can't even feel it," she said, glancing at him with pretty eyes, very blue with flecks of golden brown in the centers. Funny he hadn't noticed that years ago. But then again, he'd been lost in himself as a senior, worried about his basketball scholarship and especially whether Aimee Wilkes might go to prom with him. Yeah, the important things in life.

"Do you think there will be a terrible scar?" She directed her attention back to the doctor.

"Not if you stop talking. It moves your entire face," the doctor said. "Almost done. Hang in there."

She sighed and Kyle squeezed her hand anyway, needing to for some reason. The lights over the curtained-off cubicle turned her skin pale, but she had beautiful sable-brown hair, now falling out of her ponytail and pillowing her head on the exam table. Blood had seeped into the lines of her palm, although he'd tried to clean it for her, and a darkened handprint scarred his jean jacket.

As his gaze fell on it, he had the sudden big-brother urge to throttle her. "What are you doing playing the 400 Bar?"

"I have to go where the gigs are."

"Please stop talking," the doctor said, tying off the fifth stitch.

"But there have to be better gigs. How about dinners and receptions? That place was a brawl waiting to happen."

"Yeah, thanks to you."

"You're blaming me for the fight? Do you even know the guy who had his eyes glued to you?"

"A groupie? Hardly, but that's not new—ouch."

"Hold still," the doctor said, his patience clearly waning.

"I'm just saying that you may want to start choosing your venues with a bit more scrutiny."

"I'm trying to cut my own album. Studio time costs money," she said out of the side of her mouth. "And a girl has to eat."

"I'm assuming that still requires teeth."

"Ha-ha," she said but flashed her pearlies.

He couldn't help but smile back. Yeah, she was definitely cute. But thin, with a cross necklace dribbling over protruding collarbone. He even saw ribs washboarding through that skintight black shirt.

Kelsey's shirt. He recognized it now.

His smile dimmed and he looked away. He hated ERs. Hated the sterile, antiseptic odors, the muffled voices over intercoms, the sense of doom—and frustration—that hovered over the room.

"All done," the doctor said. He dropped the forceps into a suture tray and reached for a bandage. He peeled it out, put it over her wound, then turned to Kyle. "She may be woozy, and watch for signs of concussion. If she has trouble breathing, slurred vision or speech, vomiting, or even if she's excessively clumsy—"

"You'd better hospitalize her immediately."

"You're hilarious, Hueston." Emma sat up, then grabbed hold of the padded table as her eyes widened.

"See? What did I say, Doc?"

He smiled at them, something gentle. "Just get her home and keep her away from any more bar fights."

"For the record, I was in the band."

The doctor stood, picked up her chart. "That's what they all say." He winked at Kyle.

"Let's get you home, Bono."

He went to sling his arm around her waist, but she pressed a hand on his chest, righting herself on her own. "I know I looked like a damsel in distress back there at the 400, but I've been on my own for a couple years now. I can handle getting home by myself."

"I'm sure you can, but I wouldn't be a very good cop if I just let you walk out of here with a possible concussion."

"You're a cop?"

Something about her tone stung. "Yes," he said slowly. Why the sigh, the pained disappointment? "The good thing about cops is that we know where to get the best pancakes in town. I know this fabulous all-night breakfast place. How about a little nourishment?" *Please?* He couldn't pinpoint why, but being with her had stirred old feelings of home. Or maybe of hope.

She drew in a long breath. "Fine. I am a little hungry."

He smiled, something victorious in it apparently because she shook her head. "Kelsey always said you were overprotective."

Oh. Shoot. "Let's not talk about Kelsey, can we?"

"Agreed."

He held out his arm. "Hang on, please. I don't want you toppling over in the parking lot."

To his relief, she looped her arm through his, and they walked into the night. Tiny flakes had begun to peel from the sky, landing on her eyelashes, her nose. She leaned back, held out her tongue to catch one.

"Doesn't taste like Deep Haven snow," he said, catching one himself.

She said nothing as he opened the door to his truck.

Kyle turned the heat up for their drive to the restaurant. "How long have you been living in the Cities?"

She pulled her hands into the sleeves of her jacket, shivering. "Two years. I started at the university, but I dropped out after the second semester. My music kept me up too late for class, and my heart wasn't in it anyway."

"What is your heart into?"

The question seemed to leave her empty, just staring at him. "I'm still figuring that out."

"I get that. It took me two years of college before I figured out I wanted to be a cop. I just finished my rookie year with the St. Paul Police Department."

"My dad was a cop," she said softly.

He didn't look at her. "I know."

They pulled up to the restaurant. Inside, the lights glowed, beckoning.

He got out and moved around the truck to take her arm. The last thing she needed was another fall.

Emma held on to him as they entered, stamping their feet on the carpet. The place smelled of syrup, baked bread, and late-night conversation. They found a booth near the back, and a woman his mother's age handed them menus.

It seemed that Emma hadn't eaten this side of the New Year. She ordered the lumberjack special, gobbled down every last flapjack, drowning them in syrup, then smeared ketchup on the hash browns and went to work with renewed gusto.

He just watched, nursing a coffee and a couple pieces of French toast.

She had an enthusiasm about her, life radiating off her. That kiss kept returning to him, the surety of it, the way she felt alive in his arms.

"I want to see you again," he said, his mouth a few steps ahead of his brain. But why not? Something about being with her felt easy, right. Hometown.

She finished her bacon, holding it with two fingers as she leaned back in the booth seat. "It's about time you noticed me, Kyle Hueston. Only took you six years."

He must have been blind. "Sorry about that. I didn't pay much attention to my sister's friends."

"And I'm sure it was hard to see around the crowds of cheerleaders. I was just a band girl, playing the flute in the far section of the bleachers."

"I love the flute."

"Sure you do." She wiped her mouth, sighed. "I am stuffed. Thank you." She wore a little smile, her eyes twinkling. "Promise to feed me again and I might say yes to a date."

His heart took roost in his throat as he paid the bill, then walked her out.

"I think I'm concussion free. You can take me back to my car."

"Hey, I'm an officer of the law. I'm not allowed to disobey

doctor's orders. I'll take you home and we'll get the car in the morning."

Her smile fell a little. "I hope you're not thinking—"

"I'm staying at my buddy's place, Emma."

"Right. Good." She held out her mittens to catch more of the falling flakes.

He couldn't help it. "You know, when you kissed me, you caught me off guard. I . . . Can I kiss you, Emma? Right this time?"

She turned, and snow had fallen on her nose. "The first time was a little . . . one-sided."

"Exactly. I can do better." He cupped his hand behind her neck and lowered his mouth to hers, still sweet from the syrup. He kissed her fresh smile, tasting her buoyant spirit, the way she had suddenly made him feel strong and full of hope with the future before him. She wove her mittens into the lapels of his jean jacket, tugging him closer.

He wrapped his arms around her tiny body and deepened his kiss.

Oh yes, this was much better.

What if Emma was the girl he'd been waiting for? Sure, he'd dated women over the past few years, but apparently the kind of woman who stirred his heart hailed from the town he loved.

It made sense. Deep Haven contained everything he wanted—family, home. What his parents had. Or what they used to have.

He eased out of the kiss, moved back to smile at her. Touch his forehead to hers, ever so gently.

"So when can I see you next?"

"Tomorrow, 9 a.m.," she said, shivering a little, her smile in her eyes. "I'll take that ride please."

"Perfect." He moved her away from him, clasped her mittened

hands between his. She had tiny hands for such a proficient musician. "What would you say to coming up to visit me?"

Her smile dimmed. "Where?"

"In Deep Haven, of course."

"You live in Deep Haven?" She held up her hands. "I thought you lived here."

"I used to, but no—I've always wanted to move back and I landed a deputy job a few weeks ago, even bought a house. I came down to pick up the last of my stuff from my pal's apartment."

She had slipped out of his grip, and now as she looked at him, something of warning coiled in his chest—a feeling he got right before a suspect took off running or, worse, threw a punch.

"I'm sorry, Kyle. But I hate that town and everything about it. It's dark and a prison and as long as I live, I'm never, ever returning to the armpit town of Deep Haven."

ℼ

How did a woman forget the man she'd been married to for twenty-five years?

Eli rounded on Anne as they exited the ICU, nearly backing her into the wall.

She held up her hands. "Eli, calm down. The amnesia is probably temporary."

"I'm sorry. I'm sorry." He still gripped his hat, his eyes burning from the trip to Duluth through the blinding snowstorm that had stretched out two hours to nearly four. His hands ached and his head throbbed.

Worse, down the hall in the lounge, their seventeen-year-old son waited to hear if his mother would be okay.

Eli took a breath. "What was that in there?"

Anne didn't ruffle easily. "She's got some retrograde amnesia. It's rare—and certainly rare to have her revert so far back."

"She thinks she's in college, for pete's sake. She doesn't have a clue who I am. She *ordered me from the room!*"

Anne led him over to a bench, sat him down. "She doesn't know you right now. But you heard her; she said you looked familiar. There's a shadow of you in there, and we have to believe that you'll surface. That her life will surface. It's most likely just the shock from the fall, perhaps some temporary blood loss in the temporal or frontal lobes. I'll order a CT scan and find out what's happening. But she's responsive; her vitals are fine; her pupils are normal. The effects of the head trauma seem to be abating."

"Then why doesn't she know me?"

"Sheriff, you know as well as I do that it's common for people to forget the events leading up to a trauma. Or even a few days after."

"The woman has lost half her life, Anne." Oh, he didn't quite mean that tone. "And all of the life we shared together." Or had she forgotten only him? "Maybe we should bring Kirby in there, let him jog her memory. Certainly she's not going to forget her son."

Anne had cut her hair since he'd seen her last, lost weight, but she still retained the sense of calm emanating off her that made her so valuable in a trauma. He wanted to drink in her confidence as she pressed a hand on his arm. "The last thing Kirby needs is to see his mother confused and even not knowing him. Let's wait until morning, and then we'll assess."

"But what if she doesn't get her memory back? What if she's forgotten . . . everything? Kirby and Kyle and . . ." He cupped a hand over his mouth, drew in a breath.

His loss reflected in Anne's eyes. "The brain is an amazing organ. It has a way of healing itself. I don't have to tell you to pray, Eli, but I have seen miracles happen. However, I'm not sure we need a miracle here. It's too soon to tell how much memory she might have truly lost, if any, and if it is permanent. The best thing you can do right now is stay calm, get some rest, and trust that she's in God's hands."

Eli walked to the glass doors, stared in at his wife. She looked so broken in that bed, her blonde hair plastered to her head, tiny lines of pain on her face. When she'd looked at Anne and asked her to make him leave . . . well, he wanted to weep. How could she not know him?

Or maybe she simply didn't want to. Maybe after three years of trying to push him out of her life, trying to forget him—all of them, really—she finally had.

He rested his forehead against the glass. No, God couldn't take his wife from him. At least not like this.

"Eli."

"Who holds up a coffee shop?"

"On a day like today, maybe the thief thought he could get away, hide out in the storm." Anne cast a look at Noelle. "The clerk—a high school girl—died at the scene. I'm not sure where Noelle found the courage to run, but she is a Hueston." She turned to him, and he tried to find peace in her kind smile. "Let the Duluth police do their job. You focus on your wife. I'll get you a medical stay pass at the hotel across the street. You must be exhausted."

"I'm not leaving Noelle."

Anne gave him an expression he'd known himself to give others over the years. "Yes, in fact, you are. We'll move her out of ICU in the morning if she continues to have a good night, but it's past visiting hours, and although I made an exception, this dispensation is over. Out of my ICU, Sheriff. Go get some rest. I'll see you in the morning."

She'd moved to stand in front of the glass doors that led into the ICU. Folded her arms.

"You'd make a good cop."

"So Noah has told me. Good night, Eli."

Eli tugged his hat back on and trudged down the hall toward the lounge area. How he hated hospitals—the ever-present aura of despair, the fading hope on the faces of the weary stacked and waiting in the padded vinyl chairs.

He and Noelle had probably worn the same expressions as the doctors fought for Kelsey's life.

Kirby had dropped off to sleep, one long leg dangling over the edge of the brown love seat. His head had rolled back, caught now in the crook of the sofa's arm. Beside him, his Diet Coke dented a *Family Circle* magazine on the table. A *Sports Illustrated* crumpled on the floor where it had slipped off his lap. The kid, with his toned muscles, unruly brown hair, the blue-and-white Deep Haven Huskies letter jacket, reminded Eli so much of himself at that age—so about himself, his sports, his future.

The boy couldn't lose his mother. Not after all they'd already lost. He reached down, nudged his son with his knee. "Kirbs. Wake up."

The seventeen-year-old stirred, licked his lips, blinked to consciousness. Focused on his dad. "Oh. Sorry."

"No problem."

Kirby sat up, rubbing the heels of his hands over his face. "How is she?" He stood and stretched.

"She woke up." He didn't know what else to add.

Kirby leaned down and grabbed the magazine, setting it back on the table. "So she's out of the coma?"

"Apparently. They'll probably move her out of ICU tomorrow."

Kirby picked up his soda, making a face after he downed it. "Can I see her?"

Eli shook his head. "Visiting hours are over. We'll see her first thing in the morning. I have a voucher for a night in the hotel across the street."

"She had me worried."

Eli clapped him on the back. "Me too."

Kirby was silent as they walked through the corridors, past rooms of sleeping patients. Eli felt it too—the memories lurking in dark corners—with every beep of the machines, the smell of the carpets, the odor of sickness, the lost expressions of the bereaved in waiting rooms, bracing themselves for a nightmare.

If there was one thing he wished he could forget . . .

But would he wish to lose everything?

They rode the elevator down to ground level. Outside, the fresh snow glistened under the cleared sky. The air had warmed, the lake breezes more temperate after the storm. In the padding of night, he could hear the rumbling of snowplows, the graders on the roads, cleaning them for the morning traffic. Tomorrow, all evidence of today's ice storm might even be melted away.

As Kirby opened the car door and retrieved the window scraper, Eli stood in the parking lot, hands shoved in his pockets, searching for hope in the glistening of stars against the blackness.

4

"It wasn't his fault, Ritchie. I'm telling you, there was this groupie there—he's the one that started the fight!"

Emma sat at her kitchen table, cell phone attached to the wall charger, wincing as Ritchie Huff detailed for her the expenses the bar owner intended on charging the band—namely her—for the brawl.

"Brian says it was this guy you knew, the one who carried you out of there, that started it."

"Brian is wrong."

"Well, at the least, you're off their list of bassists, and they're spreading the word around town. I'm just hoping I can get you off the hook for liability. But if you want any more gigs in this town, keep your boyfriend away from them."

"He's not my boyfriend!" But Ritchie had already hung up. Perfect.

Never mind the fact that for about four hours last night, she'd wanted Kyle to be exactly that. Her boyfriend. She pressed the phone to her forehead, closed her eyes. Oh, why, why did Kyle have to walk—no, he'd practically barged his way—back into her life? She could still feel his arms around her. And his kiss had been every bit as perfect as she'd imagined.

You never want to return to Deep Haven? She'd hated the hurt in his voice, the disbelief.

But she could have just as easily rounded on him, accused him of the opposite. *And I can't believe you do!*

It wouldn't do any good to try to change his mind. Grief did that—set people on paths they couldn't always explain.

She'd hurt him with the armpit comment, however. And why not? Most people loved Deep Haven, a favorite vacation spot in Minnesota. Try living there, though. With the memories.

So she'd backed away from him, let him drive her home and walk her ever so gallantly to the door.

He didn't offer another kiss. She didn't suggest one.

Now she dialed the Checker cab company, gave her address, then slipped on her UGGs and a parka and went downstairs to wait. The sky hung low over the St. Paul skyline, a gray pallor that still sifted down snow, scurried up drifts. The plow had already cleared her street.

Maybe she should have scuttled her disappointment and let Kyle drive her to the 400 Bar this morning. He'd called her twice before he left for Deep Haven—making sure she didn't want a ride to her car.

So what, he could kiss her again, make her long for a life she could never return to?

What is your heart into?

His words nagged her. Even more, her answer: *I'm still figuring that out.* Yeah, that felt like the first honest thing she'd said to anyone—including herself—since leaving Deep Haven.

She pressed her hand to the foyer window, drew it away, watching the outline on the glass.

One more time through, Emma; we nearly have it.

Kelsey could travel into her head so easily, especially after a gig. The songs Emma played, regardless of the genre, always took her back to the last time she actually felt like singing. Like composing.

She'd sat on the ratty green sofa her father had stored in the attic, her acoustic guitar over her knee, experimenting with a lick as Kelsey tried a different setting on her keyboard. Kelsey had always been the flamboyant dresser between them—in this memory wearing a black vest over a lacy tank, a pair of low-cut jeans. She had curves Emma envied, not to mention golden-blonde hair that she'd recently cut to a bob, tucked behind her ears. Raspberry-rose-painted toenails peeked out from the ragged hem of her jeans as she depressed the foot pedal. "I just want to try a different harmony on the bridge."

Their song still incubated—scrawled in pencil with hash marks to delineate stanzas, the chord progressions written over the words, scratched out, repenciled. Kelsey usually came to her with the words, and Emma added the tune. Or vice versa. Emma might play a tune, and Kelsey knew exactly the words to add.

Like puzzle pieces.

No wonder Emma hadn't finished a song in three years.

"I wish Kyle were here. He's the best drummer in three counties. He'd figure out the beat," Kelsey had said.

The lake breezes drifted through the window of the attic room over the garage, lifted the edges of their scattered papers. Despite their northern location, heat had slithered into the attic, sifting up the smells of grease in the garage below. Maybe later they'd motor into Deep Haven, grab an iced coffee at the Footstep of Heaven bookstore. Or a donut at World's Best. Maybe they'd sit on the rocky beach, airing out their songs to the rhythm of the waves.

"Yeah, I agree. Call your brother immediately," Emma said.

Kelsey laughed. "It's too bad he's already in college because I think he'd love jamming with you."

Heat rose to Emma's face. "You know I'm just kidding. I've been in love with your brother since second grade and I'm not sure he even knows my name."

Kelsey came over, sat next to her on the sofa, reached for a chocolate chip cookie from the tray. "Someday, Ems, he's going to notice you. I promise."

Emma handed her a can of Diet Coke. "In my wildest dreams."

"Seriously." Kelsey took a bite of cookie. "But you have to promise me one thing."

"What?"

She looked Emma in the eyes, hers alight with tiny particles of gold. "That no matter what happens with you and Kyle, he'll never come between us. We'll always be the Blue Monkeys."

"I promise." Emma held up her pinkie finger. Kelsey wrapped it with her own and laughed.

It was the echo of Kelsey's laughter that Emma heard most often. It had a singsong melody about it that could twine inside her heart like an embrace.

Oh, Kelsey. He noticed me.

Her handprint vanished on the window.

"Hey, there you are!" Her roommate, Carrie, stood at the top of the stairs, holding her cell phone.

Emma shook herself out of the memory.

"You left your phone on the charger. I think your mom just called."

Carrie, dressed in a tie-dyed shirt, homemade flare jeans, her dyed purple hair in cornrows, trotted down the stairs. "Where are you headed?"

"I have to pick up my car from the club."

"Why?"

"There was a fight last night. I had to stop in at the ER, get a couple stitches. A friend drove me home."

Carrie lifted the brim of Emma's fedora to see the purple bruise the cut had left on her forehead. "Ouch. How did that happen?"

"I fell."

Carrie raised an eyebrow. "By the way, I saw your *friend*. Care to elaborate?"

"He's no one." But, ow, that hurt to say.

Her cell phone vibrated again. Emma checked the ID, then flipped it open. "Hey, Mom."

"I left you a voice mail, but I thought I'd try again. How are you?"

Emma knew she should call her more—her mother spent so much time keeping up their lakeside cabin-turned-home since her father died. She didn't know how she got all that firewood chopped for their wood-burning heater. Probably hired it out, but still, the picture of her mother snowbound, freezing, and without wood haunted her.

"I'm fine. I had a gig last night."

"How'd it go?"

"Fine," she said, hating the lie. But her mother would only worry, and her forehead would be healed before her mom saw her.

"I'm sure it did. By the way, your friend Nicole called, looking for you again. Do you think you'll be able to come up and play for Nicole and Jason's wedding?"

Nicole Samson. She'd played second-chair flute in the band and was marrying a guy who graduated a couple years before them. When Emma received the invitation a month ago, she'd thrown it out. "Uh . . . they didn't ask me to."

"Nicole said she sent you an e-mail. She called last week and asked for your number. Apparently their band backed out."

"My cell phone died a few days ago. I haven't charged it." In fact, with the single bar that remained, she might not have enough juice for this call. "And I haven't checked my mail recently."

Emma saw the Checker cab making its way down the street. She stepped outside, waved.

"You should check your mail now and again, Emma. No wonder I never hear from you."

"I text you, Mom. You just never text me back. You should really learn how." She opened the door, held her hand over the phone, and gave the driver the address for the 400 Bar. He nodded and she got in.

Her mother laughed. "I don't understand how you can figure out the letters. Besides, who else do I have to text? Derek lives upstairs. Just answer your phone now and again." Emma could see her, probably curled in Dad's recliner, sitting next to the fire, wearing a pair of wool socks, a down vest, the waves through the picture window frothy on the rocky shore.

Or maybe she was arriving home, a couple sacks of groceries in her arms, from one of her many volunteer shifts. The thrift store, the nursing home, the library, the school—her mother logged more hours volunteering than if she worked full-time.

"I hope you can work it out with Nicole. Derek and I would love to see you. You could catch one of his games."

And see Kirby and the Hueston clan, not to mention the entire town of Deep Haven, on the sidelines? Nope.

Oh, her grief cordoned off such brutal parameters. "I'll let you know, Mom."

Her mother paused, her voice softening. "Emma . . . do you need anything?"

Yes. Oh yes. She just wasn't sure what it was. Emma leaned her head against the cab's cold window. "No, I'm fine."

"Okay. By the way, Noelle was injured in Duluth yesterday. She's in the hospital."

"That's terrible. Did she break something?" Funny that Kyle hadn't mentioned it. She drew in a breath, tapped the cabbie on the shoulder. He pulled over.

Her mother sounded strange. "She hit her head pretty hard, I guess. A terrible storm came through here, too. We got about a foot of snow. Eli and Kirby drove down to the hospital last night."

"I hope she's okay."

"We all do, honey."

"I'll call you later, Mom."

"Stay warm, Emma." Her mother hung up.

Emma fished out a few bills to cover the fare, then got out and stood in front of the 400 Bar as the cabbie pulled away.

Somewhere under that giant snowbank was her little red Subaru.

ॐ

Grief had a way of blitzing him, of taking Kyle out when he wasn't looking. And usually just when it seemed life was playing by the rules, when the good guys would finish first, when Kyle started to believe that everything just might work out.

Emma Nelson could have been the perfect girl. For a few brief hours, she was. Sweet with laughter that could burn away the pervasive chill inside. Someone who knew him back when life felt golden.

He could still feel her in his arms. Taste her lips. It scared him how quickly his mind had written a happily ever after for them.

I'm never, ever returning to the armpit town of Deep Haven.

It wasn't like he was an official member of the Deep Haven Chamber of Commerce or anything, but her statement left a bruise.

He gripped the steering wheel, hearing again her voice this morning on the phone. *Thank you, Kyle, but I think it's best if we don't see each other.* Wow, he'd turned into some sort of sad puppy to call her again, but apparently he needed final confirmation.

He let those words rattle around in his head as he drove past the Black Bear Casino south of Duluth, the parking lot half-full on a Friday morning. By this evening, it would be packed.

Emma was right. Spending more time with her might be lethal to his decision to move back to Deep Haven. But he'd been planning to go home for three years. He'd only known Emma for one night.

Okay, longer, technically, but . . .

How had he never noticed Emma Nelson?

He glanced at his cell phone tucked in the beverage holder

between the seats of his truck. He had the urge to call his mother, to tell her that he'd seen Emma.

His mother seemed to understand his need to reroute his life and return to Deep Haven better than anyone. She too could hear the echo of Kelsey's voice in the empty hallways of the house. She knew why he had to build a life in Deep Haven, help his family find their way back. Finally be there for Kirby, his mom, even his father.

Kyle tapped the brakes as he came over the hill into Duluth, the great Lake Superior harbor spread out below. Although steam rose off the lake past the aerial bridge, the shipyard appeared gripped in the deadlock of winter. Inside the inner harbor, a rumpled, icy collision of rutted waves, inert buoys, and chunky icebergs imprisoned the ships in port. Rusty lakers at anchor dripped massive icicles from their bows. Mountains of snow, debris from yesterday's storm, mounded the parking lot by the city auditorium.

The entire city appeared to be holding its breath.

The air would only thin as he traveled north to Deep Haven. The harbor in town would certainly be solid ice, probably even shoveled and turned into a skating rink for the locals. The retirees who loved the resort town in the summer would have flown to Arizona or Florida, leaving only the hardy behind. The locals emerged when the mercury dropped, when snow covered the cross-country ski trails, turned the paths in the woods into highways for the snow machines. In the early morning, from his cabin, he could hear the barks of the dogsledders' huskies rising from the woods where they ran trails.

Sure, Deep Haven might be trapped inside winter's grasp for four months out of the year, but frankly, Kyle appreciated the isolation.

It kept the troublemakers away.

And with his picking up the reins as a deputy, he planned on making sure Deep Haven stayed safe. No one would die on his watch—not if he could help it.

His cell rang and he answered it. "Hey, Dad."

"Where are you?"

He braked as he flowed into traffic. "In Duluth. I'm headed home."

"You might want to stop by St. Luke's."

The way he said it, softly, darkly, roused memories that Kyle would rather not revisit. "Why?" he said slowly.

"Your mother took a fall yesterday. She hit her head pretty hard."

"Is she okay?"

"They moved her out of ICU this morning. But . . . Well, just stop by, Kyle. We're on the second floor, room 2112."

Kyle clicked off and tried not to let the memories find him, dig their claws into his chest.

And just when they might be finding their way back.

He wove along Superior Street, turned up Ninth Avenue, found a place in the parking ramp. His heartbeat almost echoed through the massive structure as he exited his warm truck, headed toward the elevator banks.

Last time he'd been here . . .

He wrapped his jean jacket around himself, pushed the button. Emma's handprint still stained his jacket, and now he noticed droplets of blood along his sleeve.

An elderly couple entered at the next floor, the man holding the woman's hand. Kyle looked at his boots.

The elevator opened at the skyway, and he trekked to the

reception area, then down to the second floor. He spotted Kirby on a brown sofa in the waiting area, a glass table piled with magazines in the center. He wore his letter jacket, a blue Huskies baseball hat. The kid balanced a Diet Coke in one hand and paged through a magazine with the other.

His father stood with his back turned, dressed in his brown coveralls, as if he'd just come in from fishing, a stocking cap barely balanced on his head, his hair matted as it curled out the back. He stared out over the view of frosty Lake Superior.

"Dad?" Kyle glanced at Kirby too, who looked up.

"Hey, Kyle," Kirby said, his voice sounding tired.

Eli turned. He had aged about a decade since three weeks ago, when Kyle stopped by to give him the news of his new job.

Their fight still rang in his ears. *I told you that I don't want you being a cop in this town. You'll just get yourself killed.*

Thanks, Dad, for the vote of confidence. Never mind that his father had moved to Deep Haven as a rookie, built a life there. What, his son couldn't do the same?

But nothing of their argument was betrayed in Eli's expression now as he caught Kyle's hand. His eyes were cracked with red, his beard heavy.

Dread rippled through Kyle. "What happened? What's wrong with Mom?"

"She was involved in a shooting." Eli glanced at Kirby, then back at Kyle. "I didn't want to tell you over the phone. We were just briefed by the Duluth police."

"What? Was she shot?"

Eli shook his head. "There was a holdup in a coffee shop in Harbor City. She was there, apparently. We don't know all the details, but the cashier was killed. Your mother managed to get away—"

"Oh, thank God."

"She ran into the highway, but she took a bad fall, cracked her head on the pavement."

Kyle could feel his reaction on his face. *Cracked her head . . .* "How bad is it?"

Eli blew out a breath. "She was unconscious for a few hours, but she came to early this morning, about 2 a.m. She has some pain. And residual . . . damage. But we think it will resolve itself."

Kyle stilled. "What do you mean?"

Eli met his eyes. "She had some memory loss."

Kirby rose, wearing a stricken look. "You didn't tell me that last night."

"Anne Standing Bear is treating her. She seems to think her brain will heal, that it's not permanent." Eli rested his hand on his younger son's shoulder. "I'm sure she'll be fine. But I thought seeing you two boys would cheer her up this morning." He turned back to Kyle. "Anne told us we could see her as soon as you got here."

Kyle couldn't move. "A homicide? Did they catch the shooter?"

"Not yet."

"Do they have a suspect?"

"No. Unfortunately, whoever it was got away before law enforcement could arrive at the scene. But they're hoping your mother might shed some light on the incident, give them some leads."

"I want to talk to them."

Eli frowned. "What are you going to do, Kyle? Let the Duluth Police Department handle it. It's out of our jurisdiction."

"Just because you stopped being a cop doesn't mean I will."

A muscle pulled in Eli's jaw. "Let's just take care of your mom."

"You take care of Mom. It's about time, anyway. You virtually ignored her after Kelsey's death. Why did you let her go to Duluth alone? You know how she hates driving in snowstorms."

"She didn't ask me, okay? I didn't even know she was here."

Kyle stared at him, nonplussed. "You didn't even know where she was?"

"I was fishing."

Even Eli, it seemed, realized how that sounded because he winced. Good.

Kyle shook his head. "Of course you were. You're always fishing. Well, after we see Mom, I'm going to figure out who did this to her. One of us needs to start acting like a cop."

&

Noelle liked the doctor—Anne, was it? A heart-shaped face, kind hazel eyes that had sympathized when Noelle complained of a headache again this morning. She'd been the one who agreed to move her out of ICU and nodded when Noelle asked her to call her parents again.

Maybe she should have gone into health care. But seeing people hurt, in trauma . . . the thought made her insides coil. No, Noelle didn't like hospitals at all. For some reason, they made her nauseous, although honestly, she hadn't spent much time in one. Just that time her sister had the allergic reaction to the bee sting, but that had been more of a backwoods clinic. And her brother had broken his leg skiing in Vail. But again he hadn't been treated in a large hospital like this one. She must be at the Hennepin County Medical Center off campus.

A nurse had entered after the doctor left and removed her from intravenous fluids, put a Band-Aid over the insertion point in her arm. It ached, but not like her head, which still had a long, slow throb as if her brain wanted to travel out through her eyeballs.

The sooner her parents came to pick her up, the better. Frankly, she couldn't believe they weren't sitting beside her bed when she awoke this morning. Instead, a nurse in a pink uniform had taken her pulse, checked her blood pressure, and asked about her name and her address.

Noelle Stevens, University of Minnesota. She lived in those tall Cedar Square apartments near the campus. Yes, the nurse knew of them, and she smiled at Noelle and squeezed her hand.

They'd moved her down the hall and up one floor to another room, this one with a bright window that overlooked a snowy parking lot. Outside, the morning trumpeted into the room, over the empty bed beside hers, across the linoleum flooring. They still hadn't allowed her out of bed, but she longed to get up, take a shower, put on real clothes. A girl could freeze to death in the flimsy cotton hospital gown. She pulled the cotton blankets up to her chin.

Noelle tried to remember what day it was—Tuesday? She hoped it wasn't because she couldn't miss ARTS 3105, Dimensional Painting. How she struggled with shadow and light and adding the right hues to her work. And she still had to finish that portrait for her advanced watercolor class tonight.

Her stomach growled. She could go for a Big Ten sub on whole wheat—

"Noelle?" Anne poked her head into the room. "You have visitors."

"My parents?"

"No—remember last night, when we said that you were married, had a husband?"

"Did he find his wife?" She had felt sort of sorry for the man as she'd watched him in the hallway, taking the news that she wasn't the person he thought. He'd clutched the grimy hat, shaken his head, shot another look toward her. She'd closed her eyes and pretended to be sleeping.

Anne shook her head. "Not . . . yet. He'd like to talk to you."

Perfect. She sighed, braced herself. "What does he want?"

As Anne came in, she held open the door. "I'll let him tell you."

She recognized him—what was his name again? He hadn't changed clothes—still wore those hideous brown coveralls, the filthy cap, but now had a heavy, old-man grizzle on his chin. Two younger men followed him in. The shorter one looked about sixteen, cute with curly brown hair poking out of a blue baseball cap. He wore a stained letter jacket, his hands shoved into his pockets. He looked at her with such longing that she had to turn away. The other was taller than the older man, well-built, with short bronze hair, hazel eyes. He looked like a younger replica of the older man except for the scowl.

He walked toward her. "Hey, Mom,"

Hey . . . *what?*

"What did you call me?"

He froze, glanced at the older man. Back to her. Reached for her hand. "Mom—"

Noelle yanked her hand away before he could touch her. "What kind of joke is this?" When she looked at Anne, she saw pain on her face. "This isn't funny. I told you last night that he was mistaken. What did he say to you?"

"Noelle, please, listen to us. He's not lying—*we're* not lying to you. You fell and you lost your memory. This is your husband, Eli, and your sons, Kirby—" she pointed to the younger one, who looked like he might cry, his jaw so tight she could pluck it and shatter glass—"and Kyle." She nodded toward the older one, whose piercing gaze could nearly impale her.

Anne pulled out a bag from her lab coat. "Here are your personal effects—your wedding ring, a necklace. Your clothes are in a hanging bag in the bathroom."

She gave Noelle the baggie, and she stared at the ring. Not a big diamond, and the gold wedding band fit against it, welded tight. The setting looked worn, even dirty. The necklace, tangled at the bottom, held a gold charm, a loop with two "heads" at the top. It bore the hint of tarnish.

"I don't recognize these. Or . . . them." She swept her gaze quickly across the three men, then held out the bag to Anne. "I don't know why you think I could be the mother to two grown men, but . . . I mean, really, how old do I look?"

Anne pursed her lips in a tight line.

"I'm *twenty-one*. I've never had children." She lowered her voice, leaned over to Anne. "I'm not even dating anyone." She held up her hands. "There's been a terrible mistake here. I would appreciate it if you'd leave me alone."

Eli had shoved his hands into his pockets, and he seemed to be wincing.

Kyle glanced at Anne, then at his father.

But the younger boy—Kirby?—was staring at her, shaking his head. "Mom, stop it. Just stop it. You can't be like this!" The pain in the boy's voice almost made Noelle want to believe them. He appeared so wretched standing there, his eyes glistening. "Don't you remember me—or Kyle? What about—?"

"That's enough, Kirby." The man grabbed his shoulder, a tight clamp of authority. "Just calm down. Your mother had a terrible fall. She's hurt, and she needs time."

"I don't need time. I'm fine. I just need you all to leave." She gave Kirby a sad smile. "You look like a nice kid. I hope you find your mother."

"Noelle, it's time you got up. I have to show you something." Anne reached for her, started to remove her blanket.

"Hey! Not with them here. Tell them to leave."

Kyle wore a strange, grim expression. "Don't worry," he said softly. "Everything's going to be okay."

She frowned at him. Of course it was.

"Okay, men, everyone out. Just for a moment," Anne ordered.

"I'm her husband!"

"Eli . . . please."

Kirby had already turned as if he might be fleeing.

"C'mon, Dad. We'll wait in the hall." Kyle had turned away also, reaching out for his father. Eli yanked his arm away from his son's grasp.

Noelle glared at him. This Eli person seemed downright nasty, rude, even violent. She didn't want to be anywhere near him.

Maybe his wife had run away from him—or maybe he'd hurt her, put her in the hospital.

She'd request that he not be allowed in her room.

Noelle waited until they left before she let Anne help her from the bed. "I don't like him. He's so . . . gruff."

"He's actually a very compassionate man," Anne said as she helped Noelle stand. Noelle reached for the bed rail, the room taking a wild spin. "He was the sheriff in Deep Haven for the past ten years."

"No wonder he's so hard and dark-looking."

Anne said nothing as she helped Noelle around the bed, toward the bathroom. "Listen, here's the deal. You should know that it's common for someone with your injuries to lose a little memory. Although your vitals seem nearly normal, your brain is still healing from the fall. It might take a few days, even a month or so."

"I don't have any memory loss—"

Anne flicked on the light to the bathroom.

Noelle stared at the image of the woman in the mirror. Same blue-green eyes, but the skin around them sagged, tiny wrinkles carved into the corners. Her blonde hair was smashed to her head around a bandage, patches on one side shaved off. She took a step closer, her chest tightening. Thin lines etched her mouth, her lips, and her skin appeared sallow, even sagging. She had jowls.

Noelle ran a hand along her chin, her breath knotting in her chest. She opened her mouth, but something like a whimper emerged.

Oh. No.

"Noelle, you had a C-section with Kirby. You . . . could check that out if you need more confirmation." Anne turned her, took her hands.

Noelle's breaths started to tumble over each other. *No, no—*

"It's true. Eli Hueston is your husband. You've been married twenty-five years. And Kirby and Kyle are your sons. You live in Deep Haven."

Deep Haven? She'd visited there with her family a few times, summer vacations. But she would never have wanted to live in such a dark and remote place, so far from civilization.

"This can't be true. I . . . no . . . I want my parents."

Anne sighed. "They passed away. Your father died about ten years ago, your mother more recently."

Noelle backed away from her, pressing herself against the cold tile wall of the bathroom. "No . . . that's not right." She began to shake, could feel herself coming apart on the inside. "This isn't funny. This is not right. I . . . I don't remember any of this." Her voice had begun to pitch high, her breaths shaggy, in and out, as she closed her eyes and tried to grab at anything that made sense.

She'd just talked to her dad yesterday. Asked him to go with her to look at a car.

Her mother had promised to make her lasagna if she came home for the weekend.

Noelle wound her arms around herself, slid down to the floor. Opened her eyes and stared at Anne, who crouched before her, her own eyes glossy.

"Please, please don't tell me that I've lost twenty-five years of my life."

5

ELI HAD NEVER BEEN a man for emotion. Sure, when Kyle slipped into the doctor's hands, a bubble of warmth filled his chest, and likewise with the births of Kelsey and Kirby.

And of course, nothing could describe the way Kelsey's death destroyed him, turned everything in his life gray and bleak. Other men—men who didn't have an occupation built around the lousy choices of others—might have starting hiding a bottle of Jack Daniel's in the glove compartment or the desk drawer. He'd had his work to help him forget, and besides, a cop knew how to control his emotions.

But he'd never wanted to hit anything, lash out, hurt someone like he did when he heard Noelle scream. Not a high-pitched sound of fear, but one wrenched from deep inside, places only he knew now, places she'd forgotten.

And then, the sobs. Deep and heartbreaking, they snuck out into the hallway as he stared at his two lost sons.

They lingered in the hall, not sure what to do.

He'd made a mistake bringing Kirby into the room with him. He'd thought, maybe, that seeing her son would jolt Noelle out of any residual amnesia.

Instead, it jolted Kirby into a blank stare as he listened to his mother cry.

"Kirby—"

He held up a hand, met his father's eyes, shook his head.

"I thought she would remember us when she saw you."

"You should have let me tell her about Kelsey. She'd remember her daughter," Kirby said.

"Oh, that's a great idea," Eli said, his voice low. An elderly man, tall and gaunt, held a bouquet of flowers, a tiny boy trotting along behind as he shuffled past them down the hall. "Tell her about how she had a daughter, and then what, tell her how that daughter was murdered? You don't think that might do more damage?"

He shouldn't use that tone on his seventeen-year-old son—he knew it even as the boy flinched. But the kid had to grow up, face the truth.

Compassion only made people weak. It tore down defenses and made them too trusting. Vulnerable.

Sometimes it even destroyed lives.

"No, we're not telling your mother about Kelsey. Not until she remembers herself."

"And when might that be, Dad?" Kyle, now coming to life from where he'd wandered down the hall. "Never? What, are we supposed to just wipe Kelsey out of her life?"

"I don't know, okay?" Eli's voice thundered, and he cranked it back down to something he recognized. "I think you're jumping to conclusions here, Kyle. The doctor doesn't know how long this might—"

"My own mother didn't know me. She thought she was in college, Dad. *College*. In her brain, she's *my age*." He held up his hands as if trying to push the thought away. "This can't be happening."

Eli thought he might be turning away but—

"You know, I don't blame her brain for shutting down. For forgetting us. I mean, who wants to remember the last three years? Or more? If I could, I'd wipe it away too." Kyle's voice echoed down the hall.

"Really, Kyle? You'd forget everything?" Kirby's voice shook. "You'd want to wake up thinking Kelsey was still here? Only to be told she'd died?"

Eli hiked a hand around Kirby's neck and drew him down the hall with more force than necessary. "Do you suppose we could refrain from yelling? Because I'm not sure if she heard *everything* yet."

Kyle followed them. "She's still crying in there, Dad. I don't think she's really listening to three strangers argue about her."

"Kyle—"

He seemed brewing for a fight, something more than frustration on his face even as he shoved his hands into his pockets, turned away from them.

"I just think that if we talk about Kelsey, it's going to raise questions that your mother can't hear the answers to until she's more emotionally stable. We *will* tell her. But only when she's ready."

Except the fact was, it was only devastating if she could actually remember Kelsey in the first place. To Noelle, they were strangers—unkempt, angry, unruly strangers.

She wouldn't even allow him in the room to see her in her hospital gown.

Oh, she'd love the next part . . . when they discharged her and she had nowhere to go but home with him.

Eli ran a hand down his face, then opened his eyes to see Kyle before him, his own eyes red-rimmed.

"What?" Eli said, his lack of sleep in his tone.

"I just think that maybe you could have stopped this. You should have gone with her to Duluth. Should have been there, instead of her, during the robbery. *Protected* her like a husband should." Kyle's low voice slid through him like a knife.

Eli drew a breath. "Fine. Yes, I should have gone with her. But I didn't even know she was going!"

"And that alone should tell you something."

"What was she doing here, anyway?" This from Kirby, his voice very small.

"I don't know." Eli glanced at him, his heart wringing. "Shopping, probably. Does it matter? We can't turn back time."

"Mom has. She's turned it all the way back to before she knew any of us." Kirby wiped his eye with the meat of his hand. A curse word emerged, something Eli had never heard him use. He didn't chastise his son.

"She'll come back to us. We have to believe it."

"Why?" Now Kyle rounded on him. "Why should we listen to you? You never came back after Kelsey died."

"What are you talking about, Kyle? I never left your mother."

"You didn't move out. You just moved down to the den." Kyle stared at him. "No wonder Mom wants to forget you. *I* wanted to forget you."

Eli couldn't help it. Something inside him just snapped, something angry and frustrated and—

He slapped Kyle across the face.

Kyle jerked, gasped.

Kirby stepped back, shock—or maybe fear—in his eyes.

Kyle wore an expression Eli didn't recognize.

He barely braced himself before Kyle tackled him. Around the waist, like he'd been taught in Husky football, and slamming Eli into the ground. Eli hit the ground like an old man, the impact jarring through his bones, his head. But he rebounded like a cop, ramming his elbow into Kyle's jaw, feeling sick as the kid rolled off him.

He'd never hit his children.

Eli scooted back on the floor, held up his hands. "Kyle! Knock it off."

Blood dribbled down the corner of Kyle's mouth. His eyes burned through Eli, his voice rife with vitriol. "You make me sick. First Kelsey and now Mom. She might have forgotten us, but *you* forgot us first. *You* lost this family, Dad. *You* blew it. You know, Emma was right—there's nothing to go back to in Deep Haven. Nothing but scars. Nothing but pain. Thanks for that."

Then Kyle got up and strode past Eli.

Kirby had a hand over his face, his shoulders shaking.

Eli dropped his head into his hands, wishing that he, too, could find the courage to weep.

Especially since he feared that every word Kyle spoke might be painfully, brutally correct.

Kirby finally sat down beside him. Eli felt his son's hand on his shoulder, and the gesture made him shake.

"What do we do now, Dad?" he whispered.

Eli sighed. "I guess we take this woman home and try to help her get her life back."

⚘

Kyle's mother had nearly lost her life beneath a three-way blinking stoplight, in front of a used-car dealership, a dry cleaner, and a coffee shop that shared strip mall space with a gift shop specializing in slippers and candles.

Her SUV sat, still parked, in front of Mocha Moose, buried under a crusty layer of snow.

Kyle stared at the yellow-taped doors of the crime scene and wanted to retch. He'd peeked inside the locked doors. The place still betrayed the chaos of the burglary—a cash register with the drawer open, the candies on the front counter spilled, some of them littering the floor. He'd called the Duluth Police Department, and one of the assistant deputies agreed to meet him here at the scene.

A courtesy to his father, whom he'd had to mention to get any face time with the investigators.

Kyle's jaw hurt. The bleeding had stopped somewhere between Duluth and here, but the incident replayed in his mind like a slap—shock, then a flash flood of anger, indignation, shame, all spurting out of him.

He'd tackled his father to the ground. Wanted to hit him, to put his fist in his face in an explosion of fury, of desperation. Anything to expel the roil of hurt inside. The thought now caught him up, sent a tremble through him.

He almost wanted to thank his old man for the elbow shot in the jaw. It probably saved them from an all-out brawl in the middle of the hallway.

Yeah, like his mother needed to see *that*. Not that it would jolt her memory—sure, Kyle and his father had rounded on each other a few times during his growing-up years, but his father had never, not once, hit him.

And he'd never, in all of his teenage angst, considered turning on his dad.

Even when his father had left them at Kelsey's graveside, the rain sloughing mud onto her casket.

Even when Eli started sleeping at his office, on a little cot he shoved next to his file cabinets.

Even when he bought himself the Taj Mahal of fish houses to hide inside.

Even that day when Kirby called, his voice shaking, saying Dad had come home, emptied out Kelsey's room, and gotten rid of everything, while their mother watched, knees drawn up as she sat on the floor of the living room, her eyes haunting all of them.

Not long after, Kyle had transferred to Alexandria, where he started the program in law enforcement. It simply made sense. Someone had to protect his family.

Still, it wrecked him just a little for his dad when his mother looked at her husband and didn't know him.

Or didn't want to.

"Are you Kyle?"

The voice startled him; he hadn't heard the officer drive up. Kyle turned and met his hand. "Yes, thanks for meeting me. Kyle Hueston. I'm with the Deep Haven sheriff's office. I was hoping you could walk me through the scene here."

"Marc Wrenshall." Wearing a pair of brown pants, his weapon under an insulated black jacket, and his dark hair shorn tight to his head, he had gray eyes that seemed, if not old, at least seasoned.

The deputy nodded. "I'm sorry about your mother. Your father and I had a couple cases we worked on a few years ago. How is she?"

Kyle followed him to the door. "She's . . . still recovering."

"I'll be glad when we can get a statement from her, sort out what happened." He unlocked the door. Despite the chill and the embedded smells of coffee and woodsmoke, the tinny, rancid odor of blood tinged the room.

"What do you know?"

"Not much. After your mother alerted the truck driver, he stopped, called 911. We didn't know about the burglary until later, when our deputies were doing a sweep of the area to find out what happened." He moved around the counter. "We've already checked the room for prints, but there's just too many. A cold day like yesterday . . . before the storm hit, this place saw a lot of traffic." He pointed to the back room, where an office door lay open.

The room had already been cleaned, the scent of chemicals rising from it making his eyes water. Kyle put a hand over his nose.

"Forensics has taken samples. They found skin under the victim's fingernails and a welt across her face as if she'd been hit with more than a fist. There seemed to have been a struggle, and from the blood spatter and her wounds, it appeared she'd been shot from close range." He indicated where the blood had hit the walls, the papers on the desk, the window.

"Who was the victim?"

"Cassie Mitchell. Senior over at Harbor City High."

Kyle couldn't speak. Today, a family grieved over their lost futures.

"We did find something odd." Marc backed out of the room, pointed to a painted outline on the floor. "A fishing knife. Could be the perp's—we found it on the floor next to the cash register. Maybe he dropped it when your mom took off."

"You know for certain she was here?"

"She left her purse, and her coffee, in the bathroom."

"She saw it."

"Could be. We'd sure like to talk to her."

Kyle stood behind the counter, running the scenario through his mind. His mother had left coffee in the bathroom. So she had already ordered, already waited for her drink. Had the man come in after her? Or before? Was it a spontaneous or a planned robbery?

"Does the coroner have a report back on the kind of weapon used?"

Marc shook his head. "We're going door-to-door today, doing some interviews. We'll call you if anything turns up."

"What about the log? Did anyone call in anything . . . suspicious? Out of the ordinary?"

"I went through the calls this morning. A couple cars in the ditch in the storm, a dog on the loose, but nothing that might shed some light on what happened."

Kyle moved to the bathroom. The door stood ajar and he flipped on the lights. He turned, tried to see the crime through his mother's eyes.

She had stood here, watched someone holding up the clerk. A high school student, no older than Kelsey.

No wonder she tried to save her.

He reached up, held on to the doorframe. Let the tremor that went through him pass.

"What if she opened this door, saw them—maybe ran for help?"

Marc nodded. "But why didn't he go after her or even shoot her?"

"We're right next to the highway. Maybe he didn't have time."

"There was about ten feet of visibility. No one would have seen him, or even heard, the shot over the wind."

Kyle came out to stand by the counter. Surveyed the scene. "Why didn't she go for her car? There were hardly any vehicles on the road."

"We found her keys outside by her vehicle. It's possible she tried, and he dragged her back inside."

Kyle stared out the window, the thought of some man's hands on his mother, dragging her inside, nearly killing her . . . He took a few long breaths—in, out.

Randomness. He hated every bit of it, how in a second, a person's life could be dismantled. How plans and hopes and dreams died on the tile floor of coffee shops and convenience stores. How it inflicted wounds not just on the victim or the family, but on entire communities.

It simply wasn't right that a forty-six-year-old woman could drive into a strip mall coffee shop and lose her life. Or at least, most of it.

Kyle was sick to death of randomness. Of injustice.

Marc stood by the other door. "We'll find him."

Kyle nodded. *No, I'll find him.*

&

Lee Nelson's front yard resembled one of her homemade lemon meringue pies. Snow drifted in swirls across her driveway, out toward the lakeshore. Ravenous waves from the storm the night before had devoured the ice buildup onshore, leaving only jagged crumbs, now crashing together as the current moved them. They tinkled like the wind chimes Lee hung over her deck during the summer, the wind gusting now and again to add a rattle to the pane.

Lee shivered as she stood at the picture window, zipping up a vest. Not so long ago, Clay would have covered this window with plastic to stave off the wind. She could get Derek to help her hold up one end, secure it with tape, and blow-dry it taut. But the kid usually arrived home after dark, exhausted to the bone after basketball practice, ate his dinner with a sum total of five words, and fell asleep in the spine of his algebra book.

Add to that games on Saturdays, his part-time work bagging at the grocery store, and church on Sundays, and the boy had no time for chores.

Not that Lee had extra time, either. With her volunteer positions around town, as well as her new treasurer duties at church, if she managed to cook something from scratch, she counted it a triumph.

No wonder they still had six cords of unsplit wood in the shed and a pile that needed stacking outside the wood burner.

Why on earth couldn't Clay have installed a gas heater? But no, he wanted to be efficient, and with the acreage his family left him, they could log off their own land, keep themselves in wood until the end of time.

Except he hadn't counted on leaving her with the work. Sometimes she could still see him, his body lean and strong from hours with the wood splitter, covered in shavings, smelling of poplar, cedar, and pine, grinning at her as she gathered up the wood to stack. Their Saturday morning dates. She'd bring him coffee, bundled to the gills, and they'd talk about the kids and how they would manage to send Emma and Derek to college on a cop's salary.

The wind shook the house, the sun low on the horizon, bleeding through the late-afternoon shadows that hovered over the lake.

She had to shovel if she hoped to get her car out of the garage for Derek's game tonight. She planned on surprising him. It seemed the only time they talked was when she trapped him in the car.

Lee checked the fire grate, made sure it was secure before she went into the entryway, pulled on her Sorels, her down parka, Clay's old beaver hat, and her work mittens with the wool liners. She added a scarf so that only her eyes showed, then, taking a breath, opened the door.

The chill had the power to freeze her eyelashes to her face. She shut the door quickly behind her, hating how the cold slicked up her nose, made her eyes water.

She picked up a scoop of kitty litter in a bucket next to the door and sprinkled it on the fresh snow as she packed down a new trail to the garage. They'd lived in the two-car garage for a year before they finished the cabin, building on as their family grew. Clay added an attic to the garage three years before he died, a place for Emma and Kelsey to practice.

Emma . . . do you need anything? Lee had tried not to betray her concern in her voice this morning—Emma had become so distant in the past three years, and it seemed every time she offered her support, Emma simply pushed her away.

No, I'm fine.

No, she wasn't, but Lee had no idea how to fix her. Or any of them. She just kept trying to survive a little bit better every day.

Lee hit the garage door button and let it open. A three-foot shelf of snow tumbled onto the cement. Oh, to have a snowblower, but that went out a year ago. She hadn't had the heart to ask Eli to fix it. He already did too much.

Eli.

She hated the wretched hurt in his voice last night when he'd called her. At 3 a.m. She probably should have been sleeping, but she'd been hoping he might call, if not stop by.

She hated herself a little for that—the happiness she found in his friendship. He was such a kind man, the way he showed up to cut wood, shovel, unplug a drain, mow her lawn, repair a broken faucet, help her sort out the statements from the insurance company.

Clay had picked well when he campaigned for Eli for sheriff. A better man—besides Clay—she didn't know. It helped that Kirby and Derek had played ball together since middle school; it became a natural reason to sit together at events, to become friends, to share hopes and dreams, back when they had them.

Noelle didn't even realize what she had in a man like Eli. Lee tried not to resent Noelle. . . . Okay, she probably did a little. But she could forgive her—after all, Lee had lost her past, her present. Noelle had lost her only daughter. Her future.

Hey, Lee. Eli's voice, in the padding of darkness, had made her heart do a forbidden dance. He had a deep, resonant voice, a seasoned calmness, a soft familiarity that she needed when the moon lit the lake, lonely in the night sky. "I'm in Duluth. Noelle had an accident."

"What happened?" she asked, her voice quiet. Hopefully the ringing phone hadn't woken Derek.

"She fell and hit her head outside the Mocha Moose."

"Did she break anything?"

"She has some bleeding in her brain—"

"Oh—that's horrible. I'm so sorry."

"Yeah." He sounded tired. And as if he might be talking to her in an enclosed, echoing place.

"Where are you?"

"At a hotel near St. Luke's. I'm in the bathroom—Kirby is asleep. We stopped in at the ICU. She seems to be stable, thankfully. But . . ." He sighed.

She could see the sigh. Could see him sitting on the side of the tub or leaning against the counter, dragging his fingers through that dark, curly hair. She wanted to rest a hand upon his cheek, smooth away the stress.

Lee banished that thought. It was just compassion. She knew what a midnight vigil felt like. They'd even shared it—she and Eli and Noelle.

"She can't remember me."

The words stripped her of a response. Noelle couldn't remember him?

"She looked right at me and didn't know who I was."

"Oh, Eli. I'm sorry."

He blew out a breath. "Thanks. I just wanted to let you know that Kirby won't be at tomorrow's away game. Can you ask Derek to tell the coach?"

He wanted to let her know at 3 a.m.? She had no comment for that. "Of course, Eli. And I'll be praying too."

"Thanks, Lee." He'd clicked off, and she wanted to say more, to offer something, but the words wouldn't surface.

Probably it was better that he'd hung up, that they couldn't say any more in the middle of the dark night.

Hopefully he would forget her words, so ill spoken, about

starting over. About him already being alone. She'd regretted them since the minute they left her mouth. She hadn't meant he should start over with her. Just . . . that things might be different for him, for Noelle.

But not like this.

The snow had turned heavy today, and Lee could only tackle the top layer, tossing it feebly to the side before going back for another dip. At this rate, she'd be out here until the spring thaw. Maybe she'd just put on the four-wheel drive and back out her SUV like a monster truck the entire sixth of a mile to the road.

She leaned down for another shovelful, filled it up, lifted.

It was then she felt it, the hitch in her neck, as if something slipped. The pain, sharp, bright, lit up inside her.

Then it was gone. But her arm hurt, an ache that scooted the length of it.

She tossed the snow away, and the pain shot down to her fingers as if someone had taken a match and lit.

"Ow—oh—" Her voice seemed feeble in the encroaching night. Shaggy, snow-laden trees muffled the sounds of the road, protected the house from the sight of neighbors. If Lee collapsed in the snow, no one would find her until tomorrow.

If Derek didn't come home after Saturday's game, then maybe not even then.

She put the shovel down. The pain burned brighter, creeping up to her neck, clenching the muscles there. Oh, she'd done something bad.

Ice. She needed ice, and quickly. Turning back to the garage, she hiked along the tiny trench she'd made, set the shovel on its hook, then trudged to the house. By the time she reached the door, she could barely lift her arm to grab the handle.

Shaking off her coat, her hat, her gloves, she piled them on the bench. She wanted to scream as she bent down to remove her boots and finally kicked them off and headed toward the freezer.

She pulled out an ice pack and positioned it on her neck. Then she hobbled to Clay's recliner and climbed in.

Hey, babe, you all right?

In her mind, Clay came over, sat on the hearth, his strong hands picking up the knit afghan his mother had gifted them for their wedding. He draped it over her, then pushed her hair back and pressed a kiss to her forehead, right above her eyebrow. Sometimes she could still smell him, feel the caress of his fingertips on her skin.

The sun had all but disappeared, the final brilliance of light nearly blackened. She searched for early stars high above but saw nothing.

In the hearth, her fire had started to die, embers crackling.

No. No, Clay, I'm not.

The pain pulsed down her neck, seeping into her bones as the night wind shook the cabin. And in the echo of the wind, Lee heard a tiny whimper.

Her own.

6

NOELLE MIGHT AS WELL have been a prisoner. There had to be some sort of law against the hospital releasing a patient into the hands of virtual strangers. But as Eli so brutally pointed out, where else would she go? Especially since her headaches had diminished and she otherwise felt fine.

Noelle rode in the front seat of a black truck, beside the man who claimed to be her husband—although she had to have been cracked in the head long, long before this to have married someone who looked like he'd emerged right beside Grizzly Adams from the depths of the forest, having just wrestled a bear.

The man even smelled like wildlife.

The only reason she got into the truck at all and didn't just check herself into some church shelter was Dr. Anne Standing

Bear's vigorous belief that not only was this her life, but Eli was a safe, good man.

Right.

But Kirby could make a girl rethink her headstrong ways.

She liked the boy. He had a gentleness and compassion in his green eyes that convinced her that, even if she didn't know him, she might have been proud to be the mother of such a son. Over the past day, he'd sat by her bed, told her stories of his life. He played basketball—a point guard, apparently—and football for the Deep Haven Huskies. He hoped to land a scholarship next year to the University of Minnesota at Morris or Duluth. Or even the Twin Cities campus.

He had a kind smile, too, and fetched the nurse once for her when her migraine overtook her and made her retch.

All the while, Eli—her husband—wandered in and out of the room like a prowler.

The man gave her the willies, with his dark demeanor, his wary, even angry eyes. If he hoped she'd recognize some life they shared together, he might not want to walk around with his bristly side out.

So far, she didn't even recognize her own body. She was . . . well, she was *fat*. She sat in the bathroom last night, staring at all the unmuscled, flabby flesh around her stomach, at the faded white scar of a cesarean section, running her finger into the stretch marks below her navel.

She had given birth—twice.

Which meant . . . She glanced at the man beside her, then looked away. Oh. My.

"I haven't said much to anyone about . . . well, you know. About your memory thing," Eli said.

Her memory thing? Wow, the man had superb verbal skills. No wonder he'd barely spoken to her the entire two-hour drive into the backside of the earth, where the trees seemed to loom higher, loop over them.

Like coils of barbed wire.

"Normally we'd go to church tomorrow. But I'm thinking maybe we should stay home," Eli said.

That meant she at least still had her faith. Probably the only thing that kept her from fleeing in the dead of night.

Although, funny, she didn't feel like she and God were on a talking basis.

"I need a drink," she said.

"There's a convenience store in Little Beaver; you can get a coffee—"

"I hate coffee. But I'd love a Diet Coke." It suddenly occurred to her—"Do I have any money? A job? My own account?"

"We share everything. And no, you don't work outside the home."

She didn't? Then what did she do all day? Her question must have resonated in the little sound of confusion she made because Kirby leaned up from the backseat.

"You volunteer a lot at the school. In the concession stand and taking tickets at the games. You also help some of the little kids with their reading."

"Am I a teacher?" She never wanted to be a teacher. In fact, she didn't even like children. They had runny noses, grimy hands. They were loud and messy.

"No. You just like being a mom," Eli said.

Oh.

"What else do I like?" Indeed her tastes must have changed

considerably since she wore leggings and a baggy sweater to class, because in the plastic bag over the door of the hospital bathroom, she'd found a pair of ugly black dress pants, a flimsy blouse, and a suit jacket. She did like the killer boots, however. Clearly she hadn't lost her taste in shoes.

"You like gardening and cooking, and you do the crossword every day," Kirby said.

"The crossword." What, was she *eighty*?

"Kyle gave you an advanced crossword book last Christmas. You do one every morning. You always say it helps you to . . . not lose your . . ." Eli made a face. "Mind."

Yeah, that had worked.

"But you used to play Scrabble a lot with the kids." Eli sounded like he'd rather have his fingernails sanded off.

Kids. Right. "Where's . . . uh, what's his name?"

"Kyle? Your oldest son?"

"Please don't use that tone, like I'm annoying you. I met him for five minutes."

"You've known him for twenty-three years."

"You act like I did this on purpose. Like I really don't want to remember."

"Sorry. I'm just worried, is all." For the first time, another emotion crossed Eli's face. Sorrow? Regret? "It just feels strange to explain your life to you."

She bit back a response, hearing the fatigue in his voice. He had been at the hospital for nearly two days.

They pulled into a small town, the speed limit cutting down to thirty, and drove past a pair of gigantic Adirondack chairs, the entrance to a resort. Then a tall A-frame restaurant and a scattering of small lakeside houses all pumping out gray smoke. A strip mall advertised a restaurant, a bakery, a gift shop. Beside it, snow covered the playground equipment of a day care center connected to a one-story metal church.

Eli turned in to the gas station beside it.

"I'll get your Diet Coke, Mom," Kirby said as Eli got out to gas up the truck.

Mom. *Mom?* Oh, when would she get used to that?

And how had she ended up so far from civilization? What about her art?

Eli got back into the car, staring at his hands on the steering wheel.

"Do I still paint?"

Her voice shook a little, and she hated the fact that so much hinged on his answer. That she might have lost even that from herself.

"Not since college."

Noelle closed her eyes.

Kirby climbed into the truck. Handed her the soda. She took it, but her hand trembled.

They drove home, silence wedged between her and Eli, Kirby trying to dislodge it with the play-by-play of his last game. She wanted to weep for the boy who needed her to remember him, to cheer for him.

They drove through Deep Haven—she vaguely remembered the town, a shadow from her childhood—and continued on up the highway.

"How far out of town do we live?"

"About twenty minutes," Eli said.

She stared out the window as they curved along the ribbon of highway. The lake had a rhythm to it, the waves piling the ice upon the shore. Trees hugged the shoreline, glistening with frosting. Houses, their driveways bordered by mounds of fresh, white snow, created a storybook feel.

Maybe this place had wooed her with a mystical, still-hidden charm.

Maybe she could find the charm again.

They turned up a dirt road, followed it into the woods, the trees closing in as they turned again, this time onto a rutted driveway.

At the end sat a small Cape Cod with cedar siding, a bright-red door. Two sad dormer windows watched her. A garage sat twenty feet from the main house. Snow buried a car parked next to the garage.

A black dog trotted out to meet them, barking.

"That's Riggins," Kirby said. "She'll be really happy to have you home."

"Has she been out in the cold all this time?" Noelle opened the door, held on to the handle as she slid down and steadied herself on the snow. The dog came up to her and sniffed. Noelle patted her head. "You're a sweet girl, aren't you?"

"She has a heated doghouse and plenty of food," Eli said. "Wait there; I'm coming around to help you."

"I'm fine. I don't need help." She closed the door, however, and nearly slipped. So maybe she'd take it easy. The last thing she needed was another crack on the head.

Although, if it could snap her memory back . . .

But wait . . . did she really want it back? She glanced at Eli, who picked up a shovel near the garage and started plowing a path to the door, fresh snow flying. She had a Hansel and Gretel moment, staring at the house.

"I don't want you to fall." Kirby came around the car, stuck out his arm to her. What a gentleman. She couldn't help but wind hers through his. If she'd been his age, she would have had a crush on him.

She felt closer to her son's age than her husband's.

Weird.

Yes, indeed, she needed her memory back. She appreciated his help as they walked up the snowy path to the doorway. Then she took a deep breath.

Her life. This was her life.

She entered the house, stamping her feet. The entryway, a small room off the kitchen, overflowed with snow boots and winter jackets and hats stuffed in a bin and mittens scattered on a bench, a collection of helmets in a big basket by the door.

Didn't anyone clean? She looked at the grime on the floor, shoved into the corners. Men. *Men* lived here.

She hung up her coat, then entered the kitchen. At least this was clean. Small but functional, with a breadbox, a mixer, a view of the backyard. A round, red rug lay in the middle of the floor before the sink.

Red. She'd always been a pink person, so perhaps red wasn't too far off.

A long table with a blue checkered tablecloth hosted a bowl of brown bananas. So that was the smell in the air.

She wandered down the hallway, seeing three doors.

Kirby pushed past her. "This is my room." He opened the door to a basketball shrine. Minnesota Timberwolves, Golden Gophers, and Bulldogs paraphernalia decorated the walls; a basketball hoop hung over his bed. The place smelled like a boys' locker room. She tried not to grimace.

"You helped me decorate it."

Wow. So she'd lost her decorating style over the years, too. She found a smile, nodded.

"Whose rooms are these?" She turned toward one but Kirby shook his head. "Kyle's. The other is empty."

"A guest room?"

Kirby's smile faded a moment, and he glanced behind her. "Yeah. That's right."

"Do you need anything? Maybe want to lay down?" Eli asked. He still wore the coveralls, although he'd taken off that disgusting cap. His hair lay matted, curled and greasy.

Her head did hurt, the migraine a dull ache simmering in the back of her head. "Yes, please."

He nodded. "Our room is upstairs."

Our . . . "Uh. I don't . . . think . . ."

Eli glanced at Kirby, back to her. "Don't worry. I actually . . . I don't sleep there."

"Where do you sleep?"

He sighed. "Down here. In the den." Something in his voice bespoke shame.

But, well, good. She could only jump back into her life so far. Besides, whatever had happened between them to make him move to the den, she had no idea how to fix it.

Or if she wanted to.

He led her upstairs to one of the dormer rooms. Quaint, with a sloped ceiling. She didn't look at the king-size bed or the pictures on the dresser. A large window on the side wall overlooked their acreage. She stared out across the smooth plain of white and caught a view of the lake through the bordering trees.

Behind her, she heard Eli opening drawers, closing them.

Noelle turned. "What are you doing?"

He held clothes in his arms. "Getting some things for a shower. I need to clean up."

She glanced toward the bathroom. "You're not going to—"

He followed her glance, and an emotion flickered across his face. Pain? Frustration? "No. I'll use the bathroom downstairs." He backed out of the room. "I need to run some errands. Will you be okay? Kirby will be here, so you can call him if you need anything."

"I'll be fine. Thank you." She tried a smile, but the moment he left, she closed the door.

Locked it.

So this was her life. Her home. Truthfully, driving home in that truck, she'd expected a cabin in the woods, no running water, portable electricity. This room, however, seemed feminine, and yes, she approved of the green walls, the pink pillows, the light-blue bedspread. She studied the pictures of the two boys as babies in their frames on the dresser. They were cute; she could admit that.

In a larger frame, a woman who looked like her wore a fluffy wedding dress, holding hands with a much-younger version of the curmudgeon downstairs. He reminded her very much of his son Kyle in this picture. And look—he could smile.

Next to the bed sat a bookcase. And there, in a frame on top, was a picture she recognized.

She had always guessed herself to be about two years old in this shot, sitting on the lap of her very young father, he in a white T-shirt, boasting a crew cut and smiling down at her. Her mother sat on the arm of his chair, leaning on his shoulder, smiling at the camera.

Noelle had toted this picture, in exactly this frame, to college. She picked it up. Laid her hand upon it.

Oh.

Oh. Her breath began to leak out in soft bursts. She hugged the picture to her chest, then went over and sat on the bench in the picture window.

This life *did* belong to her.

She was the woman in the wedding photo.

Those sweet adult boys—they were hers.

And that man—that wretched man—was her husband.

She closed her eyes, the truth shaking through her.

This was her life.

But she didn't want it to be.

&

Emma had given up trying to find the lyrics.

Her chord sheet lay on the floor in front of her, abandoned as she leaned back against the ancient green sofa she'd inherited from the attic jam space and lost herself in her music. She played the leads of an E major scale, then the minor chords, up and down the frets.

Then she jumped into the key of A, played a minor pentatonic extended scale, and worked out a new lick, bending the B string down around the tenth fret, then popping over to the E string and bending it all the way up to high G. She held it for a moment, then ran the notes down the scale, adding a vibrato to the low E.

Yeah, she liked that lick.

She did it again, then strummed the A blues chords to a swing beat, just for fun.

Hard not to find a smile with the beat of a jump blues guitar.

But even behind the music, the hollowness of a song without lyrics resonated through her. Kelsey would have picked up her beat, added some piano, and come up with lyrics that scrubbed their latest drama out of their hearts.

The sound lingered, then faded into the street noise. Traffic splashed through the slimy snow and mud, and across the street, someone was having a house party, the music raucous. Two years ago, Emma had found the cheapest apartment she could within walking distance of the University of Minnesota campus.

She heard movement from Carrie's bedroom. Her roommate emerged in a slinky black dress, combat boots, a jean jacket, a patterned scarf, and long silver earrings. "You sure you don't want to come out with me tonight? I hate that you're sitting here lonely on a Saturday night."

This time on a Saturday night, she should be getting ready for a gig. According to Ritchie, she'd been blackballed in the tiny blues community, and yes, the bar owner was sticking her with part of the repair bill. Thanks for that, Kyle.

Emma got up, carried her cold mash of ramen noodles to the sink. Washed them down the drain. "No. I need a night off, probably."

"What, to brood over your lost love?"

Emma shot her a frown. "What are you talking about?"

"I'm not blind to the hottie who walked you to the door the other night. And by the way, everyone's talking about how he came in and started a ruckus when he saw one of your fans flirting with you."

"That's not how it went down."

Carrie picked up her purse and set it on the counter, riffling through it. "Whatever. He's cute. And I'm not sure why you sent him packing."

Emma washed the bowl, set it in the rack to dry. "I sort of

worshiped him in high school, and yeah, we had a nice night. But he lives in Deep Haven, which if you know anything about Minnesota is about five hours north of here."

"And your hometown. So do you have feelings for him?"

Did she? She used to. There was a time when she would track the sightings of him through her day. And she could hardly forget how it felt—finally—to be kissing him, the smell of him, the way, for a few hours, he'd made her feel found.

"I guess so."

"Then what's holding you back? He's got the goods, sweetie. Tall, blond—"

"And the brother of my best friend who died." Emma wrung out the washcloth, laid it across the double sink to dry. "And I might have already mentioned that he wants to live in Deep Haven?"

"A federal crime." Carrie pulled out a couple old ticket stubs and dropped them into the trash. "This might be news to you, but last time I checked, you *can* play music in Deep Haven. At least I think they changed the zoning laws up there. Didn't you say they had a blues festival and a great music scene? I'm dipping way back into my brain cell–damaged memory here, but didn't you tell me once that's where you heard the music best? Where you felt as if it came alive inside you? I'm not dreaming up the fact that you haven't composed one new song since you moved here—"

"I've composed plenty of songs—"

"Excuse me. You haven't *finished* a song. You need something called *lyrics* too."

Emma glanced at the scattered papers on the rag rug in the living room. "I just . . . I don't know what to say."

Carrie gave a slow nod. "Find the lyrics, and I'll bet you can figure out a way to go home again." She snapped her purse closed. "Last chance to change out of your yoga pants, maybe have a little fun."

"Nope. Don't get into any barroom brawls."

"Oh no, honey. You're the bruiser here." Carrie winked at her. "Don't wait up."

Emma sat down again with her music. *Find the lyrics.* Yes, if she could do that, then she could go into the studio, record a demo.

Put some feet to her dreams.

She picked up her guitar, played a few scales.

On the table, her cell phone rang. Putting the guitar aside, she picked it up. She didn't recognize the caller. "Hello?"

"Hey, Emma, it's Nicole."

Oh, Nicole. Emma had finally read her e-mail and was still trying to figure out how to say no.

"Did you get my e-mail?"

Lying would be so easy sometimes. But it wouldn't help her here. "I did. But . . . I don't think it'll work, Nicole."

"Please, please help me out, Emma. Our entire ensemble has backed out—they don't want to drive all the way to Deep Haven with the storm we just had. I need someone who can handle everything—the wedding, the reception. Please, please? For me?"

Wedding *and* reception. That could mean enough money to cover the bar fight bill and even another month's rent. By then, maybe she'd find the right words.

"When is it?"

"Next weekend. At Caribou Ridges Resort."

Technically not in Deep Haven.

"Fine. Okay. Do you have anything special you want me to play?"

"Aerosmith's 'I Don't Want to Miss a Thing'?"

"Yeah, of course. Although I'm thinking that might need more than just my guitar."

Maybe Ritchie could fill in—he gigged now and again as a keyboardist. And she could ask Tim to help on drums. He probably knew the truth about the fight.

"Oh, Emma, you're the best. Thanks so much! I'll see if I can track down a drummer and a keyboardist—I saw Kyle Hueston back in town. He used to play in a band with Jason. Maybe—"

Shoot. What was with this guy? A dry spell for her entire life, and suddenly it was raining Kyle Hueston everywhere she looked.

"I'll find my own drummer—"

"Don't worry; I'll ask him myself. I saw him yesterday at the donut shop—or I guess it's the cupcake shop now. He was sitting in the booth with the other deputies. He looked downright hot in his uniform."

"Thanks for that, Nicole. But really—"

"I don't mind asking. Thanks again, Emma. You rock."

Nicole hung up and Emma dropped her head back on the sofa. Perfect.

When hadn't Kyle Hueston looked hot? She'd never missed a home basketball game when Kyle played. Would wait for him to pass her in the hallway on the way to Mr. Dorrin's social studies class.

Kyle could still make her forget where she was . . . and where she was going.

But he planned on planting himself in Deep Haven. She had no plans to plant herself anywhere near it.

Emma got up, put her guitar away, then grabbed a jacket and opened the door to the tiny balcony off their apartment. The city lights sparkled, red and white, constellations against the galaxy of the city. She could see her breath and drew in the crisp air. Sitting on a metal chair, she propped her feet on the railing and leaned back, searching for stars.

In Deep Haven, the stars seemed so close she could breathe them in, feel them sparkle inside her. She could trace the Milky Way and sometimes even spot the undulating ribbons of pink, lavender, and turquoise from an aurora borealis.

Not here in the city, however. The bright cityscape ate away at the darkness, the stars dim and hidden. Perhaps it was simply too early to see them, the night still so young, but nothing of hope twinkled in the sky.

Find the lyrics, and I'll bet you can figure out a way to go home again.

If only it were that easy.

⅋

Eli wanted to track down Derek Nelson and wring his neck. Two days and Lee's drive still hadn't been plowed? He saw the track marks where Derek had parked his father's Subaru down by the road, the footprints from where he hiked to the house and back.

But no tire tracks leading out from the driveway. Which meant Lee had been snowed in since the storm hit.

Yes, he'd kill Derek when the kid returned home from wherever he'd run off to. Probably shooting hoops down at the community center.

Kirby liked to hang out there too—might be there now if he wasn't worried about his mother.

Eli hauled the snowblower from the back of his pickup, yanked the zip cord to start it. The motor churned to life, and he started down the middle, throwing snow toward the banks. Icy particles landed on his face, flaked into his eyes.

Okay, someone *had* tried to shovel. As Eli drew near the garage, he spotted a feeble swath near the edges. Someone had cleared about a three-foot chunk. Working by hand, it would take one person a week to shovel this drive. Why Lee didn't hire one of the snowplow services from town baffled him.

Maybe she just didn't want to bother anyone. What was it about these women in Deep Haven that made them so insistent on managing life on their own? Noelle still mowed their acres of grass by herself. And more than once Eli had come home to her covered in snow, blowing out the driveway.

At least, the old Noelle. The new Noelle had stared at their home with a sort of abject horror. He'd always thought it cozy, the dormer windows like sleepy eyes gazing out over the forest. They heated with propane, so it lacked the ambience of a woodstove-heated home, the sleepy relaxation of a crackling fire, but it had kept them warm and dry for twenty-five years.

He'd always intended to build Noelle a fireplace someday. Just never quite got around to it.

Eli turned and cut another path down the center, all the way back to the highway. He'd started to work up a sweat underneath his parka and wool cap. He'd need another shower when he got home.

But wow, he might never erase from his brain the look Noelle gave him when he'd said he was taking a shower. Now *that* made him feel dirty.

Noelle hated him. Couldn't stand the sight of him, if her body language communicated correctly.

He turned again and cut the trail wider. At least now Lee could get her Jeep down the drive, but it took three more passes before his truck would manage it. By then, ice encrusted his collar, and icicles hung on his eyelashes.

Funny that Lee hadn't even come to the door to wave. Eli loaded his snowblower back onto the truck, debated a moment, then turned down her driveway.

He had somehow always preferred Clay's house to his own. The man hailed from a family of lumberjacks and had built it with his own hands, carved out the logs, unearthed the stones for the tall fireplace. Now a two-story log home with a loft, it seemed the perfect fit under the arms of the white pine and birch that surrounded their place. He noticed that Christmas lights still edged the house—he hadn't had time to take them down—and now, as darkness approached, they twinkled, adding a homey glow to the forest.

Sure, they'd started in the garage, but the Nelsons had added on as they had money, which meant that Clay left Lee free and clear, without a mortgage.

But also without a man to help her take care of the cottage in the woods.

He knocked on the door, noticing that someone had sprinkled kitty litter on the trail between the house and the garage. So perhaps she had ventured out. "Lee?"

"Let yourself in, Eli."

He heard the voice through the door, opened it, and stuck his head in. Usually the Nelson home smelled of something freshly baked—cookies, bread, a casserole. Today there was nothing but the hint of ash as if a fire had long ago gone out. And the house felt cool.

Even cold.

"Lee!"

"I'm here, Eli." Her voice sounded wrung out.

He toed off his boots, then ventured into the house, and his breath seized. Lee lay in Clay's recliner, her chin tucked into her chest, her arm drawn up, shivering under a white afghan. The fireplace lay unlit, cold.

"What's going on? It's freezing in here."

She looked brutal—or would have if she wasn't so pretty even in her pain. Her hair hung down around her face in a tangle of curls, and smudges of makeup marred her eyes as if she'd been crying. She wore yoga pants, a pair of wool socks. She tried to move as he came toward her, but she winced, crying out.

"Lee! For pete's sake!" He knelt before her, his voice softening. "What happened?"

"I was shoveling and I think I must have pinched something in my neck. It's just . . . I can't move. Everything hurts, right down to my toes."

She looked at him so morosely—oh, how he wanted to run his finger down her face, push her hair away from those sad eyes. Instead he got up, went to the wood box, and fished around for kindling.

"How long have you been like this?"

"I hurt myself yesterday, before Derek's game. I wanted to drive over to Ely to watch it, but I couldn't get out."

Eli built a tepee with the kindling, then stuffed it with bundles of the lavender Lee grew as a fire starter. "Where is Derek?"

She looked at him, frowning. "They had back-to-back games; don't you remember? Today's was away too, so Derek stayed in town last night. I guess Kirby didn't make it back for that one, either?"

"No. We just got home from the hospital."

"Oh." She adjusted herself in the chair, made a sound that turned his heart. "How's Noelle?"

He lit the fire. Immediately it added a trickle of heat to the cold breath in the room. He fed the remnants of the wood to the stove, then closed the glass door. "I'll get you some more wood."

"Eli."

Her voice stopped him, and he drew in a breath before he turned. She had such a gentle smile—no wonder Clay had proposed to her the day after high school graduation. Eli had always been a little jealous of how easy it came for them—they'd dated since they were fifteen, knew from the day they met that they belonged together.

Lee had grieved, of course, after Clay's death, but she didn't let it destroy her.

"How's Noelle?" She gave him the smile that always knew how to find the coldness inside, how to warm him from the inside out. She was just so easy to talk to.

He shook his head. "She still doesn't know me. In fact, I think the last thing she wanted to do was come home with me."

"Why would you say that? This is her home. It'll help her get her memory back."

"I'm not sure she wants it back."

"That's a terrible thing to say. To not remember your children—not remember Kelsey? Of course she wants her memory back."

Eli sighed, shoved his hands into his pockets. "We aren't telling her about Kelsey."

"What—no, Eli, that's not fair. How are you going to do that?" She wore the same expression Kyle had, and it brought him back, just for a moment, to that horrible tussle on the floor with his eldest son.

He'd hit the boy. It still made him sick. "You know I already took out Kelsey's things long ago. But I made Kirby go through the house while Noelle's napping to remove any extra pictures, the scrapbooks, anything that might trigger a memory of Kelsey."

"She deserves to know—"

"No. I'm right about this, Lee. Think about it. You know how she was when Kelsey died. She barely left her room for six months. And when she did, she was so distant. As if she'd lost herself inside that dark place. Frankly, I think she forgot about me—about us— even before she fell."

"Eli." Lee's voice softened and had the power to soothe the frayed, angry parts of him. "She didn't forget you. She just had to figure out how to cope, like the rest of us."

"But you didn't lock yourself inside your house."

"I had my extended family. My parents. And I didn't lose my only daughter."

Eli sighed. "How long since you ate?"

She hesitated. "It just hurt too much to cook—"

"For *two days*? Why didn't you call me?" Except what was he going to do? Leave his wife to come help Lee? He saw the truth on her face, and thankfully, she didn't voice it.

She wrinkled her nose. "I considered it a fast . . . I needed time to pray, anyway. I don't see the sunrise too often. It's so beautiful over the lake in the morning, like pink molasses."

"I'm cooking you dinner."

"You'll have to buy food first." She gave him a sheepish grin. "Or thaw some venison. I was going to make Derek some stew, but . . ." She shifted and he flinched when she cried out again.

"You need to get that looked at. You might have done serious damage."

Her face said it then—that despite her brave front, all the talk about praying and making stew, she'd been sitting here thinking that very thing since yesterday.

While he'd been with the woman who didn't want to remember him.

"I'm taking you to the hospital."

"I can't move—"

But that didn't matter because he walked over and picked her up, blanket and all. And after she whimpered, she settled herself against him.

Eli refused to let the words rise, to hear the voice inside that suggested that's where he wanted her to belong.

7

THE CRACK WOKE HIM. Sharp and bright, like a gunshot, it sparked through Kyle, grabbed him from sleep, jerked him to a sitting position, his heart choking off his breath.

Outside the picture window of his two-room cabin, way up the hill above Deep Haven, the night had receded across the lake, the sun just nudging over the eastern horizon, turning the canvas of the earth to fire.

He listened above his racing heart for the crunch of feet in the snow, a creak of his deck boards that might betray an intruder, all the while reaching over to his bedside table. He nudged open the drawer, slid his hand around his 9mm Glock—still in the holster, safety on—and nestled it on his lap. He unsnapped it, drew it out, but didn't take the safety off quite yet.

He heard nothing.

Pushing the covers aside, he climbed out of bed and padded across the floor to the window. He hadn't bothered with drapes or even real furniture when he moved in a month ago. Who needed curtains anyway? No one could see him, standing here in his bedroom window in his pajama bottoms, barefoot, bare-chested, holding a Glock.

But he'd make a great target for a sniper in the woods. He moved away from the window, his breath catching for a moment.

Oh, his father's words had simply dug too far into his brain. *A small-town cop is one of the most dangerous jobs. You let your guard down because you want to trust your neighbors. And that's when they pull out a gun and shoot you.*

Or someone you love.

His father didn't have to reach too far to cite an example.

Kyle had expected him to be more wary, even distant, after Kelsey died. But suddenly he'd become less of a hometown peace officer and more of a truant officer. He treated everyone as if they might be criminals.

Perhaps, in his eyes, they were.

Despite public sympathy, he'd been voted out of office, his ten years as the sheriff over. Rather than stay on the force working under a new sheriff, he took an early retirement.

But maybe his father was right.

Grabbing a blanket from the pile of sheets he'd requisitioned from home, Kyle shook one out, then retrieved a hammer off the kitchen counter, a couple of tacks from the utility drawer, and hung it up over the bedroom window.

He did the same across the matching window in the family room.

His heart began to settle back into his chest as he listened again. He was just hyperaware now that he'd been walking around town for a month in his uniform, a sort of target. And with his mother's assailant still free . . .

He glanced at the clock. Probably should get up and work out, anyway. He'd been hanging around Lucy Maguire's World's Best Donuts and Cupcakes too much.

He did like those red velvet cupcakes, though.

After changing into a pair of jeans and a T-shirt, he washed up, filled a water bottle, grabbed his uniform and gear, and headed out to his truck.

His boots crunched against the snow, the air crisp in his ears. He guessed it was about ten above today, a nice day for snowshoeing or skiing.

As he threw the bag inside, another crack split the air.

He froze. And then grimaced at his own foolishness. The weight of the snow on the trees had caused them to break, the cracks resounding through the forest like gunshots.

See how easily a guy could jump to conclusions?

He got into the truck, wove along the drive to the road, then down the highway to Deep Haven. This early, deer peeked out from between trees, poised to dart across the highway to the lake in a dangerous real-life game of Frogger. Sometimes he got lucky and spied a moose or a red fox. An eagle lifted from a ratty nest high in a tree, then soared low along the ditch, searching for carrion.

How could his mother forget their lives? Kirby had been calling him with bleak updates, the stories he'd told her, the pictures—carefully selected—that might jog her memory.

Always with Kelsey absent.

How was his mother supposed to remember her life without including her daughter?

Kyle turned down the heat in the truck, tapped his brakes as he entered the town limits. The memory of the fight in the hospital could still rouse fury deep in his gut.

He wasn't sure at whom anymore.

The fitness center glowed, early morning athletes on treadmills, stair-climbers, ellipticals. Their new football coach was at the pull-up bar. Kyle had heard about Caleb Knight and his missing leg, a casualty of battle. Mostly, however, he'd heard about how he took the team to the play-offs this year and the very real hope that next year, they might win state.

Another former soldier, Sammy Johnson, his curly blond hair tied back with a red bandanna, worked out at the bench press. Sammy had played defensive end during Kyle's sophomore year of high school, then graduated and joined the Army. Kyle had a vague memory of reading about him in the local paper a year ago—maybe winning some military honor? Now he worked on a logging crew.

Jason Backlund spotted for Sammy as he benched. Jason and Kyle had put together a little band their sophomore year, more fun than pretty. It gave Kyle a place to use the drum set he'd worn out doing solos in the basement. Now Jason had a lucrative winter gig running a plow for the county.

Lucky Jason—he was living Kyle's hopes, building a life with the girl of his dreams in Deep Haven.

Shoot, but he couldn't get Emma out of his head. Over the past three days, Kyle had remembered her more. She'd worked at the gas station in town with Kelsey, and he remembered seeing her in the band during his basketball games. If only he hadn't been a senior during Kelsey's freshman year, he might have known her friends—like Emma—better. But he'd had his eyes on a scholarship and spent most of his time in the gym.

He dropped his gear into a locker, the echoes of high school conversations too easily conjured, then returned to the weight room.

Upper body. He warmed up with a few push-ups, then grabbed the free weights to work on his biceps, doing some preacher curls.

He'd made a routine of working out while in high school, and by college it became a way for him to focus. To remind himself that he hadn't lost control of his life. Even if it seemed to be careening out of his grasp.

Like today.

He switched to skull crunchers, working his triceps.

Oh, God, please help Mom get her memory back. It was more of a thought than a prayer, because after Kelsey, he'd wondered if God was really on his team.

It certainly seemed as if He'd abandoned the Hueston family when Kelsey lay bleeding behind the bakery stand, dropped there by a shot to her upper body on her way to the freezer.

Yes, God had dropped the ball there—especially for a family who had spent their lives in the pew and doing service projects, trying to live as God-fearing people.

If God would start playing by the rules, it would sure be easier to trust Him.

He switched to the military press, working his shoulders until his muscles nearly gave out.

"Hey, Kyle." Jason came over to the leg press. "How's your mom?"

Hard to escape the small-town grapevine. "She's still recovering." He moved the bar behind his head to work his delts.

"Can't believe it happened again." Jason shook his head as he worked his thigh muscles. "Any word on who did it?"

"No." He put the weights back, then grabbed a twenty-pounder and held it to his body as he started sit-ups. "They don't have a lot to go on. No witnesses, and any tracks wiped clean with the snow."

"Quite the storm. I was up all night plowing. I do the stretch between Silver Bend and Deep Haven. Terrible night. Thankfully, with the winter storm advisory, there weren't many cars out. I called the patrol for two I saw in the ditch. One was Ryan Nickel's old beater."

"I know Ryan," Sammy said, passing near them to grab a towel. He hung it around his neck, holding on to the ends.

"He was a year older than you, wasn't he? Played point for the Huskies?" Kyle said.

"Yeah. And safety on the football team. He holds our record for most interceptions. When we went to the play-offs, he painted his car blue and white and put his number on the hood, a football helmet on his back window."

Jason switched legs. "It was a real sweet thing, an old Dodge Dart."

"I'm not sure how it stays running, but I remember him driving it through the fields out by his place," Sammy said. "It's nearly rusted through—I think there's plywood on the floorboards. I'm not sure it's even legal to drive."

Kyle finished his sit-ups. Leaned back on his hands. "Does he still own it?"

Jason was breathing hard and quit his reps. "I don't know. It wasn't Ryan pushing it out of the ditch. Two guys though, a skinny one in the car, the other one giving it a heave. It looked like they'd just spun out and banged the back end against a tree. I called it in, but by the time I came back to plow the other side of the road, they'd gotten free. Not sure if a patrol car came out."

Kyle got up. "Where was this?"

"A couple miles out of town, maybe. Near the Crescent River lookout."

Kyle scrubbed a towel down his face, then draped it over his head. "Do you remember what time?"

"About eight o'clock or so? I can't remember."

Eight o'clock. About ninety minutes after the robbery. Kyle had called down to the Lake County deputies, the next county over, just to sort through the logged calls from the night of his mom's accident. No suspicious vehicles.

The suspect had simply vanished.

Unless he'd kept going north. Toward Deep Haven.

And perhaps the current owner of Ryan Nickel's car had seen someone, or something, on his drive up the shore.

Sammy flicked the towel at him. "Glad you're back, Hueston. You should join us for Sunday afternoon hoops."

Kyle nodded.

"I'll see you at the game tonight. Kirby's a real star—got a great three-point shot." Sammy gave him a smile. "You Huestons always know how to get the job done, but you might remind him to pass the ball now and again."

Yeah, well, passing the ball required trust that someone would catch it. Sometimes it was better to be a one-man team.

Jason headed for the locker room also, then turned back. "Hey—did Nicole talk to you about playing drums for us this weekend for the wedding? Apparently she's hired someone out of Minneapolis to play guitar, but she mentioned needing a drummer. I'd have to pay you in wedding cake, but we'd really appreciate it."

Kyle followed him into the locker room. "Who's the guitarist?"

"She's from Deep Haven, a couple years younger than us. The Nelson girl—I think her name's Emma. Remember her?"

Kyle smiled. Maybe God was finally playing fair. "Yeah. Yeah, I think I might."

❦

What had Noelle done with the last twenty-five years of her life?

She hadn't even graduated from college, from what she could tell. And forget her painting, her photography. The only pictures on the wall were cheesy oils one might pick up at a discount art store.

Stepping on the scale had made her march down to the kitchen and pull out the tortilla chips, the ice cream, the Oreos, and the Nutty Bars and throw them in the trash. She did notice that Kirby came along behind her, fished out the ice cream, and stuck it in the basement deep-well freezer.

Fine. Carrot sticks and salad for her.

Now she stood at the stove, separating egg yolks from the whites, a pan heating on one burner, a teakettle on the other. A couple pieces of lightly buttered wheat bread lay on a plate. She'd found the loaf shoved way back in the freezer, as if her old self had briefly resurrected and made a feeble attempt at healthy eating.

She hadn't bothered to figure out the coffeemaker—even when Kirby came out of his room yesterday morning inquiring about a cup of coffee on his way to school.

What, was she a short-order cook too?

And what had happened to her personal style? Stretchy lounge pants, T-shirts, oversize sweatshirts with embroidery on the front? She'd turned . . . frumpy.

No, no, no, this couldn't be her life, but the longer she lived here, the more the truth sank in. She'd found a collection of art books in a box in the basement storage room. And a wedding dress that matched the one in the picture. And finally, her old high school letter jacket hanging in a hall closet.

Oh, the waste.

She poured the egg whites into a pan, began to scramble them. The smell rose, taunting her empty stomach. She'd hidden in bed this morning until she'd heard Eli's truck start up and grumble its way out of the driveway.

She'd dreaded yesterday, her first day alone with him after Sunday's long, drawn-out silences, Kirby trying to make her feel at home. Thankfully, Eli had pulled out right after Kirby and been gone most of the day, so she'd wandered around the house looking for clues to her life. She opened the other two bedrooms—one of them so clearly Kyle's, with a picture of the two of them standing on a basketball court, giving the camera a thumbs-up. She looked younger, but not by much.

The other room was barren—no sheets on the double bed, a crisp, unused chill to the room. She doubted they'd had guests here anytime in the last decade.

And did she have any friends at all? Because no one called. Not one person to inquire after her. Was she a miserable loner, devoid of a life?

She finally couldn't take it and spent the day cleaning out the cupboards, waiting for Eli to return. He pulled in after dark, covered in wood chips, his face red as if he'd been outdoors all day.

He dropped his coveralls in the entryway, then headed down to shower in the basement.

"Did you cook supper?" He'd asked her that as she sat watching the news—what had happened to President Reagan?

She'd frowned at him and could see the war inside him as he bit back something and managed to surface with a tolerant smile. Supper. *Really.*

Her role here had obviously sunk to that of domestic slave. Indeed, she unearthed very few feminine touches in the house— even the downstairs television room boasted team pennants and a full-size decal of a Minnesota Viking, number twenty-eight.

Even the dog had surrendered her femininity. Who named a female dog Riggins? The poor thing had found Noelle sitting in the family room, watching the waves of snow outside the window, and set her floppy mug on Noelle's knee, her sad eyes blinking as if confused.

Yeah, me too, Rigs.

Noelle scooped the eggs onto one of the slices of bread, then turned off the heat. She added salt and pepper and put the plate on the counter near the high-top chairs. She went in search of the tea she'd seen earlier as the kettle whistled.

She was opening cupboards when Kirby emerged from his room, a blue sports bag over his shoulder. He wore a button-down shirt, a tie, and a pair of dress pants.

Yes, she liked this young man. He'd arrived home last night after school, also after dark, smelling of the gym. After showering, he made himself a grilled cheese sandwich and joined her in the family room, giving her a play-by-play of practice. Apparently he was working on his three-point shot.

"Kyle holds the record for the most outside shots in a game. He had a signature swish shot from the top of the key that he nailed every time."

Ah, her shot. Maybe Kyle *was* her flesh and blood. "I played guard all through high school. Lettered, too. We should shoot some one-on-one after the snow melts. . . ."

Kirby had grinned at that but her words wound tight inside her.

How long did she intend on staying here? The thought tossed her in her sheets all night until she finally got up and stared at the moonlight, so bright on the snow.

What if she never regained her memory? Would she stay here, in this place, with people she didn't know?

And looking at Eli, at the debris of a life she couldn't believe she'd created, did she truly want to get her memory back?

"Morning, Mom," Kirby said, dropping his bag in the kitchen. "Perfect, breakfast. You remembered!" He sat down, pulled the sandwich to himself, picked it up.

She stilled, glanced at him, at his broad grin, his green eyes bright.

Oh, she hated to—

He must have seen her expression, for his dimmed. "Oh. Well, you always make me breakfast on a game day." He put the sandwich down. "Sorry; is this yours?"

"No, it's for you . . . Son. Eat up." She turned away, the endearment ringing inside. *Son.* Okay, she could admit some feelings of affection building there.

She pulled down a tea bag, opened it, and dropped it into a mug. Pouring in the hot water, she let it steep. "What time is your game?"

"Four o'clock. You're coming, right?"

Uh . . . "I don't know anyone there, Kirby."

"You know me." He looked away, and she hated the hurt on his face.

"I'll try."

He gave her a soft smile then.

"By the way, do you know where your father went? He left again this morning, early."

Kirby was gobbling down the sandwich. "No. Maybe he went fishing. He does that a lot. Or sometimes he goes into town and eats breakfast with the deputies at World's Best."

Seriously? The man would leave her alone to eat with friends? But then, did she really want him here?

"Kirby, can I ask you what happened between your dad and me? Why is he so . . . distant? And angry?"

Kirby swallowed the last of his sandwich slowly. Didn't look at her when he wiped his mouth. "It's been a hard few years. You and Dad were . . . Well, it's not all his fault, Mom."

It seemed to pain him to admit that, and she resisted the strange urge to press her hand to his, to comfort him.

"Did something bad happen?"

Kirby wiped his mouth again. Took a breath.

In the entryway, the door slammed. Eli stood in the kitchen doorway. "I changed your tires, Kirby. You should be good to go."

Kirby had gone a little pale and now slid off the stool. Picked up his bag. "Thanks, Dad."

Eli nodded, then disappeared, probably to dispense of those awful coveralls. Please.

Kirby lingered in the kitchen, looking at her, waiting, it seemed, for something.

"Have a good day?" she offered.

His smile failed him.

"What am I not doing, Kirby?"

"You always pray with me before I leave for school, especially on game day. I just thought . . . aw, it's no big deal."

See, she *was* a woman of faith. Even if she couldn't feel it. "Okay, uh, how do we do this?"

"You usually put your hand on my shoulder."

She could do that. She gripped his shoulder, trying to think of a blessing, of anything.

Then suddenly she heard, "Lord, we ask for Your blessing on Kirby today as he plays basketball. Protect him in the game, and help him to play for You to the best of his abilities. Amen." Eli lifted his hand off Kirby's other shoulder. "Have a good day, Son."

Noelle stared at him, nonplussed, as Kirby gave him a hug, then grinned at her and headed out the door.

Eli's voice—solid and affectionate for his son—nudged a feeling of warmth inside her. Perhaps she'd been a smackle too harsh on the man.

Once upon a time, she'd loved him enough to marry him. To stay with him for twenty-five years. Which meant that, deep down inside, there was something about this man worth knowing.

"I'm going to go clean up," Eli said.

Noelle nodded, picking up Kirby's empty plate. She took two more slices of bread, toasted them, and separated two more eggs as she heard the shower running downstairs.

She had just slid the new eggs onto her plate and settled down with her tea when he reemerged. He smelled clean, of fresh soap, and he'd shaved, his hair combed. He had curls like Kirby, and they corkscrewed around his ears. In a pair of jeans and a white-and-black flannel shirt, he might be considered handsome for a man his age. He rolled up his sleeves above his elbows, revealing strong forearms.

She wasn't sure why she said it, but, "Would you like me to make you some eggs?"

When he turned, she noticed his eyes. Reddened, as if he hadn't slept much, but a pretty brown. They examined her for a long moment. Then he shook his head. "I'll just make some coffee. But . . . thank you."

He turned away from her, grabbing the carafe from the coffeemaker.

"Eli? How did we meet?"

He turned back, coffeepot in hand. "I rescued you."

She set down her tea. "You *rescued* me? From what? A raging moose?"

"No." He filled the pot with water, returned to the coffee-maker, and poured it in. "Up under your hair you have a scar."

She raised her fingers to her scalp.

He came over, took her hand in his, moved it over to a bump. "There. You hit the windshield."

He had a tenderness in his touch, but she appreciated that he stepped away, resumed his coffee making.

"What happened?"

"You were on your way here to visit your parents. They'd taken a cabin for the summer, and you were driving up pretty late at night." He added coffee grounds. "You T-boned a deer, slid off the road, and hit a tree. I was on duty that night."

"So you arrived on the scene, pried me out of the car, and asked me on a date?"

He switched on the machine, and the coffee started to gurgle as he turned, leaning against the counter. Now that he'd taken off his coveralls, he didn't seem quite as rotund. In fact, he had lean hips, strong legs, a wide, powerful chest. "Something like that. I knew you were staying with your parents, so I stopped in to see how you were." He smiled, and she could imagine that, twenty years ago, he might have been sweet and charming like Kirby. Or Kyle.

She might have said yes to a date back then.

Noelle ran her thumb down the side of her cup, considering him for a long moment. "I'd like to get my memory back, Eli. I would like to remember our life together."

Eli blinked at that, then looked away, an emotion she couldn't place flickering across his face. He did want that too, didn't he?

"Do you want me to remember, Eli?"

He looked at her, the curmudgeon briefly resurrecting. "Of course I do." Perhaps he saw his words reflected in her expression, for he sighed, his voice softer. "Yes, of course I do."

Oh. Maybe that emotion had been hurt or grief. She hadn't really thought about what it might be like for him, for her to lose the life they'd shared.

Then he came over, his dark eyes solemn. "It's just that I'm not sure you're going to like what you find, Noelle. And I'm not sure either of us is ready for that."

Home games had the power to dissolve her, to erase every day of victory Lee had managed over the past three years and reduce her to that raw, devastated woman she'd been standing beside Clay's grave.

The sounds of the game emanated from the gym—the high-pitched scuff of shoes on a wooden court, the pop of the basketball being dribbled, the shrill whistle of the refs, the cheers of the home team. They lured Lee to the door and she took a breath, coaxing back her courage from the dark corners where it had scurried.

She could do this. Once inside, she'd see familiar faces, smiles now void of sympathy. Time did that—it erased the memory of another person's grief from their countenance.

Sometimes she wondered if she was the only one who remembered Clay Nelson, hometown hero.

"One ticket," she said quietly and held out a five-dollar bill. Amy, the athletic director, took it, gave her a ticket, and she edged into the gym.

Back in her day, they'd played their games in the smaller gym with the cement bleachers. She could nearly hear the echo of the cheers every time she passed by the closed doors. Now they used it for the middle school games and community activities.

This new gym could house the entire town. A sea of blue-shirted fans packed the home bleachers, waving signs, some with their faces painted. The Huskies weren't undefeated, but this close to the end of the season, they had won enough to fight for a place in the play-offs.

Lee glanced at the scoreboard. The Huskies were up by two, still early in the game, but she hated that she hadn't accounted for the extra time it would take to ease herself out of the car, hobble to the gym.

A slipped disk in her neck. In the ER, she'd had X-rays, and the doctor had given her a painkiller, but it was her chiropractor who gave her the most hope of recovery. And Eli.

What would she have done without his help? He'd not only plowed her driveway, but shoveled her walk and made a pot of venison stew that just might rival Chef Ramsey's. In between chopping wood all day Monday to refill her supply, he'd brought her ice packs, then driven her to town for her appointment. He'd even offered to carry her again, but she could make it alone.

Really.

Today he'd come over too early for even the dawn and filled her wood bin, then let himself into her house and made a cozy fire.

She hadn't heard from him the rest of the day, but as she scanned the crowd, she spied him on the Huestons' usual perch, five from the top, wearing a long-sleeve black T-shirt with the Huskies logo emblazoned on the front. He was watching the game, leaning forward, arms on his knees.

Walking the gauntlet behind the basket to the bleachers, the eyes of the town scrutinizing her, could skewer a woman's courage. Sometimes she imagined Clay beside her, holding her hand. How many times had they walked into this gym when Derek played JV, dreaming of the day when he'd start for varsity?

They'd had one son and wished the entire world for him, not to mention the dreams they had for Emma.

She swallowed, affixed her smile, and waved to Lou, the UPS man, and Jenny, her hairdresser. Joe, their local author, sat next to Mona, who owned the bookstore, as they cheered their son to victory. She glanced up toward Eli again as she approached the bleachers, searching for her empty spot. The Huestons and the Nelsons could practically carve their names of ownership on that row.

Eli erupted into a cheer as the Huskies sank a basket. She turned to see Derek grinning as he ran down the court.

Shoot, she'd missed it.

Beside Eli, wearing a black cap, her hair pulled back, sat Noelle. She had her hands tucked between her knees, her gaze intent on the game.

Maybe that's why Eli hadn't called. Maybe Noelle awoke this morning, her memories restored.

What might that be like—to remember afresh the grief? Oh, Lee wouldn't wish that on anyone. Especially now that she'd grown some calluses.

And now that Lee had managed the walk to the bleachers and found her aisle, she discovered the breath that had abandoned her by the door.

She might be alone, but she was Derek's mother. Emma's mother. And she had a place in the stands.

As she reached the row, Eli glanced at her, a funny look on his face a second before a smile emerged. "Hey, Lee!"

She scooted in beside Noelle, glanced at her friend, and patted her knee. "Hey, Noelle."

Noelle looked at her, then to Eli and back. Smiled.

Eli caught Lee's eye, gave his head a tiny shake.

Oh.

Around her, the crowd cheered as the Huskies stole the ball. She leaned over to Noelle and spoke quietly. "I'm Lee. We're friends."

Something like relief crested across Noelle's face. "I was starting to wonder if I had any friends." She stuck out her hand and Lee glanced around before she took it, shook quickly.

How long did Eli think he could keep Noelle's injury quiet?

"We've been friends for a while, since our boys started playing basketball together back in middle school. And of course, we knew each other from when Clay worked as one of Eli's deputies."

"Deputies?"

How could Eli not mention—?

"Eli was the sheriff here for many years. I'm sure it'll come back."

Across from her, a muscle pulsed in Eli's jaw.

"Yes, that's right. He mentioned that. Where's your husband? Will he be here?"

For a second, it felt fresh and raw. She hadn't had to tell anyone for so long. But the answer might raise too many questions. "No," she said quietly.

"Which one is your son?" Noelle asked.

"Number eleven. He's playing the baseline right now."

"He's got great hands for a forward. And boxes out really well. He just made a jump shot."

"Your Kirby isn't bad either. He's been starting guard since his sophomore year. He's really nailing his three-point shot this season. But basketball runs in your family. Kyle was all-state, and they won the state championship. I think there's a trophy in the case. I'll show you at halftime."

"Thank you, Lee."

Eli glanced at her too, warmth in his eyes.

Lee let it sink in, possibly too much, as she turned back to the game. Noelle had no idea what a treasure she had in that man.

Kirby managed to swish five three-pointers, Derek driving for the basket for sixteen points before the first half ended. The Huskies topped the Blue Streaks by four points going into the locker rooms.

Lee nudged Noelle. "C'mon. I'll show you those trophies."

"I could go for a bag of popcorn. It smells fabulous."

Noelle hated popcorn. At least ever since she'd cracked her tooth on an unpopped kernel at a game a few years ago, when Kelsey played volleyball.

Lee led her down the bleachers, Eli rising behind them. They hit the floor as the band began to play.

"Hey, Noelle, wait up!"

THE SHADOW OF YOUR SMILE

Lee turned to run interference as Jill Markson caught up. Her son played fullback for the Huskies but rode the bench most of the basketball games.

"I was wondering if you'd fill in on concessions for me next week," Jill said. "Brandon is playing on JV and their game is scheduled during the slot I volunteered for."

Noelle's eyes widened and she drew in a breath.

"I'll do it," Lee said quickly. "No problem."

"Thanks, Lee," Jill said. She made to turn away but then glanced back at Noelle. "I heard that you fell on the ice or something. Are you okay? I missed you at spinning this morning."

Noelle nodded, but Lee could see her smile didn't touch her eyes. "Just fine. Thanks."

Jill scooted off and Lee looped her arm through Noelle's. "Jill Markson. She runs the fitness center. And is the spin instructor."

"Spin instructor?"

"Stationary bicycles. We call it spinning."

"So that was my 8 a.m. appointment at the fitness center. Eli and I spent the day poring over my weekly schedule. I do a lot of volunteering—the school reading program, the library committee, the thrift store, and I also work at the care center?"

"You read to the folks there. And help some of the more able seniors in assisted living with art projects."

"Art? So . . . I haven't completely given up painting?" There was a desperation in Noelle's tone that stopped Lee.

"Uh . . . Noelle, I've only known you well for about five years, but really, you've mostly been a mom. I don't know anything about you doing any painting."

Noelle swallowed, her face pale.

Eli had come to stand behind her, wearing a stricken expression.

It almost looked like guilt.

Noelle drew in a long breath. "Show me the trophies."

Lee glanced at Eli as she led Noelle to the hallway. Jammed with people, it smelled of popcorn oil, pizza, and hot dogs on a roller grill, and her stomach roared. But she still had venison stew on the stove and would eat with Derek after the game.

She refused to let him eat alone.

She pointed Noelle to the display case. Inside, each sport had its own shelf, except for the football team, which spilled over. Yet there in the center sat the display for Kyle's championship basketball team, their picture emblazoned on a plaque, the names of the team listed below it. Their trophy sat in the case next to the picture.

Noelle seemed to drink it in. She began to examine the other trophies, moving to the football section, the volleyball team.

The same team that had placed second in state during Kelsey's junior year.

Oh—

Lee glanced at Eli, who had gone pale.

"Hey, there's a girl on this plaque with our last name. Hueston. Kelsey Hueston." Noelle turned to Eli. "Do we have relatives here?"

Lee wanted to cry for him. Because as much as she disagreed with this abhorrent idea of keeping Kelsey from Noelle, how much more tragic for Eli to have to erase his daughter too.

"Not anymore," he said quietly.

Lee closed her eyes. She let the noise of the crowd, the kids' voices, the sounds of the community fill her. Life went so brutally on, left others standing in the dust. *Not anymore.*

"I'm going to get some popcorn," Noelle said.

Lee looked at Eli as his wife moved to the concession line. He appeared bereft.

Perhaps she wasn't the only one alone at this hometown basketball game.

8

Eli felt like he'd brought home a stranger.

No, worse, he felt like he'd taken her prisoner, returning her to a life she didn't recognize. A life she didn't want.

That counted as twice Noelle had asked about painting. Sure, she'd been an art major when he'd met her, but he'd considered it a fill-in major until she might decide to do something real. And to his knowledge, she hadn't painted anything besides the kids' rooms their entire marriage.

Who was this woman he'd brought home from the hospital?

He sat in the truck, motor idling, flakes peeling from the dark sky and skimming across his hood, watching Lee move around inside her house. He'd just wanted to make sure she'd arrived home all right after the game.

Today's excursion into Noelle's schedule had made him wonder if he knew her at all. Even before the accident. He knew about the spinning, the thrift store, and the school. But her appointments simply didn't add up. Like the space of time on Tuesdays and Thursdays from 2 to 4 p.m. She designated the time as *fitness*, but when they'd gone to the athletic center in hopes that it might trigger a memory, he checked the schedule.

There were no spinning classes scheduled in that time slot.

And then there was this memo on Friday mornings. *Classes.* But as she'd stood in the elementary school hallway, examining self-portraits the fourth graders had painted, he'd asked the secretary, who confirmed that no, she didn't volunteer on Fridays.

It didn't take his skills as a sheriff to realize that Noelle's calendar contained unexplained holes.

He watched Lee picking up before she went to bed. Wow, he'd nearly hugged her at the game today when she slipped right into her role as Noelle's friend . . . and when she stood with him after the potential bomb about Kelsey.

Do we have relatives here?

He cupped his hand over his eyes, let out a trembling breath. Not a flicker of memory about their beautiful daughter.

A knock at the passenger-side window startled him.

Lee stood in the snow, wrapped in a blanket. She opened the door, the cold sliding into the warm cab. "What are you doing out here?"

He shrugged. "I don't know."

She gave him a look of tenderness that only made the bubble in his chest grow. Then she got in, pulling the door closed behind her. She wore her pajamas under the blanket and a pair of snow boots, snow glistening in her auburn hair, falling over her shoulders.

He looked away. "She didn't even know Kelsey's name."

Lee said nothing.

"And the worst part is, as I sat there at the game listening to her cheer for Kirby, suddenly I felt as if she'd come back to me." He ran a thumb under his eyes. "She hasn't cheered in three years. She goes to the games and sits there, says nothing."

"I remember when she used to paint her face with Kyle's number."

"She lived for the kids' games, would drive to every one, even if it was five hours away."

"She was a sports mom—of course she did."

"But she vanished after Kelsey. And tonight . . . tonight she was back. I thought she was going to run down to the court and start brawling with the refs when they called Kirby on that travel."

"I could have sworn she offered to help the coach with some tips." Lee smiled at him. "Yes, she was . . . better. Which sounds strange because she doesn't even remember Kirby."

He knew she didn't mean to bruise, but he felt her words right below his sternum. "Or me. Which frankly, Lee . . . was kind of nice."

"Oh, Eli, c'mon."

"I'm serious. She actually high-fived me once, and sitting there, it felt like we were a couple again. Even though, yeah, she considers me the guy who kidnapped her."

"Don't talk like that."

"It's true, though. She keeps asking me about whether she painted anything. Seriously? She never mentioned painting in all the years we were married."

"Never? Not once?"

He hated how Lee's words had sharp points tonight, skewering him. "I don't know. Maybe."

Lee pulled the blanket tighter around her. "I used to play the piano classically; did you know that?"

"Not a clue."

She smiled. "Clay went to a couple of my recitals, but we couldn't afford a piano, so I just . . . I quit. I haven't touched a piano for thirty years."

"I'm sorry."

"It's okay. Emma inherited my musical genes. I probably enjoy listening to her play more than if I played myself. But the point is, people let go of things to pursue others. Noelle was a mom. There's not a lot of room for painting time there."

"Except maybe there was." He handed her Noelle's appointment book. "Tuesday and Thursday afternoons, Friday mornings. She wasn't at fitness class or school."

She looked at the book, then returned it. "You have no idea where she was?"

He closed the book and stared out the window. "Kyle and I had a terrible fight at the hospital. He said . . ." He clenched his jaw, the words still so sharp they might wound coming out again. "He said I forgot our family long before Noelle did. He said it was my fault she had forgotten everyone."

"That's absurd. You were taking care of everyone, Eli." Gently she reached out and pressed her hand on his arm. "You never abandoned anyone."

As he looked at her hand, he wanted to slide his over it. She had pretty hands, and suddenly he could imagine them playing the piano. He would have liked listening to her.

"Is it terrible if I hope she doesn't get her memory back?" He said it so softly, it seemed he might have just thought it.

But Lee drew in her breath, withdrew her hand. "Why?"

He played with the keys on a chain—he'd picked up Noelle's from the hook, not wanting to dig around the pockets of his coat to find his. She always left her keys just so on the rack. "I liked her tonight. I liked knowing that she'd forgiven me."

"It wasn't your fault, Eli."

His mouth tensed around the edges. Yes, in fact, it was.

"You couldn't have known that kid was on his way into Deep Haven to cause trouble. You knew him."

"I trusted him. I should have never let my guard down."

"That's what small-town cops do—they have to figure out how to keep the peace and live with their neighbors. You have to stop blaming yourself."

He fingered each one of the keys. "Tonight, sitting beside Noelle, her memory wiped clean, I did. I felt free. Like I never have to return to that night again."

"But neither does Noelle."

He turned to her, thankful he had a friend who would sit in a cold truck listening to him. "And that's the point. Maybe this is our chance to start over."

She nodded, her mouth a tight line, but her eyes offering kindness.

He couldn't help it. He reached out, took her hand, squeezed. "Thanks for listening, Lee. I don't know what I would do without you."

&

Noelle could drown in the immensity of her king-size bed. Or freeze to death. She lay in the middle of the bed, curled into a tight ball.

Would it never stop snowing? She watched through the dark window as snow flurried outside, the wind now and again shivering the house.

She'd heard Eli leave an hour ago, shortly after they'd returned home from the game. Not before they'd celebrated the win with Kirby, however. Apparently the Huestons had a tradition of ice cream sundaes after a win.

Now *there* was something of herself she might recognize. She took a small scoop, nothing decadent—after all, someone had to take care of this body the old Noelle had bequeathed her.

That's how she saw it somehow. The old Noelle—about whom she could admit feelings of anger—and herself. The woman who had stepped into the molded footsteps that should be her own but still seemed an awkward fit.

She wished she could sense anything—a nudge, a shadow of memory—but as far back as she reached, it seemed she just swatted thin air.

She wanted to remember. Really. Because sandwiched between Eli and Lee tonight, she had sensed that yes, she'd been a part of something bigger than herself. She lost herself in the game, cheering for Kirby and the Huskies, a warmth building inside that she longed to attribute to memory but was probably just the absence of fear.

She belonged here; she could admit that now.

But if they wanted her to stay, someone would have to turn up the heat.

Noelle kicked off the covers and went to the dresser, where she found a pair of wool socks. She added a blue Huskies sweatshirt with the number thirty-five on the back. Probably Kyle's—she'd noticed his number tonight when reading the trophies.

Kelsey Hueston. The name had lodged into her brain, but for no other reason than Eli's pale face, the way he appeared, just for a moment, as if she'd slapped him. It seemed an innocuous question—*do we have relatives here?*

Not anymore.

Maybe Kelsey was a cousin.

She went downstairs to the desk in the kitchen, searched for a phone book, flipped it open to the Huestons. *E. Hueston.* No others.

Perhaps, like he'd suggested, they'd moved.

She replaced the phone book and patted Riggins, who nudged her knee. Noelle bent down, caught the dog's jaw in her hands. "Fur, that's what I need."

Maybe she could find another blanket. It still felt rude, however, to root through the closets. Nothing felt like it belonged to her. She stopped in the bathroom and opened the closet. Towels, but no extra blankets.

She turned and stood at Kirby's room a moment, his door ajar, the glow of the snow upon his long, lanky body in bed.

The warmth returned when she looked at him, too.

She stopped at the next door, Kyle's room. He'd arrived at the end of the game—she saw him walk in wearing his deputy's uniform. What a handsome man, with that bronze hair, those high cheekbones. He glanced at her, sent her a smile, but didn't sit with them.

She tried to decide if the feeling inside could be labeled disappointment.

Entering Kyle's room, she switched on the light and read his various trophies, caught a picture of him with a girl who might have been a date for a homecoming dance. She was pretty—long blonde hair, blue-green eyes. They both stuck their tongues out at the camera.

More pennants lined the walls, along with a framed newspaper article about the state basketball championship. She ran her finger down the image of his senior picture. He sat holding a basketball, his eyes shining. She would like to remember this happy season with him.

Flicking off his light, she crossed the hall to the guest room. The unmade mattress seemed so forlorn in the middle of the room.

She opened the closet. Behold, blankets. She pulled them down, found a mattress pad and sheets, and smoothed them on the bed. The patchwork quilt bore the colors of the Huskies. Perhaps it had belonged to Kyle—what if she'd made it? A graduation present? Would she have done such a thing?

She returned to the closet and found a pillow, the case still on it. Noelle held it for a moment, then, inexplicably, brought it to her nose. Inhaled. Besides the scent of fabric softener, she smelled something sweet, powdery, almost floral. She inhaled again, and the scent settled into her bones next to that warm place. This was what a home should smell like.

She placed it on the bed, then found a knit afghan on the floor of the closet. This she wrapped around herself like a cloak. It too smelled sweet, floral. Lilac?

The made-up bed had transformed the room to something friendly. Even welcoming. Noelle fluffed the pillow and went to the window. She couldn't explain it, but the snow seemed to glisten, illuminating even the darkness. Riggins wandered in only to crumple at her feet with a sigh.

She liked this room. Probably because it felt the most like

her—forgotten. But it just needed a little redressing, a little patience, a little love.

It hadn't been lost on her that sitting beside Eli at the game, being around him tonight, had made her feel safe. Or perhaps it was the way he'd driven her into town earlier, helped her sort out her daily schedule. She had a busy life—spinning in the mornings and working with Sharron at the thrift store. Sweet that Eli arranged for Sharron to cover her shifts for the next week. He'd taken her to the school and she'd stared long at the self-portrait paintings the fourth graders had done. She might not be able to accomplish even that right now.

They'd stopped by the care center, and it didn't matter that she didn't know the residents' names. The way they greeted her, some of them with eyes, others with hands that touched hers . . . yes, deep down inside she felt she knew them. Especially the ones who sat in their wheelchairs staring out the window as if wondering where their lives had gone.

One couple in particular moved her. The woman, her white hair like spun sugar upon her head, sat in a wheelchair, her eyes distant. Her husband sat next to her, reading the Bible aloud.

Noelle had stopped, drinking in the words.

"O Lord, how long will you forget me? Forever?
How long will you look the other way?
How long must I struggle with anguish in my soul,
with sorrow in my heart every day? . . .
But I trust in your unfailing love.
I will rejoice because you have rescued me.
I will sing to the Lord because he is good to me."

The man's voice shook at the end as he touched his wife's hand.

"Arlene and Hitch Johnson," Eli had said into her ear. "They used to attend our church. She's had Alzheimer's for about six years now. He broke his hip eight months ago, finally moved in next door to his wife. They've been married fifty-six years."

Fifty-six years. Did Arlene still remember him, even just a shadow of their life?

Her throat tightened.

"O Lord, how long will you forget me? Forever?" The words had found her bones; now they clung to her as she drew the blanket tighter around herself.

If she was a woman of faith, why did it feel as if God had forgotten her? She pressed a hand to the cold window. "Are You there, God? Do You know me? Do You remember me?"

She waited, listening in her heart, but heard nothing in reply.

Lights scraped the trees, wiped across the house. Eli's truck came up the driveway, then eased into the garage.

Where had he been at this time of night?

She tucked her hand inside the blanket and watched him walk into the house under the glow of the outside motion lights. He was hunched against the cold, his expression fierce.

Yes, he looked like a sheriff.

She heard the front door open, heard him stamp his feet, then the tumble of his shoes as he kicked them off.

Not long after, the door to the basement shut as he lumbered downstairs to the den.

"But I trust in your unfailing love. I will rejoice because you have rescued me."

She turned away, went to the bed, and climbed in, her head on the pillow, relishing the smell. The chill had receded from her bones, the blanket giving sufficient warmth. She tucked her nose inside it, sleep finally curling through her.

Perhaps tomorrow, she'd wake up and remember everything. Perhaps tomorrow, her life would return to her.

Find me, God. Please, don't forget me.

❦

Sometimes Emma's imagination could run away with her, chase her all the way into her dreams.

Sometimes it even put her inside Kelsey's skin.

Although Emma knew it couldn't have happened quite this way, the reports she'd read, testimonies of others, and her own knowledge of Kelsey and her father crafted a story that haunted her in the wee hours of the morning.

She would always be standing behind the counter, the lights over the gas station pumps like an oasis as the early evening twilight fell like a blanket over the town. She'd be ringing up Hitch Johnson's bait, minnows scurrying in the Styrofoam container, while she kept one eye on the pumps outside.

No matter how hard she looked, however, she never saw him drive up.

The reports said he drove an orange Chevy Camaro, and she didn't know if she placed it from her memory or simply created it on her own, but in her dream, it just appeared outside, the motor rumbling.

And then she turned toward the next person in the checkout line.

He simply materialized, like the car had. Parker Swenson.

Those who knew him came forward in the *Deep Haven Herald*

to comment on the days when he played football for the Huskies, although everyone knew he'd spent more time on the sideline than the field. He had a record, though—possession from the year he lived in Minneapolis. But because he was a hometown boy, no one bothered to do their homework.

Sheriff Hueston had seen him that day but made no mention of errant behavior.

Still, in her dream, as Emma looked at him through Kelsey's eyes, she only saw the stringy hair tied back in a ponytail, the stubble of his unshaven face. The smell of cigarette smoke and the odor of grease lifted off him, curdling her stomach. He wore a grimy brown ski jacket and stuck his hands in his pockets as he said, "A pack of Pall Malls." His voice scored through her like razors.

She looked above to the stock of cigarettes. Pulled down a pack. Dropped it onto the counter. "ID please?"

The doctors speculated that he might have simply snapped, although the autopsy showed traces of marijuana in his system. Neither motivation gave him a bye for pulling the gun, for pressing it to her forehead, the barrel cold against her skin.

She raised her hands, met his dark eyes. "Please."

Emma always said a feeble *please*, her heart in her throat. But she had no doubt Kelsey—born from Hueston stock—said something more. Whatever it might have been, it made him hesitate because they found her between the bakery rack and the cooler as if she might have been escaping.

He'd shot her twice, once in the back.

That's when Emma longed to awaken. She tried, but the dream had tentacles, held her tight, forcing her to watch as a man walked in. He wore the brown uniform—dark pants, pale shirt, his utility belt around his waist.

The dream slowed then, bowed out and became like molasses. Parker turned, took one look at the deputy, and shot.

Every time, shock tore through her. Every time, she hated herself for not crying out, for not warning the man. Every time, she caught his gaze as he fell, his chest torn open at close range.

Every time she heard her voice, screaming. *Daddy!*

"Daddy!"

"Emma—wake up!" Carrie's voice at the door.

Light splashed over her as Emma kicked her way from the dream. Her heart pummeled her chest; sweat beaded over her body. She lay in the tangled sheets, catching her breath, making a noise that frightened her.

Daddy.

Carrie sat on the bed and caught her hand. "You have to stop having these. You're going to wake the neighbors and they'll think I'm in here with a knife."

Emma ran a hand over her forehead. "Every time my mother calls, I have nightmares for days afterward."

"Maybe you shouldn't take the gig this weekend. Maybe it's too soon."

Emma sat up, pushed her hair from her face. "I need the money. And it's not in Deep Haven—it's at a resort about ten minutes out. I'll go, play the wedding, leave. Easy."

"Do you want me to go with you?"

Emma shook her head. "I can do this."

"I'm not so sure. I know I said you have to make peace with this, but it's been three years, Emma. Someday you're going to have to forgive yourself."

Emma wrestled her way out of bed. The cold air shocked the rest of the dream from her mind. She stared out at the street, early morning light now dribbling over the city, turning the buildings to pewter, dingy brown. "How do you forgive yourself for surviving?"

"You weren't even there."

"But I was supposed to be." She turned and gave Carrie a sad smile. "I was supposed to work, but I had a band concert at school. The stupid flute. I hated the band."

Carrie got up, came to the window to stand beside her, looping her arm through Emma's. "You didn't hate the band. You hate the fact that you feel guilty for living."

Emma flinched. "After Kelsey died, I thought I'd come down to the Cities, get into the music scene, and start playing her songs. Keep her alive, you know? But . . . I'm gigging as a backup bassist, I haven't had my own show for two years, and I'm not making it, Carrie. I should just go home. But I can't. Everything about home reminds me of how I've failed."

"Including that hot guy you met the other night."

Kyle. The hot guy. Oh, if only she could erase him from her thoughts, but he dogged her. That smile, suddenly directed at her after all these years. And the way he'd kissed her, so impossibly gentle, so delightfully perfect.

He made her want to go home.

"That hot guy was Kelsey's brother."

"You told me," Carrie said. "You're trying to live Kelsey's dream down here, aren't you?"

"It was our dream. Kelsey's and mine. We shared it."

Carrie turned away from the window. "Whatever you say."

"Carrie, I want to be a musician."

"True fact: you can be a musician in Deep Haven."

"Not and hit it big."

"How big do you want to hit it, Emma? What do you want

136

your life to look like? Gigging every weekend in dives? Because I don't see you in the studio, I don't see you adding words to those reams of music, and frankly, I don't see you loving the city life."

"I love the city life."

"I think you love Deep Haven more. In fact, I think the reason you don't want to go home has less to do with the tragedies in Deep Haven and more to do with the failures here. Go back. Maybe the nightmares will end." She squeezed Emma's arm as she walked out of the room, closing the door behind her.

Emma got back into bed. Pulled the covers over her head. *Go back. Right.*

Her nightmares didn't have a prayer of ending.

9

Kelsey lay in her bed, curled into the pink afghan their grandmother had knit for her.

No, no, not Kelsey. Mom.

Kyle stood in the hallway between his room and Kelsey's, unable to move.

Mom lay asleep on Kelsey's bed, wrapped in Kelsey's blanket.

Had her memory returned?

For a moment, as he'd tiptoed down the hallway, he'd seen the open door and a crazy old memory rose. Kelsey, collapsed on the bed, having dragged in late from work, the sun draping lazy early morning arms over her body, her hair golden upon the pillow.

It could take his breath away as he half expected—no,

desperately longed for—Kelsey to roll over and flash him an annoyed wrinkle of her nose.

Crazy hope, because of course, it could never be. Yet his breath deflated and he felt a terrible scrape of disappointment inside when he realized his mother had wrapped herself in the afghan and fallen asleep on Kelsey's pillow.

"She's been having trouble sleeping." Eli tiptoed up behind him, wearing a pair of sweatpants, wet hair plastered to his head, a bathrobe hitched at his waist. He moved past Kyle and shut the door. "Don't wake her."

Kyle kept his voice low. "What is she doing in there? She hasn't stepped foot in Kelsey's room since . . ."

Eli lifted a shoulder. "I don't know."

His dad seemed more rested today. Last night at the game, sitting beside his mother, Eli nearly resembled the father Kyle knew, the man who'd attended his home games, the man who'd drilled into him the three-point shot.

He hated how much that memory wooed him.

He wanted to sit in the stands, cheering his own sons. Longed to set an example they might follow.

"What are you doing here so early?" Eli said.

Kyle turned in to his room. "I came to pick up my drum kit. I'm playing this weekend at a wedding. By the way, the forensics guys are done looking at Mom's SUV. I have a pal driving it up from Harbor City later today."

"Thanks, Kyle." Eli stood in the doorway, watching as Kyle began to unscrew his high hat.

Kyle didn't look at him. "Do you remember Emma Nelson?"

"Emma?" His father's voice hitched just a little. "Yeah, sure. Lee's daughter."

"I saw her last weekend in the Cities. She was playing at a blues club. Got into a bar fight—"

"Emma got into a fight?"

"No—there was a fight around her. She got hurt—"

"She was hurt? How bad?"

He glanced at his father, at the worry on his face. "She's fine, Dad. A couple stitches. But that's not the point. I was just . . . Well, we had a good time together. She's the one I'm playing with this weekend."

"Which is why you've decided to sharpen your rusty drum skills."

"I'm not that rusty, and frankly, I was pretty good."

"I remember a lot of noise." His dad smiled at him, teasing in his eyes.

Kyle had missed that. "Uh, about the hospital—I'm sorry, Dad."

Eli looked at the floor, examining it as if there were a vital piece of evidence there. "Me too."

Kyle set the high hat on the bed, then turned to the cymbals.

"Just . . . remember, she's getting on with her life. You don't want to mess with that."

He didn't? He glanced at his father, who was now staring at something out the window, lost for a moment.

Maybe he was thinking of Kelsey, how he'd feel if Kelsey had fallen for a hometown boy. Only, that didn't seem like such a crime. After all, his father had been a hometown boy, and his mother hadn't objected to living her life so far from the city.

Kyle finished with the cymbals, loading them and the high hat into a padded case. He lifted the snare from its stand and slid it into the container.

A weighted pause behind him made him glance up. His father always had a presence about him—the way he walked into a room and folded his arms could cause his sons to sit up at attention. He wore his cop look, the face that said, *Tell me your story and I'll see if I believe it.*

"You're investigating the incident, aren't you?" Eli said.

"What makes you say that?"

"I saw Norm yesterday in town. He mentioned you'd received the autopsy report on the victim."

"A courtesy from the guys down in Duluth. She was shot with a 9mm Glock. And cuffed across the face, leaving a welt."

"Anything suspicious on the log? Did they dig up anything from the witnesses?"

See? His father couldn't stay away either.

"Nothing that's flushed out any leads. However, Jason Backlund was out plowing, saw Ryan Nickel's car in the ditch. He's had a few tickets, so I tracked down the plate and registration on the car—apparently he still owns it. Seems he might have been on the road about the time of the incident; maybe he saw something. I'm headed up to the Nickels' place today."

"It's imperative that we nail this guy, Kyle."

The smallness of his voice, the worry in it, rattled Kyle. In that moment, his father appeared not like the Deep Haven sheriff but like a victim. Lines creased his face, his eyes troubled. "If this guy took a look at your mom, he might believe she's able to identify him. The longer he goes free, the more danger she faces. We'll let our guard down and one day—"

"I'm not going to let that happen, Dad. I'm not going to let him find Mom."

Eli met his eyes, the cop in him now searching.

Kyle returned his gaze. "You just help her get her memory back. I'll find this guy."

Eli nodded, a sigh rattling out of him. "We spent the entire day yesterday going through her daily life. It jogged nothing, not even the game. She . . ." He glanced at the closed door. "She even saw Kelsey's picture in the case at school and didn't have a blink of recognition."

"Then why is she sleeping in her room this morning?"

Eli scrubbed a hand down his face. "I've been thinking . . . maybe it would be better if she never remembers—"

"Don't say that."

Kirby stood behind Eli, skinny and bare-chested, his hair in knots. He needed a cut, but he'd filled out over the year as he'd lifted weights. He wore a sort of desperate fury on his face. "She's already remembering. She made me breakfast yesterday, and I saw her in the stands. She was her normal self."

"Her normal self before Kelsey's death," Eli said, then laid a finger to his lips. "Keep it down. She's in there sleeping." He nodded to Kelsey's room.

"See. She *does* remember. Maybe she just doesn't know it yet."

"We all hope so, Kirby, but what you're seeing isn't memory. It's who she is. When I first met her, I took her to a few games. She loves to cheer. And I think you stole her breakfast from her."

Kirby's mouth pinched into a tight line. "She remembers. You just wait."

"But is that what you really want for her? To remember losing her only daughter?"

"She still has us, Dad," Kirby snapped.

"Yes, she has us . . . even if she never gets her memory back. But before, she was so distraught, so beaten. Maybe this is better."

"She was getting better. Much better. You just didn't see it because you were never around."

Kyle recognized his brother's tone; he'd heard it in himself.

"I was around, Kirby. I just couldn't take losing your mom, too."

"Is that why you cleared out Kelsey's stuff?" Kirby turned to Kyle, his eyes venomous. "Did you know that he came home one day and packed it all up? All her clothes, her journals, her pictures. He took down the family photos, the scrapbooks, the photo albums. Everything. He even stripped her bed. I came home from track practice, and she'd vanished from our lives. Mom was hysterical, but guess what? Dad was gone."

"Yes, you told me," Kyle said softly. He turned to his father. "You can't erase Kelsey from our lives."

"I wasn't erasing her. I was trying to get us past it without a daily reminder of who we lost. She got better after that, didn't she?"

"I'm not sure she ever forgave you, though."

Eli swallowed hard. "Now do you see why it's better that she doesn't remember?"

"So she'll forgive you?" Every emotion Kyle had tried to ignore since the hospital rose. "I can't believe how utterly selfish that is."

Eli rounded on him. "You know what? Maybe it is. Maybe I want the woman I fell in love with back. I want her to be like she was—"

"She was trying!" Kirby's voice rose, and Kyle shot a look at the door to Kelsey's room. "She even started painting!"

Eli hooked Kirby's arm, dragged him into the kitchen, Kyle close behind. His voice ground to low. "What are you talking about?"

Kirby shook out of his grip. "At the art colony. They rent out space. She had a little room there on Tuesdays and Thursdays and sometimes on Fridays."

"How do you know?"

"It wasn't a secret, Dad. She showed me some of her work. It was pretty good."

But clearly it had been a secret, at least to their father. Kyle watched the truth dawn across his face. He looked away and for the first time felt sympathy for his old man.

Still, the bruises from the fight at the hospital lay fresh on him. He drew in a long breath. "Dad, I'm thinking that in order for you to help Mom get her memory back, you might want to learn who the woman you lost was."

Lee lay in bed, staring at the exposed beams of her ceiling, the morning sun having already flushed through her room. Derek had left over an hour ago for school, and she'd done the practical thing on a frozen, below-zero morning, after she'd stoked the woodstove and lit a fire.

She'd returned to the heat of her bed.

At first, after Clay passed, she'd hated lingering in their double bed—had even slept downstairs on the sofa for a few weeks. But she liked the view from their loft, overlooking the lake, split by a trio of birch and the shaggy outline of black pine. Here, too, she felt less alone, although she'd long ago washed Clay's smell from the sheets and started to sleep in the middle of the bed.

She closed her eyes, remembering Eli's hand on hers. *I don't know what I would do without you.*

Something dangerous had moved inside her then. An emotion

she shouldn't linger on, an urge that frightened her. She'd smiled, then bid him good night and escaped the truck.

But the emotion remained, settled in her chest.

I don't know what I would do without you either, Eli.

He'd become a part of their lives, as natural as breathing, over the past three years. Listening, caring for her, reminding her that she wasn't alone.

She'd wanted to invite him in.

Banging on the door outside jerked her upright, and a residue of pain speared down her arm. She groaned, then climbed out of bed, slid her feet into slippers. She'd already changed into her yoga pants and a T-shirt, but that had seemed suitable sleepwear, too.

"Lee!" More banging and then the door opened as she descended the stairs.

Eli barged inside and stood on the mat, snow sloughing off his boots. He seemed lit up, his eyes dark. "Why didn't you tell me?"

She folded her arms over her chest. "What are you talking about?"

"I'm talking about Noelle's painting studio at the art colony. She's been renting one for two years. Did you know that? Because I sure didn't."

The way he looked at her—half-pleading, half-angry, mostly hurt—stripped away the indignation she should feel at his accusation. She schooled her voice. "No, Eli, I didn't."

He turned away and ran a hand through his hair. Breathed out. "Can you come with me?"

The tremor in his voice could make her say yes to anything. "Of course. Let me get my boots."

While he radiated fumes of frustration downstairs, she cleaned up, pulling her hair back in a ponytail, throwing on just enough mascara to recognize herself. Then she pulled on her parka, her UGGs, and tromped outside behind him.

He opened the door for her and helped her into the truck. Probably because she'd groaned as she put on her coat. Even in his distress, he had a way of watching out for others. She liked that about Eli Hueston.

He climbed behind the wheel, started up his truck. "She was sleeping on Kelsey's bed this morning."

Lee shot him a look. "Do you think she remembers anything?"

"I don't know. I left her there, wrote her a note." He backed out of the driveway and turned onto the highway toward town.

"What happened, Eli?"

His knuckles blanched on the steering wheel. "Kirby seems to know about some art studio his mother rented. Apparently—" he glanced at her, his eyebrows up—"she *has* been painting."

Oh. "No wonder she kept asking."

"Do you think she knew that, deep inside?"

Lee shook her head. "I don't know." She touched his arm. "Really, I had no idea."

He glanced at her before he took one hand off the wheel and wove his fingers into hers. Sighed. "I believe you."

The art colony had purchased the old Baptist church in town decades ago and since then added on two wings. Lee herself had taken a pottery class there from Liza Beaumont, their local potter, a few years ago.

Eli parked outside and held on to her elbow as they walked in. "I'm fine, Eli—"

"I don't want you to fall." He said it with a touch of heat in his voice.

They found the director, a slim, tall brunette in a smock and clogs. She looked at Eli with some surprise when he asked to see Noelle's studio.

"We keep the studios private, Eli. She might not be ready to—"

"Let me in the room, Jane. Right now."

She swallowed and bit her lip. "Fine. But I'm going to let Noelle know—"

"I promise you, she won't care."

Lee followed him up the stairs, her heart aching for him. When she'd gone through Clay's life after his death, she had discovered a few online gambling accounts—nothing with real money, but he'd logged sufficient time on them for her to wonder if he would have ever put them in jeopardy. It had rocked her world enough to erase it from her mind, to focus on the man she knew.

Thankfully, Clay had never hidden a private room from her. She had the sense of prying into Noelle's journal as they stood before a tiny door.

"I don't have a key," Jane said.

Eli held the ring out to Jane. "These are Noelle's."

Jane picked through the keys, surfaced with a silver one, and inserted it in the door. "What's going on, Eli?"

"I'm not sure," he said as he pushed past her.

"It's okay," Lee assured Jane.

Eli was standing in the middle of the room, completely still. Lee followed him in and closed the door behind her.

The studio measured about ten feet square, with a two-paned window overlooking the town of Deep Haven, the harbor with the lighthouse, a frozen skating pond. A blue armchair with tiny peach flowers sat near another window, a sketchpad on the ottoman before it. In the middle of the studio, a large easel held an unfinished watercolor. She recognized the background features as

Artist's Point, the craggy breakwater that protected the lee side of the harbor. An unfinished section of white contained a pencil sketch, the forms of two girls sitting on the beach, one with a guitar.

Her heart expanded in her throat, lodging there.

Eli had moved over to a stack of paintings, some large, others on smaller frames. Most of them featured landscapes or close-ups of rocks, fence posts. One was a detailed watercolor of a pair of red Converse tennis shoes. It seemed she'd seen that picture before.

"These are watercolors of Kelsey's photography." He held up a photo of a pine tree, the perspective from the base to the top, as if Kelsey had stood hugging it, looking up. The next picture showed a coffee cup set on a bloodred maple leaf, perched on the grainy wood of a green picnic table.

Photographs hung by clothespins from a piece of yarn that extended across the far wall.

"Kirby said she was getting better. That she was trying to heal." Eli turned to her, his eyes wide. "She was trying to recapture Kelsey."

"I thought you emptied the house of Kelsey's things."

"I did. But maybe she already had these." He went over to examine the photos. "She was really talented."

"Kelsey?"

Eli drew in a breath. "Noelle." He shook his head. "What is this? Why didn't she tell me that she was painting? Did she think I wouldn't care, wouldn't listen?"

Oh, Eli. Lee set down a painting of Kirby's rusty Neon. "Maybe she just couldn't let you in." She bit her lip, hating the way he flinched.

He sat on the chair. Sank his head into his hands.

She couldn't help walking over, sitting on the ottoman across from him. Taking his hands from his face. "Everyone grieves in their own way. This didn't mean she was betraying you."

"No," he said, his eyes red-rimmed. "It means I betrayed her. Kyle was right—I didn't even know her."

"That's not true. You just went through so much, Eli. We all did."

He met her eyes, searching. Swallowed.

And then, just like that, he kissed her.

She didn't expect it, hadn't ever contemplated it—not really. His kiss was urgent and desperate, and she knew it was wrong. But she hadn't been kissed in so long, and the feelings of a man desiring her, needing her, flooded through Lee.

She touched his face, felt the bristles of his overnight whiskers, and kissed him back. She kissed him because, oh, he had a strength about him that she longed for.

And then, as abruptly as he'd leaned forward, Eli jerked away, his breath harsh in his lungs. "Oh . . . Lee, I'm so sorry." He held his hands up as if pushing her from him, even though she hadn't moved, then got up and stalked across the room.

"It's okay, Eli—"

"It's not okay! What was I thinking?" He let out a word she'd never heard him use. "I'm not that guy—I don't cheat on my wife."

"Eli, she doesn't know you. It can hardly be called cheating when the woman can't even remember your vows."

Lee wanted to clamp her hand over her mouth, take the words back, but as they lay out there in the silence, she realized the truth.

She didn't want Noelle to retrieve her memory. Never. Because then Eli wouldn't have to stay with her, would he?

The thought must have flashed across her face because his jaw tightened, and he shook his head a long time before the words came out. "I'm not leaving Noelle for you."

His words slapped her, but she managed to find her feet. "Uh, you kissed *me*, Eli. I didn't start this. And I never asked you to leave Noelle." But inside, she could hear her own indictments. "You need to take a good look at your life. Your wife, even before she lost her memory, was sneaking around, keeping things from you. What else was she hiding, do you think?"

His eyes widened, and she could only imagine what might be scrolling through his mind.

"And frankly, you cheated on her long before you kissed me."

"I never—"

"Stop lying to yourself, Eli. You spend nearly every day at my house, helping me. Listening to me, being my friend. And when you weren't at my house, you were fishing or hunting or snow-mobiling. You didn't want to be in that marriage because if you did, you would have *shown up*."

He flinched, but Lee didn't care. She whirled around, nearly knocking over a painting. She righted it and turned back to him. "You'd better figure out what you want because guess what—I *do* remember. I remember everything. And I'm not so sure I'd want you anyway."

She didn't slow down to see if her words landed. She just ran down the steps—ignoring Jane, who lifted her gaze from her desk—and outside, where the crisp air froze her tears to her face. Oh, she was an idiot. Such, such an idiot.

And she hadn't driven. Or brought her keys so she could hike to the school and take Derek's car home.

How she hated being at life's mercy. Hated the fact that other people's choices could destroy her own.

Emma had been right to leave this town, to kick off the snow and find a new life.

"Lee?"

She didn't turn. "Take me home."

Eli said nothing but held out his arm for her.

She ignored it. She could manage just fine on her own, thank you very much.

⨎

Eli dug his fingers into the steering wheel as he drove up the slick road toward his ice house.

He just had to get somewhere to clear his head, figure out how to erase the feel of Lee in his arms, or reel back time to that moment when he'd lost his mind.

Lee had been sitting there, the compassion in her expression almost too much for him to bear. And he'd simply reacted.

He needed someone who needed him.

But even as he kissed her, even as he'd thirsted for a way to hide from the reality of his fractured marriage, he knew Lee couldn't slake it. And when he'd pulled away, seen the surprise—the hope—in her eyes, he knew he'd pitched headfirst into a place he didn't want to go.

He wouldn't be a cheater. Even if his wife couldn't remember him.

Eli slowed his truck as it bounced over the rough road.

What hurt worse, however, were Lee's words, sandpaper on his ego. *You didn't want to be in that marriage because if you did, you would have* shown up.

What did Lee expect of him? His daughter had died. Been

murdered. And frankly, he wasn't sure that the entire thing wasn't his fault. Of course he'd been distant.

Besides, Noelle had hardly shown up either.

The paintings, though—they had the power to undo him. He'd thought he'd been doing them all a favor by taking away reminders of Kelsey. Of course he planned on returning everything someday.

When they were healed.

But maybe Noelle had figured out her own way to heal.

He stopped the truck at the landing. There in the middle of the lake, his silver ice house glinted like a trophy in the sunlight. He backed the truck up to a snowbank, opened the back, and drove the snowmobile off it.

He should have stopped off at home, put on his gear, but . . . well, he couldn't look at Noelle. Even if she didn't know him, didn't care, he couldn't bear to see her beautiful eyes, beginning to trust a man who had so abominably failed her.

He gunned the sled out onto the snow, not caring how the particles hit his face. He shouldn't be driving without a helmet, but then again, he shouldn't be doing a lot of things.

Like kissing Lee Nelson.

He drove faster, catching some air as he hit a drift, liking the speed, the buzzing of the machine against the crisp blue silence of the day.

He reached the ice house. Icicles hung off the roof, long spears that could dissect a man. Inside, he could light a fire, make it cozy.

Camp out here for a few days.

A week.

Maybe even until the end of the month, until they made him drag it off the ice at the end of February.

He closed his eyes, now stiff with flakes in his lashes.

You'd better figure out what you want because guess what—I do remember. I remember everything. And I'm not so sure I'd want you anyway.

He'd blown it big with Noelle—and with Lee, who deserved better than to have him show up on her doorstep at all hours of the night.

Honestly, he should be surprised that the kiss hadn't happened sooner. He'd been harboring feelings for Lee for a good long time. Just never wanted to admit it.

He banged his hand on the handgrip. She hadn't spoken to him the entire ride home, had gotten out of the car and slammed the door.

He hadn't missed her grimace as pain shot through her body. He should probably swing by later, see if she needed a ride to the doctor.

No. Wait. He shouldn't.

He gunned the sled, zipped out again onto the lake, and opened it up, leaning into each turn. The snow plumed up behind him, and he opened his mouth to let out a cry that the motor easily ate.

Round and around—he wore a path, then cut through the middle around the ice house.

Back when they'd first married, he would take Noelle on long snowmobile rides, her arms tight around him as they cut through deer paths in the forest. She knew how to hang on, to move with him, and for Christmas that first year, he'd given her a snowmobile helmet.

He had no idea where it might be now. Probably in the basement with the other unused equipment in their life—tents, snowshoes, skis, bicycles, her tackle box and fishing pole. Before they had children, Noelle had been the kind of wife who joined him in his outdoor pursuits. How many times had she sat in the bow of the boat, rain plinking on her hat, her line deep in the lake, waiting for a nibble? Or even after Kyle was born, she'd hiked out to the woods early in the morning, leaving Kyle with a sitter, and sat with him in a deer stand. He thought she might alert Bambi to his demise, but she'd stayed quiet as he made his shot.

Noelle had learned to hunt, to fish, to camp. She'd joined his life.

And he'd learned . . . ?

He slowed the machine, turned off the motor, put his feet down on the snow. They crunched in the crisp white field as he leaned back on the seat—built for two—and stared at the sky. Faint cirrus clouds looked watercolored upon a blue canvas.

After Kelsey's death, he'd filled his life with all the things that made him feel safe. But he'd done it alone. No, he hadn't exactly invited Noelle into his life, so she'd had to create her own. Reconstruct the one she'd loved.

When he closed his eyes, he heard Kyle's soft voice with its lethal accuracy. *Dad, I'm thinking that in order for you to help Mom get her memory back, you might want to learn who the woman you lost was.*

It didn't matter if she didn't remember their vows, their life. Because *he* did. And hadn't he been out on this very lake a week ago, asking God to help him be the husband she needed? How to love her?

He mashed the heels of his hands against his eyes, found them wet.

He'd been about to give up.

In fact—he sat up, the realization ringing through him—he'd

been about to give his heart to Lee. He shook his head, hating the man he'd nearly become.

He spoke aloud, letting his voice puff out in the cold as if seeing the words form before him added power to them. "God, I want to do the right thing. Help me want to do the right thing. Even if she doesn't ever know me, help me be her husband. Even if . . . even if she never remembers me."

It was time for Eli Hueston to show up.

10

Emma always knew that Deep Haven had a lethal ability to woo travelers to the north. Something about the fairyland forest with its frosted trees, the lure of the lake as it murmured mystery from the depths, the footprints of foxes and deer in the snow, the low-flying eagles along the highway. The town could lure someone close with its song, make her forget the reasons she'd fled, and entangle her forever.

The reason you don't want to go home has less to do with the tragedies in Deep Haven and more to do with the failures here.

Oh, Carrie had a knack for words that reminded Emma of Kelsey. Both girls could always pinpoint exactly what Emma was thinking but didn't have the courage—or poetry—to express.

Indeed Carrie might have looked into her soul and seen the

truth because driving along the shore, drawing closer and closer to Deep Haven, didn't stir up the dread Emma had expected.

The town turned magical in the grip of winter. The lake sparkled under the sun where skaters glided over the clear ice in the harbor, and curly smoke rose from the coffeehouse. She'd expected a stab of pain as she passed the convenience store, but only the memory of her and Kelsey rolling their eyes over one of George Whitehall's jokes surfaced. He came in every Saturday morning for a coffee and a banana muffin.

Why can't a blonde dial 911? She can't find the eleven!

Oh, Kelsey had been such a good sport.

When Emma passed Artist's Point, she heard the waves churning through her memory. She and Kelsey must've come here a hundred times to put together a new song, try out lyrics while tucked into a pocket of rocky shoreline.

She spied a customer emerging from World's Best Donuts and heard her father ordering two glazed raised. They'd eat them together at the picnic table, watching the lake, even in winter. She could almost see his laughter, crystallized in the crisp air as she read aloud the crazy police reports from the weekly paper.

Yet somehow she passed through Deep Haven without tearing open old scars.

If only she could manage not to see Kyle Hueston, she might escape with her brain—and her heart—intact. He had no right to linger in her mind after a week. Oh, she hoped Nicole hadn't lined him up to play drums.

She didn't want to see him; she didn't want to see him. Maybe if she kept saying it, she'd find herself believing it.

Who was she kidding? She longed to catch a glimpse of him. More than a glimpse. She kept thinking about that kiss, the way his smile could turn her to syrup. Indeed, feeling as she did right now, he just might have the power to make her change her mind.

Return to Deep Haven.

Okay, right now, she didn't know what she wanted.

She pulled into her driveway, glad Derek had kept up with the shoveling. His car, however, wasn't there. As she climbed out, she drank in the smell of home. Woodsmoke, the scent of pine in the air.

Why had she been so afraid?

She walked up to her house, pushed open the door. "Mom? I'm home."

"Emma?"

She stomped her feet, slid her coat off, hung it on the hook. Her mother had risen from the recliner, but Emma hardly recognized her or the house. Laundry lay unfolded on the family room floor, dishes scattered on the counter. Lee came toward her, no makeup, her hair pulled into a messy ponytail. She wore sweatpants that dragged on the floor and an old Deep Haven sweatshirt.

"Mom, are you okay?"

Her mother hooked her arm around Emma's neck, pulling her close. "I'm fine." But as she moved back, she didn't look fine. Lines edged her eyes, and they appeared reddened. And she held her arm close to her chest. "I slipped a disk in my neck about a week ago. It flared up again."

Emma dropped her bag on the floor. "Oh, Mom, why didn't you tell me? I could have come home."

"You're so busy, Emma." Her mother touched her cheek, smiled into her eyes. "You've lost weight."

"Just a little."

"I'm sorry; we ate the last of the venison stew, but I think there is lasagna in the freezer."

"Actually, I'm on my way to rehearsal up at Caribou Ridges. The rehearsal dinner is tonight, the wedding tomorrow."

Her mother wandered back to the recliner. Her tiny moan wasn't lost on Emma.

"How about if I make you a sandwich before I go."

Her mother lifted her good arm. "I'm fine, honey. So you're playing for Nicole's wedding?"

"Yes. She roped me into it. Where's Derek?"

"Basketball practice. He'll be home later."

Emma picked up the laundry, put it into the basket. "He should fold these."

"I needed a clean pair of pants and didn't want to drag this upstairs to fold."

"How long have you been like this?"

"Just a week. Really, I'm okay." But she sighed, and the smile didn't reach her eyes.

Emma picked up the poker and opened the fire curtain, prodded the fire to life, then added a log. She closed the curtain, replaced the poker. "What aren't you telling me, Mom?"

Her mother shook her head. "It's nothing. I'm just so glad you're moving on with your life, Emma. I really hope to get down to the Cities and hear you play. And I can't wait for Derek to get his scholarship, move down to the Cities, too."

"What about you?"

That empty smile again. "I'll move too. I'm tired of living in Deep Haven."

The words froze Emma, cut through her. "I don't understand. You love it here. It's your home—our home. Dad built you this house. Your friends are here; your life is here. You can't leave."

Her mother raised an eyebrow, gave a chortle. "It's time I

stopped living a life that's over. I need to start new. Away from Deep Haven. Like you."

Emma stared at her, the way she curled into herself on the recliner. Yeah, like her. "I'll be back after rehearsal, Mom. It might be late."

"Don't worry about me, honey. Have fun, and stay out of trouble." She winked but it looked more like a wince than her usual cheery good-bye.

&

If he could, Kyle would rewind his week back to the sight of his mother in Kelsey's bed and relive it without the eerie feeling that dogged him until he'd finally found someone home today at the rutted junkyard of the Nickel place. Just being inside the cabin had turned his stomach, from the putrid odor of a septic tank backing up somewhere, to the mangy dog eyeing him from where he chewed a deer leg in the middle of the dirty linoleum in the kitchen, to the sense that mice might be living in the ratty sofa that held down the shag carpet.

He had stopped home to shower before dressing up for the rehearsal this afternoon.

Still, his conversation with Billy Nickel ran through his head as he drove to Caribou Ridges.

Ryan hadn't been home, but on the sofa sat a beanpole of a boy, greasy blond hair hanging tangled out of an orange hunting hat. He wore a pair of jeans smudged with grease, a flannel shirt. His hand rode the knee of a girl who nearly snarled at Kyle as he'd knocked on the door. Or perhaps it just looked like she snarled with the two tiny spikes protruding from her bottom lip, her shocking red hair, tied in two low pigtails, adding to the surly effect. She got up, propped the door open with her foot, and folded her arms over her chest.

Kyle flashed his badge. "I just need to talk to Ryan."

"He doesn't live here. That's his brother, Billy." She jerked her head to the rail on the sofa.

Billy looked stoned even as he lolled his head toward Kyle. "Hey."

Kyle shot a look at the Dodge Dart parked in the snow and noticed a taillight had been smashed. Maybe from the skid into the ditch. With the blue paint job, the *State Champions* wording now flecking off the side, a giant helmet painted on the window, Kyle figured he'd tracked down the right vehicle. "That your car?"

"It's my brother's."

"Are you driving it?"

Billy lifted a shoulder. "When it runs."

"Were you driving it the other night, during the storm?" He tried to keep his voice friendly, no big deal. He looked at the girl for permission, and she pursed her lips as she stepped aside. He stood in the tiny kitchen, a grimy green sweatshirt jacket hanging over a chair at the round kitchen table. It reeked of fish and woodsmoke.

Billy sat up. Reached for a cigarette. Kyle pegged him at nineteen at the most. "Why?"

"A week ago, there was a shooting at the Harbor City Mocha Moose. Someone was killed."

He watched the kid for a reaction, and there it was, the narrowing of the eyes, the way Billy looked away from him.

"There weren't many cars on the highway that night, and Jason Backlund mentioned you were pushing yours out of the ditch."

Billy blew out a stream of smoke. "Uh-huh. Real slippery."

"Who was with you?"

His gaze shifted to his girlfriend and back. "No one."

"Really? Because Jason said there were two—one at the wheel, someone else pushing." He glanced at the girl. "Was it you?"

For a second, something like fear flashed across her face. Then she shook her head.

"Relax, Yvonne." Billy crushed out his cigarette. Stood. "It was just a friend of mine, okay? What is this, a federal investigation?"

Kyle held up his hands. "No problem. I just wanted to know if you two might have seen anything as you passed through Harbor City. Maybe a car driving too fast up the highway—"

"I didn't see nothing, okay?" He came up behind Yvonne and slipped grimy hands over her shoulders. He wore a class ring, bulky on his skinny finger, a ruby in the center. A ring that could hurt someone, leave a welt, or more. Fury boiled up inside Kyle, and he had to take a breath as Billy responded. "I was with my girl all day. I wasn't even down in Harbor City. Right, babe?"

Babe glanced at him, back at Kyle, nodded.

Billy pulled Yvonne away from the door. "I think you should leave."

Kyle kept his cool smile. "Thanks for your time. By the way, you'd better get the taillight fixed. You drive that around in town, you might get a ticket."

Billy shut the door behind Kyle with more force than necessary.

As he climbed into his cruiser, a van drove up. Big man at the wheel, maybe in his late twenties. He wore a beard, his hair a chin-length mop. He got out of his vehicle, a white, dented Caravan that looked as if it might have been used off-road, and stared at Kyle as he rounded the back end and headed to the house.

Kyle drove away, watching him in the rearview mirror, the fine hairs rising on the back of his neck.

He couldn't dislodge the pair from his brain, nor the feeling that they knew something.

He'd spent the rest of the day serving papers, although he'd answered one call for a disturbance and found Duane Hoglund breaking in to his own house after his wife locked the door.

"You should carry a key," Kyle had said.

"No one carries a key in Deep Haven."

Which, of course, might have been true for other families.

He stopped in at World's Best, said hello to Joe and Jerry, who were exchanging football draft opinions with the new coach, Caleb Knight. He spotted Seb, one of the former Husky all-stars and current basketball coach, serving up red velvet cupcakes and nearly fell over when Lucy flashed him a ring.

Look at that—Lucy Maguire, tying the knot.

See, this was the town for happily ever after.

Which was exactly what he hoped to convince Emma Nelson, Miss I Hate Deep Haven, of this weekend.

Although perhaps he should have thought a bit harder about saying yes to playing an instrument he hadn't touched in six years. He set up the drum kit in the reception hall of Caribou Ridges, a room with a view of the lake and a crackling fireplace. Jason and Nicole had clearly planned an intimate wedding, with only six round tables and a head table at the front of the room, adorned with pine boughs, red roses, and a hurricane candle. Twinkle lights hung on the pine tree decor and wound around the windows, and a nest of lights curled over the mantel, mixed in with more greens, more red roses.

Romantic.

He warmed up with flat flams, then paradiddles, then a number of sticking exercises he'd developed back when he was serious. He followed with single stroke rolls. In between he stretched his hands, arms, then his feet, working first with his heel down, then rolls, and finally in more vigorous toe-up positions.

He could easily break a sweat and more while drumming.

Long ago he'd learned how to read sheet music and chart out his own drum parts from the lead sheet notation. If Emma had a list of songs, he'd download them tonight and chart those out. He'd also learned a few of the standards and warmed up on a couple, his iPod playing in his ear.

He didn't hear her come in, wrapped up in John Cougar Mellencamp's "Hurts So Good," the split track on his iPod allowing him to play the drums without competition.

Emma set her gear on a chair, propped her guitar on the table, and stood with her hands on her hips, not smiling.

He removed his earbuds. "Aw, c'mon. You have to be a little happy to see me."

"What part of 'I don't think we should see each other' did you not get?"

He did a drumroll. "I can tell when a girl is bluffing. I'm a cop—I know these things."

She pinched her mouth a little at the edges as if trying not to smile, and it set off all sorts of crazy explosions inside his chest.

She looked good, too, in a pair of skinny jeans, a button-down shirt, a patterned pink-and-blue scarf around her neck. Her dark hair fell around her shoulders, under a knit hat with an appliquéd pink flower on the side, her eyes so blue they had the power to make him forget his name.

He twirled a stick between his fingers. "Admit it—you're glad to see me. You can't get me off your mind. Your heart did a jig when you saw me."

She rolled her eyes, but more of that smile appeared.

"In fact, you might even admit that you're glad you're back in Deep Haven."

"Near Deep Haven, and let's not get ahead of ourselves."

"C'mon, we're at a wedding, in a terribly romantic pocket of the earth. You have to admit that this is fate."

"Fate? Fate would have been you noticing me years ago when I wore a 'Vote for Kyle' shirt for three days to get you elected homecoming king. This is not fate; it's an ambush."

"You really wore a 'Vote for Kyle' shirt?"

"Kelsey made me. And I should have never told you that."

"But you did. Which means I owe you for your vote."

"Absolutely. At the very least a sandwich." She unzipped her guitar case. "Do you know anything about playing the drums, or are you just here to look cute?"

"You think I'm cute?"

"Listen, Your Highness, I need a real drum player."

"I can play. Give me the lead sheets and I'll chart them out. I promise."

She raised an eyebrow. Then her smile vanished and she came near him, all tease gone. "Kyle Hueston, this gig means serious money for me. And maybe references later, so if you mess this up for me—"

He held up his hands. "Emma. Seriously. Protect and serve, right?"

There was that smile again.

"Okay, Deputy, let's see what you got."

⅋

Drummers are so hot. Emma heard Kelsey's voice in her head even as Kyle donned a pair of oven mitts and opened his oven to grab the pizza he'd made from scratch. He wore a pair of Levi's, but he'd slid out of his boots and socks and was walking around barefoot in his cabin nestled in the woods. And it didn't help that his thermal long-sleeved shirt outlined perfectly all those basketball muscles she remembered. Actually, he looked better than high school, his shoulders broader and confidence rather than swagger in his walk.

And he had drumming chops. She could hardly stop the swirl of joy inside when he'd charted out his beat to the songs she'd picked for the wedding reception, almost without effort. She'd handle the ceremony, located at the tiny harbor chapel, but his rhythm would add a festive vibe to the reception.

They'd ended with a jam session, something that had her wanting to sing, if she only knew the words. Kelsey would have made up something on the spot, taken the mic and added her bluesy voice in between their riffs.

Emma had so much fun, she forgot to be angry. And she even agreed to a late-night pizza at his place. Just this once.

She liked his house. Small, with one bedroom and a sparse amount of furniture, it had two Palladian windows—one in the bedroom, one in the family room—that overlooked the hamlet of Deep Haven. The pine floors appeared recently refinished, the smell of linden seed oil rising from their shiny surface. The kitchen looked like it'd been remodeled also—stainless steel oven and fridge, black granite counters.

She could live here. Sure, it needed a girl's touch, but she could stand forever at the picture window, overlooking the night, with the starlight trickling onto the lake, the pine trees laden with snow.

"I love your cabin."

He put the stone with the pizza on the counter, took a roller, and began to cut it into squares. The smell of garlic and chicken, the sweet scent of fresh basil, rose to make her stomach do curlicues. "Thanks. I bought it from Noah and Anne Standing Bear. They were hanging on to it in hopes they'd move back after Anne's residency, but apparently they needed the cash for one of Noah's inner-city initiatives. He's setting up a youth center in Duluth. I know the cabin is small, but I loved it even back when Noah was building it. I was about twelve when he moved here and started the summer camp. I helped him roof the place and always secretly wanted it."

She slid onto a rustic stool, made from stripped birch, and hooked her stocking feet around the bottom rung. "I can't believe you made me homemade pizza."

He slid a piece onto a plate. "Is this better than the sandwich I owe you?"

"Maybe." She picked up the piece. The crust crunched in her mouth, the garlic and basil a perfect mix in the white sauce. He always fed her so well. "What about Pierre's?"

"They don't deliver. And they don't make a decent thin crust."

She caught a string of mozzarella cheese on her chin. "I used to go to Pierre's every Wednesday for their lunch buffet. A bunch of us would pile into Kelsey's car—"

"*My* car. I bequeathed it to her."

"So *that* was the smell. Gym socks." She grinned at him. "We'd head down there with bodies hanging out of windows, gobble down the buffet, and charge back up the hill before the bell rang for fifth hour."

"Jason and I used to go to the taco place during lunch. They had those puffed shells that could make my mouth water just thinking about them."

"It's a Thai take-out place now."

"About time they added Asian food to the repertoire here in Deep Haven."

Emma took another square. "They make a cute couple—Jason and Nicole."

"Yeah. Lucky bum." Kyle put pizza on his own plate and came around to sit on the other stool.

But she got up. "Let's eat outside."

He frowned, but she ignored it and grabbed a quilt from his sofa before stepping out onto the deck overlooking the lake.

The brisk air seeped up under the quilt, but she wrapped it around herself and sat on the edge of the deck, conveniently under the overhang of the house.

"It's cold out there."

"Get out here, Heat Miser. I promise you won't freeze to death."

He'd slipped into his boots, pulled on his jacket, and now dusted off the deck before he sat down. "My pizza is cold."

"But look at the stars." They glistened against the night, and she reached out as if to grab one. "You can't see stars like this in the Cities."

"I guess I never noticed."

"Never noticed the stars?" She shook her head, took a bite of pizza. Oh, even cold, his garlic chicken pizza could make her eyes roll back into her head. "Kelsey and I used to lay out in your yard on a warm July night and watch for shooting stars to make a wish."

"What did you wish for?"

She glanced at him. "I'll never tell."

He narrowed his eyes, a smile tweaking his face. He had pretty whiskers—light but with flecks of red. "Playing gigs in the Cities?"

More like dating hometown basketball players, but—"Not really, no. Kelsey dreamed of doing something with our music;

she had an entire future worked out for us. I . . . I used to like Deep Haven. I thought I would live here the rest of my life."

He considered her a moment, then finished off his piece. Put his plate on the deck. "I never wanted to live here."

This time, she was the one to frown. "I thought you loved Deep Haven."

He tucked his strong hands between his knees. Okay, so maybe it had been a bit foolish—albeit romantically hopeful—for her to drag him outside into subzero temperatures.

"I did, but I thought maybe it was too small for me. I wanted to play basketball for the Timberwolves or, better, the Lakers or the Bulls. I only saw my future."

"It was a good future. Sports cars, big houses. Cheerleaders."

But he didn't smile at her tease. "I was cut from the U of Minnesota, Duluth, Bulldogs after the first year."

"Cut? How can that be?"

He looked away. "I took my fame too seriously. Started partying on campus, didn't show up for a few practices. They benched me, and then I lost my scholarship." He stared at his hands. "I was pretty selfish back then."

Oh, Kyle. She had a feeling that he had just entrusted her with little-known information. "I'm sorry."

"Yeah, well, Kelsey's murder sort of woke me up to the fact that I was derailing my life. I transferred to Alexandria Technical College's law enforcement program and decided to return to Deep Haven, keep it safe."

Because he couldn't do it for his sister. Suddenly his devotion to their small town made sense.

"Are you?"

"Am I what?"

"Keeping it safe? How is your job going?"

"I don't know. I'm trying. I stopped a raccoon from eating Mrs. Schultz's garbage yesterday."

"Had to use your weapon for that one?"

That nudged out a small smile.

"I'm also trying to solve the homicide in Harbor City."

"What homicide?"

"You didn't hear about it?"

She shook her head.

"It's the same incident where my mother was hurt. A robbery at the Mocha Moose there. The clerk was murdered, but my mother escaped."

"Oh, that's terrible."

"We have very few leads and there are no suspects yet."

"Did your mother see them? Maybe she could identify them."

He shivered, and she was just about to suggest they return inside when he said, "My mother hit her head, and now she doesn't remember anything."

"Nothing?" Her mother had mentioned something about Noelle falling.

He drew in a breath, blew it out like smoke in the air. "Actually, she's forgotten the last twenty-five years."

Emma stilled, no words in her.

"She doesn't remember marrying my father, or any of us kids."

"Kelsey."

He shook his head. "She doesn't remember her life or her death."

Emma pressed a hand to her mouth. Stared out at the blackness. "I'm so sorry, Kyle. Your family must be devastated."

"Of course, she doesn't remember the accident either, which

puts her at risk because we don't know who the suspect is. If he figures out who she is, he might come after her, not realizing that she can't identify him."

He shivered again, and the action, along with his words, made her open the quilt to draw it around him. "You'll find him, Kyle. I have no doubt."

He caught her eyes for a moment. The high school hero had vanished, leaving someone she liked better. A real hero.

He scooted in next to her, his leg warm against hers. "During the daytime, you can see the entire town from here. The harbor, with the lighthouse along the break wall, and the Coast Guard station. The fish house—"

"I used to think all towns smelled like hickory smoke."

He laughed. "The municipal campground, with all the motor homes, and even Artist's Point."

"Kelsey and I used to hang out there, compose songs. She said the water made her think better."

"You're an amazing guitar player," he said. "I wish I'd known you back in high school." He glanced at her, so close she could see the moonlight in his eyes. "I mean really known you. We would have had some fun jam sessions, you and me and Kelsey."

"She always wanted to invite you, but I wouldn't let her."

"Why?"

She gave him a look.

And that's when he kissed her. Sweetly, just like in the parking lot, his fingers against the line of her jaw, drawing her close. He tasted faintly of garlic and sweet basil and smelled like a man in jeans and cotton, strong and able to protect and serve, just as he claimed. She wove her fingers into his hair and kissed him back, just as sweetly.

Kyle pulled away, a smile tipping his lips, and bumped his forehead to hers.

"Because you were too tempting," she whispered. "I would have stopped playing and simply started watching you play the drums."

"Drummers are hot, you know."

She opened her mouth, leaned back. "What?"

"Kelsey would stand in the doorway to my room, listening to me practice, and say that. Like it was an incentive to learn or something."

"She always said guitarists were hot, too."

"They are," he said softly and kissed her again, this time letting his touch linger.

She'd stopped being cold but didn't mind when he tucked her under his arm, drew her close to his chest. "Maybe Kelsey was trying to set us up, all those years ago."

"Maybe," he said quietly, "it finally worked."

11

KYLE DIDN'T WANT to be jealous, but the beast prowled around, nipping at him as he watched Jason dance with his bride.

Twilight had begun to descend, spilling amber light across the tables, a fire crackling in the hearth of the cozy reception hall. With the hurricane candles and the smell of the pine boughs, he could imagine himself outside, a campfire burning.

Even better would be if Emma were pillowed up against him, her head on his shoulder, swaying to the harmony of the waves on the shore.

Sort of like how Nicole rested her head against Jason's chest, his eyes closed as Emma sang Aerosmith's "I Don't Want to Miss a Thing."

It took every ounce of discipline not to grab Emma, pull her out onto the dance floor. But then who would play the music? He'd have to come up with something.

"Don't wanna close my eyes, I don't wanna fall asleep,
    'Cause I'd miss you, babe, and I don't want to miss a
thing. . . ."

Indeed every word could belong to Emma. He might never forget her cute frosty nose peeking out of the quilt his mother made him for graduation or the way she'd let him kiss her, then tucked herself against him.

Maybe Kelsey was trying to set us up.

He should have listened. But a few years ago, he hadn't been ready for a girl like Emma. He'd wanted a big-city girl, some-one who fit into the sports-car life he'd dreamed for himself. But Emma . . . unraveled him in a way he found intoxicating. Like sitting out in the cold last night under the full smile of the moon.

He'd make her love Deep Haven, make her long to return—in fact, he thought he might be halfway there. And then he'd walk her down the little Deep Haven Chapel aisle.

Start the life that he'd plotted out in his mind that terrible day Kelsey died.

He'd seen it all as if it might have been his own day as he sat in the back row during the wedding. The tiny church held about thirty-five guests, a small group for a hometown wedding, but perhaps they had their reasons.

Jason and Nicole didn't even have a dance at the reception, just this sway in the middle of the floor. That bum, Jason, he had his life planned out. No surprises. No derailments.

When Emma finished the song, Jason released Nicole, smiling into her eyes.

"How about a little Righteous Brothers," Emma whispered to Kyle as the couple kissed to the tinkling of glasses.

He found his beat chart as she stepped up to the mic.

"Oh, my love, my darling,
    I've hungered for your touch . . ."

He kept the beat. Wanted to nod.

What was it about Emma Nelson that had consumed him? More than her smile or her music . . .

Kelsey would have approved.

He swallowed. Wait. He didn't like Emma just because she'd been Kelsey's friend, did he?

She glanced at him, smiling. Her eyes seemed to settle on him, and he felt his throat tighten.

He was ready for this, right? Ready to woo Emma back to Deep Haven, into his life? When she'd kissed him in the alley outside the 400 Bar, his life had clanged right into place.

The last of the song faded. The guests began to gather their things as the bride and groom made their way to the door. He heard shouting, then cheers as they left the building.

Emma started to pack up her guitar. "Thanks for playing with me, Kyle. You were fabulous. I'll give you part of what they pay me—"

"I didn't do it for pay, Emma." He knelt next to her. "And you're not leaving that fast, are you?"

"I should stop in and see my mother before I leave town. She was upset last night, and I got home too late to talk to her about it. It's been hard for her with my dad gone, only Derek here. He's gone a lot with basketball."

"Don't go yet. Please."

She looked at him, a smile crawling up her face. "Why?"

"We haven't had our dance."

"Um, *we're* the music, Kyle."

"I have my iPod."

"You're so romantic." But she rose and he pulled out his iPod, searching desperately for something that might draw her close. Oh, good, an old Lonestar album. He called up "Amazed."

He took out his earbuds, wiped one off, then handed it to her. She raised an eyebrow but put it in, and he pushed Play.

"See?"

"Country music?"

"You're *in* the country, baby." He wrapped his arm around her back, took her other hand. "My mother used to dance with me in the kitchen."

She fit into his arms and let him lead her as they did a gentle two-step.

"'Every time our eyes meet, this feeling inside me is almost more than I can take . . . ,'" he sang softly. He stood a head taller than her, and she looked up at him with eyes that could name every reason why he couldn't let her go.

She giggled, and it turned him inside out with joy. "My dad would dance with me sometimes."

"I'm sorry he's not here to dance with you," he said quietly.

"He would have been happy about us, Kyle. He chased off every boy who tried to date me, but I think you would have met with his approval."

"I would have tried. And I think I'm terribly jealous of every guy you ever dated."

"There wasn't a big list, I promise. I was pretty consumed with my music."

"Me either. My MO was to ask out a girl for prom about four days ahead of time."

"I didn't go to prom my senior year."

He leaned back. "What?"

She shook her head. "It just felt . . . with Kelsey gone, I . . . No, it wasn't right."

No prom. "Oh, Emma, I'm so sorry."

"It's okay. Deep Haven holds so many memories I'd like to erase."

"Even the ones this weekend?"

The slow grin she gave him warmed his toes and worked its way up. "What do you think?"

Perfect. He rested his chin on her head. "So admit it: you're falling just a little bit in love with Deep Haven again."

But she stiffened ever so slightly at his words. "I don't know, Kyle. This thing with you . . . it feels so perfect, but it's not real."

"It's real to me."

"You don't know everything about me."

"I know that I like you. That I am a fan."

She met his eyes then, with something that looked like pain, and disentangled herself from his arms. She handed him back the earbud. Walked over to the window to stare out at the dark lake.

"Every time I even think of Deep Haven, all I see is Kelsey, lying so perfectly in the coffin as if she's sleeping. Everywhere I go in town reminds me of her. The coffee shop where we hung out during third hour, when we skipped class, and Artist's Point, where we'd sit and compose songs as the waves hit the shore. I think about the prom party your mom threw us our junior year at the supper club and watching fireworks over the harbor, snuggled in a blanket even during July."

Her voice shook a little, and a hot feeling of panic slid through him.

"I haven't written one song since Kelsey died. I can't seem to find the words."

He had the precarious sense of standing on the edge of dark, ragged cliffs, a hand slowly pressing to his back. Especially when she glanced at him, her expression wretched.

"And then there's my dad. He's not here, and I can't think of living here if he's not."

He wanted to weep at her words. Because, yes, he understood how it felt to return home to find no one waiting.

"I'm sorry," he said softly. "I remember the day I came home about three months after . . . after she died. My mom was still barricaded inside her grief, and Kirby and my father barely spoke to each other. I lay there in my room, listening for Kelsey's voice across the hallway."

"She said you two always talked at night, before bed."

"We'd tell each other the best and worst of our days; then we'd cheer each other up, remind ourselves that tomorrow it might be better. Sometimes she'd sing me that stupid chicken song."

"I remember that song." She sang softly, "'Oh, I had a little chickie, but she couldn't lay an egg—'"

He laughed. "'So I poured boiling water up and down her leg.'"

Emma turned, and his throat tightened at her shaky smile. "'Oh, my poor little chickie, how she hollered and she begged.'"

"'Then my poor little chicken laid a hard-boiled egg.'" He

wanted to cry now too, because suddenly he saw Kelsey in Emma's eyes. Bright, funny, beautiful.

He turned away, hating the sudden rush of emotion over a stupid song.

And how impossibly soft Emma's voice was when she tiptoed up to him, put her hand on his shoulder. "I know how hard it was for you to come home after she was gone."

He closed his eyes, finding them wet. Wow, this wasn't quite the picture of romance he'd envisioned.

He could still hear the Lonestar song playing softly in the background.

Kyle shut it off, stared at his iPod. "It was awful. But what was harder was knowing I wasn't here. I felt so helpless."

She looked at him a long moment. Then she eased his iPod from his hand. Ran through the playlist. "I can't believe you're a Garth Brooks fan." She found a song, picked up his earbud, put it in her ear.

"'Looking back on the memory of the dance we shared 'neath the stars above . . . ,'" she sang, her beautiful eyes in his.

He gathered her into his arms, something breaking inside. "Deep Haven is more than the sad memories, Emma. I have to believe that—you have to believe that. You don't have to remember only the tragedies. Maybe . . . maybe we can help each other remember the happy times too."

She stared at him as if his words had pinged inside her.

"Don't you have happy memories?"

She drew a breath. "Of course I do. I just . . ."

"Let me help you find them, please. Don't say good-bye, Emma, not yet. Not until we finish our dance."

᪥

Not until we finish our dance.

Emma drove home with the stars winking at her and the memory of Kyle's scent, his amazing arms around her.

In two days, he'd managed to mute the haunting memories of Deep Haven, to make her listen for something more.

So maybe she'd stay in Deep Haven just a little longer.

She pulled into the driveway of her dark house. After the wedding, Kyle had driven her to his cabin, tucked her into a baggy snowmobile suit, and lured her onto the back of his sled. With her clinging to his parka, he'd motored them through the woods down to town and over to Honeymoon Bluff, where they could watch the moon trace silver ripples on the lake.

He stopped the engine and let the song of the night spill over them, his voice crisp and small in the darkness.

"The summer before I went away to college, we all took a canoe trip to McFarland Lake. Kelsey and I were in one canoe, my dad and Mom and Kirby in the other. We set up camp, and my dad made his favorite biscuits on a stick. I think the dog ate every single one of them. But the best part was the fact that Kelsey made us all get up at the crack of dawn, before the sun was even up, and look for the morning star. I'll never forget—we sat in the canoe, our paddles on our knees, shivering and waiting for Venus to appear over the horizon. She said it was her favorite part of the day—God's reminder of His faithfulness right before the dawn."

Emma had climbed off the machine then, sat on a picnic bench, her snowmobile suit crunching under the stiff grip of cold. "She had great faith, Kelsey did. Always made me a bit angry that she could look at life so positively. Like nothing touched her."

He came and sat beside her, their shoulders brushing against each other. "Things touched her. Like when Jazz, that kid from my class, was killed in a snowboarding accident. She mourned him even though she barely knew him."

"I remember him. Loved Dr Pepper?"

"I think the randomness of it shook her."

"She wrote a song about him, you know. About the people that pass through life, leaving their imprint in the grace of fresh snow."

"She had amazing poetry." His breath crystallized as he spoke. "Kelsey told me once that faith wasn't about trusting God when it was easy. Faith appeared when God seemed farthest away."

"Like right before the dawn, when the stars have faded?"

"And the morning star appears."

His voice was like a melody, sweet inside her.

But maybe she was simply stuck in the nighttime.

They'd sat there on the bench, talking way too long about memories of Deep Haven. He recounted the state championship basketball game but then moved on to his training days in Alexandria. She'd told him about Tim and Brian and the other guys she'd gigged with, and he'd gotten real quiet when she mentioned some of the venues.

Finally, when she had started to shiver, he piled her back onto his snowmobile and headed home.

She'd wanted to stay in the enclave of this fairy tale, warming herself to the fire he'd built in his fireplace, but it would do no one any good for her to wake up in his arms. Even if he'd been the gentleman he'd promised he was in the parking lot of the pancake house.

He did, however, invite her out for pancakes the next morning. And what girl could say no to that smile?

He drove her to her car, lonely in the parking lot at Caribou Ridges, and she left him there, crunching into her own driveway long after midnight. Standing in the glow of the garage light, she listened to the breezes, the waves, the faintest lullaby of music in her heart. Instead of going inside, she climbed to the garage attic, where she traced the moonlight over the old brown chair and saw Kelsey there.

Kelsey sat, of course, strumming her black Gibson. She only played enough to find the chords, and now the sheets lay at her feet.

What took you so long? I've been here for hours. Listen to this new song. It's not done, but it's a start.

Emma walked over, sat next to her. Kelsey flicked her blonde hair back before picking out the tune. Emma could already hear where she might add a lick, change up a chord, but soon, the words of the song pulled her in.

"There are broken rainbow moments,
   And dandelion wishes that don't come true.
   There are times it don't seem fair,
   Like He's never there.
   But He's watching over you."

Emma closed her eyes in the stillness of the attic, letting the song cascade over her, Kelsey's strong vibrato resonating through her.

She finally flicked on the light. A round wool carpet covered the plywood floor, and on the table were papers that bore Kelsey's handwriting, some of Emma's. They hadn't finished the song. She picked up the papers, stared at the pages, and debated fetching her guitar.

She sang a cappella, her voice emerging weak and feeble. "'There are wishes on shooting stars that finally come true . . . for you.'"

She put the pages down, wishing Kelsey had finished it. In her mind, Emma saw Kelsey look up, grin at her as she began to hum.

"What happened to the ending?"

"I just made it up. I don't know how it ends."

Me either, Kelsey.

She heard Kyle then, humming in the darkness tonight as they'd danced to Garth Brooks's song about leaving life to chance, opting for the pain if they could only have the dance.

But see, she'd never operated with a belief in chance, in fate. Which only left her with the option that God had taken Kelsey.

Instead of her.

Emma let that thought slide through her—cold, brutal. She turned off the light and headed inside.

She woke the next morning to the fragrance of bacon, the whine of the floorboards, and for a second she was seventeen.

Hey, Ems, want some breakfast?

She had always known when her father came home from a night shift, or left for a morning shift, by the creak of the floorboards above her basement bedroom. She'd had to train herself not to listen for the groan of the house, smell the eggs he made every morning.

She lay there, one arm flung over her head. What was it with the sudden onslaught of memories? But perhaps they weren't so bad. Her father, standing in the kitchen in his uniform, pouring her a cup of coffee. Her mother, pink bathrobe cinched tight, kissing them all before they left for school, for work.

What had Kyle said about helping her find happy memories? Last night, Kelsey and her song. Today, her father.

So maybe she could fall in love with Deep Haven again, find a way to live here.

Especially with Kyle in the picture.

She could help her mother, move into the attic, start to play weddings and gigs around town. She knew plenty of musicians who made a living playing around the county.

Emma kicked off the down comforter, the chill slicking through her. She shivered and pulled on her bathrobe, then slid her feet into leather slippers.

The stairs creaked as she climbed, and she hid a crazy shard of disappointment when she spied her mother at the stove, cooking eggs in a cast-iron pan.

"Hey, Mom."

Her mother turned. She looked brighter today, a sort of energy radiating off her that seemed almost surreal. "Emma! I'll cook you eggs too."

"No, that's okay. I . . . I have a breakfast date."

"Oh." But her smile didn't fade. "Well, me too, actually. I need to get going. I just thought I'd make up something for Derek." She slipped the eggs onto a plate. "Now he can reheat them." She put the plate in the fridge, turned, and headed toward the door. She sat on the bench, reached for her boots.

"Aren't you going to church?"

"Not today."

Emma frowned at that. "If you want me to go with you, I will."

Her mother looked up, surprise written on her features. Then she shook her head and bent back to her boots. She winced a little.

"Is your neck still hurting you?"

"It'll be better." She stood, grabbed her coat. "You probably need to get going. Call me when you get home."

"Actually, I might stay a few days."

"You don't have any gigs lined up?"

"I have . . . a few days free."

Her mother raised an eyebrow but then turned and picked up her purse. "Perfect. You can help me pack up your room. I've been thinking of going through it anyway."

"Pack up my room?" She had the feeling of watching a car careering out of control on ice, and she wasn't sure how to stop it. "Why?"

Lee wore a smile that seemed too bright, too eager, and seeing it, Emma felt her chest tighten, although she couldn't exactly put a finger on why.

"Because I'm going to meet with a Realtor, Emma. Like I said, it's time I leave Deep Haven."

⬥

Kyle could only wait so long before he had to report for duty. He'd sat in the Blue Moose Café, waiting for over an hour, but Emma never showed.

Once he'd changed, been briefed, and checked the log, he'd driven by Deep Haven Community Church. The service was just letting out, and he felt a little like a stalker as he sat across the street, cataloging the people exiting the building.

He saw his father's truck, and the presence of it gave him pause. To his knowledge his father hadn't attended church since Kelsey's funeral.

Then again, Kelsey's death had derailed all their faith in some way. His own words, spoken under the canopy of brilliance last night, beautiful Emma breathing out puffs of captured breath beside him, came back to him.

Kelsey told me once that faith wasn't about trusting God when it was easy. Faith appeared when God seemed farthest away.

God hadn't seemed simply far away after Kelsey died. It felt like He had disappeared. Trust had to be earned, didn't it?

Fact was, a large part of him missed God, had missed asking Him to help with his basketball games. Missed knowing that God was on his team.

Missed trusting Him. He sighed and drove down the hill toward the highway. According to the log, a 911 call had come in about a domestic disturbance near Spoon Lake. It nagged at him. Especially since the address listed was near the Nickels' place.

He'd just check it out, make sure everyone was okay. The way Billy Nickel had curved a possessive hand over his girlfriend's shoulder bothered him.

Then he'd drive by the Nelson place. Emma had probably overslept. After all, he had gotten her in pretty late.

He'd barely slept a wink, his brain churning up too many possibilities. Maybe he could get her a gig at the Lucky Penny, the supper club in town. And certainly Caribou Ridges could add her to their list of wedding musicians. What about a job with the music association in town? Hadn't he seen an ad on the grocery store board listing a job opportunity?

She wanted to stay. He could see it written in her eyes, shining as he kissed her, holding on to the hood of her snowmobile suit.

He was braking at a stop sign when a red Subaru bled past him. He clocked it at twenty-one miles over the 30 mph speed limit.

That called for lights, a bleep of his siren. He pulled out, but the car didn't slow. He bleeped again.

The driver braked, then slid over to the shoulder. Kyle got out and walked to the passenger side. Knocked on the window. The driver leaned over, rolled it down, and looked up.

Emma. She had capped her head with an embroidered tuque, wrapped a pink scarf around her neck over a fleece jacket. Her suitcase and guitar lay in the backseat, her Fender speaker in the passenger seat.

She glared at him.

"Uh, hi, Emma. I . . . Where are you going?"

"Home, okay? Was I speeding?"

"Just a little. I had you at fifty-one. It's a thirty here."

"Fine, whatever. Ticket me." She sat back in her seat, wrapped her mittened hands around the steering wheel.

Ticket her? "I don't want to ticket you. What's going on?"

She held up her hand as if to push him away, but he noticed her chin trembling. He bent over into the open window. "Emma, are you okay?"

"Just give me my ticket and let me go, Officer."

Officer? "I don't understand. I thought we had a breakfast date today. And not only do you stand me up, but now I find you pulling a Dukes of Hazzard out of Deep Haven. I thought you were going to stay—"

"I'm not, okay? This is over, Kyle. It's time I faced reality—stopped playing around."

Her words hit him as if in the gut. "I wasn't playing around, Emma. I like you."

She had blades in her eyes. "Yeah, why? Why do you like me, Kyle?"

Her question froze him. Because . . . because . . .

"That's what I thought. You don't know. Well, I'll tell you

what—*I* know. You took one look at me and said, 'Oh, there's an adoring female I can manipulate.' You Huestons are all alike."

What—? "I have no idea what you're talking about."

"You wanted someone who could adore the great Kyle Hueston. But that's not me—okay, it was me, but not anymore. I don't need you tangling up my heart in some fantasy. My life is not in Deep Haven. Leave it at that."

"No, I'm not going to leave it at that! You love it here—you know you do. But you won't admit it. And I don't know why!"

"You don't want to know why." She turned back to the windshield, watching the oncoming traffic.

"Try me."

"No! Listen, maybe you can act as if it never happened, as if some crazy kid didn't drive into our little town and shoot two people we loved. You want to put a big Band-Aid over it and call it fixed—"

"That's not true."

"Then what? Why do you have to live here?"

"Because it's my home! And because maybe I can make sure that it never happens again!" He didn't mean to raise his voice and schooled it now. "You have no idea what it's like to get a phone call from your father while you're a hundred miles away telling you that someone killed your sister."

"And you have no idea what it feels like to be the one who should have died instead."

What—?

"I was supposed to work that night, but I had a band concert at school. Kelsey worked in my place. The worst part is, she was going to go with your mother to watch your basketball game." She looked away. "So, see, I don't even know why you would want to be with me, Kyle. If it weren't for me, she'd be alive."

Oh, Emma. His anger deflated with the sorrow in her words.

"It's not your fault," he said quietly. "You didn't know Parker was going to lose it and shoot my sister. Or your dad. Do you seriously think I'd be angry with you for being the one who *lived*? That's crazy."

"Now you see why I can't live here."

"That's not true, and you know it. You just want to believe that because it's easier than facing the real problem."

"And what is that, O All-Knowing One?"

"It's easier to ignore the memories than to believe that God can fix them. It's easier to walk alone in your pain than to share it."

Her eyes glittered. "Yeah, well, maybe it is. Maybe we don't need you Hueston men trying to comfort us. We have this figured out, thanks."

He recoiled. "I'm not trying to comfort you, Emma. I'm trying to—"

"Seduce me?"

Oh. Wow. That hurt more than he expected. "If you'll notice, I've been nothing but a gentleman—or tried to be. I'm not sure where that came from, but—"

She wiped her mitten under her eye, and despite the fact that he wanted to throttle her, he had the urge to get in the car, pull her to his chest. But he was in uniform. He cut his voice low. "Please, don't leave. Let's talk."

"No. I'm not going to be the convenient girl that swoons into your open arms. I'm not her."

"I never thought you were convenient, Emma."

"No, you just thought I was easy. You didn't have to work at it with me—I came prepackaged to fall for you. Well, guess what, Hueston? I'm no longer a fan. Either give me a ticket or back off."

He searched her face, read the fury there, and stepped back, nonplussed. "I don't understand what's going on, Emma—"

She pulled out and tore down the road.

Convenient?

He gritted his teeth so hard his jaw cracked. *Convenient?*

Kyle climbed into his cruiser. Clocked her at forty-seven.

He waited until she was over the hill, where the speed limit changed, and then turned and headed up the hill toward Spoon Lake, winding his way into the woods.

Prepackaged? Didn't have to work at it?

Okay, maybe the fact that she'd once liked him had attracted him, but . . .

Why do you like me, Kyle?

Did he have to have a reason?

Maybe if he knew the answer, he wouldn't be traveling down Spoon Lake Road and would instead have his sirens on, chasing the runaway out of town.

He turned north, toward the Nickels' place, and was passing the gravel pit, now a field of glistening snow, when a flash of blue caught his eye. He slowed, then put the cruiser in reverse.

There, behind a pile of debris and snow, he glimpsed the trunk of a car. A Dodge Dart. The taillight was smashed.

Kyle pulled in, parked a few feet away from it. The helmet painted on the rear window tightened his gut. He got out.

The air smelled crisp with a hint of woodsmoke, balsam. His boots crunched in the snow as he approached the car. It seemed to be wedged into the bank, snow cascading over the front end.

Someone had made a poor attempt at camouflaging it with pine boughs. He pulled them off the hood so he could look inside.

Nothing seemed amiss—a ratty blanket lay on the backseat; a dirty, broken piece of plywood covered the floorboard on the driver's side. Fuzzy white dice hung from the rearview mirror, the logo for a local casino emblazoned on the side.

He walked around the car. At the back end, black footprints marred the snow.

Kyle went to his car, fished out a crowbar from his trunk, and returned. Wedging the crowbar into the Dart's trunk, he worked it, the sound of crunching metal whining into the air. Suddenly the trunk popped open.

And there, crammed inside, lay the skinny body of Billy Nickel.

12

NOELLE DIDN'T KNOW the words, but she felt them, and they lingered inside even as the congregation finished singing, then filed out of the sanctuary.

> I'm finding myself at a loss for words,
> And the funny thing is it's okay . . .

She had no words for the kind people around her, shaking her hand, asking her how she felt. No words for the way Eli had changed over the past three days, his demeanor patient—like now, as he stood beside her, not touching her, but close enough to intercept friends, to say their names a moment before they greeted her.

As if he was running interference. Protecting her.

No words, either, for the feeling, ever since the morning she woke up in the guest room, that something had changed. A presence lingered deep inside her and left her with the sense that she wasn't alone.

Even if she had no idea who was wrapping an arm around her neck, hugging her into a mohair scarf.

"When I heard about your fall, and then you weren't here last Sunday, I thought, *Oh no. Not more trouble for this precious family.*" The woman had fluffy white hair, kind eyes. She wore the purple scarf over a black two-piece leisure suit.

"Thanks, Edith," Eli said.

Apparently a leisure suit was appropriate attire for church.

Do I wear sweatpants to church? She'd hollered this out the bedroom door this morning, downstairs to where Eli sat reading. Perhaps his Bible, although she didn't get a good look.

"Sometimes!" he hollered back. "But mostly jeans."

Jeans? To church? Instead she found a pair of gray wool pants in the back of the closet, a black sweater, and tied her hair up into a sleek bun. Then she'd added a pair of silver earrings, a necklace, and heels.

Eli stared at her all the way down the stairs.

"What?"

"You look nice."

She wasn't sure why the compliment warmed her—she still hadn't rooted up any real feelings for the man. But a girl could love a look of appreciation, right?

Now she nodded at the white-haired woman as Eli steered her away. "Usually we go home for lunch, but I thought maybe I'd take you out."

He held up her coat while she slipped into it. "Really? I cook on Sundays?"

"Pot roast. And yes, you cook every day."

She shook her head. "I am a terrible cook."

He opened the door for her, offered his hand as they skated out into the slick parking lot. "You *were* a terrible cook. You got better. Lots better." He covered her hand with his—a simple gesture, but it heated her to her bones. "I was hoping you might give me a haircut this afternoon."

Kirby caught up to them as they reached the truck. Eli opened the door, helped her inside. Kirby hopped in the back.

Noelle waited until Eli climbed in the opposite side. "A haircut? I cut hair too?"

He started the truck and turned down the heat until the engine warmed. "Uh-huh. You've been cutting my hair for twenty-five years. Still shave Kirby bald every summer."

"All that luscious, curly hair?"

Kirby leaned forward. "See, now, two weeks ago you would have called it a greasy mop." He winked at her as they pulled out.

She snapped on her seat belt. "I don't know, Eli. I can't remember my haircutting days or techniques. What if you end up bald?"

"Hair grows. And I have hats." He drove down the hill, braked at the stop sign, then looked to pull out.

She followed his gaze.

"Hey, there's Kyle," Kirby said.

Indeed. Standing at the passenger side door of a red Subaru, dressed in his uniform. He seemed to be arguing with the driver.

"Probably a local trying to talk him out of a ticket," Eli said.

His cynicism jarred her. "People do that?"

He laughed as he pulled away, nothing of humor in his tone. "Everyone is hiding something. But that's the problem with being a small-town cop—when you recognize someone, you can't treat them like a criminal."

"Even if they broke the law."

"Depends on what law they broke. But yes, you have to live next to these people. You have to watch how you treat them. Unfortunately, that kind of mentality can get people killed."

His face had changed as he spoke, grown harder, and briefly he returned to the man she remembered from last week.

Angry. Hurt.

Something had happened to him on the job. The realization jolted her, and for the first time, she wished she knew his life, more than her own. What must it feel like for him to lose his wife, to get back this stranger?

"I'm sorry my memory hasn't returned."

He glanced at her and frowned. "The doctor said it would take a while. You'll get it back."

"I really do want to remember."

"I know."

But the little lilt at the end of his voice made her wonder.

They dropped Kirby off at a fellow player's house—apparently he planned on working out after church, joining his teammate's family for lunch. She missed him already as he slid out of the car, lifting his hand to them as they drove off. What had she been thinking—a greasy mop?

Noelle and Eli ate at a tiny hometown diner with pictures of past football and basketball teams hanging on the wall and sat at a table under a poster-size map of Lake Superior. Next to it, smaller pictures depicted the town in the early days—1910, 1930.

Eli ordered the voyageur's special, a venison-and-wild-rice omelet. She opted for the yogurt parfait, a glass of orange juice.

"You mentioned that we used to have family in the area," she said, sipping her juice and looking at him over the rim of the glass. "Why did they move away?"

He fiddled with the gold ring on his hand. "My parents died, actually, and my brother and his wife live in Ely. He's with the border patrol."

"Oh. I suppose they move people around a lot. Like the military."

He nodded but didn't look at her, appearing almost relieved when his meal arrived.

He did need a haircut—his dark hair long and curly, brushing against his collar. But after Noelle appeared in her outfit, he'd cleaned up for church, wearing a pair of brown dress pants, a white shirt, a patterned blue-and-brown tie.

"You like your parfait?"

She nodded. "I gotta figure out where my girly shape went."

"Three babies," he said, then stiffened.

She stared at him, the words like a knife through her. "*Three* babies?" Oh, no wonder they had a guest room. Probably, at one time, she'd wanted to fill that with another child.

He didn't look at her. "We lost one."

She reached out to take his hand. "I'm sorry. I wish I could remember that. Did we know if it was a boy or girl?"

His breath leaked out, tremulous, and he pulled away. "A girl."

A daughter.

She'd had a daughter. Was it a miscarriage? Stillborn? She longed to ask, but suddenly she felt like a voyeur into his grief.

Eli had returned to his food, as if he'd very much like to drop the subject.

Okay. Well, she'd give him his privacy. At least until she remembered more.

But the silence opened between them as they finished their meal, the chatter of the café rising to fill the void. As Eli paid, she could read trouble on his face.

He didn't speak again until they reached the truck. Then he stood at the door, considering her. She shivered, her wool jacket too light for this northern breeze.

"I have to show you something," he said quietly. He opened the door and helped her in, then went around to the other side and put his key in the ignition. "I've been trying to figure out how for the last couple days. See . . . I didn't know about it, and I have to admit I was a little shocked. But I think maybe it would help."

"What on earth are you talking about?"

Eli backed out, drove them away from Main Street, up the hill, took a left, and finally stopped before a quaint little white church.

"What is this place?"

He sighed, opened his door. "The art colony."

Noelle met his eyes as she got out, holding on to his arm. "The art colony?"

"Yeah. It's a place where local artists rent rooms to work in."

Meaning pulsed between them. "And you just found out about this place?"

He raised his eyebrows, and she heard his voice ring back at her. *Everyone is hiding something.*

Why would she hide a room at the art colony? What had she been doing there?

He held out his arm for her as they crossed the street, but stiffly, without welcome. The door was unlocked, and he opened it, followed her in. "Upstairs, to your left."

She liked the place. A wooden floor in the main area downstairs, posters advertising everything from pot throwing to textile classes to print work—even a dancing class. Framed art lined the staircase as she climbed to a loft.

"Your space is to the right." He held out a key dangling from a key ring.

Your space. The words rippled inside her.

She inserted the key, turned the knob. The door swung open.

If she could design a space to create in, it would look exactly like the room before her. Bright windows overlooking the town, the lake, an armchair with an ottoman, sketchbooks stacked on the floor. Pictures dangled from yarn stretched across the far end of the room. And along the wall, canvases of finished watercolors.

"I *do* paint."

"Yes," Eli said, his voice sounding funny. "Apparently you do."

Noelle walked over to the unfinished picture of a rocky point. A sketched form of two bodies in the middle evidenced more to paint. "Who was I going to put here?"

He shrugged, his hands in his pockets. For a moment, her heart went out to him, the way he stood at the door as if afraid to enter. He appeared old. Forsaken.

"You didn't know about this place?"

"I just found out a couple days ago. Kirby knew, but he didn't bother to tell me."

"Why would I keep this from you?"

The question played on his face, emotion ringing his eyes. "I'm sure you had your reasons."

She turned back to the painting, tracing the unfinished outline with her finger. "It looks like a couple of girls . . ."

"It's your painting."

It was her painting. As were the rest. She picked one up. "Why would I paint red Chuck Taylors?"

Eli shrugged again, and if his feet hadn't been standing completely still, she would have guessed he was in an all-out sprint away from her.

Wow, this room really hurt him.

She picked up another painting. This one of a tree. "I love the angle of this picture. As if I'm standing at the bottom, looking skyward. Did I take this photo?"

He turned away, not answering.

She put down the painting, walked over to him. Touched his shoulder. "I don't know why this room bothers you so much, Eli, but don't you see—this is good news. I didn't lose myself all these years. I recognize my style in these paintings. Maybe if I try to paint something, my memory will come back."

He looked at her then, his eyes wet. Then he breathed out, a long exhale. As if he'd been holding in something for far too long.

"I would be very happy if you would paint me a picture, Noelle."

&

"How old is this house?"

Jenny Carlton entered the house in front of Lee, stopping to admire the fireplace, the beams overhead in the front room. Lee wanted to retort something along the lines of "About ten years older than you," but that wasn't quite accurate. Jenny had to be at least twenty-one, right? She wore her blonde hair down, tumbling out of her lime-green knit hat. She had a matching lime-green ski jacket and a pair of mukluks that on anyone else would have looked like a fashion faux pas. But apparently you could get away with anything when you were young and skinny and not an old widow who whittled away her youth every day dragging in logs for the stove her husband had insisted on building and cleaning off a walkway that got longer with every snowfall—

"Mrs. Nelson?"

Lee dropped a pile of wood in the bin and closed the door behind her with her foot. "About twenty-eight years old. My husband and I built it together, piece by piece."

"It certainly is beautiful." Jenny took pictures of the stone chimney before she stepped into the kitchen. "Although you're going to have to make some upgrades if you want a fair investment out of it. Most people want granite countertops." She smoothed her hand along the Formica counter, tested the water pressure.

"We have our own well. And delicious water."

"Lovely," Jenny said, but Lee had the sense she hadn't heard her. "So you'll be pulling up this carpet, then?"

"I hadn't thought of that. Why?"

"Carpet in the kitchen?" Jenny made a face.

Okay, when Lee went to talk to Robby at Seagull Realty and he said he'd send out his best agent to help her prepare for her listing, she expected someone older than this middle schooler here. "The floor gets very cold in the winter."

"Maybe you could install an electric floor pad under the wood—everyone loves a wood floor. Bamboo is really in, recyclable and all."

Bamboo. Didn't you eat bamboo?

She followed Jenny into the bathroom, where she received the expected nose curl at the pink tub. "I like my pink tub," she said before she could stop herself. Or maybe not wanting to. "It's big. And rare."

"And pink." Jenny had pasted on a smile. "The entire bathroom could stand a redo."

"My husband bought me that pink tub."

Jenny raised an eyebrow but left her words mercifully unspoken.

Lee drew in a breath. "You're the real estate agent. You know what sells."

"I actually do, Mrs. Nelson. I've sold more houses in this area, even with the housing slump, than any other agent in the county."

Lee didn't want to comment that it might have something to do with her jean size.

No! No, that wasn't right. If Clay had suggested that, she would have popped him upside the head.

"That's wonderful. Thank you for coming out."

"It's a lovely house. It just needs some decluttering, new floors, an updated bathroom . . ." She disappeared downstairs and Lee braced herself. "And probably carpeting on the floor down here."

"I thought cement floors were in." Lee descended the curved staircase.

Jenny stood in the middle of the room, peering into the heater at the bottom of the stairs. "What's this?"

"When we first moved in, we lived in the basement. This was our source of heat."

"And do you still heat with wood?"

"Yes. We also have a gas furnace in case we run low."

She closed her notebook, took a few more shots. "That will be a selling point."

"How about the fact that we have nearly two hundred feet of lakeshore?" Should she take the girl back up to the front windows, show her again the view of the lake?

"Oh, most definitely, Mrs. Nelson. But the fact is, buyers who can afford lakefront property usually also expect a certain level of . . . amenities."

"My husband and I added amenities as we went."

"I can see that."

"Well, can you see the craftsmanship in the beams here? How each one is hand-carved? Clay did that, one by one, every Saturday for a month before our wedding . . . before we even had a house to put them in."

"They're lovely. But really, it's very dark down here. You may want to consider painting them white."

White.

"Get . . . out." Lee didn't realize that the words had slipped out until she saw Jenny's expression.

"What?"

"I'm not sure I'm ready for this." This was nicer, and she added a smile. "I'm sorry, Jenny."

Jenny set her camera down. Her smile gentled. "Listen, I understand. My parents put their house up for sale last year and moved to Florida. It nearly killed me to see the place go—watch them paint over the lines in the doorway where they measured our height, and repaint and carpet the room where I doodled my high school pain on the walls. But they moved on, and they're loving their life in Florida." She touched Lee's arm. "And you will too."

"I'm not moving to Florida," she said softly.

Jenny picked up her camera, wandered to Emma's bedroom for a picture. Oh, Lee might never forget the expression on Emma's face yesterday when she told her what happened between her and Eli.

She hadn't meant to—it just came out.

Moving? What do you mean you're moving?

Emma's voice had shrilled and Lee raised a hand to silence her. "I haven't exactly told Derek yet."

"When, Mom, do you plan on moving? And when were you going to tell your children?"

She had grown up so much in the past two years—probably from life in the big city. The best thing Emma ever did was move away from this town.

"I'll move after Derek is done with school."

"But what about your life here—*our* life here?"

"Emma, you don't have a life here anymore." Oh, she hadn't quite meant it how it emerged, betrayed in Emma's flinch. She softened her tone. "I mean, of course, Deep Haven will always be your home, but you've moved on; you're building a life in the Cities. Soon you'll meet someone nice and get married."

Another flinch. With it came the slow, cool realization that perhaps Emma had already met someone. Maybe that's what had kept her out late the last couple nights.

"Sweetheart, what's wrong?"

She shook her head, turned, and opened the fridge. She stared into it as if it might contain some answers. "Nothing. I just think you should have told us you were moving."

"Have you met someone?"

She shut the door. "I don't know."

"Is he from Deep Haven?"

The rise and fall of her shoulders suggested he might be.

"Honey, this is a bad idea. This town is too small for you. You need to build a life outside Deep Haven—"

"Why, Mom?" She'd whirled around, her pretty blue eyes lit up. "You seemed to do just fine here."

"Really? Because last time I looked, I was alone here, Emma. Alone." She regretted her tone, but someone had to wake up her daughter. "And there's no one knocking at my door, asking me out on a date."

But as soon as the words left her mouth, the image of Eli kissing her, his hands cupping her face, flushed through her. She turned away, hoping to get control of herself.

It didn't matter that his wife didn't know him, right?

His words burned through her. *I'm not leaving Noelle for you.*

Sheesh, she hadn't asked him to. He'd been the one showing up on her doorstep the past three years. He'd been the one with desire in his eyes.

"Mom?" The touch on her shoulder had startled her. Emma turned her. "What's going on?"

Lee shook her head, but her eyes had filled and she couldn't blink the moisture away without Emma seeing. Her daughter brushed a tear from her cheek. "Did someone hurt you?"

She shook her head again. "I have to go."

But Emma didn't let her go. "Mom, tell me what happened." She had that look now, the one that she got when she knew she was right, when she knew she would get her way.

"Eli Hueston." She shouldn't have told her probably, but Emma no longer lived here, and it felt so good to push his name out, away from her soul where it burned. "Eli Hueston kissed me."

"He kissed you? Like *came on to* you?"

Her tone made Lee want to grimace, the words so ugly. She nodded.

"I knew it. He was around here too much after Daddy died. Like a prowler."

"He was trying to help us, honey."

"He was trying to help himself. He's probably been in love with you for years, and now he saw you lonely."

"No, I think I was just convenient."

Her word brought Emma's eyes up. "*Convenient?* What, like he needed someone to care about him and you were there?"

She lifted a shoulder. It sort of felt that way. "I think it surprised him as much as me—"

"He didn't mean to kiss you?"

Lee turned away from her and walked to the window. "I don't think so. He's confused right now. His wife lost her memory."

"It doesn't mean you're supposed to fill in for her."

"Emma!"

"Sorry. I wasn't accusing you. It just seems so . . . planned out. As if he knew your weakness and tried to exploit it for his own needs. *Convenient* is exactly the right word." She stared out past her mother.

"Emma?"

Emma looked back, now smiling. "I gotta get back to the Cities."

"Agreed. Promise you'll call?"

Emma came to her, wrapped her arms around her. "Stay away from Eli Hueston, Mom. He's trouble."

Lee had nodded into the sweet smell of her daughter's embrace, locking it inside.

"Where are you moving, if not to Florida?" Jenny emerged from Emma's bedroom and headed for the stairs.

Lee followed her up. "I'm not sure yet. I just know it'll be away from Deep Haven. You get me a list of what I need to change—I'll make sure it happens."

13

Eli couldn't avoid the sense that Noelle was coming back to him. Because as he came upstairs this morning from his bed in the den, he caught her making oatmeal.

For the dog.

Their black Lab sat, her button tail tapping the carpet, waiting for Noelle to add the milk, stir, and put it on the floor.

Eli stood there, shaking his head.

"What?" She looked pretty this morning, the way she'd flipped her hair out and wore a pair of faded jeans, a pink shirt. She'd added a teal-and-royal-blue scarf around her neck, highlighting her blue eyes.

"How did you know that Riggins liked oatmeal?"

"She nearly jumped into my lap the other day as I sat at the table with my bowl, and then, when I didn't finish it, I found her on the table, lapping it up." She wiped her hands on a towel. "Oatmeal, really?"

"You've been spoiling her for years."

She knelt in front of the dog, rubbed her ears. "Me spoil you? I don't think so. It's pure survival. We women need to stick together in this household of testosterone, don't we, baby?"

Riggins lifted her head, licked her on the chin. Noelle laughed.

Eli stared at her, words vacating him. She'd let the dog *lick* her?

Noelle climbed back to her feet. "What do you want for breakfast? I found a pancake recipe that looks well-worn."

She'd been trying out every manner of recipe this week— including a batch of chocolate chip cookies, double the chips, that seemed as rich as her smile, her laughter. Last night she'd beaten Kirby in Scrabble and then wandered outside, wrapped in a blanket, and watched Eli change the spark plugs on his snowmobile.

"Is it fun?" she'd asked.

"I'll take you for a ride, if you want." He'd looked up at her standing in the glow of the garage lights, the sky watching above, and something about her soft smile made him feel young again.

As if he didn't have any faults. As if they'd just met, their relationship without dings and scratches, wounds and scars.

He wanted to lean into that freshness, free of the brambles of the past, but fear lurked in the back of his mind that one of these days, she'd wake up.

Remember.

Maybe even ask him to leave.

But he wasn't that guy anymore, the one who would have barked back an angry "Fine with me," hopped in his truck, and hidden out in the woods. Or at least he was trying not to be.

He hadn't gone to Lee's house once this week. Despite the fact that missing her had left a hole in his life. He missed her kind words, her friendship.

The way she looked at him without accusation.

But so did Noelle now, didn't she?

"Are you going to the studio today?" he asked, returning his attention to Noelle as she moved around the kitchen. "I can give you a ride."

She was pulling out flour, baking powder, sugar, eggs. He liked how her hair curled against her shirt, and he sort of wanted to touch it.

"I want to, but frankly, Eli, I'm starting to give up. It's been three days, and for all my talk, I can't remember how to paint."

She turned, shook her head. "I keep staring at the paper, but I see nothing. It's so strange—it's like I used to be able to see the picture in my head before I even painted it. But there's nothing there." She pressed her hands to either side of her head. "How can there be nothing there?"

He couldn't help it. He went to her, took her hands away from her face. "Stop trying so hard. It'll come when it's time."

She looked at him, her eyes wide, beautiful, without cynicism. "You believe that?"

"I believe in you," he said softly.

Oh, he wanted to kiss her. The urge rose inside him, rushed through him, shook him. He wanted to pull her into his arms, to feel that comfort they used to bring to each other, that intimacy of knowing they'd created life together.

But this woman didn't know him. She didn't know their history, their triumphs, their hurts. She was just a bright, beautiful replica of the woman he'd shared his life with.

And she certainly didn't love him.

Swallowing, he backed away. "Maybe you should . . . I dunno, do something else for a while. You know the studio is there now, whenever you want it. What else do you want to do?"

He retreated behind the counter, slid onto the stools, his heart a little too large in his chest.

She consulted the recipe, then grabbed a measuring cup and dove into the flour bin. "I think I'd like to plan a graduation party for Kirby." She dumped the measured flour into the bowl, followed by the sugar. "I know it's a few months away, but even if I can't remember his growing-up years, that doesn't mean other people can't. And maybe as I pull out old pictures and plan his party, I might be able to piece together my memory."

Noelle melted butter in the microwave, then added it to the mix. Holding an egg, she looked at Eli. "Will you help me?"

She cracked it with one hand, then tossed the shell into the sink. Probably didn't even notice that as she picked up another egg.

"Of course. What do you want me to do?"

She tossed the other shell into the sink, grabbed a teaspoon, and measured out the baking powder. "I want you to go through all the old pictures of the family and pull out Kirby's and date them. I want to build him a time line. I think I'll create a basketball theme—"

"Like his bedroom?"

She wrinkled her nose. "Better. Maybe make a cake with a big basketball, and we could have one-on-one competitions in the driveway." She turned the mixer on. "I just want it to be special."

Her movements, her words, had only dredged his heart into his throat. Of course she didn't remember having nearly this same conversation the year Kelsey would have graduated. He forced a smile, looked away. "No problem."

Noelle finished mixing the batter. Smelled it. "There's something missing." She opened the cupboard, turning the lazy Susan, fishing through the spices.

"Cinnamon?"

"Is that what I put in?" She kept searching.

"I don't know. They just taste good."

"Oh, how about this. Nutmeg." She opened the cap, sniffed it. Dashed some into the batter. "That smells right."

He stared at her as she started the fire under the griddle and waited for it to heat through. *God, are You giving me back my wife?*

He'd been praying every day, reading his Bible in the mornings, trying to be the guy who showed up, who became the husband she needed. The verse Hitch Johnson had read at the nursing home hung in his mind. *"How long must I struggle with anguish in my soul, with sorrow in my heart every day? . . . But I trust in your unfailing love. I will rejoice because you have rescued me. I will sing to the Lord because he is good to me."*

And today his wife had added nutmeg to the pancake mix.

She placed the finished pancake in front of him, a bottle of Log Cabin syrup beside it.

He fixed up his plate. Smiled as he took the first bite. "Yes, that's right. Delicious, Noelle."

They finished breakfast, and Eli loaded the dishwasher while Noelle washed the griddle. She wiped her hands. "How about that snowmobile ride?"

"Really?"

"I think the best thing for me to do to find inspiration is to be out where I am inspired."

"I know just the place."

He found her a snowsuit, warm gloves, a scarf, and even unearthed the helmet he'd given her years ago. "I'm just trying it on you for size." He lifted the visor. "You okay in there?"

"I feel like I'm Luke Skywalker in an X-wing fighter."

"May the Force be with you. By the way, they made three more of those movies."

"You're kidding."

"The Force for a whole new generation. Kirby and Kyle ran around the house with light sabers for years."

She laughed, and he could feel the world lift from its moorings.

He took off her helmet, then loaded everything into the truck, heading for McFarland Lake. The sun bathed the snowy paths that wound farther into the forest, the sky a pristine blue.

"Where are we going?" she asked.

"Someplace I should have taken you long ago."

He pulled up to the dock landing, then backed the truck up to the snowbank. "Stay here."

Backing out the snowmobile, he let it run as he parked the truck. Noelle climbed out, pulled on her helmet.

"I promise I won't go too fast."

She lifted her visor. "Don't slow down on my account. I feel the need for speed!"

"See, this is the problem with a girl stuck in the eighties."

She wrinkled her nose at him and climbed aboard. He liked the feel of her weight in the upper seat, how she wrapped her arms around his waist.

He motored out onto the sparkling white surface of the lake.

Wind had drifted over his old tracks from days before. He

buzzed around the lake, Noelle leaning into the curves with him as if they were one, the snow billowing out behind them.

Once she leaned back, put her arms up, but a bump made her grab for him. He smiled under his helmet.

They circled the lake twice before he parked in front of the shiny ice house.

"What's this place?" she said, lifting her visor.

"It's my ice house," he said, climbing off. "Actually it's really nice inside—want to see?"

She nodded and took off her helmet, her hair damp and curly underneath. He unlocked the door, kicked snow out of the way to clear a path, then opened it. The cool scent of the house—the oil embedded into the walls, the pine woodwork—floated out.

He stepped back and let her enter.

"This place is huge. And you have a television!"

Eli followed her inside. "And four bunks, a fridge, and a heater. I could stay here for a month."

At one time, he'd seriously considered it.

She opened the bathroom, made a face, then sat down at the table. "What are those holes in the floor for?"

"That's where we drill through to drop our fishing lines in."

"Seriously? You sit here and fish all day?"

He sat at the table with her. "It's fun. I have a depth meter, so I can actually watch the fish nibble at the hook. And I get satellite reception, so with my generator, I can watch TV."

"So we come out here, sit in this little cozy hut, and watch TV and fish."

He cleared his throat, tasting how easy it would be to lie. But he hated the lies, the biggest being Kelsey. It loomed before him, growing larger every day. Anytime now, it would pop and bleed out betrayal and anger between them.

And then, even if she didn't remember the jerk he'd been before, he'd start a whole new batch of dark memories.

Why had he ever thought hiding their daughter from her might be a good idea?

No, he was sick of lies, and even if he couldn't figure out a way to tell her about Kelsey, he'd come clean about their life together.

"*I* came out here, sat in this cozy hut, and watched TV and fished. Alone."

For a moment, hurt crossed her face. As if she cared. Then, "Oh. Well, maybe ice fishing just wasn't my thing?"

I wasn't your thing.

He looked away.

Silence pulsed between them.

"It's more than that, isn't it, Eli? This is where you came to escape me."

She might not remember their lives, but she had the uncanny ability to read him. He gritted his teeth, nodded. Couldn't meet her eyes.

"You want to tell me why you were sleeping in the den before I fell?" Her voice was so soft, without judgment, and it freed him a little.

He stared at his snowy gloves, gripped in his hands. "We weren't getting along."

"Why?"

The truth landed on his tongue, turning hot there. *We lost our daughter.* No, it was more than that. *I made a mistake. And because of it, our daughter was killed.*

But the words wouldn't emerge.

"I'll find out someday, Eli."

Yes, she would. But not today, with the sky so blue, with her holding on so tight to him.

She leaned back. "Or maybe it doesn't matter anymore. Maybe what's gone is gone."

But that didn't feel right either.

He shook his head. "We just grew apart, Noelle. Like most married couples do. We had our share of problems and hurts and we couldn't find our way back."

He looked up when she reached across the table and touched his arm. "We're finding our way back now, aren't we?"

Oh, he hoped so. He nodded and was a weak man for relishing her innocent, sweet smile.

We're finding our way back.

Her words lingered as he raced them around the lake again, then through the deer trails of the forest. Finally, long after lunch-time, they returned to the truck. Noelle set her helmet and jacket on the seat as they drove down the snowy road, then leaned back, closed her eyes.

"Does your head still hurt?"

She nodded. "Sometimes. But I'm sleeping better, so that's good."

He wanted to cry when she curled up against him, falling asleep on his shoulder as he drove.

Maybe they were finding their way back. Maybe they could start over, no secret rooms, no secret lives.

He didn't wake her when they arrived home, just picked her up and carried her into the house. He debated a moment, then brought her to Kelsey's room, laid her on the bed, and pulled the blanket over her.

Eli heard the phone ringing but let it go to the machine as he eased off her boots. The message was just kicking in as he came into the kitchen.

"Noelle? It's me, Eric. Call me soon. I'm starting to get worried."

Eli played it three times, his heart thundering in his chest, before his finger hovered over the button.

Then, with a push, he erased it.

&

"Thanks for faxing the file over, Marc. I think our vics are related here." Kyle sat at his cubicle, a desk lamp spotlighting the autopsy report, the forensics lab report, and the crime scene report of the coffee shop shooting in Harbor City. "It looks like the bullet pulled out of Billy Nickel matches the bullet used on Cassie Mitchell." He always preferred putting a name to a victim—kept it more personal, his attention engaged.

"Did forensics pick up anything from your crime scene?" Marc asked. He'd been überhelpful since Kyle had called him with Billy's murder and their new evidence.

"I sent the car to Duluth, to the crime lab there. We'll have results in a few days. I did notice, however, Billy's missing class ring. A real bruiser—it had a ruby, his year written on it."

"Could be a robbery. Those rings are worth a bit of nice change," Marc said.

"I'm going to alert the pawnbrokers in Duluth, see if it comes through them. Did you ever get a hit on that fishing knife you found at the scene?" Kyle was paging through the papers and pulled out a photograph of the knife.

"No usable prints. We have two fish houses in town—both of them confirmed using a similar type of knife. However, their knives are stamped with the name of the processing plant. This one's blank."

"I'll check the fish house in Deep Haven, see what I come up with. Most of the kids in town do a shift or two during the roe season, and Billy had a coat that reeked of fish. But as far as I know, the season ends before Christmas."

"Let me know if you find out anything. In the meantime, I'll check on the pawn places for you, if you can find me a picture of the ring."

"Appreciate it."

"Hey—how's your mom?"

Kyle had turned to a picture of the crime scene, the body of the young high school clerk sprawled in her own blood. His voice tremored. "Alive. But she still can't remember anything, so . . ."

"So we need to find this guy before he finds your mother."

"Thanks, Marc."

Kyle hung up, grabbed his coffee, and walked to the break room, shoving the cup into the microwave. There were only so many times you could reheat a cup of coffee before it was considered nuclear waste. Still, it kept him awake.

That, and the image of Emma's face—angry, hurt—as she glared at him. *Convenient?* He still couldn't get past that word.

He wanted to call her. But what, exactly, would he say? He'd given it his best shot, tried to convince her that Deep Haven could call her home.

When the microwave beeped, he pulled out the coffee. It burned his lips, tasted like tar. He poured it down the sink.

He just didn't like failing, was all.

Returning to his desk, he grabbed his coat and the picture of the knife.

The Harborside Fish House remained one of the few enterprises that sent out fishermen in the morning who returned with a catch of herring, trout, and whitefish by noon. As a kid he'd watched them head away from the harbor, their nets dangling over the side, and wondered what mysteries he might find out there beyond the mist. During the summer, the fish house offered fresh fish cakes, fish and chips, and smoked fish—a delight of the tourists.

Throughout the fall, the smokehouse turned out smells that made for free advertising, as they hauled in trout heavy with red roe. Employing as many menial laborers as they could scrounge up, they armed fifteen-year-olds with fillet knives and taught them how to clean a fish, collect the roe. This they packaged and slapped with a designer price.

Kyle's father had taught him how to find the roe, and they made their own caviar at home.

Since the beginning of Deep Haven time, when fishermen rowed out in the lake, the Steg family had run the fish house, their daughters marrying seamen, their sons taking over the fleet. But like a dock under relentless waves, they'd eroded down to only Bonnie and her husband, Chuck, weather-weary, resilient Norwegians.

Kyle found Bonnie in a pair of insulated rubber boots and a green Army jacket, leaning over an ancient PC in the back room of the fish house restaurant. They only opened for lunch hours during the winter, few people hankering for chilled herring when the mercury dropped to twenty below. The café overlooked the snowy, waveless harbor, the open waters still promising mystery beyond the break wall. Fish in icy drifts lay openmouthed in the glass cases.

He had the sudden craving for a herring sandwich. "Hey, Bonnie, you got a second?"

"Kyle. I haven't seen you in years. Look at you all spiffy in your new uniform." He had a feeling she barely suppressed the urge to pinch his cheeks.

"I'm here on official business, although I could do with a herring sandwich. Or some of that homemade trout chowder."

"I'll fix you up both," she said, shucking her coat and moving behind the counter. "How can I help you?"

"Do you know a kid by the name of Billy Nickel?"

She grabbed a Styrofoam soup container. "Sure. And his brother, Ryan. They worked for me. Good workers—Billy especially could clean a fish in record time."

"So he worked here this past season?"

"Longer, actually." She ladled out a scoop of the trout chowder, and Kyle was nearly woozy with the smell. "I kept on a skeleton crew, processing the fish and the roe we brought in until the lake got too cold. Billy was one of my best cutters."

She put the cap on the soup container, set it on the counter. "I gave him and the rest of the crew their bonus and cut them loose about three weeks ago."

"Bonus? Cash or check?"

"Cash, but it's all legit, of course. Billy was going to use his to buy a ring for his girl. Yvonne." She reached into the case and pulled out a premade herring sandwich wrapped in cellophane.

"I met her. She and Billy were definitely together, but I didn't see a ring."

Bonnie bagged the lunch items. "Well, maybe he hasn't popped the question yet. He did tell me that he was headed down to Duluth to see what he could find. You know, this close to Valentine's Day and all."

"I'm sorry, Bonnie." He fished a ten out of his wallet. "Billy was found dead in his car up at the Spoon Lake gravel pit."

She stared at him as she took the ten. "No, that can't be. I just saw Hugh yesterday and he said that he and Billy would be coming back in the spring."

"Who's Hugh?"

She shook her head. "Billy was such a promising young kid. Had his problems, for sure, but he showed up on time, did his work."

Promising? Maybe Kyle had seen the wrong kid. "Billy Nickel? Thin kid, blond?"

She nodded, her eyes glistening.

"Can you describe his friend Hugh for me?"

"I don't know. Big. Dark hair, about chin length. I made him wear a hairnet. Might have played football, but I don't think he was from around here. I thought he might be related to Billy—he recommended him."

He sounded like the man Kyle had seen outside Billy's. "Also a nice boy with promise?"

"No. He was . . . rough. I never felt comfortable with Hugh Fadden around. But he could clean fish, once I taught him how."

"Did you give him a bonus too?"

"He and Billy came in together. I think maybe they were both on their way to Duluth."

He held up the picture of the knife. "Does this look familiar to you?"

She took the picture, her mouth slacking. "That's my daddy's knife. I thought I lost it while I was teaching the new cutters how to clean fish." She returned the picture to him. "Where did you find it? I'd like to get it back."

"Actually, it was involved in a homicide in Harbor City."

His words registered on her face in a ripple of shock. "Oh. My."

"Do you have any idea who might have taken it?"

She shook her head. "I sometimes would put it down and then forget it."

"Are you sure this is your father's?"

"It has to be. The rest of our knives have our logo stamped on the handle. And—" she reached for the picture again—"this handle, the grooves? That's my daddy's work. It was hand carved and passed down to me. It's my knife, all right."

Kyle picked up his bag of lunch. "Let me know if Hugh comes by again, will you?"

"Will do. He told me he was working at a restaurant in town. Don't know where." She handed him back the ten. "I was always a fan of your old man, even after the tragedy with your sister. It wasn't his fault. Sometimes life just backfires on you, is all. Lunch is on me, Deputy. Keep us safe out there."

14

"ARE YOU ANGRY with me for some reason?"

Noelle sat on the truck seat beside Eli. He could feel her eyes on him, burning, lifting the layers he'd bundled over himself since hearing the phone call yesterday.

I'm starting to get worried.

He shouldn't have deleted the message. An impulsive, angry, desperate act, driven by panic.

Who was Eric?

"No," he said, but it came out more clipped than he meant.

"Right," she said. "I know I don't remember much of our marriage, but I do remember the man who brought me home from the hospital. You might not be angry at me, Eli, but I know you well enough now to recognize when something is eating at you."

She knew him well enough now. And he felt as if he didn't know her at all.

But he wanted to. For the first time in longer than he could remember, he wanted to know—again—this woman he'd spent the majority of his life with.

"I think we need to call the doctor in Duluth, see if I can get another brain scan. There has to be some reason I'm not getting my memory back."

He said nothing, not wanting to argue with her. But what if bringing it back only brought back Eric, too?

"When do you want me to pick you up?" he asked as they arrived at the art colony.

She wore a blue parka, pink knit mittens, a cute knit beanie that had once belonged to Kelsey. For a second, as she'd emerged from the mitten bin with it, he'd seen his daughter. Bright, smiling, those beautiful blue-green eyes so full of life.

Noelle had often joked that Kelsey was her clone. Indeed.

"A couple hours. If I haven't started anything by then . . ." She lifted a shoulder. "I'm beginning to think this is futile."

He reached out for her—not sure why, just following a desperate urge to keep her in this pocket where he was still her hero—and squeezed her hand. Smiled.

She smiled back.

Eli waved as she entered the art colony, then drove down to the café. He just needed to feel normal again.

After hanging his jacket on the coatrack near the door, he passed by the table with the usual suspects—Jerry the mayor, Anthony the hotel owner, Pastor Dan, Joe Michaels. Caleb Knight had pulled up a chair at the end. Their plates, runny with egg yolk or syrup, had been shoved to the center of the table.

"Eli. How are you?" Jerry lifted his cup to him. "Heard about your wife's fall. How's she doing?"

"Better, thanks," he said, not stopping, not meeting Pastor Dan's gaze. Thankfully his usual spot in the back was open, a newspaper stuffed into the otherwise-empty menu holder. He slid in, opened the paper, read the police report. A few reports of disturbances, one speeder, a couple drunk and disorderlies. On the page next to the blotter, the report of a death at the Spoon Lake gravel pit caught his attention.

Billy Nickel. Eli had ticketed his brother Ryan a few times for speeding. Kyle would probably catch the case.

"Hey, Eli." Melanie set the menu down. "I'm dropping this off, just in case, but do you want your usual?"

"Please." He pushed the menu away. Two eggs over easy, a slab of French toast. And coffee, black.

She picked the menu back up. "Good to see you. I missed my favorite sheriff last week."

Melanie had voted for him, even when the town rejected him. But she had a son in the Army, one who might not have gotten in if it weren't for Eli's willingness to go easy on him when he'd busted the kid for buying liquor with a fake license.

Actually, Eli could eat free all over town if he called in the favors he'd done over the years.

He turned to the front page, reading the weather report.

"Hey, Eli." Dan slid into the seat opposite him.

Normally he liked Dan, the town pastor and volunteer fire chief. He had a hands-on idea of church, a desire to help people as he preached the gospel. Brown hair, warm smile, the look of a man who ate a few donuts while he counseled the lost. But Eli had seen him pull men out of burning buildings and talk a man down who had found himself at life's precarious edge.

And he'd been a friend, or tried to be, during those dark days after Kelsey's death. But they were past those days now.

Eli continued studying his paper. "Pastor."

"Nice to see you at church on Sunday. It's been a while."

Eli grunted.

"And of course, we're all grateful Noelle is okay, especially after the shooting. Terrible. How is she doing?"

Eli ground his jaw. The entire thing exhausted him. Finding answers for others, for himself. He reread a sentence about the hospital board meeting minutes.

Dan just sat there, the annoying man, saying nothing.

"What?"

"It's just that . . . well, I thought that might be a rough time for you both, Eli."

"Noelle's fine." He wasn't sure where the heat came from, but he glanced around to see if anyone had heard him.

Two snowmobilers sat at the counter. Joe and the others had left.

He stared out the window at the lifeless sky.

"I see," Dan said, but apparently he didn't see because he stayed right there in the booth.

"What do you want, Pastor?"

"I want to know who kicked you in the teeth. Why you stormed by our table like you didn't know us. Why you look like you've lost your best friend."

"I don't have any best friends. Not since this town turned on me."

"No one turned on you, Eli. They were afraid. And you were hurting. You needed to be home with your wife."

Eli pursed his lips.

"But that's not what's eating you, is it?"

Melanie set down a cup before him and poured his coffee. "Eggs will be out in a jiff. Pastor, you want a cup?"

No, please.

"Absolutely. Thanks, Mel."

She grabbed one from the counter, filled it. Dan lightened it with creamer to a soft mocha color.

"Pastor—"

"Eli, I'm your friend. Even if you don't know it. And I'd like to help."

"Okay, answer me this. Maybe you can help me figure out how to forgive my wife for something she doesn't remember doing."

To his credit, Dan didn't crack a facial muscle. "Forgiveness is not optional, Eli. God expects it from us regardless of the crime because He first forgave us."

"I figured you'd say that."

"Do you want to tell me what your wife did that she doesn't remember?"

Eli shook his head. "It doesn't even matter, I guess. Maybe she didn't do it, but we wouldn't know because, see, Pastor, my wife can't remember me."

Oh, the relief of letting that truth out.

Dan frowned at him, sat back. Folded his arms.

"Yeah," Eli said. "When she fell, she lost all twenty-five years of our marriage. She can't remember Kyle or Kirby—"

"Or Kelsey."

"Right. And especially me. It's taken two weeks for her to trust me, but the crazy thing is . . . we haven't gotten along this well in years. It's like I have my old wife back, the one I married, before we had kids. She's funny and sweet and she makes oatmeal for the dog. And even though I know she can't remember anything, it's like there's a part of her way down inside that does remember. A shadow of the woman she used to be—or maybe could have been if . . ." He looked out the window again. "If I hadn't taken it from her."

"What are you talking about?"

"I don't know." He played with the rim of his cup. "When I met her, she was a junior in college. She was an art major, but I thought it was one of those fill-in majors that people declare when they can't think of anything else. We had this whirlwind summer romance, so I admit I didn't know her that well. When I asked her to marry me, she dropped out of school and moved up here, and I had no idea that she liked to paint."

"She's an artist?"

"Apparently. She rented a studio at the art colony—has about ten paintings, all of photographs Kelsey took."

"I had no idea."

"Imagine how I felt when I discovered them. It's like I'm finding things out about her . . . things I'd forgotten or things I didn't know, and . . . I feel like a creep because a big part of me doesn't want her to return to the woman she was. I was losing her—I knew it, and I didn't know how to stop it. And then . . . then she gets this call from some guy named Eric."

Dan leaned forward. Met his eyes.

"Yeah, I don't know who he is. In fact . . . I deleted the message he left on the machine."

Dan raised an eyebrow.

"Don't look at me like that—I already know. I should have let her hear it, should have kept the number. But what if . . . what if he's . . ." He gritted his jaw and looked away, hating the sting in his eyes. "What if my wife was going to leave me for another man?"

"Eli. That doesn't sound like Noelle. She's always been a God-fearing woman."

Eli pinned him with a look that held everything dark he knew still stirred inside him. "Yeah, but I haven't been a God-fearing man. After Kelsey died, something went with her, and I started wandering. I didn't . . . I didn't have an affair, but I wouldn't have stopped it if I could have." The image of Lee looking at him, his hands tangled in her hair, made him wince. "I substituted fishing and hunting and anything else I could do to get out of the house for my wife."

"For intimacy."

"Maybe."

"Absolutely, Eli. When we lose someone we love, of course we grieve the part that has been ripped away, that part of us they take with them. And it leaves us hollow and empty, desperate to fill it. Your marriage is missing the intimacy God intended to heal it."

"I don't even know what intimacy is, Pastor."

"It's belonging and believing and being loving to each other. It's vulnerability to the one person you trust most. It's saying, 'Here's my ugly, battered, wounded heart. I'm going to let you see it and trust you with it.' Did you ever let her see your grief?"

Eli leaned back as Melanie set the eggs down in front of him. Only, he wasn't exactly hungry anymore.

"It wasn't like I didn't want to. It just . . . it wasn't easy."

"Who said marriage and intimacy—the way God wants them to be, a depiction of His intimate love for us—would be easy? Marriage is not a conditional act. It's loving no matter what. It's how we're supposed to be with God—trusting Him with all our fragile parts."

"Yeah, and what if God never shows up? What if He doesn't care?"

"He always cares, Eli. That's the loving part—He loves you. He wept with you over your daughter's death, and He longed for intimacy with you, to care for you, for you to have faith in Him. And I know you were afraid you wouldn't get the right response—that He'd let you down. After all, He hadn't protected Kelsey."

"That was my fault."

"Oh, deep down, Eli, you believe more than that."

Maybe he did. Maybe that was the bigger problem.

"That's where your faith really kicks in. Trusting God, being vulnerable even if you don't get the response you want. You're doing the same thing to Noelle you did to God—you're afraid your wife can't love you the way you need to be loved. And maybe she can't, not right now. But that doesn't mean you're not supposed to love her, be intimate—at least emotionally—with her."

Eli pushed his uneaten food away. "I don't know. Yes, I'm afraid that she'll get her memory back, remember this Eric guy, and leave me." He shook his head. "But I'm also afraid of her never getting it back, never knowing her daughter. And I feel like such a jerk for not telling her—"

"She doesn't know about Kelsey?"

"No. I thought it would be best, but it was such a stupid idea. And now I don't know how to tell her without her feeling completely betrayed—"

"And destroying this new relationship you've built with her."

He nodded. "Then there's the fact that I wasn't a real prize before the accident, and I don't want her to remember that. I want her to remember me as the guy I'm being now . . . or trying to be."

He scrubbed his hand down his face. "It's all a giant mess and I don't know how to figure it out."

"Your job is not to solve this. I know you're a cop and that's what you do, but your job is to love your wife, however God gives her to you—memory or not."

Melanie came by, eyed the uneaten eggs, but didn't stop.

"I've known you for a long time, Eli. Back when you were going home for lunch with Noelle. Back when you and she sat together for every basketball game, when you attended all of Kelsey's play performances. You were good once, but maybe God is giving you a chance to be better."

"Even if she doesn't remember us?"

"It says in Song of Songs, 'Place me like a seal over your heart . . . For love is as strong as death.' When you two pledged yourselves in marriage before God, He sealed you both for each other, and that is stronger than the death of the last twenty-five years. Faith is believing that. And faith pleases the Lord, even when it feels overwhelming."

Overwhelming, like admitting that he'd made a mistake that got their daughter killed. Overwhelming, like wishing he could take it back, protect his wife from grief. Overwhelming, like him two weeks ago, sitting at the lake, not sure how to love his wife.

Maybe God was bigger than even *overwhelming*.

Dan met his eyes. "Let your wife into your life, Eli. Tell her about your daughter. For both your sakes."

"I know. I just have to figure out how," Eli said. "I guess I'm supposed to buy your coffee now?"

Dan gave him a slow smile. "Probably."

Eli handed Melanie back the eggs as she passed by, then dug out his wallet. "I need to run by the station, check on Kyle."

"He's doing a good job. Give him some room to find his feet. By the way, I saw him last weekend at Nicole and Jason's wedding. Played the drums. I didn't know he was so musical." Dan got up and Eli followed him, handing Melanie a ten for a breakfast he hadn't eaten.

He shucked on his coat at the door. "I called it noise, Pastor. Until all hours of the night." But he grinned. Yeah, those were good memories—Kyle and Kelsey jamming together in the basement.

He wanted to share that with Noelle. That and Kelsey's journal of lyrics. He wanted to show her the crazy Converse shoes she'd designed to wear with her beautiful red prom dress, and the pictures of the summer she dyed her hair blue. He wanted to play for her the album Kelsey had cut as a Christmas gift her senior year, and show her the scrapbook of newspaper clippings from every theater performance she'd starred in.

He wanted to introduce his wife to the amazing, beautiful, talented, breathtaking daughter God had given to them for seventeen incredible years. Noelle deserved that.

Eli waved to Dan, then climbed into his truck, sat there in the cold. He was tempted to lean his forehead on the steering wheel, but people in this town might call an ambulance, thinking their former sheriff had passed out.

So he pulled out, drove down to the harbor parking lot, and stared at the gloomy sky.

"Oh, God, please forgive me for my fear—for not trusting You. For my betrayals. Please, even if You don't bring Noelle back to me, give us a new future." He blew out a breath. "And help me figure out how to tell her about Kelsey."

He closed his eyes then, breathing the cold air into his chest. And for the first time, it didn't rattle through all the hollow places.

He drove to the art colony. It hadn't been quite two hours, but maybe she'd let him sit in that chair by the window, let him watch her, trace the beautiful angle of her face.

Maybe she'd let him rediscover his wife.

He climbed the stairs and was about to knock on the closed door when he heard a hiccup, a shudder of breath. "Noelle?"

A flare of panic made him open the door.

She sat in the blue floral chair near the window, her legs drawn up to herself, her forehead on her knees. Her shoulders shook.

"Noelle?"

She looked up, her face red and wet, her expression devastated. "Hi."

Hi? "Are you okay? What happened?"

He looked around the room. Shadows dappled the floor, but nothing seemed out of place.

"Nothing. I'm fine. I just . . . I'm so sad. I can't stop crying. It's like there's something broken deep inside me, but I can't find it, and I don't know how to stop it."

She pressed her hands to her eyes, wiped them. "I should be happy because I painted something. I actually sat down and just started painting. And it's not half-bad." She got up then and walked over to her easel, angled away from him, where she could look out the window as she painted.

She lifted the canvas off the easel, turned it around. "It's still drying, but it's pretty good, right?"

Eli stared at it, his breath leaving him, his insides dropping away. He opened his mouth but couldn't find his voice.

"I've been sitting here for the last twenty minutes trying to figure out who this is. I had her in my head when I woke up this morning. She looks like me—maybe it's a memory I have of myself, years ago. Which makes sense, because in my mind I still think I should look like this—"

"It's not you, Noelle." He walked over to her and took the canvas, stared into those beautiful blue-green eyes, his own filling. "You caught her perfectly. Those incredible eyes, so full of life, and her hair—it always had those golden highlights, like it was made from the sun. And her smile. Like she was teasing you, but she loved you so completely, it didn't matter what you did." He closed his eyes, rubbed his thumb and forefinger into them, his breath ragged.

"Eli, what are you talking about?" Noelle's voice was soft, almost worried. "Who did I paint?"

He looked at her then, his heart turning over, and cupped his hand on her cheek, running his thumb down it. "Oh, Noelle. You painted our daughter, Kelsey."

15

SHE HADN'T KNOWN Eli for long, but after two weeks Noelle thought she understood him. A strong man, unflappable, brave, even a bit on the too-tough-for-emotions side.

She didn't recognize the broken man before her. The man who covered his face to hide his grief, whose shoulders shook, his breath ripping out of his chest.

"What do you mean, *our daughter, Kelsey?*"

His words didn't make sense, although deep inside, she felt something lock into place. Some truth that had been floating in the murky darkness, something she'd been trying to wrap her fingers around but had proved slippery.

Not unlike how she felt when she painted the face, those eyes looking at her. She knew them; she just didn't know how or from where. Painting this . . . this Kelsey had seemed like an exhale, almost, as if she'd been holding her breath for two weeks.

But with it had come this wave of unnamed sadness.

She never guessed it was for their daughter.

"She didn't die at birth?"

Eli looked at her with an expression so wretched she wanted to wrap her arms around him. Even if she wasn't in love with this man, he'd been her husband—or rather, still was—and that truth made her heart soften.

"Oh, Eli, please tell me what happened."

He shook his head, his eyes wet. "I'm so sorry, Noelle. I should have told you from the first day, but I was afraid, in your fragile state, that it would do more damage. See, you weren't the same after Kelsey died. You left us, and . . ." His breath trembled in. "Or maybe I left you. I don't know. But our family fractured. And I was afraid of it happening again."

She touched his arm, searched his eyes. "I'm so sorry; I don't remember. I . . . want to. It's like a shadow back there in my mind I can't get a good look at."

He nodded with what looked like a grimace. "Maybe you don't want to know. Maybe . . ."

"I want to know."

He swallowed, then took her hand, brought her to the chair. He sat on the ottoman before her and hung his head.

"Kelsey didn't die at birth. I implied that, and I'm sorry for that too." When he lifted his head, he tried a tremulous smile. "She was amazing. Seventeen years old and she knew what she wanted. She loved music and wanted to be a singer, a composer. She had already been accepted to a college in St. Paul, and her entire life was before her. I remember, you two used to sit in her room at night, and she'd play you songs that she'd make up on the spot. I was jealous sometimes because you were so close, but it was unique. You two had a bond that seemed unbreakable by teenage angst and mothering fears. You always said she was your clone. I shouldn't have blamed you for falling apart when she died."

"I fell apart? What about my faith?"

"I have no doubt that you did a lot of praying. But . . ." He sighed. "We were already struggling, you and me. I am sure you felt utterly alone."

"As did you, Eli." She touched his hands, wanting to share in his pain, feeling like such a spectator to the tragedy they'd shared. "How did she die?"

He closed his eyes, rubbed his thumb over one, then the other. "It was a stupid, hometown mistake. I picked up a kid for speeding outside town, and I recognized him. Parker Swenson. He went to school with Kyle and played football with him. I thought he was a good kid, and sometimes people get a little heavy on the pedal when they're coming into Deep Haven. I didn't run his plates to check, just gave him a verbal warning."

He shook his head again. "I should have been more alert. A better cop. I just . . . well, I trusted him. But he'd robbed a gas station and killed a cop in Minneapolis, and there was a BOLO out for him. If I'd run his plates . . ."

He was fading back into that moment; she saw a darkness filtering into his eyes. And inside her, panic began to swirl, something unfamiliar. "It wasn't your fault, Eli. You didn't know. You trusted him—"

He pinned her with a desolate look. "His next stop was the gas station where our daughter was working. She asked him for identification when he requested a box of cigarettes and he pulled out a Glock—taken off the cop he'd murdered—and shot her."

She stilled, unable to breathe. Unable to speak.

"Actually, Kelsey was his second victim. Lee's husband, one of our deputies, came into the shop right as Parker pulled the gun on her. Parker turned and shot him point-blank in the chest. Kelsey had the presence of mind to hit the alarm under the counter; then she took off running. Parker caught up to her by the bread aisle. He shot her twice—once in the leg, then in the back. By that time I arrived on the scene, along with the other officers in the area. Parker took one look at us and put the gun to his head."

His face had hardened, his voice tight as he spoke. "Kelsey wasn't dead. We airlifted her to Duluth, but her injuries were too dire. She and Clay Nelson both died a few hours later."

"That's awful."

He nodded, licked his lips, let out another breath. Then he got up and walked over to one of the pictures—the one with the red sneakers—and picked it up. Outside, snow had begun to drift from the sky, lazy, free-falling.

"You were in Duluth visiting Kyle. I caught you on the way home, and we met at the hospital. I should have warned you, should have intercepted you, but the doctor came out of surgery with the terrible news right about the time you arrived. You were completely blindsided. I know I should have told you before this . . . but I didn't know how."

"And you still can't forgive yourself."

Her eyes had long ago started burning, and she let the tears flow down her cheeks, not bothering to wipe them away. "C'mere, Eli."

He turned to her, his face crumbling. "When you lost your memory, I thought it was sort of a gift to both of us. I thought maybe God could let us start over. But how do I start over when every time I look at you, I see how my mistakes destroyed our lives?" He pointed to the painting of Kelsey. "See? Even though you can't remember her, you still know. You still know who we lost, what we lost."

"Eli." Noelle stood and walked over to him, laid her hand against his cheek. "We lost a daughter, but we didn't lose each other. God gave that back to us, even if we can't understand His ways. Maybe He does mean for us to start over."

He reached out to rub a tear from her cheek. "Why are you crying, Noelle? Do you remember her?"

She brought his head down to her shoulder, wrapped her arms around him, held him. "No, Eli. I'm crying for you. I'm crying for all you went through, alone, and the pain you felt when you couldn't help me. I'm crying for your grief and the horrible fact that you blamed yourself for this. And I'm crying for your family—our family—and the tragedy and unfairness of this world."

She lifted his face to hers. "And I'm crying with joy that God would see fit to give me such a wonderful husband twenty-five years ago. A husband that I know I must love dearly."

He looked at her, then tucked her into himself and wept.

Emma didn't expect Kyle to call, not after the way she'd raced out of Deep Haven last weekend, his lights flashing in her rearview mirror.

It didn't keep her from ducking into the kitchen of Mulligan's, leaning against the stainless steel double fridge, and fishing her cell phone from her pocket. No missed calls, no text messages, not from Kyle, not even from Ritchie. Which meant that getting a job at Mulligan's waiting tables—thanks, Carrie—hadn't cut into her gig schedule after all.

The kitchen reeked of onions, grease, and the chaos of too many bodies flipping burgers in the heat.

"Corned beef and cabbage panini, a fish-and-chips, and a bangers and mash, table three, up." The chef hiked the plates up under the warmers.

Emma pocketed her phone, loaded the plates onto her tray. She hefted the tray to her shoulder and smiled her gratitude at the owner, Michael, when he held the door open for her. "The guy at table five is wondering when our live music will start," she said as she passed by.

Michael, tall and thin, with dark hair and the requisite Irish green eyes, shot a glance at his watch. "Soon, I hope. I called our musician's cell, but it rolled over to voice mail."

She entered the dining room, the sounds of voices rippling through the tiny corner pub on this chilly Thursday night. She'd walked by the place a thousand times on her way to the grocery store and finally decided to stop in during an open mic night. Then she'd upgraded to dragging her guitar along, sitting on the stool under the spotlight for her two songs, always playing one of the Blue Monkeys' old standbys. Landing this waiting job meant that maybe she'd also be able to sidle up to the mic now and again, when Michael needed a fill-in.

She hoped.

Emma set down her tray on a caddy, unloaded the plates before the patrons, got their drink refill orders, then swung by table five, where a man and woman sat, probably on a date. The woman, a redhead, toyed with the stem of her wineglass.

"Our musician is on his way," Emma said.

The man in the booth looked like a musician himself, in a derby hat, a sports coat, jeans, and a narrow tie. He glanced past her at the empty stage. "I guess I'll need another Guinness, then."

She added his empty glass to the tray. "Your shepherd's pie will be up soon."

"Do you know what kind of music is on tap for tonight? Celtic?"

"I don't know; I'm sorry. Mulligan's is more of an eclectic mix even though we have an Irish menu. I'll check."

She returned to the kitchen, stopping by the bar to deliver the drink orders. Michael was behind the grill, the hands-on owner now flipping a couple of top sirloins. "Do you know what kind of music the musician—?"

"He's not coming," Michael snapped, clearly stressed. "He just called—was in a fender bender. Apparently he's banged up. I'm trying to track down someone else."

She glanced at the clock, back at Michael. "I could fill in until you found someone else. Or . . . just fill in?"

He pulled the sirloins off the grill, plated them, and handed them to the chef. "We need you on tables."

"It's not that busy, and I'll ask Carrie if she can cover for me. And if it gets too busy, I'll just hop off the stool and pitch in. I can handle it; I promise."

He gave her a long look, then finally said, "All right."

"I live a half block away. I'll go get my guitar and be back before the shepherd's pie is up. Thanks, Michael."

"Walk—don't drive!"

She was already untying her apron, pulling on her jacket.

The night wind nipped at her ears as she jogged down the

street, glad someone had cleared the sidewalks. She'd play a few covers from Fleetwood Mac and Stevie Ray Vaughn. Maybe some Otis Rush, and then shift over to Janis Joplin and Aretha Franklin. An eclectic mix, for sure, but she'd tweaked them all for her voice, her tone.

And if she felt brave, she'd pull out a couple tunes from the Blue Monkeys. Bring Kelsey along tonight.

She unlocked her apartment, the rush of the opportunity making her shiver. She hadn't sat under the spotlight, just her . . .

Ever. The thought stopped her, made her stand for a moment in the quiet apartment. She'd always played with Kelsey at the mic. Sure, she'd had her solos and had played for Ritchie when she'd auditioned, but other than her open mic nights, she hadn't landed a solo gig.

She picked up her guitar, held it to herself, and remembered suddenly Kyle's arms around her as he'd swept her up, carried her out into the alley.

Oh, who was she kidding? She should be back in Deep Haven, not here in St. Paul, trying to hustle up a musical future. Why had she left—no, fled—Deep Haven?

Certainly not because any of her accusations to Kyle were true. *Convenient.* She wasn't sure why that word flew out of her mouth. Probably she just wanted something to spring her out of the magic spell Kyle seemed to cast over her. Within twenty-four hours she'd seen herself returning to Deep Haven, gigging at local restaurants . . . or even better, starting a life with Kyle. Teaching music to the youngsters in town, maybe even working for the music association, organizing events.

She hadn't run from Kyle. Or Deep Haven. She'd run from the fact that it felt too good, too comforting. Too perfect.

She still couldn't wrap her head around Kyle's retort when she suggested she should have died instead of Kelsey. *Do you seriously think I'd be angry with you for being the one who lived?*

Why not? She was angry at herself.

Or maybe she was angry at God.

Emma hiked her guitar over her shoulder, then jogged down the street, the fight still so fresh, she thought he might appear.

It's easier to ignore the memories than to believe that God can fix them. It's easier to walk alone in your pain than to share it.

Maybe. Because going back to Deep Haven would mean that she'd have to let God heal her. And frankly, she was just too angry at all He'd taken from her. It *was* easier to walk alone.

The heat of the kitchen burned away the chill of the street, and she shrugged off her jacket, hung it on the hook next to her hat, then made her way to the front.

"I delivered your shepherd's pie to table five," Carrie said as she knelt next to Emma, helping her pull out her music and arrange it on the stand. Emma tugged the strap over her head, began to tune the guitar.

"By the way, a couple people came in, said they knew you. From Deep Haven? They're sitting in my section. Although the entire pub is my section now, isn't it?" Carrie winked at her.

Emma glanced toward the booth by the window. Nicole, looking tan and happy, waved. She waved back, forcing a smile. What was this, some sort of cosmic reminder of what she'd run from?

She plugged in her guitar, set the levels, then slid onto the stool and finished tuning. Finally ready, she leaned into the mic. "Hey there, everyone. I'm Emma Nelson. I know that I was just waiting on you, but Carrie's gotcha while I fill in for our missing guitarist. I hope I can do him justice. Thanks for listening."

She sat back on the stool, took a breath, then started the chords for "Blue Bayou." The words had curled inside her, aching to roll out as she watched Nicole and Jason hold hands at the far table.

"I'm going back someday,
Come what may."

Even as she sang it, yes, she wanted the courage to return. She didn't really believe her mother would move away—she was simply hurt from Eli Hueston's actions.

"Where the folks are fine
And the world is mine . . ."

Maybe that was the problem. The night Kelsey and her father died, Deep Haven became a foreign place. Kyle had made her see it as hers again.

Oh, she missed him.

She ended the song, received a hearty round of applause, and followed with James Taylor's version of "You've Got a Friend." So maybe she wasn't going to play her usual blues list. This one felt more healing, perhaps. "'When you're down and troubled . . . just close your eyes and think of me, and soon I will be there . . .'"

Kyle appeared in her mind, his nose red and cold as he kissed her. She could stay warm, right there in the pocket of his embrace.

The image gave heart to her song, and the crowd whooped for her when it was over. If she had a drummer, she might have tried a little Steely Dan. Instead she dove into "You Are So Beautiful" by Joe Cocker. She would have enjoyed remaking "Up Where We Belong," but she'd need Kyle for the duet.

Wow, her little gig had her imagining all sorts of fantasies for a girl who had left him standing on the shoulder in the dirty snow. Apparently she wasn't done dreaming about Kyle Hueston in her life.

The romance of the night, the rapt attention of her audience, led her to end the set with "Hooked on a Feeling" in the old B. J. Thomas style.

She sang it as if Kyle might be in the crowd. Since he wasn't, she wasn't exactly risking her heart. But she poured it out anyway.

She noticed that Jason held up his cell phone like a lighter through the whole song. Cute.

"I'm going to take a break and see if Carrie needs any help with refills. I'll be back in about twenty minutes."

Emma set her guitar on the stand, then headed over to Carrie, leaning against the bar. "What can I do?"

Carrie grinned at her. "You're making tip money like crazy, girl. Just keep playing those oldies. By the way, the couple at table five wanted you to stop by."

"Probably mad about their cold shepherd's pie."

Carrie rolled her eyes. "Take a compliment, will you? They're waiting for a couple Irish coffees, by the way." She lifted two mugs of Killian's, overflowing with foam, onto her tray and headed off to her table.

When the barkeep put up the coffees, Emma carried them by the handles to the table, setting them in front of the couple. "Carrie said you wanted to talk to me?"

"I'm Brenton O'Hare, and this is my associate Terese Lawton. We're music producers for Peace Records down in Nashville. We were in town reviewing a couple acts." He handed her a card. "You've got a good voice, and I see you know your way around a guitar. Do you have anything original you could show us?"

She drew in a breath, swallowed. "Yeah. Of course."

"That's great. We're actually on our way out of town, but we'll be back in a couple weeks. How about you give me a call tomorrow and we'll set up an audition time."

Emma nodded, smiled, nodded. Tried not to hear the tiny siren in the back of her head. Original songs. Maybe she could find something that she and Kelsey had written.

Brenton picked up his coffee. She backed away, nearly fleeing to Nicole's table.

"What are you guys doing here? I thought you were on your honeymoon." She tried not to let her glance boomerang to table five.

"We're on our way home. Can't you see the tan? Cancún, baby." Nicole lifted her sleeve. "You were awesome."

Emma was staring at Brenton's card.

"What did they want?"

She looked up.

Jason grinned. "The table behind us. We saw you talking to them."

She handed over the card. "They're record producers. He wants to audition me."

Jason read it, looked at Nicole, then at Emma. "That's fabulous. You were amazing. In fact, I got the whole thing right here. Just posted it to YouTube."

She froze. "You did what?"

"You need fans, Emma. Let us be the first to sign up for the official Emma Nelson fan club." He returned the card, glanced at his phone. "Hey, I already have a view." He scrolled down, reading something. Smiled.

"Fan number three appears to be Kyle Hueston."

⁂

"C'mon, pick up, pick up." Kyle let the phone ring until it rolled over to voice mail, but he didn't leave a message. Maybe he'd turned into some sort of lovesick fool to believe the song Emma had sung on YouTube might be directed at him.

As he'd watched her sing, despite the grainy darkness of the video and the raspy, crackled audio, he'd traced her face, let her sweet voice churn up all the memories he'd tried to bury this past week. Only a week? It felt like an eternity.

Why do you like me, Kyle?

He'd stopped trying to figure that out, just retorted—in all his imaginary conversations, of course—*I just do, okay? Does everything have to make sense?*

But see, he'd nailed the problem, the one thing that had kept his finger off the dial all week. Everything in his life made sense— at least the things he could control. His career choice, returning to Deep Haven. Even his cabin on the hill. It all fit into the plan he'd envisioned for his life after Kelsey's death, as he watched his mother unravel, his father turn into a walking corpse. He would never let life destroy him like that. Never live on the edge.

Never find himself helpless. Without a plan.

And Emma fit perfectly into that plan. Hometown girl. She even loved music.

"I'm hooked on a feeling . . . that you're in love with me."

Kyle couldn't actually pinpoint what love might feel like—was it wanting to hear her voice, thinking about her smile, tasting her kiss as if she were right there with him? Was it longing so badly to be in the audience there in St. Paul that he carried his cell phone out of the restaurant where he'd been listening to the local band

JayJ Bump and played the YouTube video? The video had posted to Jason's Facebook page, appeared on Kyle's news feed.

Okay, so maybe he'd been rude to surf Facebook while sitting with the other deputies, but he couldn't listen to any more shop-talk. Not when it meant remembering that he still hadn't found his mother's attacker. And a murderer—not just in Harbor City, but here in Deep Haven.

Kyle had spent the day tracking down the alibis of the fish house workers whose names Bonnie had given him. Every one of the seven employees, with the exception of Billy and the currently AWOL Hugh, alibied out. He had stopped in to a couple restaurants in town, asked if they employed a man matching Hugh's rough description, but no one seemed to recognize him.

At the very least, he wanted Hugh for questioning.

If only Billy's girlfriend hadn't gone missing. That bothered him more than he wanted to dwell on.

Especially when Marc called from Harbor City with the report that Duluth Pawn had a class ring matching the description of Billy's, pawned only two days earlier. They were sending him the digital footage from their surveillance camera.

Whoever had murdered Billy and Cassie Mitchell and hurt Kyle's mother could be seated at the tavern right now and he wouldn't even know it.

Facebook seemed the only escape.

Now Kyle sat down on a cold bench outside the restaurant, in the park overlooking the harbor, flakes still drifting from the sky, and replayed the YouTube video. So beautiful. So—

His phone vibrated in his hand.

He was smiling before he answered and probably betrayed himself in his eager "Emma?"

"Sorry I couldn't take your call earlier. I was finishing my second set."

"I'm sorry; I shouldn't have called you so late."

"It's not late—oh, well, I mean, we just closed up here."

"Where are you?"

"I'm walking out of Mulligan's. Made about twice as much in my tip jar as I did waiting tables tonight."

"I'm not surprised. You were . . . you're amazing." He wished he could see her, although he already knew she was wearing a pretty blue shirt with sequins and a pair of jeans. Her hair up but waterfalling around her face. He wanted to yank out the hair band, let it fall over her shoulders, weave his fingers through it. He took a breath. He had to remain calm. Remember that the last time he saw her, she had broken speed limits escaping from him. That should keep the sweat from piling up on the back of his neck. That and the way his words crystallized before him as he spoke in the sparkling night.

Behind him, the restaurant pulsed out Bump's beat. The fresh snowfall glistened on the ground, the sky above moody.

"Thanks, Carrie. Good night."

"What—?"

"Oh, sorry. My roomie. She walked home with me."

He heard the sounds of doors closing, and then her voice turned quieter, more intimate. "I need to apologize to you, Kyle. I was . . . Well, it was a good weekend, wasn't it?" The lilt in her voice, one that spoke of hope, warmed him to his bones.

"A very good weekend."

Emma sighed. "I thought of you all week and the way I behaved, and I think . . . I wasn't ready for the way you made me feel about . . . Deep Haven."

It was a start, anyway.

"You know I don't think you're convenient, right? If anything, you're inconvenient, all the way down there, five hours away."

She laughed, something precious and healing in it. "You want to know a secret?"

"Always."

"There was a record producer from Nashville there tonight. He gave me his card and wants me to audition for him."

He hesitated for only a half second. "Emma, that's wonderful."

"Mmm-hmm."

"What's wrong?"

"He wants me to play some original stuff for him."

"So?"

"So I haven't written anything new—I mean, I haven't completed a song since . . . Well, see, Kelsey was the lyricist. She always had the right words. I had the tune."

"You two were an amazing pair."

"That was the plan. We'd go on the road together. We'd follow the dream together."

"And now you're following it alone."

"Right. Without Kelsey. Without her words. A half act."

"Babe, I think you're the whole act."

She drew in a breath, and for a second he thought he heard a shudder. "You're sweeter than I thought you'd be, Kyle. Much sweeter."

"What, did you think I'd be a jerk?"

She paused. "I guess I shouldn't have jumped to conclusions. I shouldn't have lumped you in with . . ."

"With whom?"

She drew another breath. "Aw, you know. Guys."

Somehow he didn't think that's what she meant, the way her words came so easily, so without emotion. He got up so he could walk through the park to keep warm. "I wish I could help you write your songs, Emma."

"I know you do. You don't do helpless well."

He could almost see her, almost see the twinkle in her blue eyes, feel her hand on his face.

He cut his voice low as he zipped up his coat all the way, tucking his chin inside. Must be below zero. "I believe in you. You have the words inside you—you just have to find them."

"I have a couple weeks."

He was already calculating his schedule.

"Where are you right now?" she asked.

"I'm trying to stay warm, walking along the harbor. I was at the basketball game earlier tonight. We won, and it was parents' night. It felt strange to see my mother accept a rose from Kirby, knowing she has no memory of attending every game since fourth grade."

"It's nearly championship season, isn't it?"

"Play-offs start this weekend. We're a good team. Kirby has a few schools scouting him."

"Do you ever wish you hadn't lost your scholarship?"

"I wish I hadn't let it go to my head, hadn't become so out of control. But I know being a deputy is what I'm supposed to be doing."

"You're a good man, Kyle."

He smiled into the phone. "Is that your way of saying you like me?"

"Not fishing or anything, are you?"

"Cut a guy some line here, Emma."

"I like you, Kyle. You win."

Oh, he wished he could reach out, kiss her. "What are you doing now?"

"I'm staring out my window, watching a drunk guy skate out to his car while his buddy wrestles the keys from him. Ouch! That couldn't have felt good."

"Come back to Deep Haven. I'll keep you safe from the troublemakers."

She said nothing. Oh, why had he said that? But yes, he wanted to. Hated that she was down there.

"I believe you would if you could," she said finally. "But I'm not sure that's in your hands. And that's the problem, isn't it? We want it to be, and when it isn't, we get angry. But the funny thing is, even when we are in control and it doesn't turn out, we still get angry. Either way, we want a guarantee that everything will turn out all right."

He drew in a breath, Bonnie's words ringing through him. *Sometimes life just backfires on you, is all.*

Not anymore. Not on him.

"You'll have your lyrics, Emma; I promise."

16

SHE'D SPENT THE ENTIRE DAY studying the life of this beautiful young woman, entering into the history of the Hueston family and seeing her own face among the pictures. Noelle would do almost anything to retrieve the memories that lurked just beyond her grasp. Pictures of their family gathered around birthday cakes, of sand castles and snowmen and Christmas trees and every major event in the past twenty-five years, told her that they'd been a happy family. A family that laughed together. A family she wanted to belong to.

Headed by a man who had suddenly started to withdraw after the closeness of yesterday's revelation. She'd felt it beginning this morning, the moment Eli began to unload from his truck the cartons of family mementos, Kelsey's belongings. He'd piled them in the living room while she stared at him, admittedly thunderstruck.

"You packaged all this up and took it away?"

Eli wore his padded jean jacket and a baseball cap, his boots leaking snow onto her freshly mopped floor. He looked at her with such remorse in his eyes she didn't have the heart to say anything else.

She remopped the floor after he delivered it all and returned to the garage to tinker with something in desperate need of repair, no doubt.

Or maybe he was simply gifting her with privacy as she examined the life of their daughter. She'd unpacked the boxes slowly, peeling back the layers of Kelsey's life. A menagerie of glass unicorns and pretty ornate boxes that held mismatched earrings. Stuffed animals—she counted no less than seven teddy bears. A tangle of necklaces, one of them made of shellacked Froot Loops, another of fishing wire and a glow-in-the-dark star. Another box held perfume and the contents of what had probably been her sock drawer. Posters, rolled up in one box, lay atop pictures in frames. Noelle pulled them out, set them around the room, chronicling the progression in age. Kelsey had worn braces, if Noelle compared the shot with her hugging Mickey Mouse to the one with her arms around a skinny, pimply boy who probably didn't deserve her. She unrolled the posters—mostly of bands, but a couple of famous photographs. She recognized the World War II shot of the sailor kissing the nurse in Times Square. So her daughter had been a romantic.

She found shoes tumbled together as if Eli had simply scooped them off the floor and dumped them into the container. The violence of it rattled her. Oh, the grief of this man to want to tear something so vital from their memories.

You weren't the same after Kelsey died.

She kept hearing that in her head. The same as what?

Whatever terrible grief that had defeated her, she felt nothing of it as she unpacked Kelsey's clothes, examining her T-shirts. She had a number from the theater department—local productions of *Annie, Hamlet, Macbeth*.

Noelle had always wanted to be an actress.

Eli had packed away Kelsey's books, too. Mostly titles Noelle didn't recognize, although Kelsey had a well-worn copy of *Jane Eyre*, along with the complete works of Jane Austen.

Tucked in with the books were journals, dog-eared and doodled in, that contained lines and lines of poetry. She read through every one, spending hours in one titled "Life Lyrics," caught in the joy of Kelsey's words.

We are the hearts of today,
 Our ages fresh and cool
 Springing for the farthest star.
 The age of second by second
 Moment by moment
 And the day is ours to find.
 Where is your hope?
 Can you not see past the lost?
 Yours may pass, and you'll be forgotten.
 So rise up,
 Hold to the moment you have.
 For, children, we are the lives of the time
 And flames of the start.

Run, and be the youth of your day
Owning each moment
As the hearts of today.

Noelle pressed her hand to it, traced the handwriting, the scratches, the scribbles. *Yours may pass, and you'll be forgotten.* How could she have forgotten this amazing girl?

She sat in the middle of the living room, the sky unblemished today, the birch trees white and majestic as they rose above the ocean of snow. *Hold to the moment you have.*

Had she held on to Kelsey? To her moments? Had her daughter known she was loved?

"Where did this come from?"

The voice made her look up. To her surprise, her cheeks were wet. She wiped a hand across her face, smiled at Kyle. He wore a brown flannel shirt, a pair of jeans, and a cap not unlike his father's. But he had kinder eyes, at least today.

"I saw you at the game last night. Why didn't you come and sit with us?"

He walked into the room and sat on the sofa, displacing a marbled unicorn. He picked it up. "I gave this to Kelsey for Christmas when she was twelve. She had a thing for unicorns."

"She has fourteen."

He weighed it in his hand. "What's going on?"

She closed the book, slid up to the sofa. "Your father brought home all these boxes—"

"I'm sorry we didn't tell you."

She hadn't really looked at the omission as deception until she saw Kyle's expression, the way his face twitched and his gaze slid away from her.

"I painted her yesterday. At the studio. I dreamed about her; then I painted her face. Your father saw it and realized he had to tell me." Noelle set the "Life Lyrics" book down. Kyle's gaze fell on it, something like pain passing through his eyes.

"I've been going through her things all day, trying to connect to her. Hoping that the feeling deep inside might surface, take form. It's like it's at the tip of my mind, and if I am just quick enough, I can grab it before it dashes away."

"Maybe you should stop trying so hard. Maybe it'll just come to you." Kyle reached out, opened the book. "I have a couple poems in here."

"Really?"

"Yeah. She was compiling a list of our poetry to give to you for Mother's Day." He looked up at her, smiled. "This was a school assignment, but you always liked it. 'Paint me like I am. Paint me serene and focused. Paint me with a basketball, sweat down my spine. Paint me blue and fast and accurate.'" He glanced at her, and she smiled at him.

"Go on."

He lifted a shoulder. "It's silly."

"Please, go on."

"'Paint me on the court, the crowd wild, bright lights above. Paint me without fear, without doubt, without limitations, without weaknesses.

"'But most of all, paint me unstoppable.'"

He blushed now, and it curled warmth in her chest. "I love it."

"You're just saying that because you're my mom."

"Technically, yes, but I have the unique position to not be bound by the constraints of motherhood. I really do love it. You loved basketball."

He closed the book and shrugged but wore a smile that made him suddenly look about thirteen years old. "I did. But becoming a small-town cop was a much better course for my life. This was what I was meant to do."

"Because of Kelsey?"

He lifted a shoulder. "I'd like to make sure that no one goes through what we did."

"Kelsey's death has such a grip on this family," she said quietly.

He said nothing as he ran his hand over the journal. "Do you mind if I borrow this?"

"It belongs to you more than me." She sighed, staring at the array of Kelsey's life around her. "I don't know how to stop trying. I see so much of the past in Eli's eyes, but no matter how I try, I can't step into it, can't shoulder it with him. I want to be there in our memories, but I can't."

"What do you feel?" He tucked the journal beside him.

"Actually, when I look at her pictures and I read her poetry and I count these unicorns . . . I feel joy. I can't explain it, but there is an unabashed vibrancy that flows out of it all—like Kelsey lived every minute for all it could be."

"That was Kelsey. She liked to live large. When she had a girls' sleepover, in the morning we'd find them all with their blankets outside on the lawn, staring at the stars. Shivering, of course."

"Did we fight? Ever?"

"Are you kidding me? You once took her door off the hinges because she slammed it too often."

"Oh."

"Yeah. When you and Kelsey crossed horns, we men ran for cover. But you were also crazy close. You never missed a performance, and once you even tried out for a play just to be in it with her."

"Did I get the part?"

"You were . . . well, you were the lion's paw in *The Lion, the Witch and the Wardrobe*."

"I was a paw."

He grinned. "Actually, you just worked a giant paw, one of two, like a puppet for Aslan's body. But to your credit, you were the best paw I ever saw."

"You're just saying that because I'm your mom."

"Yep." He winked at her. "Hey, where's Dad?"

"He told me he was going to the lake to bring in his ice house."

Kyle reached for Kelsey's Bible, lying on the ottoman. Noelle had paged through that also, reading her script, her highlights.

"I guess it doesn't surprise me that you feel joy—Kelsey's life verse was Romans 15:13. 'I pray that God, the source of hope, will fill you completely with joy and peace because you trust in him. Then you will overflow with confident hope through the power of the Holy Spirit.'" He looked up. "She always said our job was to trust. God's job was to overflow us with joy."

"Maybe that's what I feel. The joy that came from her trusting God."

She picked up a silver object—it reminded her of a credit card, only it had earphones attached, the string wound around it. "I'm guessing this is for music?"

"Kelsey's iPod." Kyle took it from her and wound his thumb along the dial. "She has some of her own music in here. Wanna hear it?"

"Of course."

He got up and walked to the stereo on the built-ins, plugged in the iPod, and turned it on.

A beat rolled out, filling the room. It had a bluesy tone to it, a pulse that made Noelle find her feet. Bob her head.

"It's the Blue Monkeys, Kelsey's band. She and another girl named Emma were in it. They cut an album, just for fun."

The vocals began with something soft, husky, shimmering under her skin, then rising high, a powerful vibrato that she felt against her breastbone.

"Daydreaming, I came across a place in my mind,
    Found you . . ."

The tones were sultry and rich, confident.

"And that's Kelsey."

A rich, joyous voice that could make Noelle's entire body thrum.

"Dance with me, Kyle." Noelle held out her hand, stepping out of the nest she'd made of Kelsey's belongings.

Kyle looked at her hand, back to her, then smiled. "Okay."

She had the moves of the untrained, but then again, twenty-five years had passed since she'd last danced. The music swam through her as she smiled at Kyle. He was shaking his head in between bobbing his shoulders, grinning crazily back.

Joy. If she couldn't shoulder the Huestons' grief, perhaps she'd collect the joy. Bring it back to them.

The song ended and another came on. "Okay, Mom. Let me teach you something. You used to make Kirby and Kelsey and me practice dancing in the kitchen after you and Dad took classes."

"We took classes?"

"When we were little. You were good." He held out his arms. "You can swing dance to the blues. Just follow me. It's a six count with a back step. Start by stepping out with your right foot."

He led with his left. She stared at her feet, but the movement did feel familiar, and in a moment she got the beat.

He led her in a turn, back again into his arms. "You always did have hot moves, Mom." Kyle had a sweet sparkle in his eye, something of joy there too, now.

"What's going on in here?"

The voice made her jerk. She turned to see Eli. He hadn't shaved yet today, his cheeks ruddy from the brisk air outside.

"Are you dancing?"

She looked at Kyle, smiled. "Yeah. Apparently you and I used to have some hot moves. Kyle was just teaching me—"

"Don't do that. Don't dance." Eli glanced at Kyle, who let her go, and then back at Noelle. He shook his head, something like betrayal in his eyes, and walked out of the house. It shuddered at the slam of the door.

She stood there with Kyle, the music pulsing behind them, as Eli roared down the driveway in his truck.

∂⅝

Eli drove to the end of the road, his chest burning. He wasn't angry. Not angry.

Jealous.

He closed his eyes, laid his forehead on the steering wheel, the sun hot on his black dashboard. Kelsey's music still threaded through him.

Noelle was dancing. With Kyle, both of them laughing.

Around the living room, bathed in the golden light of the late afternoon, lay the remnants of Kelsey's life—her pictures, her books, her music. And Noelle and Kyle were *dancing*?

Eli gritted his jaw and lifted his head. He turned onto the highway.

Was this some sort of joke to her?

That wasn't fair, but he couldn't make it past the roaring in his ears. The way his chest burned as if Noelle had driven her fist into it.

The fact was, he'd been angry with her, or something like it, since the day she'd said, *I'm crying for you.*

The sweetness of her voice had torn through him, left a jagged, raw place.

He was supposed to protect *her*, was supposed to comfort *her*. Not the other way around.

It only made it worse when he'd returned home to another message from the mysterious Eric. He wrote the number down and fought with his desire to bring it to the station and ask the guys to run it through their database.

At least he hadn't deleted the message. That counted, right?

But the fact that she had people in her life he didn't know—or once had—unsettled him.

He drove toward town, needing something. Maybe he'd stop by the fitness center, although he hadn't worked out in months. Or the Blue Moose Café, see if any of his former coworkers were chewing the fat.

The sun simmered low and full on the horizon, a blast of hazy heat that spilled like molten lava into the lake. He put down the visor, the glare almost mesmerizing in its allurement.

Out of habit, he slowed as he passed Lee's driveway.

What—*wait one second.* He turned in to the driveway, barreling down it faster than he should, skidding to a stop precariously close to her garage, and banged out of his car.

He didn't even pause to knock, just slammed his way into her house. "Lee! What's going on?"

No sound. He expected her to be in the kitchen or reading a book in the sunlight that waxed the floor. Or perhaps she wasn't home—in town doing her volunteer work.

"Eli?" Her head poked up from the basement. "What are you doing here?"

He fought the part of him that wanted to raise his voice, to lash out at her. "There is a For Sale sign in your front yard."

She came up now, wearing a pair of black yoga pants, a paint-stained yellow shirt, a red bandanna holding back her hair. A streak of tan paint marred her nose. "I should hope so. How else will I get any calls?"

"That's not funny, Lee. What are you talking about?"

She wiped her hands with the rag she held and dropped it in the sink. "I'm selling my house. I'm moving." She shrugged. "No big deal."

"No big deal?" He was shouting and he knew it. "No big deal? No. No way. You can't sell, okay? You can't leave Deep Haven."

She had eyes that could see straight through him, turn him inside out, and she used them now to silence him. "It's time. I need to leave."

"No—" He held up a finger, pointed at her, then to the air. "No—that's not right. You . . . This is your home."

"This was my home with Clay. I need a new home. Without Clay. Without . . ." She took a breath. "I can't have a place that requires so much help."

"My help, you mean."

Her voice lowered. "Yes, your help. Like you said, you aren't leaving Noelle. And I don't want you to."

"And I don't want you to go, okay? Listen—" He rounded on her, not sure why he was so angry, fearing it had more to do with Noelle, but this seemed so much easier. "You're my best friend, Lee." Wow, had he said that? He winced. "Or you were. I don't know. I'm so confused."

"No," she said softly. "You're just lonely, like I was. Like I am. And yes, I wanted you to love me. I wanted to be in that safe place, in your arms." She put her hand on his shoulder. "But it's not right, Eli. And you know it."

He swallowed. "You're just so easy to be with."

"Because you don't owe me anything. You haven't pledged your life to me. You haven't promised to love and cherish me. You can hurt me and walk away from me and shrug it off—"

"I'd never do that—"

"You *did* it, Eli. You kissed me and then practically told me it was my fault. I didn't show up day after day on *your* doorstep. You thirsted for the easy world of my friendship, and if you weren't a man who is trying to follow God, you might have pushed for more. And stupid me might have let you. I might have surrendered the woman I was for the momentary security of your arms. But then what? I'd wake up and be right back where I was, only loathing myself." She shook her head. "I need to leave Deep Haven. I need to leave you."

He closed his eyes.

"You have a wife. And you have the unique chance to start over with her. To break down all the barriers of the past and begin again. Don't run from it."

"I'm not running."

"You're here, aren't you?"

He drew in a quick breath. "She's over at the house dancing with Kyle. *Dancing.* To Kelsey's music."

Surprise showed in Lee's eyes.

"Yeah, that's right. I told her all about Kelsey. I brought home all her things from the storage center, and she's spent the day reading all about Kelsey and her life. And what does she do? Dances."

Lee stared at him until finally a slow smile crested over her face. Then she nodded. "Dances. That seems about right."

He shook his head, turned away, then back to her. "Really?"

"Oh, Eli. If anyone should dance to Kelsey's music, it should be her parents. Go home. Join in the dance with your wife." She moved forward, touched his face. "I promise it's going to be okay."

Then she rose up on her toes and gently kissed him on the cheek.

Something about the gesture, about her words, released the band of guilt around his chest. *Join in the dance with your wife.*

He caught her hand. "Thank you, Lee."

"Hey, what's goin' on?" Derek closed the door behind him, dropped his athletic bag on the floor. He regarded Eli with a strange look.

"I was just leaving. Great game last night."

Derek smelled of sweat, gym socks, the weight room. Eli could feel the young man's eyes on his back as he walked out to his truck.

Lee stood at the window, arms folded, nodding.

Maybe it *had* been easier to be around Lee because he didn't owe her anything. Perhaps he'd begun out of guilt, but after that—well, she'd stood at the door in her wool jacket, gratitude in her eyes, and it had spoken to the frustrated pieces of his heart. His wife wouldn't even let him in, yet Lee embraced the smallest things he did for her.

You have the unique chance . . . to break down all the barriers of the past and begin again. Don't run from it.

All this emotional nakedness around Noelle just seemed so . . . Well, a guy didn't walk around opening his heart. It didn't seem masculine. Or helpful. Someone had to remain tough. Solid. Put together.

But if he could admit it, he'd never felt so vulnerable—or loved—as when Noelle had cried for him.

He backed out, onto the highway, paused for a long moment.

Then he turned toward home.

Kyle's truck was gone from their snowy driveway. Eli entered the house, stamped his feet on the rug. He pulled off his boots, hung up his coat, and dumped his hat in the basket. Ran a hand through his hair. Yeah, he looked like a real prize.

Walking into the living room, he noticed it had been cleaned up with the exception of the tiny unicorns. These Noelle had lined up on the top of the piano. Little fairy-tale creatures capturing the sun, turning the ceiling to kaleidoscope colors.

He picked one up, ran his thumb over it.

Thumping came from the back bedroom.

Kelsey's room.

He headed down the hall and stood in the doorway. Noelle was hanging one of Kelsey's pictures from the box—she'd created a gallery of sorts over the bed. She'd filed Kelsey's books back onto the empty bookcase; her shoes nested on the rack hanging from the door.

And beside the bed, her journals.

"I wondered why this room was half-blue, half-purple," Noelle said softly. She didn't look at him.

"Because you and Kelsey couldn't make up your minds," he answered. "So you chose together."

She drew in a breath, and it sounded ragged, like she'd been crying. Shoot. He hadn't wanted that.

Or maybe he had. Maybe that was the problem—he hadn't wanted her to dance because he wanted her to be in misery like he was. But maybe the time for misery had passed.

Oh, he wanted to dance. Or at least to let himself hear the music.

He watched Noelle pull out the World War II poster of the kiss in Times Square. It curled over her as she tried to affix it to the wall.

Eli came over, held it up. She stepped inside the pocket of his arms to tape it to the wall. "I love this picture. It shows such an emotional moment, a man outside of himself. I have to wonder what happened next."

"Maybe she slapped him," he said.

"Or maybe she kissed him back." She turned in his arms, and now he could see that yes, she had been crying. He let go of the poster, ran his thumb down her cheek.

Why had he ever thought Lee might take Noelle's place? This was the woman God had given him, the woman who had shared children with him, the woman who deep down knew his wounds, his dreams. And most of all, the woman who knew how to celebrate the life of their daughter.

Eli couldn't help himself. She drew him in with her blue-green eyes, that tentative smile, the smell of her, so familiar, so new.

He kissed her.

Tenderly. Not sure if she might slap him or kiss him back. But she made a little sound, curled close to him, her arms winding around his shoulders. She always fit so perfectly in his embrace, and that was familiar too. It stirred up feelings he'd long ago locked tight.

He let them out, just enough, and deepened his kiss, wanting to lose himself but afraid of what might be on the other side.

And she kissed him back. Timid at first, then with something of confidence.

Like she too might be letting go, hoping.

When he finally broke away, he cupped his hand to her face. Searched her eyes.

She gave him a slow, suggestive smile.

Oh.

Oh.

His mouth dried. "I . . . well . . ."

Noelle looked away. "I'm sorry. I just . . . I want to remember so desperately, Eli. And there's something about the way you look at me, the way I feel when I'm in your arms, the way you just kissed me, that feels so right." She raised her eyes to him. "I want to be your wife again."

His throat tightened, his chest burning. His wife. Again. He could barely find his voice. "I've missed you so much. And I want that too. But . . . you don't remember us being together, Noelle. Are you . . . are you sure this is what you want?"

"We're married, right?"

He nodded.

"Then I want you, Eli Hueston. Don't sleep in the den anymore. Be my husband tonight."

He let a slow, rich smile slide up his face. "Do I have to wait until tonight?"

She grinned. "How long do we have before Kirby gets home?"

17

EMMA SAT ON A BARSTOOL at Mulligan's, red-and-yellow neon lights splashing into the dark pub, alive with conversation. She leaned into the mic, trying not to care that no one paid much attention to the girl on the black padded stool, one foot hooked onto the bottom rung, crooning out a lonely tune on a Saturday night. It ended and she received a smattering of applause.

Outside, drivers splashed muddy slush onto the sidewalks. She hated March, with the crusty, dirt-edged snow caving into the damp streets. The March thaw turned the world gray and bleak, the wind still toting a bitter edge as it stung her face.

And to make it all worse, her brother's semifinal basketball game was Monday. Right during her audition. She longed to be home, to pack the stands with the rest of Deep Haven, to cheer the boys on to state.

She could still remember Kyle in his high school basketball

uniform, the surge of excitement when he sank the final three-pointer for the win.

She segued into another Joe Cocker cover. "'Ain't no sunshine, when he's gone . . .'"

Emma had spent the past two weeks digging up new songs, probably too many from the era of angst, but they seemed to capture the tumult of fear inside her that seemed to only grow as the day of her audition approached.

Monday. She had two more days to put words to the reams of music she'd worked out, each with a fresh, tangible hope that words might swirl to the surface of her mind.

She'd even purchased a journal and sat for hours waiting for something poetic to appear. Instead, she found herself doodling Kyle's name, words that he said to her on the phone at night, feelings that arose when they hung up.

She wouldn't name it love, not yet. But something about his low, calm voice greeting her at midnight when she got home from work, as she brewed a cup of hot cocoa and curled up on her chair, as he told her about the happenings of Deep Haven that day, had seeded new feelings beyond those of any high school crush.

He told her about his life, and he listened to her music—sometimes adding a strange verbal beat to the songs she'd play him while on speakerphone.

She finished the song, let the last of the music die out, and smiled as a fresh table of college boys burst into applause. They called out requests, mostly new stuff—Rihanna, Gaga, Beyoncé. She wrinkled her nose.

"You'll like this one," she said and launched into Mötley Crüe's rowdy version of "Smokin' in the Boys Room." Then she slowed it down with Lennon's version of "Stand by Me."

Her father would have appreciated tonight's lineup.

The boys raised their glasses to her as Carrie took their orders. Her roommate wore a green tie-dyed shirt and a pair of impossibly skinny jeans, her hair in short pigtails.

Another group of patrons rose, smiled at her as they shoved some green into the tip jar, then headed for the door.

At least she'd be able to make next month's rent. But sooner or later, she'd have to face the facts.

She had failed Kelsey. And their dream.

Someone at a far table had started singing along, and the husky, twangy sound roused a memory as she closed her eyes and lost herself in the song.

Her father scooted into her memory, having changed out of his uniform, wearing sweatpants, a printed T-shirt of some ancient band, his wool slippers. He raised his hand as she looked up. "Don't stop. It's wonderful."

He seated himself across from her, in that decrepit brown tweed chair he had in college, bobbing his head. And then, as she reached the second chorus, he'd just stared at her, grinning.

Like she might be the most beautiful thing he'd ever seen.

I miss you, Daddy.

It wasn't fair how life changed, turned on her in an instant.

She glanced toward the entrance as the door opened for another diner. He came in alone, wearing a dark jacket, the light catching his bronze hair, the wide shoulders. He just stood there by the door as if waiting for his vision to adjust to the darkness, looking around the room.

Emma nearly hiccuped her words, her heart swelling, lodging inside her chest.

Kyle.

What was he doing in St. Paul? At Mulligan's? She finished the song, but by that time he'd caught her eye, smiled, and helped himself to a front row table.

Carrie set down a menu before him, then gave him a second look and shot Emma a glance.

"I'll be back in twenty, folks. If you have any requests, give them to your server, and I'll see if I can accommodate you." Emma slipped the guitar strap over her head, set her guitar on the stand, and stepped off the stage, grinning at Kyle.

He stood. "I hope you didn't stop for me because I'd just as soon you kept playing."

They stood there for a moment, and oh, she wanted to leap at him, to throw her arms around his neck. Smell Deep Haven and the woods on his skin.

But she refrained, taking a breath, waiting . . .

He reached out, pulled her to himself. "I've missed you." He pressed a kiss to her cheek.

She wanted to turn her head, but instead she released him and slid into the opposite seat. "What are you doing here?"

He raised an eyebrow.

"Please. You know what I mean. I talked to you last night— you didn't say a word about coming down."

"I wanted to surprise you. And bring you this." He pulled a folded journal from his inside pocket and slid it across the table to her.

Her breath caught at the familiar cover. "This is 'Life Lyrics,' Kelsey's song journal."

He nodded. "My dad brought her stuff out of storage for my mom to read through."

"Does this mean she got her memory back?"

"No, but she's trying."

Emma's mind went, however, to a picture of Eli kissing her mother and she shucked it from her brain. Kyle was not like his father—he was kind and funny and creative and spontaneous and . . .

And she wasn't convenient. Kyle had traveled five hours to sit across from her with that crazy grin on his face.

She opened the notebook, immediately captured by Kelsey's loose, almost whimsical scrawl. Stanzas, some circled, others crossed out, words underlined in the margins, all surrounded by doodles, betrayed the way she thought. Random. Poetic.

Pure Kelsey.

Emma paged through, found a few finished products she recognized, other half songs they'd never finished.

On the last page, she found the song Kelsey had started in the attic.

There are broken rainbow moments,
And dandelion wishes that don't come true.

Her throat tightened as she read the title. "'Emma's Song'?"

There are times it don't seem fair,
Like He's never there.
But He's watching over you.

Her breath hitched and she looked at Kyle. "She wrote this song for me?"

"Most of a song. It seemed to end right after the bridge." He leaned over, pointed to the last stanza.

There are times you want to quit;
  Let God take care of it.
  He loves you so . . .

"I was thinking you and I could finish it. You know, for your audition?" He said it in a small voice, more hopeful than confident. "And we could take some of her other lyrics, set them to music too—maybe some of your new stuff?"

She drew in a breath, paged back through the journal. The "Steps" song and "Rescue Me." Yes, she knew these lyrics—Kelsey had read them aloud to her, trying them out.

She'd heard music, even then, behind them.

"Are you sure, Kyle? She's not here to sing them."

"But you are." His eyes met hers, wouldn't let her go. "She left these behind for you, Emma. And you can give them a voice, bring Kelsey's dreams to life. I know she'd want you to have them."

She blinked away the burning in her eyes. Lyrics. Life—no, dream-giving—lyrics. She closed the book, smiled at him. Nodded. "I have one more set, and then we have work to do." She got up. "Do you have any requests?"

He seemed to consider her offer for a moment, then grabbed her hand, pulled her down into his lap. "Just one," he said softly and kissed her.

&

Noelle could fall in love with the life her former self had built. With the exception, perhaps, of the crow's-feet around her eyes and the extra padding around her waist. But like pieces to a puzzle that had lain scattered a month earlier, suddenly, when she stepped back into her life as Eli's wife, everything fit into place.

Like now, sitting beside him during the Huskies semifinals basketball game against the Eagles, their hands knit together like newlyweds in between the rush of taking to their feet to cheer.

Kirby landed another three-pointer. She turned to Eli and met his high five.

He had such beautiful eyes. Deep brown, with facets of gold when the sun found them. She loved to prop herself up on one arm, trace his jaw, the russet overnight brush of whiskers, his face so relaxed in sleep.

She loved being with him, his strong arms cradling her. Yes, this was how she'd dreamed marriage might be. Sweet. Safe. Intimate.

Other than in sleep, Eli never relaxed, his life so full of taking care of their family. In the past two weeks he'd hauled his ice house home, parked it in the woods near their house, then driven out the backhoe and smoothed over a pothole in their muddy driveway that just about swallowed her SUV whole. He'd turned in the recycling—the giant cans of plastic, glass, tin, aluminum, and paper nearly overflowing in the garage—then washed her car of the grime the dirt road had kicked onto her hatchback.

Small, manly things, but so thoughtful. So she'd responded by hauling out her cookbooks, finding a dog-eared recipe that he might like. Even Kirby smiled when she plunked a smoked ham with homemade au gratin potatoes on the table.

Indeed, their home seemed almost back to normal, or what might feel like normal, if she could remember anything.

One morning last week, she nearly had. She'd woken with the distinct sense of being late, rushed downstairs, and while putting on coffee, heard a voice call from the bathroom, something about fixing her a cup too. A high, sweet voice. She'd spun around to capture it, but it vanished in the dark silences at the end of the hallway.

Maybe she'd simply begun to heal, her brain settling down to a routine. Probably because she'd stopped trying so hard, like Kyle suggested, and started enjoying what remained, the life she had now.

Too many times, the verses she'd heard nearly a month ago resounded back to her. *"But I trust in your unfailing love. I will rejoice because you have rescued me. I will sing to the Lord because he is good to me."*

God had been good to her—good enough to give her a husband who hadn't quit on her even though he felt forsaken. Good enough to give her Kyle, who helped her find the music of her daughter. Good enough to give her this community filled with friendly faces that someday might have names.

And good enough to give her Kirby, the senior star making jump shots from the top of the key.

She'd even dressed the part tonight—a blue Huskies jacket, a pin that identified her son as a player. Kirby's mom.

Yes, maybe the key to going forward with her life was simply being grateful for it.

Derek, playing near the baseline, caught the ball, shot it back to Kirby. He rimmed his shot, and it ricocheted back out. Derek caught it, put the ball up again. Swish.

Four minutes left on the scoreboard and they were up by four.

She breathed out as the crowd lit up around her. She'd noticed Lee sitting a few rows down and felt a strange pinch inside when the woman opted not to sit by her, by Eli. Hadn't she said they were friends?

Another woman sat beside Noelle today, munching on a bag

of popcorn. "Hey, Marybeth," Eli had said when she sat down, running interference again.

Now Marybeth leaned over, popcorn in her hand. "I saw your picture in the paper with Kirby. Great shot of your family. I can't believe your last one is graduating."

"Me either," Noelle said honestly. Kirby got the rebound from the Eagles shot bouncing off the board, took it halfway down the court, and passed it to Derek. It slapped out of his hands, out of bounds.

"Hang on to the ball!" Eli's voice boomed out.

Marybeth looked past Noelle to Eli and back. "Such a dad— doesn't just yell at his own son, but the rest of the team too."

Well, that could be because Derek didn't have a father to sideline coach him. The fact that Derek's father wasn't here to watch his son turn into a basketball star sent a curl of sorrow through Noelle. She'd have to hunt down Lee after the game and tell her what a great job Derek did. Maybe even invite her and Derek over.

Noelle watched the clock tick down as the Huskies worked their next play, finally tossing the ball to Kirby. He went up for the shot. It hit the rim, bounced out, and the other team grabbed it.

Less than two minutes. The crowd had started a defense cheer and she joined in, clapping next to Eli. *C'mon, Kirbs.*

The Eagles swished a beautiful three-pointer, bringing their score one under. The Huskies threw the ball into play, and Kirby ran down to the key.

They just had to hold on to it until time ran out.

"What's the guard's name?" Noelle said.

"Cory. He's a good ball handler. They got this."

Cory passed it to Kirby, who passed it back to the other guard.

Derek ran a pick and the guard drove to the basket, then turned and shot the ball back out to Derek.

He wasn't watching for it and the ball hit his hands, flew out of bounds.

A groan rippled through the audience.

Eli's mouth tightened.

The Huskies played man-to-man coverage and nearly stole the ball from the Eagles, who played the clock brilliantly. At four seconds left, they set a screen, and their guard dribbled up, faked, and banked in a two-point shot.

One ahead, Eagles.

The Huskies crowd went berserk, screaming for a score.

Cory grabbed the ball, threw it in to Kirby, who shot an overhand long ball to their basket. The buzzer sounded in midair. Noelle held her breath as the ball arched.

It hit the backboard and bounced into the crowd.

The Eagles erupted.

Noelle stood, hollowed out along with the other parents. She looked at Kirby. He had gritted his jaw, but she saw his mouth pucker as if he might be trying not to cry.

She started to go down to him, but Eli grabbed her arm. "Leave him. Trust me on this. We'll wait outside their locker room."

He slid his hand down to take hers as they made their way down the bleachers.

She spotted Lee a few feet ahead of her. "Hey, Lee!"

In the chaos, Lee must not have heard her.

They were stopped by Jerry, the mayor, whom she remembered from a previous game, and he talked shop with Eli. She half listened, watching the crowd. So this was her town, her people.

Most wearing parkas, warm hats, mukluks. Some of them waved to her—she waved back.

"Sorry about the game," said a woman with long black hair. "I miss you at the studio—come by; we'll have coffee."

The studio? Maybe she was from the art colony.

Another couple walked hand in hand, their other hands holding on to a pair of towheaded twin boys who bounded beside them.

"Yeah, I heard about Billy," Eli was saying to the mayor. "Kyle mentioned they'd hit a dead end. Something about not being able to find the right footage from a pawnshop?"

Jerry nodded, and she heard him greet a young man wearing a Huskies football jacket and a blue stocking cap.

She wanted to tug on Eli's hand, but he knew Kirby better than she did. Maybe he wouldn't want his parents hovering.

The pastor had joined the threesome; she smiled at him, rooting for his name. David? Doug?

"I saw the picture too," he was saying.

"I wish the *Herald* hadn't run it," Eli said. "The entire thing has me on edge."

What picture? She turned now to the group, began to listen.

"The second Kirby brought it home, cut it out, and put it on the fridge, I wanted to wring Gloria's neck."

Oh, the newspaper picture—Kirby presenting her a rose for parents' night. She could still glow when she thought about it.

"The suspect could be right here in Deep Haven."

"What suspect?"

Every eye turned to her. Then to Eli. And Eli wore a look she hadn't seen since that day she'd painted Kelsey's picture. "What suspect?" she said again, slowly.

"I'll see you guys later," Eli said.

"Tell Kirby he played a good game," the pastor said.

"Thanks, Dan."

Dan. She'd remember that. But now she stared at Eli. *"What suspect?"*

He shook his head. "Your accident wasn't an accident. We didn't tell you right away because we wanted to see what you remembered, and then when we realized your situation, we didn't want you to have more trauma."

She kept her voice even, ignoring the sting of being left in the dark again. "What do you mean, more trauma?"

He blew out a breath. "You were involved in a robbery while on your way home from Duluth. The clerk was killed."

"And I got away."

"Somehow. You ran into traffic and flagged down a semi. But you slipped and took a brutal fall."

"Which wiped out my memory."

He nodded. "The problem is, they don't know who did it. He's walking around loose."

"But if I can't remember him, then I'm not any danger to him, right?"

"He doesn't know that."

Oh. Hence Eli's hovering. She could hardly be angry at him for wanting to protect her. Still, the fact that he'd hidden the circumstances of the accident from her churned inside her. She pulled her hand away from his.

A scream, then commotion from the hallway, spilled into the nearly empty gym.

"Fight!"

They heard more screaming, yelling, shattering glass. Eli took off for the hall, Noelle behind him.

A crowd surrounded two boys fighting, some of the adults around them yelling at them to stop, others—mostly kids—backing away. Glass from the shattered trophy case littered the floor.

Noelle pushed through the crowd on Eli's tail, then froze.

Kirby had slammed Derek into the wall. Derek pushed him away, following with a fist to his face. Kirby threw himself at the other boy, tackled him.

"Knock it off!" Eli charged in, grabbed Kirby by his belt, and hauled him off Derek. "Kirby!"

Blood dripped from Kirby's mouth as he glared at Derek, who bent over and hung on to his knees, breathing hard.

"You shut up," Kirby said, his voice lethal. "You just shut *up*."

"Yeah, Kirby? Why don't you ask him yourself?"

Kirby stiffened, his jaw tight.

"'Cause you know the truth, don't you? You know your dad's been sneaking over to our house to be with my mom." Derek turned to Eli. "Haven't you?"

Eli went white, his body still as Kirby jerked himself out of his grip.

"For a couple years now. Isn't that right, Mr. Hueston?"

"Derek!"

Lee emerged from the edge of the crowd, stepped close to Derek, but he narrowed his eyes at her. "You make me sick. Do you even notice that Dad's gone, or has Eli filled in so well it doesn't matter?"

She slapped him. Noelle winced, her heart tearing open at the sound. "That's a lie, and you know it."

"Isn't that why you're leaving Deep Haven, Mom? Because Eli

has gone back to his wife? The wife who can't even remember him? Maybe he thinks she won't remember that he had his paws all over you. That he was going to leave her for you."

"Derek, that's enough," Eli said, his voice bearing a heat that shook Noelle. But as he said it, it occurred to her that he wasn't denying it either.

In fact, he and Lee looked at each other and something like guilt—or shame?—pulsed between them.

She might be ill. All this time he and Lee had been . . . and then Noelle and Eli had . . . *Oh.* Noelle turned, pushed her way out of the crowd. She heard Eli calling her name, but she didn't turn. Nor did she when Kirby called out, because she wasn't his mother. His mother had vanished, leaving her to pick up the pieces, to put their life back together.

A life that was probably broken beyond repair.

⚘

"How did I do?"

Kyle could see the adrenaline on Emma's face as she launched herself through the door of studio B at Wingate Studios, a sound-proof room with warm oak floors, a carpet in the center, a micro-phone dangling from the ceiling. She'd sat underneath it for the past four hours, pouring out her heart.

She landed in Kyle's arms, nearly bowling him over. "That was so amazing."

She'd not only laid down five demo tracks, but had been joined for an impromptu jam session by a couple local musicians practic-ing next door.

Kyle had even sat in on the drums, tired of waiting in the

mixer room, studying this Ritchie guy, who was supposed to be her agent, and the record producer named Brenton, whom he'd probably have to run a search on.

Just in case.

But most of the time, he'd simply watched Emma through the glass, bursting inside.

Oh, he loved her.

The thought resonated through him as he curled her tight into his embrace, spun her around with joy.

He loved her.

He could even come up with reasons why.

Her smile, for one, slow and sweet like molasses as it slipped up her face and turned her eyes so warm he felt the burn clear through to his chest.

He loved her for her creativity and her ability to turn Kelsey's words to something with heart and soul and verve and life. He nearly wanted to cry at the beauty of Kelsey's words to Emma's playing.

And what about her spontaneity? Like last night—after a hard day of playing, she'd made him drive her downtown to the art park, where she gave him a tour under the golden moon, dodging the melting puddles and making up stories about the exotic art pieces.

Maybe just the fact that she could sit and play for hours in a sweet pocket of blues riffs and licks, drawing him into a magic place with her.

She urged him out of himself to a place he liked.

Most of all, he loved how she trusted him. How she let him help her. How she let him into her life.

"You totally dazzled him," he said, putting her down, cradling her face with his hands, kissing her.

She grinned, then stepped away from him and stooped to pick up her gear. "I don't know. It still wasn't my lyrics."

"Oh, please. It was fabulous. And you may have used Kelsey's words, but you made them fit with your song. Kelsey would have been beside herself with joy."

She looked up at him through the curtain of her dark hair. "Really?"

He knelt before her, pushed her hair back. "Really."

Brenton came out the door down the hall. "Okay, kid, that was pretty good. I'm going to get that demo back to my studio, give it a good listen, talk to my people, and I'll let you know." He held out his hand to her.

Emma rose, shook it, and he winked at her.

Yes, Kyle would definitely be checking out this record studio.

"Here's a couple copies of the CD we made," Brenton said, handing them to her. She took them and stared at them with a strange, euphoric smile.

"Earth to Emma." Kyle picked up her guitar case. "Ready for some food?"

"I'm famished, absolutely ready to keel over."

"I can't carry you and the guitar."

"I'll bet you can."

Oh yeah. Kyle grinned at that. He led her outdoors to the dark parking lot. A streetlamp pooled shiny light onto the lot. Traffic splashed by. Across the street, a Chinese place flashed an Open sign. "What do you want for supper?"

"Pizza?"

"Attagirl."

"Yours?"

"Even better."

She slipped her hand into his. "You didn't have to stay, you know."

"Yeah, actually, I did. I can afford a couple days off." He opened the door to his truck, put her guitar in the back. "And by the way, I have couch privileges at my buddy's house for as long as I need."

He didn't regret missing Kirby's game, but he expected a call from his father any minute with the score. He had no doubt Kirby would be heading to the state finals next weekend.

He climbed into the truck.

Emma was opening the CD case. "Want to hear it?"

"Absolutely." He backed out, heading onto the street. He hated March, the dingy snow piled along the curbs. Even Deep Haven, crawling out of the icy grip of winter, seemed harsh and uninviting. No wonder all the resort owners closed their lodges for cleaning by the end of March.

"So how soon do you think we'll know?" Emma asked. She leaned forward, trying to find his radio controls. He pressed the CD button, and her first track came on.

"The sky cried, and I wept,
    for the hope I had lost in time . . ."

"I don't know." He glanced at her, her pretty profile, those amazing blue eyes, her lips—he could be entranced by her lips. "Emma, what if . . . and this isn't saying I don't think so, but what if Nashville doesn't work out?" Oh, he shouldn't have said that. Immediately he saw her cringe, nod.

"You're right; it probably won't."

"Hey, I'm not saying that. I'm just . . . Well, would you consider . . . ?"

It was too early. He couldn't voice what was in his heart—how he'd yearned for her to move back to Deep Haven. But wasn't that what he wanted? To marry a hometown girl? To start a life there?

He looked at Emma, leaning back against the seat, clearly replaying the gig.

No.

The realization rattled through him.

What he wanted was Emma. With or without Deep Haven.

The thought took his breath away, and he stared ahead, shaken. What about his plan?

"Would I consider what?"

He managed a small smile. "I . . . I was just . . . I don't know."

"You still want me to move to Deep Haven, don't you?"

He made a face. "No."

"Baloney. You love Deep Haven. Your life is in Deep Haven. I've never met anyone more hometown than you. Or maybe my mom. Although even she's leaving, so I guess people can change their minds."

"Your mom's leaving?"

"Moving." She played with the knitting on her gloves. "Right after Derek graduates."

"Why?"

Her silence made him look at her, but she had turned away and was staring out the window. "I guess she just thinks it's time."

Oh, he knew a lie when he heard it. But he said nothing.

The Nelsons leaving Deep Haven?

"I never understood my mom. It's like life just doesn't faze her. Did you know that when she and Daddy first built the house, they lived in the garage? And then the basement? They worked their way up, building the house as they went. She didn't have plumbing or electricity or hot water . . ."

"She's a true north shore gal."

Emma hiked up a shoulder. "Even after my dad died, she was always so tough, so steady. She dove into volunteer work, ran the booster club, helped at the church. And she kept the house going. Do you know how hard it is to heat a house with wood?"

"I'm sure Derek helped her."

She drew in a breath. "Yeah, she had some help. . . . I think I didn't want to go home because I saw how she had her life together. I had nightmares for months afterward—still do sometimes. I couldn't just pretend it never happened."

"I'm sure your mom doesn't pretend it never happened."

"Feels like it. And when I go home, it's a reminder of what a mess my life is." She looked at him, a wry smile on her face. "Maybe this Nashville thing will change all that."

"You think getting a record contract will make you feel better about your dad's death?"

He hadn't meant it to come out quite so harsh.

"No. Of course not. But then at least I'd be living my dream."

"Your dream or Kelsey's?"

"That's not fair. You said you loved the songs I put together with her lyrics."

"I do love them. Of course I do. You're amazingly talented. But you still haven't finished 'Emma's Song.' Or written your own. Getting a contract isn't going to fix what is holding you back."

"Here we go again, Mr. All-Knowing."

"Sorry. I just . . ."

"Can't help but fix things. Well, maybe God doesn't want me to write. Maybe it's my punishment for not—"

"You have got to be kidding me!" He turned to her, glanced at the traffic, then cut off the street and pulled over at the curb. "Do you seriously think God is holding it against you because you lived and Kelsey didn't?"

"No. But why would He take Kelsey and not me?"

"You're operating under the belief that God is disappointed that you lived. That He's somehow keeping score. As if He's given you this one chance and if you blow it, then your life isn't worth what it took to save. Guess what—you're going to keep blowing it, over and over and over, and He's going to keep loving you, over and over and over."

"How can He possibly love me—He took my father!"

"And He spared you!"

She blinked at him, almost horrified. "I didn't ask to be spared."

"And that's the problem, isn't it? Going back to Deep Haven isn't about the memories of all who died. It's the fact that you lived. And because of that, you had to change your life, do something noble and big—live Kelsey's dream—because if you didn't, if you did your own thing, then it would be selfish and not worthy of the life God spared, right?"

"You're one to talk. You wanted to play basketball. Now you're a small-town cop."

"I don't want to waste my life either. I want to protect people. But not out of some sort of guilt trip. I want to be the guy I know I can be, every single minute, because that's who I'm supposed to be."

She folded her arms across her chest. Looked out the window. "I wanted to live in Deep Haven, teach music to the kids, maybe play some gigs around town. I wanted to live my mother's happy life. To grow old in our small town with a man I loved. But then Kelsey died, and she had no one else to carry on her dreams."

"Has it occurred to you that God didn't want you to live Kelsey's dreams? That yours were perfectly acceptable to Him?" He softened his voice, reached out to touch her. She didn't move. "If God wanted Kelsey to live her dreams, then Kelsey would have lived."

Her jaw tightened. "I don't like that God didn't spare her."

"Neither do I. Life can look like everything is a mess; I admit that. And it can look like God doesn't love us. But I keep thinking about what Kelsey said, how faith is about trusting God when He seems farthest away. I'm wondering if, in those moments, we have to remember what we know about God, about what He's done for us."

He almost didn't recognize himself, the words issuing from him as if with power. But perhaps they were in him all along.

God hadn't abandoned him. Kyle just didn't want to admit it. Didn't want to admit that God could be there with his sister as she was dying and that He could hold their family together as they grieved.

Didn't want to admit that yes, he could trust God in every moment. Still, it felt right to take Emma's hand, to speak the words churning inside, for himself as much as for Emma. "Let's just ignore for a second—if it's even possible—that because of God's love for us, we'll see Kelsey again. Let's stay here on earth and look at the treasures He gave us to carry us through the darkness. Don't you have any good memories?"

She wiped her cheek with her mitten. "Of course."

"Like what?"

"Um . . . like the time I was fishing and flung myself off the dock into the water and my dad had to dive in to save me."

He smiled, picturing her soggy and cute.

Oh, she was so difficult to remain angry at.

"And the time I made a chocolate cake for my mother at your house and then came back after jamming with Kelsey only to discover your dog had eaten it."

"That's Riggins. She's a little oinker. Her face swelled up for a day and we thought she might die. Thankfully she just threw up the cake on our living room carpet. Yeah, that's a great memory."

She smiled. "And then there was my junior prom. My dad did a drive-by, even came in and stood at the doorway, just to see me dancing."

"And to put the fear of Deputy Clay Nelson into your date, no doubt."

She laughed, sniffed. "Yeah, I have good memories."

He swallowed, ran his thumb over her hand. "After Kelsey died, I started going to this little church. Some of my law enforcement pals went there, and the preacher always started the service with a psalm. I loved it because David had a lot of messy emotions. Sometimes he'd get angry at God, lamenting that God had abandoned him. Sometimes he'd whine about mistreatment of others. Sometimes he'd talk about all the great things he'd done for God. Regardless, he'd always end with a statement of faith. Something about trusting in God even when it's the darkest."

She looked at his hand. "Right before the morning star shows up."

"Mmm-hmm."

Emma drew in a breath. "Maybe that's what Kelsey was talking about. Trusting when things seemed darkest."

"I'm sure it was. Because she was a believer in Jesus showing up."

His cell phone vibrated in his jacket pocket. He pulled it out, stared at the display. Kirby.

"So you going to state?"

But Kirby's voice sounded strained, even sharp, as if he might have been crying. "No, we're not. But I don't care. Did you know . . . did you know Dad was having an *affair* with Lee Nelson?"

His words reverberated through the truck.

Still, Kyle couldn't quite decipher . . . "What did you say?" His voice came out even, cool, as he glanced at Emma.

She glanced back, something of shame on her face, before she looked away. Swallowed.

Oh . . .

"Dad and Mrs. Nelson were having an affair. For a couple of *years.*"

"Kirby—"

"I just got in a huge fight with Derek in front of the entire town. He accused Dad of it in front of everyone and Dad just stood there."

"And Lee?"

"She slapped Derek. But everyone knows, Kyle. Everyone knows."

Everyone. "Mom?"

"She ran away. She just . . . left. You gotta come home, Kyle."

"I'm on my way." He closed the phone, his heart pounding, jamming through his ribs. Silence descended between him and Emma. Then, quietly, "You knew."

She drew in a shuddering breath.

"Sheesh, Emma, you knew about my dad and your mom?"

Her voice emerged small. "I don't think it was as big a deal as you're making it out to be—"

"They were having an affair! That's a big deal—"

"No, Kyle, it wasn't like that. Your dad just kissed her—"

"He kissed her, and you knew? And you didn't tell me?"

"What was I supposed to say?" She was crying, her eyes red. "What—that your dad came on to my mom, and she freaked out and that's why I left town?"

"I'm taking you home. I gotta go back to Deep Haven."

"Why, so you can solve more problems?"

He put the truck into gear and pulled out. "Yeah, maybe. My family's falling apart, okay? So someone has to figure out what to do."

"Maybe you should leave it alone. Let your parents handle it."

"My dad's a jerk, and my mom's lost her memory. I think maybe they need me." He banged his hand on the steering wheel. "I knew I shouldn't have left."

She folded her arms. "No. You should have never left Deep Haven. Because clearly, it'll fall apart without you."

18

FOR A MAN who had spent most of his life learning to control the impulses of his tongue, to curb his anger, to keep a steady head in the face of every situation, Eli had really blown it.

Coach Seb still had Kirby and Derek in his office, his grim expression betraying his emotions. Eli watched him through the glass, dressing down the two boys, who never looked at each other.

He leaned against the wall and let the fight with Noelle rebound in his head. He'd made some quick choices, standing there in the school hallway, his life, his mistakes, stripped bare before the town with Derek's accusations.

Worse, he'd looked at Lee, and the truth of Derek's words had burned in his chest. *Maybe he thinks she won't remember that he had his paws all over you. That he was going to leave her for you.*

He hadn't actually planned to leave Noelle—though yes, he'd let himself care for Lee. Too much.

But he couldn't choose her over his wife. So he left Lee there to deal with the fallout and sprinted after Noelle. He'd chased her out into the parking lot, where the sky drizzled into the night, turning the black asphalt into an ice rink, glaring under the streetlights.

He closed his eyes, even now seeing Noelle round on him, the rain smashing her blonde hair to her head, tearing down her face. "You deceived me, Eli."

"I know; I'm sorry. I don't love Lee—"

"It doesn't matter if you love her or not. You made me believe we had this perfect life, that we were in love, that we had an amazing family despite our wounds. You showed me a world that I wanted to live in again."

"I never said we were perfect. In fact, I remember warning you that you might not like what you found."

Her eyes turned sharp. "So it's true, then, about Lee. You *were* having an affair."

"No—it wasn't like that." He'd shaken his head, not sure where the truth was. "I cared—care for her, yes. She needed my help, and it felt . . . Well, I could actually *do* something for her. And you wouldn't let me in."

"Did you even try, Eli? Did you wrap your arms around me, hold me, cry with me?"

He looked away, her words like fingernails scraping his heart. "No."

"I wondered about that." She shook her head. "The fact is, if you had, I might not have lost anything, including my memory. I keep asking myself—what was I doing in Duluth? My life is here. Was I shopping? Going to the doctor?"

Feeling her reeling out of his grasp, he wanted to lie. *Yes, you were shopping.*

"Did I know about the affair, Eli? Did I know and go to visit a divorce lawyer?"

Her words stung him, and that's when he lost possession of his thoughts, when they spiraled out until his dark fears, his anger, grabbed hold. "I don't know where you were, Noelle, because you didn't tell me. Like you didn't tell me about the art colony. Or Eric."

She didn't flinch, didn't move. Finally, as the rain saturated his skin, turning his body to ice, she said, "Who's Eric?"

"I don't know. You tell me."

"Oh, that's fair. I'll just dig around in my vault of memories. *Who is Eric,* Eli?"

He looked away from her, gritting his teeth. "I don't know, okay? He keeps calling our house and leaving cryptic messages. Maybe he's your lover."

The minute he said it, the sentence ripped a hole through him, and he couldn't breathe.

She stared at him like he might be a stranger. Perhaps, in that moment, he was, even to himself.

"You're a jerk, you know that?" she said, her voice shaking. "I should have followed my instincts back at the hospital when I told you to *stay away from me.*"

"Yeah, well, maybe I should have just left you there and come home to a woman who could actually *remember* me."

Oh, what was wrong with him? He felt his life, the last month, especially the sweetness of the past two weeks, shattering.

No. He softened his voice. "Noelle—"

But it was too late. "Have at her, baby," Noelle said icily. Then she turned, stalking toward his truck.

"Where are you going?"

"I don't know. Away from you. Far away, where I can forget you and Deep Haven and start over."

Like an idiot, he'd watched her get into his truck. But she didn't have keys, so—

The truck started up. Eli searched his pockets, found nothing. Then he remembered. As he had for twenty-five years, he'd handed Noelle his keys to store in her purse during the game.

He stood there in the parking lot, rain sluicing down his back as he watched her pull out. Her taillights, like little red eyes, glared at him until they disappeared into the night.

By the time Eli returned, Lee had vanished too.

Seb finished his lecture, and Kirby exited the office without a glance at his father. Eli followed him to the Neon, glad for the silence between them.

"Where's Mom?" Kirby said when Eli slid into the passenger seat.

"At home." He hoped. Where else did she have to go? But her words thundered through his head. *Far away, where I can forget you and Deep Haven and start over.*

Kirby drove in silence.

"It's slippery out. Be careful."

His son said nothing. Finally, "This is my fault." His hands were white on the wheel as he took a long breath.

"No, Son—"

"Dad, I started the fight." His voice emerged small against the pattering of the icy rain.

Oh, please, let Noelle be at home. He hated to think of her driving in this. "What do you mean?"

"I was mad at Derek for missing the pass at the end, for letting the other team get the ball. So I called him a name and said something about having bricks for hands."

Eli considered his son. "What did Coach Seb say to you?"

"He said that I betrayed the team." When Kirby glanced at him, Eli bit back a suggestion to keep his eyes on the road. "He said that we are always about unity, that we have each other's back, that we're stronger together than we are on our own, and that we have to stay committed to that, despite our mistakes. He said we have to believe in each other, believe the best, and believe the highest. He's always telling us how we can be amazing if we reach for it, and that no matter what, we believe in the good intentions of our teammate, that he's giving his all."

Kirby shook his head. "We're supposed to love each other. Forgive. And be patient. And make sacrifices—like our pride. I didn't forgive him, Dad. I was angry that he biffed the catch and that we lost the ball. I heard the crowd and I wanted the win. I wanted it for me. I was angry for me—not seeing how he might be angrier with himself than I was. I betrayed Derek, and I betrayed our team."

He looked at Eli again. "I was the one who told Derek about Mom's memory being gone. I don't know what happened with you and Mrs. Nelson, but we almost had Mom back, Dad." He didn't say any more, but the words came loud and clear.

Eli had betrayed his team too.

He hadn't stayed committed to Noelle, hadn't believed in her, hadn't encouraged her. And most of all, he hadn't loved her. Hadn't been patient, hadn't forgiven. Hadn't truly sacrificed. He'd just wanted to be left alone, to handle his grief on his terms.

But marriage didn't work that way.

In fact, it seemed as if he'd heard Kirby's words before.

It's vulnerability to the one person who you trust most. It's saying, "Here's my ugly, battered, wounded heart. I'm going to let you see it and trust you with it."

Pastor Dan's words rose from where he'd pocketed them inside.

It's how we're supposed to be with God—trusting Him with all our fragile parts.

But Eli hadn't trusted God with his broken places. It felt too vulnerable to let God inside, to let Him see his mistakes, his shame. His wayward heart.

He'd wanted to fix everything on his own.

"Do you still love her, Dad?" Kirby had braked, now was turning up their road.

"Of course I do, Son." But the words came too easily, without emotion. Did he? He watched Kirby's headlights scrape against the dark forest, cut over the dirt road.

Bringing Noelle home, letting her back into his life, had been like that. Light cutting through the darkness. He'd discovered the woman he'd forgotten, her laughter, the way she could make him feel young and fresh and whole.

He'd wanted to be the one in the living room, dancing with her.

And finally for the last month, he'd been the husband he'd wanted to be with her. Protective, nurturing.

Yes, he loved her. She had woven herself back into his heart, balmed all the wounds, reminded him of who they'd wanted to be together. Resilient, committed, joyous.

For the first time in years—even when he'd been a cop, long before Kelsey's death—he felt like the man God wanted him to be. A man built to bless his wife. To love her intimately and be loved back just as well.

Like the psalmist had said, God had heard his broken heart and answered. He'd given Eli back his wife, though he hadn't deserved her. Indeed, God had been faithful even when he hadn't. *I'm sorry, Lord. I'm sorry for my stubbornness, my pride. Help me be a man—a husband—who seeks to bless his wife, not himself.*

"She's not here." Kirby pulled into the driveway. No truck parked in the garage, the house lights off.

Eli got out of the car, saw fresh tire tracks, footprints. She'd been here.

He opened the door, probably with more force than necessary, and heard the panic in his voice. "Noelle!" But only the dog greeted him. Not bothering to shuck his boots, he bounded upstairs to their room.

The dresser drawers had been flung open as if she'd yanked out clothing. The bathroom drawers were empty, her makeup and toothbrush gone.

He stood in the chaos of the room and noticed, in the middle of the bed, the gold glint of her wedding band.

Eli scooped it up, closed it in his palm.

His brain plowed through destinations as he walked downstairs. Maybe her art studio? Or . . . no, she wouldn't go to Lee's house. Who else did she know? Or rather, who else did she remember? Maybe she'd called Kyle.

Kirby stood in the doorway, hands in his pockets.

Eli couldn't look at his son. He pushed past Kirby for the answering machine.

The messages had been erased.

"Where's Mom?" Kirby asked, his voice weak.

It was time for Eli to do more than just show up. "I don't know. But I'm going to find her."

❧

Of all the cosmically ironic moments to get a flat tire. Lee wanted to scream as she rounded her car and opened the trunk, the rain plastering her parka to her body, turning her wool hat soggy, freezing her to her core.

The tire had been sinking for days—why hadn't she changed it? Sometimes, in the back of her head, she still operated as if she were married.

Clay could have jumped out, changed the tire, pulled her out of the ditch, kept her on the road.

But Clay wasn't here anymore, was he? Just Lee and the dark highway, her Jeep crippled in the ditch.

A mile to home. She could walk. Or unbolt the tire, jack up this wretched car, try to change it. But even the jack seemed to weigh a thousand pounds as she pulled it from the trunk.

She threw it back inside, slammed the hood, and hated her life. Of course she had to hoof it home on this lonely stretch of pavement in the darkness. Maybe she'd get hit by a car. Or run over by a moose.

Grabbing her purse, she locked the door and pulled up her collar.

Water dribbled into her eyes and she brushed it away, Derek's filthy words scraping through her mind. *You make me sick. Do you even notice that Dad's gone, or has Eli filled in so well it doesn't matter?*

She'd stood there, naked in front of the community she'd known her entire life, watching her son unravel, and knew he'd seen right through everything. It only made it worse when Eli didn't deny it. Then Noelle turned, pushing her way through the crowd, and Lee wanted to be ill right there.

But what hit her hardest, like a blade through her sternum, was watching Eli run after Noelle.

Oh, Lee had lied to herself. She'd believed, somewhere in her bandaged heart, that Eli cared for her, that she had been noble to push him back to his wife, to sit elsewhere in the stands, to smile on the edge of the crowd, watching Noelle and Eli hold hands.

She told herself that it was just for show.

Lee started into a jerky, slow run.

He loved Noelle. Not her.

As she had stood there, seeing Eli chase after his horrified wife, as Coach Seb grabbed Derek and Kirby and hauled them into his office, as the crowd dispersed around her . . .

No one spoke to her.

She'd been abandoned by Deep Haven.

Lee slowed, her breath sawing in her lungs. She wanted to scream, to hit something.

It wasn't supposed to be like this.

She and Clay were supposed to grow old together in the house he'd built her. They were supposed to cheer on Derek as he played college basketball and walk Emma down the aisle. They were supposed to enjoy their grandchildren, go on vacations, rekindle their romance after so many years raising children.

He wasn't supposed to walk into the gun of a punk kid.

She turned and flung her purse out toward the lake where it frothed onto shore. She watched it bounce, settle on the beach, out of the reach of the waves.

"Why did You do this to me?" Lee looked up at the starless night, rain spitting on her face. "Why did You do this? Why couldn't You have spared him?" She wanted to curse, but the power of her anger frightened her. She cupped her hand over her mouth. She didn't expect an answer—she had stopped listening years ago.

Shoot, she'd probably broken her purse. When she stepped into the crusty snow lining the highway, she nearly fell, the ice scraping her ankles, but she plowed through to the beach. The shiny stones crunched under her footsteps. Her purse lay like a dead goose; she picked it up and smoothed her shaking hand over it.

It wasn't fair. None of it. Noelle had a perfectly good man she couldn't even remember. And Lee had no one. Not even her hometown.

She closed her eyes, sank onto the ground and pulled up her knees, not caring that the stones turned her to ice. She'd spent three years trying not to break down, and . . .

Her own sobs had the power to hollow her out.

She sat there, shivering, not caring that she might get sick. Why care? No one else did.

Lee pulled her hands into her sleeves. She couldn't feel her fingertips. Exhaustion wrung through her. Oh, she was tired. So very tired of trying to survive.

She closed her eyes, put her forehead on her sodden jacket.

Listened to the waves churning on the shore, the water pelleting her coat.

Listened to the steady thump of her heart.

So very, very tired.

Get up.

She raised her head, listening. Not a voice, more of a sense.

Get up.

She stared out over the lake. Far off in the distance, a row of lights revealed a laker, probably headed to Duluth. The lights pierced the darkness like eyes.

Go home.

What if Derek was there waiting for her?

She found her feet, trudged back to the road, her entire body sopping wet now, so cold she'd begun to tremble.

Go home.

She stared at the pavement as she forced one foot in front of the other.

Lights spilled over her, along with the sound of a motor creeping up behind her. She didn't turn, not wanting to see anyone she might know. Anyone who might confirm the awful sense of abandonment as they splashed past her.

The car pulled ahead of Lee, veered to the shoulder, stopped. The driver's door opened and a figure got out. "Is that you, Lee?"

Lee stared at the woman in the darkness. "Liza?" She ran a pottery shop next to the bookstore in town. Lee had an entire collection of her seagull pottery at home, the ones with Bible verses scrolled into the design, and had at one time taken classes from her. "What are you doing out here?"

"I'm house-sitting for Edith Draper up the road a ways." Liza came closer, squinting as the rain doused her. "You're soaking wet, and—" she reached out, grabbed Lee by the arms—"you're shivering. Get into my car right now."

Lee's teeth had started to chatter and she put up no fight as Liza drew her around to the passenger side, all but shoving her inside. She hated to turn the interior of Liza's car into a swimming pool. It was an older model, a Bonneville, maybe, with plush velvet seats and the defrost cranked to high. Liza turned the heat up to blazing when she got in. She took Lee's hands and held them in her warm grip. The kindness of the act warmed Lee more than the car's radiator.

"You're freezing to death," Liza said. "What are you doing out in this storm?"

Lee's teeth had reached a low-level buzzing. "I . . . I wassss . . . attttt . . . the game."

"Was that your Jeep I saw back there?"

Lee nodded.

"Wow, I'm glad I came along. You're a mess."

"Th-th-thank you."

Liza grinned. "I meant that in the nicest of ways, of course. Let's get you home." She pulled out onto the highway. "By the way, I was at the game too. Great game. So sad for the boys. Derek did a fabulous job."

Liza was at the game? And . . . afterward? Lee looked at her, searching her face for judgment. "Did you hear . . . the fight?"

Liza said nothing for a long moment. Finally, "I think it doesn't matter what the town thinks, Lee. What matters is that you were on the road alone tonight, in the freezing rain, and you didn't call for help."

Oh, so she had been there. But really, who did Lee have to call? Besides, she was tired of being needy. Needy got her humiliated by the entire town.

She held up her hands to the heat pumping from the vents, not answering.

"I remember when Mona married Joe. I was secretly devastated. We were best friends, did everything together. Worse, I had to find a new place to live and fix it up myself. I was so angry at her—and angry at myself for being angry. How could I resent her for her happiness? It wasn't her fault. But I was angry that God hadn't given me a man, too."

Liza shook her head. "Men are a little hard to come by up here in Deep Haven. But God's given me something beautiful while I wait. I've had an intimacy with Him, because I've needed Him so much, that I might not have had if I were married. Yes, of course I'd like to get married. This world is designed for couples. But God has filled that empty place, overflowed it, even. That was when I started my white line of pottery, vases and pitchers and coffee cups with Psalm 16 written on them. David says to the Lord, 'Apart from you, I have no good thing,' and that God fills him with joy in His presence. It helps me remember that I'm not alone."

She braked as they came to Lee's driveway. "This is your road, right? I remember when Clay ordered that pottery set for you for Christmas. I delivered it here."

Lee nodded.

"God never intended for us to go through life alone. It feels like it sometimes, but every time I get that urge toward self-pity or desperation, I think of it as an invitation for a deeper relationship with God. The point of life, in marriage or singleness—even widowhood—is that it should bring us to that intimate relationship with God. And that relationship should fill us—all the way up to our secret and ashamed places—so that we are overflowing with love for Him. Then we stop searching. Then we are filled with joy."

Joy. Lee hadn't felt it in so long that she'd forgotten the feeling. The joy of holding her newborns, the joy of seeing Clay after a long day on the job, the joy of standing on the lakeshore on a summer night, the waves on her toes, Clay roasting marshmallows at the fire pit.

Joy was what she'd had. But joy could be her future, too. She had survived—nobly, but not well. Perhaps it was time to lean near to God, let Him be her provider, the husband to the widow.

I'm sorry, God, for not letting You in to heal me. For substituting everything else for Your intimate love. The prayer pulsed inside her, only the beginning of what she had to say.

Liza pulled up to Lee's house. Derek stood at the window. As Lee reached for the door, Liza grabbed her hand. "I don't want to find you out in the freezing cold ever again, Lee. You hear me?"

Lee smiled, but Liza didn't. She dug into her pocket, still holding Lee's hand, and slipped a card into it. "And if you start to think you're alone, I'm happy to remind you that you're not."

Lee managed a trickle of a nod. She got out, and as Liza backed down the driveway, Derek opened the door. He stood silhouetted in the light, grief on his face. Then he ran out, barefoot, onto the driveway. "Mom!"

She met him at the end of the walk, let him throw his arms around her, let him apologize into her ear.

"Of course I forgive you, Derek."

He held her as the night cried over them, and Lee realized that she was no longer cold.

❧

You should have never left Deep Haven. Because clearly, it'll fall apart without you.

Emma's words singed the back of his brain, turning the drive home from St. Paul into one giant shouting match.

A singular shouting match.

Except Emma was winning.

Your father is at home, isn't he? Isn't this his problem?

He needed to turn off her voice in his head.

You're just afraid that he'll fail. That he won't find her. That something worse will happen to her.

Maybe he was. But his father had failed before. And he'd failed big.

You don't seriously blame him for the shooting.

"Stop talking to me, Emma," Kyle muttered. He turned on the radio, flipped through the stations, found nothing in this no-man's-land so far north of the Cities. He hit the CD button and Emma's first song queued up.

"The sky cried, and I wept,
    For the hope I had lost in time . . ."

"The Rain Song." One of Kelsey's first, and Emma put it to a soulful ballad. It could draw him in with its husky, intoxicating sweetness.

"My faith twisted, out of control.
    Or so I thought.
    And as I rained . . . I sang."

He gauged the road conditions. He'd seen cars spin out, roll over into the ditch on nights like this. The clock pushed past midnight, and his neck had started to ache.

"I sang of the thing in which I had lost
    The courage to carry on.
    I spoke in song,
    Asking for strength and hope."

He could almost see Kelsey at the mic, smiling at him, or sitting on her bed, guitar on her lap.

"And as I reached the chorus of my words . . .
   I felt Him.
   All around me."

But Emma had a voice that could turn him inside out. Kyle had no doubt she'd land a recording contract, move to Nashville. Kyle turned the song up and let the vocals fill the car. Red and blue flashing lights and flares ahead made him slow. He passed a semi jackknifed in the ditch.

"Drops on my heart, the sky cries,
   Not for me, not for my loss,
   But for what I found . . . in the rain."

What had he found? Maybe his own fears. He saw himself making the mistakes of his father and it shook him to the core. No wonder the man had retreated into himself.

He hated the rain, the darkness, the unpredictability that could surprise a guy and skid him into the ditch. Hated the crimes committed during storms, the way they could wipe away crime scenes, hide suspects.

Kyle turned off the radio, let the last of the notes find his soul.

He couldn't control the rain. Just like his father couldn't control every person in their town, couldn't read their minds. Predict their sins.

You should have never left Deep Haven. Because clearly, it'll fall apart without you.

No, maybe he'd fall apart without it. Maybe being a cop in Deep Haven meant he could hold together the world he'd grown up in, where kids rode bikes around town without fear of kidnapping, where teenagers slept out on the rocky beach, where most people kept their doors unlocked.

Please, God, take away the rain.

But He wouldn't. There'd always be rain, always be darkness.

Chaos.

Crime.

Pain.

But perhaps there was more to find in the rain, if he looked closer.

He eased off the gas as the car ahead of him braked. It swerved, and Kyle held his breath until it straightened itself.

His windshield wipers now ran with cakes of sleet, scraping the windshield like fingernails with each pass. He should stop in Duluth, get a hotel room.

His cell phone vibrated on the seat next to him. Grabbing for his earpiece, he wrangled it into his ear and answered the call.

"Hey, Kyle."

"Dad." He stiffened, his voice crisp. "Where are you?"

"I'm headed to Duluth. I think your mom's going back there."

"In this storm? Dad, what's going on? Kirby called and told me everything. Emma knew it too. You and Lee?"

"What do you mean Emma knew it too? Emma Nelson? You were with her?"

"Yeah. We're sorta . . . we were dating."

"Were?"

"It's not going to work out." Saying it made him hurt, right down to his bones.

"What happened?"

"Sheesh, I dunno; you tell me. *You* happened. You and Lee, and Emma knew about it and didn't tell me."

"There's nothing to know, Kyle. Lee and I weren't having an affair. We were just—"

"Oh, please, I can't wait to hear this. Any sentence that starts out *we were just* is *so* full of truth." He lowered his voice. "Gimme a break, Dad."

He waited to hear something sharp and defensive, wanted it, his adrenaline stirring hot.

"Okay, you're right. I did spend way too much time with Lee. And yes, I had feelings for her, but it was wrong, and I know that too. I wasn't a good husband all the way around. You were right that day in the hospital, Kyle. I blew it. But I love your mom, and I want to find her and fix this. I want to put our family back together again."

Kyle wasn't sure why the words from his father made his chest hurt, why his eyes burned. "Good," he managed. "I'm glad to hear that. Because . . ." His voice shook and he put a clamp on it. "We all missed you a lot."

Silence. The rain pattered on the windshield.

"I'll help you find her, Dad."

A breath in, then, "Thank you."

He was about to hang up when—

"Kyle? You might want to call Emma and tell her you're sorry that your dad was a jerk and ask her to forgive you for being a little like him."

"Yeah. Maybe. But maybe it's not such a bad thing to be like my old man. See you in Duluth."

19

NOELLE HAD NEVER feared thunderstorms. As a child, she would lie in her bed, covers tucked up to her chin, delight rippling through her as lightning crackled and thunder rumbled through the house.

No fear, just an awe at the power, knowing she was safe in her home.

Even the ice storm didn't frighten her now, despite having to drive Eli's truck at nearly half speed to Duluth. She'd watched the ice form on the windshield, the calming rhythm of the wipers nearly wooing her to sleep.

No, she didn't fear the storm.

She feared the aftermath. The cleanup. The debris in the yard, the broken fences, the shattered trees.

Once, in her yard, a giant cottonwood had fallen, the branches shearing off like amputated limbs. She couldn't bear to see it and had avoided the backyard for a month until her father cleared it.

Noelle didn't want to return to a life where Eli had betrayed her and figure out how to forgive him.

She wanted, frankly, to forget.

She reached the hotel long after midnight, put the room on her credit card and tried to sleep in a large, lonely bed that refused to surrender warmth. Instead, she rewound the fight in her head until she finally arose before dawn and watched Venus blink to life in the dark sky. It settled her a little, like a hand over her heart.

She'd found Eric and his number on her cell phone, under the recent calls made. By ten o'clock she had dressed and found his office at the Duluth Art Institute, located in the old train station downtown. As she parked in the lot and hiked to the brown cobblestone building with Gothic turrets, a giant arched door, it nudged something inside. Yes, she'd been here before.

Maybe he's your lover. Eli's voice scraped through her.

Oh, please, she hoped not.

She took the stairs to the fourth floor and found the offices of the institute. Eric Hansen's secretary recognized her, greeting her and offering her a seat on the slick black and metal sofa. Abstracts along the lines of Picasso hung on the wall. Behind the secretary, out the window, she could see the harbor, the dockyard busy now that the ice had broken.

"Noelle. I'm so glad you called."

Tall, good-looking, with curly brown hair, glasses. Eric wore a tweed jacket, jeans, square-toed shoes. And a smile that said they were friends.

She swallowed. He ushered her inside.

His office overlooked Lake Superior on two sides, a sleek black desk angled in the corner, a row of pictures behind it on the near wall, gallery style. A black sectional sofa made of leather and steel matched the one in the lobby and sat opposite a pair of orange molded chairs.

The place smelled modern, new, although paintings from all genres filled the walls—abstract, modern, impressionistic, even classical and Renaissance styles. She could stand for hours taking each one in, analyzing the techniques.

"How are you? I was concerned when I didn't hear back from you." He didn't sit at the desk but found a place on the black sofa, unbuttoning his jacket, crossing his legs, like they were here for a friendly chat.

Noelle sank into an orange chair. "I had an accident."

He uncrossed his legs, leaned forward. "Are you okay?"

"Getting better, but that's why you didn't hear from me."

He was an attractive man, maybe midfifties, and he had groomed, precise hands. They folded now in front of him.

She searched for a feeling, anything inside that might alert her to their . . . relationship? But of course, nothing surfaced.

"Well, have you decided?"

Decided. What? To leave her husband for him?

"I can hold your position for a couple more weeks if money is an issue. We just need your confirmation one way or another. These positions are coveted and we have a long waiting list. And of course, if you still want housing, we can arrange that also."

Oh. Oh! Her breath leaked out and for the first time, she found a smile, relief breaking through her chest. "I'm a student here."

He raised an eyebrow. "Not yet, but we hope so. Next year. Is that a yes?"

"I . . . I don't know." She touched her temple, her head suddenly starting to ache. She hadn't had a migraine in weeks. Please, not today. But the truth began to wash over her. She had planned on leaving Eli, on going back to school. Was divorce a part of those plans? Apparently the old Noelle had given up on her marriage as much as Eli had. And she hadn't cheated on him, but she'd certainly kept secrets.

"Did you get a chance to look at our financial aid package?"

"I . . . That's not the problem."

"What did Eli say?"

Hmm. Clearly she hadn't told Eli about Eric. But Eric knew about Eli.

"Can I ask you a strange question?" She leaned forward, clasped her hands together.

"Sure."

"Do you know why I applied to this school?"

Eric frowned. She smiled, expecting that.

"Why does anyone apply to art school? I suppose you love art and wanted to pursue it. Let's see—you told me that you'd loved it in college but you never finished your degree, and now that your son was graduating from high school, it was time for you to go to college again. Did I get it right? Is this a test, Noelle?"

She watched the movement on the harbor through the window, a huge tanker breaking free of the ice, lumbering out to the lake. "It's not a test." She looked at him, his kind smile. "I don't know who I am, Mr. Hansen. In that accident I mentioned, I lost my memory. I didn't know, until this moment, why I applied here. Who you even were. I've lost myself, my family, my life." She shook her head, the words oddly cathartic. "I just woke up a month ago and thought I was twenty-one. I had no memory of my husband. He took me home, took care of me."

He *had* taken care of her. Gently. Wooed her back to him.

"And I . . . well, I learned to care for him again. And our two amazing sons. The problem is, I found out a few things about our life that . . . I'm not sure I want to go back to. I'm not sure it's a life I want to remember. I feel like I've wasted the last twenty-five years. Like I don't even know who I am anymore. Maybe it's best to forget everything and just . . . leave it behind."

He stared at his hands, took a long breath. "Like the memory of your daughter?"

Oh. "You know about her? You know about what happened?"

He gave her a soft smile. "Of course I do. You wrote a long essay about your painting and how it helped you recover from your grief over your daughter. Our selection committee was extremely moved. But even more so by your paintings." He considered her a long moment, his lips together. "Noelle, would you like to see the portfolio you sent us for consideration?"

"Yes."

Eric got up, went over to a large bookshelf behind her, knelt, and opened a bottom panel. After a few moments, he returned with a thin black portfolio.

"We often hide pieces of ourselves in our paintings. You tell me what you see here."

She opened to the first page. A watercolor of a rock, white with brown etchings—a peace sign, a giant *K*, a cross. It lay in the palm of a young hand, the sun golden behind it.

"I don't know. It looks like something a child made."

"You titled this *Faith*."

The next was a picture of darkness, not pitch-black but just dark enough to accentuate the pale star over the horizon, bubbling with the dawn.

"I recognize this. The morning star."

"You called this one *Hope*."

The final picture was of five hands stacked on top of each other. A male hand was turned up at the bottom, the others palm down on top of it. She recognized Eli's hand, her own, Kyle's, Kirby's, and on top, it must be Kelsey's. The sunset bled out behind it, a shadow of a cross cascading over the stack.

"And this, this was *Love*."

She wanted to fit her hand into this picture, to feel Eli's in hers, Kyle's on top. She wanted to belong to this family, to love them.

To remember them.

She closed the portfolio. Rested her hand on it.

Eric sat back down. "You tell me, Noelle. Was this worth twenty-five years of your life?"

She met his eyes, hers blurry. Nodded.

He let a beat pass. "Perhaps you'd like more time in making your decision about the future?"

She wiped her cheek. "Yes, I would." Perhaps she needed time to rethink everything. As she rose, she held out her hand. "I wish I could remember you. I have a feeling you were very nice to me."

He laughed. "Nice to see you—to meet you again, Noelle. I'll save that spot for you as long as I can."

She took her time as she exited, lingering before the paintings in the hallways, walking by open classrooms, people working. She missed the creative hum of a studio.

Maybe she'd start painting again at the art colony.

She paused at a metal sculpture on her way out. An oval, it formed a head at the top, curved around to a smaller head below it. Like a mother holding a child up to kiss its head.

Her hand went to the charm around her neck. She fit her thumb into the circle, felt the two grooves. Oh.

Then Noelle ran her thumb over her naked finger, now indented without the ring. It felt hollow, light.

She wanted her ring back.

Pushing through the door, she discovered the sun had arrived, burning off the clouds, the brutality of the night before. She walked toward Eli's truck, digging the keys from her purse as she crossed the wet parking lot.

Noelle felt the movement more than she saw it out of the corner of her eye. A blur of white. She turned.

Froze.

A van thundered toward her, a heartbeat away on the slippery ice.

She jumped as a shot cracked the air.

"Noelle!"

She didn't have to find the voice to know it, nor the arms that locked around her, tackling her to the soggy ground.

Eli.

They landed between cars, her on top of him as the van careened past.

"What—?"

"Shh. I got you, honey. Are you hurt?"

She pushed herself up, looked at Eli. He appeared ragged, unshaven, his dark eyes troubled.

"No, I'm fine but—" Behind them, she heard the van spin out of the parking lot.

He pulled her to himself, crushing her. "Oh, I'm sorry, Noelle. I'm so sorry."

"It's okay, Eli. What happened?"

"Ask Kyle. He thinks it was—"

"Eli, you're bleeding." She had leaned back and seen the blood soaking his jacket.

He looked down at the wound. "I . . . oh . . ." His face whitened as his gaze returned to hers.

She cupped her hand behind his head, pulled off her scarf, shoved it into the wound. "Just stay still, honey. Just . . . help! *Help!*" She turned back to Eli, finding a voice that seemed suddenly very familiar. "Don't you die on me, Eli Hueston. I'm not done with you yet."

&

"I've seen that van before."

Funny how five words could change everything. One minute Kyle and his dad and Kirby sat in the parked truck, staring at the old Union Depot, the home of the art institute, waiting for his mother to emerge. The next moment his father had barreled out of the truck, running full-out for his mother.

There'd been ten minutes of waiting between when Kyle spotted the white van and the moment Noelle appeared, ten minutes of eternal frustration as he had called his office in Deep Haven. As they'd run the plate on the van for him.

They'd confirmed Hugh Fadden as the owner.

Then there was the casual drive-by. The man had a wide face, chin-length brown hair, a red baseball hat.

Same guy Kyle had seen outside Billy Nickel's house.

Add to that the woman seated beside him, her shocking red hair messy around her face. So there you went, Yvonne.

As the van drove by, the pair inside didn't even blink away from watching the door of the art institute, not unlike what they'd been doing since Noelle went inside.

When she appeared, Eli leaped from the truck. Then a shot rang out and the next seconds were a blur as Kyle floored it out of the parking lot, hot after the van that had nearly mowed down his mom.

Somewhere in there, he also had a memory of his father's voice. *What is she doing at an art institute?*

He'd ask later, after he alerted the Duluth police to Hugh and the need for them to arrest the man, if not for attempted homicide, then for the way he plowed through Duluth traffic at a high rate of speed.

Too high, even for summer when the roads hadn't glazed over, when ice didn't crackle from the trees. Thankfully, the sun had risen and begun to bake away the danger. Still, Kyle fishtailed going around the corner at First Street.

Nearly hit a car.

Kirby grabbed the handle above his seat. "Don't kill us."

"Just hang on. I have to keep him in my sights until the locals find him." Deep Haven had patched him in to dispatch in Duluth, and he'd already alerted them to the cross streets. "I'm turning northwest onto Fourth Avenue."

Duluth, with its San Francisco–style steep streets, plunging to the lake below, could be lethal. Worse, the snowy street concealed potholes and black ice.

"He's cutting up the hill on Mesaba," Kyle said to dispatch, his stomach knotting. Instead of heading toward the highway, Hugh had opted for an escape toward the clogged Mall area.

Or not. "He cut off onto Skyline Parkway." The last thing they needed was for Hugh to race through tiny neighborhoods. Through school zones and pedestrian crosswalks.

Oh, he wanted to get his hands on this guy. Wanted to slam his fist into his face, to expel the memory of fear in his mother's expression.

"Where's our backup?" Kirby said, his voice tight.

Kyle almost hit another car as the truck spun wide. He straightened it, ignoring Kirby's comments from the backseat as Hugh now turned southeast on Eleventh Avenue, toward the knotted neighborhoods. "I'm just south of Chester Park, headed for Portland Square."

"Officers are on their way, Officer Hueston," said the female voice in his ear.

Not soon enough. The van nearly plowed into the oncoming cars at a four-way stop. Kyle hit the brakes, slid into the intersection, then pumped the gas when he missed a little sedan.

"The mom in that car just flipped you off."

"Kirby—put a sock in it."

"I'm just saying, don't kill us. Or anybody else."

"Don't you want to get this guy?"

"I wanna go back and see if Dad's okay! I think he shot him!"

Kyle glanced in the rearview mirror at Kirby. The kid wasn't kidding. "Are you sure?"

"I don't know, but it looked like he got hit."

Kyle bit back a word. Watched as the van turned onto Fourth Street.

Sirens sounded in the distance, too far off yet to be of any help. He tapped his brakes. *God, please, make me smart. Help me not to make a stupid mistake.*

Hugh turned southeast toward the lake on Nineteenth.

Kyle kept going through the green light.

"What are you doing?"

"I thought you wanted me to pull back."

"Not let him go!"

"I'm not letting him go," he said to Kirby. "I'm trying to stay ahead of him. If he thinks he's being chased, he's only going to get someone killed. But more than that—" he turned southeast on Twenty-First—"Nineteenth Avenue is torn up with road construction."

He cut onto Third Street, a one-way. "Please, please." He gave his location to dispatch.

Ahead, the street hadn't been plowed, evidence of the stall in road repairs. Ice hooded the cars parked before ornate Craftsman houses, still tucked into the snow.

He slowed just enough to brake for pedestrians.

"I see him!" Kirby said.

Indeed—the van had barreled through the orange construction signs and skidded into a hole of road carnage, its wheels spinning in mud as the driver gunned it.

Kyle pulled into the intersection, threw the truck into park. "Wait here." He jumped out.

Hugh must have seen him coming because he opened his door and flew out.

Kyle leaped on him, tackling him into the mud. "Oh no you don't!"

Hugh flung an elbow at him, but Kyle dodged it, grabbed his arm. He slammed Hugh's face into the dirt with an arm bar, his knee powering into the man's spine.

"Get off me!"

"Sorry, dude, but you're under arrest."

Hugh struggled beneath him. "Says who—you're not a cop."

"Yeah, actually, he is." Kirby hadn't stayed put, clearly, and in fact had made his own collar. He had Yvonne by the arm.

She was crying, red-faced, shaking. "It was all Hugh's idea! He followed that lady down here! And he was the one who killed Billy and that clerk at the store. It was him! Not me!"

So now she was willing to talk.

"Good catch, Kirby."

He expected a grin, but Kirby's mouth tightened as cruisers appeared on the scene. A couple of uniforms jumped out and Kyle identified himself as they took Hugh into custody.

Yvonne had a few words of protest when they slapped cuffs on her also. Apparently she'd been an innocent bystander.

Kyle briefed the officers and then found Kirby sitting in the cab, his cell phone pressed to his ear. He slid into the seat. "What?"

Kirby shook his head. "Dad's at St. Luke's. He's in surgery."

&

Two bowls of Lucky Charms, a half-eaten bag of popcorn, and nine Hershey's Kisses left over from the Valentine's heart Emma's mother had sent her hadn't driven Kyle's voice from her mind.

Has it occurred to you that God didn't want you to live Kelsey's dreams? That yours were perfectly acceptable to Him?

She sat on her bed, cross-legged, Kelsey's lyric book open to the last song. She'd spent most of the night and some of this morning reading through the lyrics.

Remembering.

Hearing Kelsey's laughter, her voice. But also hearing her own, listening to her own dreams.

Kyle had nailed it exactly. It did hurt to remember. But he'd also shown her the sweet memories collected in Deep Haven. Bittersweet, in total. Especially the dreams, however simple, of raising a family in her small town.

If God wanted Kelsey to live her dreams, then Kelsey would have lived.

Brutal, his words felt upon her heart. Even more brutal the betrayal on his face when he realized that she hadn't told him about his father and her mother.

Why not? Fear, maybe. Or maybe, like in every other part of her life, she thought if she could run from it, it didn't exist. If she kept herself busy pursuing Kelsey's future, she wouldn't have to stop. Turn around.

Deal with the debris.

Let God heal her.

She strummed her guitar, looking at Kelsey's song—no, *Emma's* song. She sang the words, softly.

"There are wishes on shooting stars that finally come true . . .

For you.

The sunshine always comes in the morning.

Let the storm pass on by.

Don't let the night leave you blind.

Leave it all behind . . ."

The words left an eerie echo inside. As if Kelsey had known. Or perhaps she was simply writing about the everyday angst of a teenager. But suddenly the words seemed to unlock, spill out over Emma. She *had* been caught in the night. Had been blinded.

Had stopped looking for the morning star.

She could never get very far from the fight she'd had with Kyle, back when she'd been escaping Deep Haven. When he'd accused her of wanting to ignore the memories rather than believe that God could fix them.

Maybe it was easier to walk alone in her pain than to share it.

Or maybe . . . She remembered Kyle's face last night when she'd launched herself into his arms after the audition. Pride. Joy. Sharing her triumph with her.

Perhaps sharing the pain *would* ease it.

Especially if she shared it with God.

But words . . . she had none. She bowed her head, letting her fingers strum out the tune in her heart. A minor, an octave change, a lick back down to E major. She liked the lick. It felt like something of a catharsis.

She started again with A minor, strumming a blues pattern. The words formed in her chest, born of the tune.

God, I don't want to spend my life running. Or ignoring all the good things You've given me.

She added the B7, did an E string bend, climbed up the pentatonic blues scale, then down the frets.

Like my family. Kelsey. My dad.

Her throat tightened. She played the minor scale in A, held it at the B string, the long moan of her heart.

Kyle.

She added a swing beat, a few jazz tones. Moving into the sound. She imagined Kyle, his head bobbing as he added his finesse on the drums.

What a surprise he'd been.

She threw in another B7 chord, then an E9, and then an F-sharp 9 for a turnaround back into the main beat.

Oh, how she loved him.

The thought caught her, stilled her hand on a C-sharp minor 7, a high, almost-tenuous chord.

She loved him?

The chord faded into the walls of her room. Yes, she loved him. Not the high school fan crush but the kind of love that might make a girl want to face her inadequacies, her fears. She loved him because he *knew*—he knew that she was running, and he'd gently urged her back to a world she'd longed for. She loved him because he wouldn't give up on her.

Or hadn't, until she'd betrayed him.

But perhaps . . . What had he said about making mistakes, over and over, letting God love you anyway?

She finished the song with another pentatonic blues, fast, landed on the E9, then down to an F diminished, adding a hint of tension before she popped it out for a final lick down to the E. A power chord.

She strummed it, looking out the window at the sky, the sun making an appearance, finally, after last night's rain.

Lord, I want to turn around, to see the memories. To let You heal me. I don't want to live Kelsey's dreams. Or even mine. I want to live Your dreams for me.

God's dreams for her.

Yeah, that seemed like an answer she might be able to settle into, embrace. Find the music, even the words to.

She glanced at Kelsey's unfinished lyrics, words stirring in her head.

Don't let the night leave you blind . . .

"Emma! You have a phone call." Carrie poked her head in the

door. She wore a towel, her purple hair dripping. "You left your cell phone in your bag."

"Sorry."

"I think it's the guy from Nashville."

Emma took the phone. "Hello?"

"Emma. Glad I caught you. It's Brenton O'Hare. Listen, I'm sitting here in the studio with my guys, listening to your demo, and it just keeps getting better. You've got real talent, and we need you to come down here. How soon can you get on an airplane?"

Real talent?

"I . . . I don't know. I don't have money for a ticket."

"I'll get you a ticket. How about today, this afternoon? There's a flight leaving Minneapolis around five."

"I . . . uh . . ."

Carrie had returned to the door, wearing a bathrobe now, towel drying her hair. "Whatever it is, say yes!"

"I guess so."

"Perfect. You're the voice we've been waiting for, Emma. Can't wait to see you. I'll e-mail you your ticket info as soon as we get it booked."

She hung up, stared at Carrie. "I'm going to Nashville."

Carrie threw her towel in the air, then threw her arms around Emma. "I knew you could do it!"

Emma grinned. "Yeah, well . . . I couldn't have done it without Kyle." She opened her closet, pulled out her carry-on, dropped it onto the bed.

Next to the suitcase, her phone vibrated again.

Carrie picked it up. "Well, it seems Kyle thinks so too." She held up the phone to show her the display. "It's Deep Haven calling."

He'd been here before. Eli recognized it at once, hated it, wanted to recoil out of the memory, but it pushed him forward as if there were hands on his back.

Again he found himself standing outside the Lucky 7 convenience store, hearing the sirens, the lifeless body of Parker Swenson bloody on the concrete.

He'd seen that kid earlier—had stopped him, warned him, let him drive on into Deep Haven.

Officer Clay Nelson lay at the door. Eli had to move him to get inside. He knelt beside Clay and rolled him over. He'd been shot, his chest wound too awful, probably fatal. Clay gasped for air.

Eli let go a curse, shoved his hand against the wound in Clay's chest, not caring that the hot blood spilled between his fingers.

"Hang in there, buddy. Help's coming." He radioed in the report of an officer down at the scene, just as Clay gripped his wrist.

"Kelsey."

Eli's world stopped at her name. He met Clay's eyes, saw in them too much. No—no. Kelsey wasn't supposed to be working today—she'd gone to Duluth with Noelle. *No!*

"Daddy?" The voice rang out from someplace he couldn't see. "Daddy, are you here?"

He stood, scanned the store. *Please, let her be okay, hiding behind the counter or in the cooler.* "Baby, I'm here—"

And then he saw the blood puddling under the bread stand, her legs crumpled where she fell.

Oh, please, Lord. He ran, jerked the bread rack out of the way, letting it crash to the floor as he knelt beside her. She'd been shot once in the back, a through and through that tore open her chest, and again in the leg. He whipped off his belt, wrapped a tourniquet around her leg. Turned her onto her back. She cried out.

"Honey, it's going to be okay." But he couldn't possibly be reassuring, the way his words cut out around his jagged breath.

His sweet daughter stared up at him, her blue-green eyes watching him, fear in them.

God, please make me strong. For Kelsey.

"Oh, Kels . . ." He closed his mouth, lest he betray his own fear. Swallowed. "Help is on the way. It's gonna be here." He pulled off his jacket, put it under her head, pressed his hand to her chest wound.

She flopped her arm over herself and settled her hand over his. "I tried to run away, Daddy, but . . ." Blood trickled out of her mouth, and he ran his thumb over it to clear it away. He was shaking, his breath thick.

God, please, where are You? Please, send help—please!

"Oh, honey, you were so brave. You called the police."

"Emma's dad—he . . . he shot Emma's dad."

"Shh." He was on both knees now, sliding his hand under her. Maybe he could prop her against him, stop the bleeding in her back. She groaned, crying out as he found the wound.

"I'm sorry, Kelsey. I'm sorry. I'm just trying to stop your bleeding." There was so much blood, it saturated his uniform, dripped down his arms.

She stared up at him with those beautiful eyes that could make him say yes to nearly anything. His eyes burned, and he gritted his teeth. "Hang in there, Kelsey."

She gulped a breath, another, labored. Then, a look of surprise. "Oh . . . oh, Daddy. I . . . It doesn't hurt anymore."

He shook his head. "Kelsey, you just stay with me now. Your mom, your brothers, we need you." His voice strained, and he fought to control his breath.

Her hand upon his had begun to loosen. He grabbed it back, and blood spurted from her chest. "Now, Kelsey, you look at me. Look at Daddy. Like that, yeah."

He had her eyes again, but it seemed she wasn't looking at him, not really. She was smiling. "I can hear it. Wow, Daddy—what is it? Can you hear it?"

"What do you hear, baby?" He could hear sirens, his heartbeat rushing through him, the sound of his wail inside.

"Music. Oh, it's beautiful—it's so . . ." She came back to him then, for a moment. "Daddy, it's joy. I can hear the joy." Her eyes started to close.

"No, Kelsey, don't—*Kels*! Please . . ." He was unraveling; he knew it as his daughter faded into herself, that smile still tipping her lips.

"No! God, no—not Kels—Kelsey!" He was shouting now. "Don't you leave us. Don't you leave me!"

"Eli, move aside." Ellie Matthews crouched beside him, her light-brown hair pulled back, shooting out the back of her blue EMT cap. She put down her first response bag. "Let me in there."

He scooted back and Ellie stepped in. Kelsey had paled, her breaths so shallow he could barely make them out. He held up his hands. They shook, blood dripping off them.

Five feet away, Joe Michaels was administering CPR on Clay while Dan fed something into his vein.

Eli looked at his hands. At Kelsey.

And for a brief second, everything stopped. Went silent. Ellie slapped on an oxygen mask while her partner shoved padding into Kelsey's wounds. But he couldn't hear them, couldn't feel it.

No. Because in that moment, he too heard the music. Singing or maybe just instruments. Yes, instruments, but voices too. They flowed through him, filling him, capturing him.

Holding him together.

Yes, Kelsey, I hear the joy.

"We're losing him." The noise returned, only he was no longer kneeling in Kelsey's blood, no longer watching it drip from his hands. No longer at the Lucky 7.

He lay on the table, doctors bending over him. "He's in V-tach."

I'm sorry, Noelle. I'm so, so sorry.

20

Two cops and a preacher sat in the waiting room of St. Luke's surgical unit when Kyle returned from his search of vending machines.

This did not bode well.

He'd always feared that someday he'd come home from school to the appearance of two of Deep Haven's finest, along with Pastor Dan, sitting in his living room. In fact, whenever he spotted a cruiser in his driveway, a fist of tension tightened around his chest until he walked into the kitchen, spied his dad seated at the table, eating an apple or reading the paper.

Alive.

But his father wasn't sitting in the waiting room. He'd been in surgery for the better part of three hours. Kyle's mother had disappeared, although Kyle guessed that she'd gone in search of a chapel.

He'd been praying too. Because as he'd sat in the waiting room, Kelsey's song echoing in his head, he realized . . .

He'd found God in the rain. In the helpless place. In the cry of his heart.

In the chaos and randomness of life.

He could trust God and His unfailing love to comfort and heal and restore, even when it felt like everything had turned dark.

Earlier, sitting in the waiting room, his mother holding Kirby's hand, holding Kyle's—it felt like they had become more of a family again than they had been in years. Even without her memory.

"We'll get through this," his mother had said. "Together."

Together.

Maybe that meant the family of Deep Haven also, because as Dan stood to shake his hand, Kyle noticed that Ellie, Dan's wife, sat beside him. Sitting in the chairs opposite, his friends Jason and Sammy, looking like someone had pulled him out of bed. And Joe Michaels—he and Dad had been friends since nearly the day Joe pulled into town, when Joe had been accused of sabotaging the Footstep of Heaven bookstore. And basketball coach Seb Brewster sat with his fiancée, Lucy, who had brought cupcakes, evidenced by the open box of goodies on the table.

Seb had his arm around Kirby.

"Did the doctor come out yet?" Kyle said.

"A nurse came out, said he was still in surgery. There'd been a few complications."

Kyle let those words sink in, glad he hadn't yet opened his Cheetos. "Did my mom come back?"

Dan shook his head.

Kyle sat down on the heating grate, glad his pants had finally dried from his takedown of Hugh. The department had given him time to check in at the hospital, to find out the status of his father before they took his statement.

"A van matching this description was seen at two liquor store robberies this weekend," one of the officers had told him as Kyle described his leads on the Mocha Moose case.

It helped that Yvonne gave a full confession of how Billy and Hugh had come back from the casino with empty pockets, spied opportunity at the Mocha Moose. How Hugh suspected Billy had betrayed him to Kyle and killed him for his silence. How Yvonne had waited in the car, terrified, kidnapped—she called it—as Hugh pawned Billy's ring.

How they'd waited outside the school, after the game, for Noelle, followed her to Duluth, looking for an opportunity to force her off the road. Only the icy conditions and fear for their own safety kept Noelle alive until the next morning.

And his father's instincts.

Or perhaps the instincts of father and son.

That felt good. Working together with his father.

Please, God, let Dad live so I can keep learning from my old man.

Kyle kept checking his phone. Emma had said she'd call him from the airport.

Nashville had called. He let that thought spread heat through his chest. That, and the way Emma had greeted him when he'd talked to her.

As if he hadn't been a jerk. As if she could look past that horrible moment when he'd dumped her on the sidewalk outside her apartment and hit the road. As if she could remember, instead, the moments when he'd been the man he'd wanted to be.

"Of course I forgive you," he said to her apology. "My dad and I had a huge talk last night when we met in Duluth. He said the whole thing was his fault, that he'd been over there at your mom's, being her friend. He said he never meant it to get out of hand. He was feeling pretty bad."

"I talked to my mom, too. She said the same thing—it was her fault for leaning on him too much. For being afraid of being alone, for believing she'd been abandoned. I'm not sure what that last part meant but she said she was going to put moving on hold for a while. Especially since she likes how she fixed up the house."

He'd found a corner in the hospital where he couldn't be overheard. "Emma, I know this is a huge opportunity for you, and I just want to say that I . . . I'm totally behind you going to Nashville."

He heard silence and couldn't read it.

"So you want me to go to Nashville?"

Something about her voice . . . "Of course I do. It's amazing and wonderful. I'm so proud of you."

"Oh."

Again, that texture—almost disappointment? Maybe he'd read this all wrong. "I was thinking that if it worked out, uh . . ." He blew out a breath, cupped his hand behind his head, smiled at a nurse walking by. "I could come down there. Visit. Or . . . well, they probably need cops in Nashville, too."

Her breath caught. "Really?"

Now that was more like it. "Yeah, really. I mean . . . oh, Ems, I'm just crazy about you. I am so sorry I tried to talk you into moving to Deep Haven. I should have said I would follow you wherever you want to go. Because that's the truth. Nashville, California, Mars. I'm good."

"I'm not sure they need peace enforcement on Mars."

"Trust me on that one. Definitely Mars." He softened his voice. "Blue Monkey, we'll make a little Deep Haven wherever we live."

She had giggled then, and it uncoiled the pain in his chest. "I'll call you from the airport."

He looked again at his phone now. No call, no text.

He felt Kirby's gaze on him. Offered a smile.

Kirby rolled his eyes.

But hallelujah, the phone vibrated in his grip. "Emma!"

Her voice could turn any dark day to pure light. "Hey! Sorry it took so long."

"Are you all set? Did you get your ticket? Are you through security?"

"I've got everything under control here, Officer. Nearly arriving at my destination."

"I thought the flight didn't leave for two more hours."

"I'm not going to Nashville. Look up."

He froze. Looked down the hall.

Emma. She wore a green trench coat, a light-blue beret, her guitar in its padded case over her shoulder. She lifted her phone and waved.

Kyle didn't care that the entire town watched him as he sprinted down the hall. He threw his arms around her, captured by the way she curled hers around his neck. Oh, she smelled good—apples and cinnamon and chocolate and surprise.

"What are you doing here?" He let her go. Grinning.

"You mean that in the best of ways, right?"

"Are you kidding me? I'm . . . I'm beyond words."

"Then show me." She smiled, winked.

So he kissed her, sweetly, because the town was watching. But enough to make it clear.

"I'm convinced," she said quietly, her eyes sparkling.

"But . . . what about Nashville?" He shook his head. "Babe, you should be on a flight for Tennessee."

"I called Brenton and told them that if I was the superstar they wanted, they'd have to wait for me."

"But—"

"Nashville can wait. Your dad can't. I'm here because I belong here." She looked past him toward the cluster of Deep Havenites. "With them." She cupped her hand on his cheek. "With you."

"I couldn't agree more," he said, sliding his hand up to hers. "You brought your guitar."

She wound her fingers through his. "I wanted to sing you a song I wrote. Or maybe a song I finished. Finally."

&

After she'd visited the chapel, left her prayers there, Noelle found herself in the maternity ward, staring at the babies.

Little packages of joy. She watched their eyes blink, their little mouths curve open in a yawn, before they settled back into the embrace of sleep.

She'd wanted one—or more—of these. Had dreamed about holding a baby, smelling innocence on his or her skin, curling the child to her breast.

She'd dreamed about watching that child grow up, fling his or her tiny body into her embrace, curl chubby arms around her neck. She pressed her hand to the glass. *God, I wanted this.*

After two hours on her knees praying for Eli, her sons, for their lives, for their pasts, it seemed natural that the Almighty might appear, breathe truth into her.

You had this.

Yes. She had. But she couldn't remember it.

Or . . .

She closed her eyes and something fleeting appeared, like a child playing hide-and-seek behind a curtain. She saw it, and then it vanished. A smile. A tiny hand wrapped around hers. A smell. Powder and a fresh bath. She heard a giggle. High-pitched. Joyous.

She opened her eyes. Around her, the bustle of the maternity ward told her that nothing had changed, but she felt different.

Less alone.

As she was leaving the ward, she spotted a plaque by the door. A photograph of a tiny hand, that of a preemie, wrapped around a finger. The words at the bottom threaded through her.

"Can a mother forget her nursing child? Can she feel no love for the child she has borne? But even if that were possible, I would not forget you! See, I have written your name on the palms of my hands."

She stared at the photo, repeating the words, wanting to fit her hand around the finger.

Kelsey was written on her heart; she knew it. And God knew it. Noelle would just have to trust Him to bring her back.

She exited the maternity ward and found her way to the surgical waiting room. The nurses at the desk had given her a pager, and of course she had her phone, but Kyle hadn't called.

She'd changed, finding one of Eli's shirts in the tangle of clothes she'd thrown into the suitcase in her dash from their house. There had been so much blood.

Why hadn't she simply believed in him, waited for him?

Instead she'd run off to Duluth to find a piece of her that didn't seem to fit anymore. Or maybe it did, just not the way she'd intended before her accident. The entire meeting with Eric made her feel as if she might have been running away.

She should have been running toward.

She should have never hidden her desire to attend school. She shouldn't have let Eli hide out at that ice house or lose himself in his garage. At the very least, she should have gone with him.

Instead of caving in on herself. By herself.

How had they expected to survive grief alone when they were supposed to bear it together? No wonder they'd been frail, their marriage breakable.

She bore half the blame for letting it become fragile in the first place.

Not anymore. She intended to enlarge the picture she'd painted of their hands, to put it in their family room. The Hueston five, one member already home.

She clasped Eli's shirt around her, breathing in his musky smell as she headed down the hall to the waiting room. Music, a sweet voice, lifted, ribboning down the hall.

"There are broken rainbow moments,
And dandelion wishes that don't come true . . ."

The voice sounded familiar. Not Kelsey, or maybe . . .

Another memory brushed her, this one clearer, fresh, as if it had just happened. The hallway around her flickered away and she saw in her mind's eye a young woman sitting on the beach, her guitar on her knee.

"There are wishes on shooting stars that finally come true . . .
For you."

The waves of the lake caressing the shore. It shimmered, deep blue in the sunlight, turning her hair to gold.

"Don't let the night leave you blind.
　　Leave it all behind . . .
　　He's there for you."

She looked up, eyes so blue-green they took Noelle's breath.

"The star will come in the morning.
　　Believe it's true . . ."

She wanted to reach out, touch her, wrap her in her arms, hold her. The girl looked at her and smiled.

"'Cause I'll be waiting there . . .
　　For you."

She let the last notes linger, staring at Noelle, nodding as the music faded.

Kelsey, don't go—

Noelle was standing in the hallway still, tears running down her face.

"Mom?"

Kyle appeared. Blessed Kyle. He'd looked triumphant, albeit rough around the edges, when he showed up at the hospital. "Did you remember something?"

She stood there, breathed in the fragrance around her. Cottony, with a hint of lilac. Just like Kelsey's blanket. Perhaps . . .

"Yes. I think I did."

"I knew you would." He took a step toward her. "Mom, I want you to meet my friend Emma."

The pretty girl holding Kyle's hand, petite, with brown hair under a blue beret and shining eyes—this girl she didn't know. But she wanted to. In fact, even as she held out her hand, smiled at her, a warmth filled Noelle's chest—a peace, a familiarity, a joy.

"Emma Nelson. I . . . I was friends with Kelsey."

Noelle glanced at Kyle's hand, woven into Emma's. "And my son, I see."

Kyle grinned at her. Then at Emma. There was something in his grin, the way he looked at this girl, that seemed so . . . right.

"The nurse just came out, told us Dad was out of surgery. The doctor is on his way."

Oh, thank You, Lord.

Kyle looked past her then, and she turned. The gray-haired doctor introduced himself as "Robert Mitchell, chief of surgery." He wore blue scrubs, a puffy blue hat. "Eli is stubborn, and although his heart tried to give out, he fought back. We had him out in recovery earlier, but we had to take him back in, so we monitored him for a bit and now he's awake. And he's asking for his wife."

"That's me," Noelle said, glancing at Kyle. She took his free hand, then reached for Kirby's. "I'll be back as soon as I can." She met their eyes, squeezing their hands. "Together, boys. We'll get through this together."

She followed Dr. Mitchell down the hallway into a recovery room filled with beds, pink and blue curtains hanging between them.

Eli lay on a bed, slightly propped up, tubes running from his chest, his arms, an oxygen mask over his mouth.

He saw her and smiled.

It was the smile that undid her. He looked at her the way Kyle had just looked at Emma. Like she gave him a reason to live.

And that too felt familiar.

She moved toward him, took his hand. "We gotta stop meeting like this."

He pulled his oxygen mask to the side, his eyes tired but teasing. "Who are you?"

"You're real cute."

His smile dimmed. "Are you okay?"

"Are you serious? You jumped in front of a bullet for me, Eli. You saved me."

"Of course I did. I'm your husband."

Oh. Yes, he was. She didn't need a declaration of love yet, but—

"I love you, Noelle. I've always loved you, but . . . I know I blew it. If you'll let me, I'll try to help you remember our life and why it worked, and fix the things that didn't. Marry me again, and let me be the husband you deserve."

"I don't know."

"Oh." She heard surprise, even disappointment, in his tone.

Noelle leaned close to him. "I'm already married to this guy I'm crazy about. He's a little old for me, but I think he's exactly the guy I've always wanted to be married to. So, you see, I'm taken."

She touched his hand to her face. He opened it, pressed it against her cheek.

"I'm sorry I didn't tell you about the art institute."

"I'm sorry you had to hide it from me."

"I think we were hiding a lot from each other."

He drew in a breath.

"Like ourselves," she said, meeting his eyes. "I forgive you for Lee."

"Thank you."

"If you forgive me for . . . Eric."

He raised an eyebrow.

"It's nothing like that. It's just . . . well, I don't think another man should know more about my life and my dreams than my husband."

He nodded. "Your husband is going to start listening to them. Noelle, if you want to go to art school, I'm right behind you. We can sell the house, move to Duluth. I'll figure out something to do."

"I was thinking you might teach me how to fish."

"You don't like fishing."

"Really? I don't remember that." She winked at him. "Nor do I remember how to cut hair, but I am not married to a hippie. We're tackling your curls the moment we get home."

"You're frightening me a little," he said as he drew her hand to his chest. His smile dimmed. "Do you think you'll ever really remember me? Or our family? Kelsey?"

"I know I will. I already have, I think. But you know, Eli, I never did forget you." She leaned close to him, her lips a breath from his face, kissing him in his favorite spot, in the pocket right below his eye. "In the back of my mind, I always remembered—and always loved—the shadow of your smile."

A Note from the Author

EVER LOOK BACK on your life and think, *What happened?* I know I do. Where is the woman who wanted to work in a New York ad agency? Where is the runner, the outdoor enthusiast, the girl who wanted to own a ranch in Colorado? (I clearly had mixed goals!) Oh, wait, she married this cute guy who wooed her from the back of his motorcycle and whisked her off to be a missionary in Russia. Then she had these four kids. And then she started writing books (and spending a lot of time in her office rather than outside!). I'm not complaining—I love my life. But looking back, twenty-two years ago I couldn't have imagined being where I am today.

What if you could reset your life? Would you do the same things? And what parts of your life would you keep . . . or cut out? These were the questions that hounded me as I began to write *The Shadow of Your Smile.* I read an article about a man who had fallen and lost his memory of the past twenty-five years, and from his story I launched my own exploration into the what-ifs of starting over. It also happened to be my daughter's senior year of high school, and watching her prepare to be on her own, while exciting, also strummed sorrow in my heart. I will miss her. I let my imagination wander into dark places a bit and wondered how, if anything should happen to her, I might go on without her. I've met women who have lost their children, and their wounds are deep and abiding. I myself have lost four children to miscarriage. That dark place of grief made me wonder—would it be better to start over, or would the joy of the memories be worth the pain?

Maybe our grief comes not from the loss of a child, but from a different loss, a regret, a mistake . . . anything that has wounded us so deeply we long to erase it all. But we can't erase it, so what do we do?

That question drove me to Psalm 13: "How long must I struggle with anguish in my soul, with sorrow in my heart every day? . . . But I trust in your unfailing love. I will rejoice because you have rescued me. I will sing to the Lord because he is good to me."

What does it mean to have the Lord be good to us—especially with our open wounds? I think the answer lies in this passage also: because of God's unfailing love for us, because He has rescued us from death, we have hope.

One of my favorite verses is Romans 15:13: "I pray that God, the source of hope, will fill you completely with joy and peace because you trust in him. Then you will overflow with confident hope through the power of the Holy Spirit." Our job is to trust. God's job is to overflow us with joy.

That's hard to imagine when we're sitting in dark places. I know—I've been there. If you've read any of my other books, you'll find some of my stories in the author's notes. But even in those dark places, I think hope is found in something Noelle discovered: "Maybe the key to going forward with her life was simply being grateful for it." Being grateful for all we have, grateful for all we will have, grateful for the unfailing love of God—this is the foundation of hope.

Psalm 16 says, "Apart from you, I have no good thing." This is the one thing I hope to never forget. This is the one thing that I take with me into the future. I have God. I have good things.

I hope you've been encouraged by the power of love through Noelle and Eli's story. There are new beginnings even for "worn-out" marriages. There is hope because of God's unfailing love.

In His grace,
Susan May Warren

About the Author

SUSAN MAY WARREN is the RITA Award–winning author of more than thirty novels whose compelling plots and unforgettable characters have won acclaim with readers and reviewers alike. She served with her husband and four children as a missionary in Russia for eight years before she and her family returned home to the States. She now writes full-time as her husband runs a lodge on Lake Superior in northern Minnesota, where many of her books are set. She and her family enjoy hiking, canoeing, and being involved in their local church.

Susan holds a BA in mass communications from the University of Minnesota. Several of her critically acclaimed novels have been chosen as Top Picks by *Romantic Times* and won the RWA's Inspirational Reader's Choice contest and the American Christian Fiction Writers Book of the Year award. Four of her books have been Christy Award finalists. In addition to her writing, Susan loves to teach and speak at women's events about God's amazing grace in our lives.

For exciting updates on her new releases, previous books, and more, visit her website at www.susanmaywarren.com.

Discussion Questions

1. At the beginning of the story, we see Noelle Hueston heading home on snowy roads after doing something she doesn't want her husband to know about. What is it and why does she keep it from him? Have you ever kept a secret like this from someone you love? Why, and how did it affect your relationship?

2. We first meet Eli Hueston as he's fishing in his ice house. What does he believe about his marriage as the story opens? What factors have contributed to this situation? Have you ever been in a place where you felt like Eli does?

3. Noelle wakes up from her accident having lost her memory of the past twenty-five years. When she sees Eli, what does she think about him? What is her reaction to the fact that he is her husband and that she has children? What would you have done if you found yourself in her situation?

4. When Noelle returns home, she discovers that her life has turned out differently than she expected. What dreams did you have as a younger person that turned out vastly different? What dreams came true?

5. Eli can't believe his wife has forgotten him—and their family—and makes a radical decision to keep information from her. What information does he hide? Why? Given his situation, do you agree or disagree with this decision?

6. When Noelle returns home, she begins to "sense" her daughter without knowing it. What are some examples of this? Do you think it's possible for a parent to truly forget his or her child?

7. Why doesn't Emma want to live in Deep Haven? Have you ever been afraid or reluctant to return somewhere? Where and why?

8. Kyle Hueston started out with dreams of being a sports star but changed his plans to become a cop like his father. Why does he want to be a small-town cop, and what are some of the challenges Eli talks to him about? Do you agree with his concerns?

9. Why does Eli spend so much time with Lee? Do you think they crossed lines they shouldn't have even before the surprising moment in the art studio? Do you believe what they did constituted an affair? Why or why not?

10. Do you think Emma should have told Kyle about what she knew about Lee and Eli? What would you have done in her situation?

11. After the blowup at the basketball game, what does Lee finally realize about how she's handled her grief? What part did she play in her relationship with Eli? How do you think things will change for Lee after her conversation with Liza?

12. What realization does Eli have that allows him to rekindle his marriage? Likewise, what realization prompts Noelle to try to make their marriage work?

13. Have you ever longed to forget something in your past? Would you be willing to forget *everything* in order to forget that one thing?

14. How have you seen God come to your rescue despite difficult circumstances you have faced?

Her perfect romance, right next door . . .

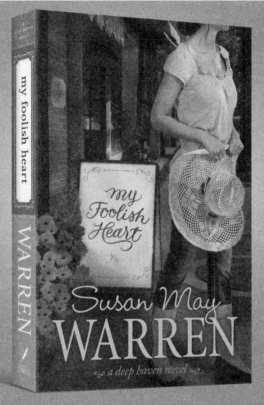

A story of first impressions and second chances, *My Foolish Heart* demonstrates the power of love to break us free from prisons of our own making.

Please turn the page for a preview.

FOR TWO HOURS A NIGHT, Monday through Saturday, Isadora
Presley became the girl she'd lost.

"Welcome to *My Foolish Heart*, where we believe your perfect
love might be right next door. We want to send special greetings
out to KDRT in Seattle, brand-new to the Late Night Lovelorn
Network. BrokenheartedInBuffalo, you're on the line. Welcome
to the program."

Outside the second-story window of her home studio, the
night crackled open with a white flash of light and revealed the
scrawny arms of her Japanese plum, cowering under a summer
gale. Issy checked the clock. Hopefully the storm would hold off
for the rest of her show, another thirty minutes.

And the weather had better clear by tomorrow's annual Deep

Haven Fisherman's Picnic. She couldn't wait to sit on her front porch, watch the midnight fireworks over the harbor as the Elks launched them from the campground, and pretend that life hadn't forgotten her.

Tomorrow, she'd watch the parade from her corner of the block, wave to her classmates on their annual float as they made their way toward Main Street, then linger on the porch listening to the live music drift up from the park. Maybe she'd even be able to hear the cheers from the annual log-rolling competition. She could nearly taste the tangy sweetness of a fish burger—fresh walleye and homemade tartar sauce. Kathy would be pouring coffee in the Java Cup outpost. And just a block away, the crispy, fried-oil tang of donuts nearly had the power to lure her to Lucy's place, World's Best Donuts. She'd stand in the line that invariably twined out the door, around the corner, and past the realty office waiting for a glazed raised.

She'd never, not once in her first twenty-five years, missed Fish Pic. Until two years ago.

She'd missed everything since then. She swallowed down the tightening in her chest.

"Thank you for taking my call, Miss Foolish Heart. I just wanted to say that I listen to your show every night and that it's helped me wait for the perfect man."

BrokenheartedInBuffalo had a high, sweet voice, the kind that might belong to a college coed with straight blonde hair, blue eyes. But the radio could mask age, race, even gender. Truly, when Issy listened to her podcasts, sometimes she didn't recognize her own voice, the way it softened with compassion, turning low and husky as she counseled listeners.

She could almost trick herself into believing she knew what she was doing. Trick herself into believing that she lived a different life, one beyond the four walls and garden of her home.

"I'm so glad, Brokenhearted. He's out there. What can I do for you tonight?"

"Well, I think I found him. We met a few weeks ago in a karate class, and we've already had three dates—"

"Three? Brokenhearted, I know that you're probably smitten, but three dates isn't enough to know a man is perfect for you. A great relationship takes—"

"Time, trials, and trust. I know."

So Brokenhearted listened regularly. Good, then maybe Issy could slow her down, help her to part the heady rush of the "love fog"—another of her coined terms.

"Then you also know you don't develop that in three dates, although Miss Foolish Heart does advise calling it quits after three if there is no visible ten potential."

"But it feels like it. He's everything I want."

"How do you know that?"

"I have my top-ten list, just like you said. And of course, the big three."

"Big three essentials. Sounds like you know what you're looking for."

"That's just it—he has *most* of them, and I'm wondering if it's essential for him to have all of them. Isn't . . . let's say, seven out of ten enough?"

"You tell me, Brokenhearted—would you settle for a seven romance? Or do you want a ten?"

"What if I don't know what a ten feels like?"

What a ten feels like. Yes, Issy would like to know that too.

"Good question, Brokenhearted. I think it must be different

for everyone. Stay on the line and let's take some calls and see if anyone has a good answer. Or you can hop over to the forum at the *My Foolish Heart* website—I see that Cupid27 has posted a reply. 'Love feels as if nothing can touch you.' Nice, Cupid27. Any other callers?"

She muted Brokenhearted and clicked on another caller. "TruLuv, you're on the air. What does a ten feel like?"

A gravelly, low voice, the two-pack-a-day kind: "It's knowing you have someone to hold on to."

"Great response, TruLuv. Here's hoping you have someone to hold on to." She muted TruLuv. "Go ahead, WindyCity."

"It's knowing you're loved . . . anyway."

Loved, anyway. Oh, she wanted to believe that was possible. "Love that, WindyCity. Anyone else?"

The forum had come to life, replies piling up. On the phone lines, PrideAndPassion723 appeared. Pride called at least once a month, often with a new dilemma, and kept the forum boards lit up with conversations. Issy should probably give the girl a 1-800 number.

She clicked back to Brokenhearted. "Do any of those replies feel like what you feel?"

"Maybe. I don't know."

"Miss Foolish Heart suggests you hold out for the ten, Brokenhearted. The perfect one is out there, maybe right next door."

She went to a commercial break, an advertisement for a chocolate bouquet delivery, and pulled off her headphones, massaging her ears.

Outside, the rain hummed against the house, a steady battering with the occasional ping upon the sill, although now and again it roared, the wind rousing in anger. Hopefully she'd remembered to close the front windows before she went on the air. Lightning strobed again, and this time silver leaves stripped from the tree, splattered on the window. Oh, her bleeding heart just might be lying flat on the ground, after all the work she'd done to nurture it to life.

The commercial ended.

"I see we have PrideAndPassion on the line, hopefully with an update to her latest romance. Thanks for coming back, Pride. How are you tonight?"

She'd expected tears—or at the very least a mournful cry of how Pride had stalked her boyfriend into some restaurant, found him sharing a low-lit moment with some bimbo. Pride's escapades had become the backbone of the show, ratings spiking every time she called in.

"I'm engaged!"

Issy nearly didn't recognize her, not with the lift in her voice, the squeal at the end.

"Kyle popped the question! I did it, Miss Foolish Heart—I held out for true love, and last night he showed up on my doorstep with a ring!"

"Oh, that's . . . great, Pride." Issy battled the shock from her voice. No, not just shock. Even . . . okay, envy.

Once upon a time, she'd dreamed of finding the perfect man, dreamed of standing on the sidewalk at the Fisherman's Picnic with Lucy, hoping they might be asked to dance under the milky starlight of the August sky. But who had the courage to dance with the football coach's daughter? And as for Lucy, she simply couldn't put her courage together to say yes. Sweet, shy Lucy, she'd used up her courage on one boy.

It only took Lucy's broken heart their senior year to cement the truth: a girl had to have standards. She had to wait for the perfect love.

Issy had come up with the list then, refined it in college. A good, solid top-ten list, and most important, the big three must-have attributes in a man besides his Christian faith—*compassionate*, *responsible*, and *self-sacrificing*—the super evaluator that told her if she should say yes to a first date.

If any came around. Because she certainly couldn't go out looking for dates, could she?

"Oh, Pride, are you sure?" Silence on the other end. She hadn't exactly meant it to come out with that edge, almost disapproving. "I . . . just mean, is he a ten?"

"I'm tired of waiting for a ten, Miss Foolish Heart. I'm twenty-six years old and I want to get married. I don't want to be an old maid."

Twenty-six. Issy remembered twenty-six, a whole year ago. She'd celebrated her birthday with a jelly-filled bismark that Lucy brought over, and they'd sung ABBA at the top of their lungs.

And as a finale, Issy ventured out to her front steps. Waved to Cindy Myers next door, who happened to be out getting her mail.

Yes, a red-letter day, for sure.

"You're so young, Pride. Twenty-six isn't old."

"It feels old when everyone around you is getting married. I'm ready, and he asked, so I said yes."

Issy drew in a breath. "That's wonderful. We're all happy for you, right, forum?"

The forum, however, lit up with a vivid conversation about settling for anything less than a ten. See? Not a foolish heart among them.

"Good, because . . . I want you to come to the wedding, Miss

Foolish Heart. It's because of you that I found Kyle, and I want you to be there to celebrate with us."

Issy gave a slight chuckle over the air. High and short, it was a ripple of sound that resembled fear. Perfect. "I . . . Thank you for the kind offer, Pride, but—"

"You don't understand. This is going to be a huge wedding. I know we're not supposed to reveal our names on the air, but I am so grateful for your help that you need to know—my father is Gerard O'Grady."

"The governor of California?" Former actor–turned–billionaire–turned–politician?

"Yes." A giggle followed her voice. "We're already planning the wedding—it'll be at our estate in Napa Valley. I want you there, in the front row, with my parents. You've just helped me so much."

"Oh, uh, Pride—"

"Lauren. I'm Lauren O'Grady."

"Okay, Lauren. I'm so sorry, but I can't come."

"Why not?"

Why not? Because every time Issy ventured a block from her house, the world closed in and cut off her breathing? Because she couldn't erase from her brain the smell of her mother's burning flesh, her screams, the feel of hot blood on her hands? Because every time she even thought about getting into a car, she saw dots, broke out in a sweat?

Most of all, because she was still years away from breaking free of the panic attacks that held her hostage.

"Our station's policy is—"

"I'm sure my father could get your station to agree. Please, please don't say no. Just think about it. I'll send you an invitation."

And then she clicked off.

Seconds of dead air passed before Issy found the right voice. "Remember to visit the forum at the *My Foolish Heart* website. This is Miss Foolish Heart saying, your perfect love might be right next door." She disconnected just as Karen Carpenter's "Close to You" signaled the close of her show.

Yeah, sure. Once upon a time, she'd actually believed her tagline.

Once upon a time, she'd actually believed in Happily Ever After.

The next show came on—*The Bean*, a late-night sports show out of Chicago that scooped up the scores from the games around the nation. She had no control over what shows surrounded hers and was just glad that she had the right to control some of the ad content.

Stopping by the bathroom, she closed the window, grabbed a towel, and threw it on the subway tile floor, stepping on it with her bare foot. She paused by her parents' bedroom—it hadn't seen fresh air for two years, but she still opened the door, let her eyes graze the four-poster double bed, the Queen Anne bureau and dresser, the window that overlooked the garden.

For once, she left the door cracked, then descended the stairs. Front door locked, yes; the parlor windows shut.

Light sparked again across the night, brachials of white that spliced the blackness. It flickered long enough to illuminate the tiny library across the street and the recycle bin on its side, rolling as the wind kicked it down the sidewalk. A half block away, and down the hill toward town, the hanging stoplight suspended above the highway swayed. The storm had turned the intersection into a four-way stop, the red light blinking, bloody upon the glassy pavement.

She pulled a knit afghan off the sofa and wrapped it around herself, letting the fraying edges drag down the wooden floor to the

kitchen. Here, she switched on the light. It bathed the kitchen—
the spray of white hydrangeas in a milk glass vase on the round
white-and-black table, the black marble countertops, the black-
and-white checked floor. Part retro, part contemporary—her
mother's eclectic taste.

Thunder shook the house again, lifting the fine hairs on the
back of her neck. How she hated storms.

She snaked a hand out from the blanket, turned on the burner
under the teakettle. She'd left the last donut from her daily Lucy
delivery upstairs in her office. Her gaze flicked to the index card
pasted to the cupboard. *"If God is for us, who can ever be against us?"*
Indeed. But what if God wasn't exactly for you? Still, she wasn't
going to ignore help where she might get it.

Another gust of wind, and something tumbled across her back
porch—oh no, not her geraniums. Then, banging on her back
door. The glass shuddered.

Why her mother had elected to change out the perfectly good
solid oak doors for one solid pane of glass never made sense to her.

The kettle whistled. She turned the flame off, reached for a
mug—

A howl, and no, that wasn't the wind. It sounded . . . wounded.
Even afraid.

She swallowed her heart back into her chest. She knew that
kind of howl. Especially on a night like this.

Tucking her hand into her blanket, Issy moved to the door,
then locked it. She turned off the kitchen light and peered out
into the darkness.

No glowing eyes peering back at her, no snaggletoothed monster groping at her window. She flipped on the outside light. It
bathed the cedar porch, the cushions of her faded teak furniture

blowing in the wind, held only by their flimsy ties. Her potted geraniums lay toppled, black earth muddy and smeared across the porch, and at the bottom of the steps, the storm had flattened her bleeding heart bush.

At the very least, she should cover her mother's prized Pilgrim roses.

Issy dumped the afghan in a chair, rolled up her pant legs, grabbed a Windbreaker hanging in the closet near the door, and pulled the hood over her head.

Unbolting the door, she eased out into the rain. The air had a cool, slick breath, and it raised gooseflesh on her arms. The deluge had stirred to life the Scotch of her white pine, a grizzled sentry in the far corner, its shaggy arms gesturing danger.

But who would hurt her here, in her backyard? Not only that, but her father had built the Titanic of all fences, with sturdy pine boards that hemmed her in, kept the world out, with the exception of Lucy, who used it as a shortcut on her way to town.

It wasn't like Issy actually locked the gate. Okay, sometimes. Okay, always. But Lucy had a key to the gate as well as the house, so it didn't really matter.

Splashing down the stairs, she dashed across the wet flag-stones, past her dripping variegated hosta, the verbena, the hydrangea bush, too many of the buds stripped. The rugosa, too, lay in waste.

She wouldn't look. Not until tomorrow. Sometimes it worked better that way, to focus on what she could save. On what she still had.

Reaching the shed, she dialed the combination and opened it. She grabbed the plastic neatly folded on the rack by the door, scooped up two bricks, and dashed back to the porch. Rain couldn't quite smatter the roses here, under the overhang. Still, just in case . . . she weighted one end of the plastic with the bricks on the porch, then unfolded it over the flowers. Grabbing stones from the edging of her bed, she secured the tarp, then ran back to the shed for another pair of weights.

The howl tore through the rain again, reverberating through her.

She froze, her heart in her mouth.

Something moved. Over by the end of the porch.

The sky chose then to crack open and pour out its rage in a growl that lifted her feet from the earth.

And not only hers.

Whatever it was—she got only a glimpse—it came straight at her, like she might be prey. She screamed, dropped the bricks, and sprinted for the porch. Her foot slipped on the slick wood and she fell, hard. Her chin cracked against the wood, and then the animal pounced.

"No! Get away!" But it didn't maul her, didn't even stop. Just scrambled toward the door.

The pane of glass waterfalled onto the floor as the beast careened into her kitchen. Issy froze as the animal—huge and hairy—skidded across the linoleum.

It came to a stop, then lay there, whining.

A dog. A huge dog, with a face only a mother could love, eyes filled with terror, wet and muddy from its jowls down.

"Nice doggy . . . nice . . ."

Lightning must have illuminated her, and the animal simply panicked. It turned and shot off through her house. Toenails scratching her polished wood floors.

"Come back!"

In the front parlor, a crash—not the spider plant!

The dog emerged back out into the hall and shot up the stairs.

"No! C'mere, boy!" Issy's bare feet stopped her at the threshold. The glass glistened like ice on the floor. Perfect. "Don't break anything!"

She darted off the porch, around the path of the garden, opened the gate, and ran through the slippery grass to the front of the house.

Thumper the rabbit still hid the key, and now she retrieved it and inserted it into the door.

The squeal of rubber against wet pavement came from her memory—or perhaps she only hoped it did. Then a crash, the splintering of metal, the shattering of glass.

She turned. *No.*

Under the bloody glow of the blinking stoplight, a sedan had T-boned a minivan. Already, gas burned the air.

Her hand went to her face, to the raised memory on her forehead, and she shook her head as if to clear away the images.

She should call 911. But she could only back into her house.

She shut the door and palmed her hands against it, the cool wood comforting. *Just . . . breathe. Just . . .*

Her breath tumbled over her, and she felt the whimper before it bubbled out.

God, please . . . What was her verse? *"If God is for us" . . .* No . . . no, the one Rachelle had given her. *"God has not given us a spirit of fear and timidity, but of power—"*

She heard shouts and closed her eyes, pressed her hand to her chest, heat pouring through her.

Just breathe.

Issy slid to the floor.

You're safe. Don't panic. Just breathe.

More great fiction from

SUSAN MAY WARREN

THE PJ SUGAR SERIES

PJ Sugar came home looking for a fresh start. What she
found was a new career as a private investigator.

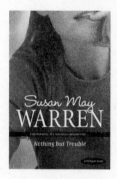  

THE NOBLE LEGACY SERIES

After their father dies, three siblings reunite on the family ranch to try
to preserve the Noble legacy. If only family secrets—and unsuspected
enemies—didn't threaten to destroy everything they've worked
so hard to build.